Also by

The Taylor & Graham Mystery Series:

Death of an Ordinary Guy

Sainted Murder

On The Twelfth Night of Christmas

PEARLS BEFORE SWINE

Jo A. Hiestand

HILLIARD HARRIS

HILLIARD HARRIS

P.O. Box 275
Boonsboro, Maryland 21713-0275

This novel is a work of fiction. Names, characters, places and incidents either are the product of the author's imagination or are used fictitiously. Any resemblance to actual persons, living or dead, events, or locales is entirely coincidental.

Pearls Before Swine Copyright © 2006 by Jo A. Hiestand

All rights reserved. No part of this book may be reproduced or transmitted in any form or by any means, electronic or mechanical, including photocopying, recording, or by any information storage and retrieval system, without the written permission of the Publisher, except where permitted by law.

First Edition-September 2006
ISBN 1-59133-178-1

Book Design: S. A. Reilly
Cover Illustration © S. A. Reilly
Manufactured/Printed in the United States of America
2006

To "Scott Coral" — Brenna's colleague — for your support and brain power. And for your friendship. Who knew where that first ride-along was going to lead…

Acknowledgements

An author may devise plot and character, but it is with the addition of practical knowledge that the plot works and the characters react believably. My characters' intelligence is the omniscience of many people, whom I appreciate more than I can ever express. Thanks to Dr. Ruth Anker, for taking time away from autopsies to answer all sorts of medical questions; Detective-Sergeant Robert Church and Detective-Superintendent David Doxey (ret.), Derbyshire Constabulary, for keeping my cops and nomenclauture on the eastern side of the Atlantic; Jed Flatters, John Taylor Bellfounders Ltd, for enlightment on the two Big B's of this book: bells and beer; Chris Eisenmayer, for her sketches that grace the pages of this novel; and 'Scott Coral,' for all other "cop stuff," including the rudiments of tailing, fight management, and insights into the police officer's heart.

Any information that may have become garbled in translation to the printed page is my error.

Jo A. Hiestand
St. Louis, August 2006

CHARACTERS:
The Titled and Their Relatives:
Roger, Lord Swinbrook: Titled Earl, owner of Swinton Hall

Geneva, Lady Swinbrook: Countess, wife of Roger

Kirk Fitzpatrick: Brother of Geneva

Noreen Fitzpatrick: Wife of Kirk

Lyndon Fitzpatrick: Son of Kirk and Noreen

Austin Swinbrook: Roger's younger brother, earl by right of succession

Dulcie Burgess: Austin's fiancée

The Staff and Their Family:
Mona Griffiths: one of Roger's household staff

Ben Griffiths: Mona's husband, chef at a restaurant

Sibyl Griffiths: Daughter of Mona and Ben, friend of Lyndon

Friends of The Titled:
Barry Sykes: Ex-husband of Geneva, former business partner with Roger

Ed Cawley: friend and former business partner with Roger

Sharon Seddon: friend of Geneva

Not-so-Friends of The Titled:
Baxter and Eileen Clarkson: retired couple who moved recently to the village

The Police of the Derbyshire Constabulary:
Detective-Sergeant Brenna Taylor

Detective-Chief Inspector Geoffrey Graham

Detective-Sergeant Mark Salt

Detective-WPC Margo Lynch

Constable Scott Coral

Sergeant Erik Davidson

DC Byrd

DC Fordyce

Jens Nielsen: Home Office forensic pathologist

Faye Usher: Home Office forensic biologist

Dean Hargreaves: civilian Scientific Officer employed as police photographer

Detective-Superintendent Simcock

CHAPTER ONE

I'VE BEEN IN more romantic surroundings than a cold, drafty bell tower—the middle of a London motorway at rush hour comes to mind. And felt more warmth from a good night hug than from the police lights that illuminate this scene. Particularly on Valentine's Day. And right now, though I was engaged with a dozen or so lads from the Derbyshire Constabulary, it was anything but my idea of a dream date—especially with a dead body at my feet.

The dozen or so lads and I were in the bell tower of Swinton Hall, a stately, medieval home huddled in a tree-choked vale of the Derbyshire Peak District. This national reserve of rugged dales, mountains, rivers, caves and windswept moors is as renowned for its natural beauty as it is for its picturesque villages, most of which had endured centuries of battering snow, rain and wind.

Right now the February wind seemed to be sweeping across the tower's stone floor and freezing everything it touched. Which included my ankles and feet, despite the protection of my woolen socks and expensive designer-label leather boots. I picked up my foot, looking sadly at the police-regulation paper bootie that encased the polished leather, and thought that fashion wasn't all that it was touted. Warmth had its advantages over chic many times.

Relief also had its advantages over dignity, I thought as I stepped out of the way of a police constable rushing for the stairs—presumably to puke outside. In spite of the situation, I smiled. Hadn't I done the same thing as a probationary constable on seeing my first dead body, a victim of a car crash on one of the district's twisting roads? It was an occupational hazard, even plaguing some senior officers if the crime scene was particularly gruesome.

Not that our present body or scene was. It was a serene spot, a fifteen foot square chamber of whitewashed stone with a small leaded glass window that would let in western daylight. A door in the southern wall opened to stairs that led down to the ground floor. One gained access to the room above by the wooden ladder fastened vertically to the wall. An aged wooden plaque was screwed into the opposite wall, the wood blackened with age and carbon from the burning of countless candles. Beside the plaque an iron hook waited to hold something. Perhaps a jacket or cardigan, I thought, noticing the hook's height from the floor. Several mouse-nibbled hymnals, a broken wooden stool, and a half dozen worn bell ropes cluttered the room's southeast corner. A small wooden box, about 3-foot by 1-foot, squatted in the southwest corner. Iron chains disappeared into holes in its top. A wooden cask—probably filled with beer—squatted on top of this wooden box, a metal tap protruding from its side.

"You thinking about last November?"

I pulled my attention from the ropes dangling from the holes in the ceiling. Mark Salt was grinning beside me. Mark was a detective-sergeant in the Derbyshire Constabulary, as I was. He was tall, muscular, good looking and inclined to think of himself as cock of the walk around women. Me, in particular, these days. I begrudgingly admitted—to myself or to my friend Margo Lynch—that he did have a bit of animal magnetism, but I wasn't about to be the lamb for this wolf.

I nodded and pointed toward the rope nearest the dead body. "But this rope appears to be intact and there seems to be no question of a hanging." I was referring to the previous November when we had worked on a case during a village's Guy Fawkes celebration.

"Also seems to be rather straight forward," Mark replied. "One bloke, alone, hits his head on the edge of the ceiling hatch, falls from the ladder. The End. Suspicious, I grant you, when someone dies alone, but it doesn't scream murder."

"You know anything about change ringing, Mark? PC Byrd said this death might involve change ringing bells, the huge tower-hung things. Like the Hunchback of Notre Dame liked to swing on."

Mark shrugged as if to say he wasn't that interested in bells, just the police work. His eyes followed the length of the ropes upward. "I've not rung, if that's what you're asking. But one of my mates used to. I'd go over and watch sometimes. Sounded like a bunch of noise. No melody."

"But the bells themselves...."

"Change ringing bells are hung in towers such as this one. Each bell's fixed at right angle to a wooden wheel. The rope..." He nodded toward the six ropes hanging in front of us and disappearing through the small holes in the ceiling. "The rope's attached to the wheel. When the rope's pulled, the wheel revolves, which tips the bell over to ring. It's not strength that's needed for this—that's where the wheel and ball bearings come in. You control the bell by feeling the action of the swinging bell on the rope."

"Like feeling a horse's mouth through the bridle reins."

"Yeh. Something like that."

"I hear they're heavy."

"What? The bells? Yeh. Several hundred pounds all the way up to tons. That's where the wheel is so brilliant in all this. Marvelous invention. There'd be no way in hell you could tip a bell weighing that much with just a tug on a rope."

"So it's dangerous, then."

PEARLS BEFORE SWINE

"Can be. I've heard of accidents involving arms and hands getting caught in the moving rope. Blokes getting hung. Easy, when you've got a ton of dead weight on the other end of the rope hoisting the poor bloke, where he literally cracks his head on the ceiling."

I shuddered and looked at the six ropes that swayed slightly in a cold blast of air. Someone must have opened the tower door downstairs. Perhaps Graham had arrived.

"You said you never got involved in change ringing," I said.

"You neither, from the questions you asked. Is that because you're not C of E, or not religious, or just not mathematically inclined? I know you're into music, so that's not the reason." He grinned. "Or maybe it *is*. Bing bong tin tan clunk. Bells rung in a jumble, it sounds like to me. Maybe you like music *too* well to change ring. Maybe you miss the melody—it's no tune you ring on these things. Is that why you're not a ringer?"

"Time's the main culprit. How can a cop commit to anything on a schedule, like 7:30 choir practice, or an evening cookery class? I'd miss more classes than I could attend." I didn't want to begin confiding in Mark, telling him I wasn't really a believer or church-goer. Once I started baring my soul and childhood hurts I would establish ourselves as friends. And, even though we certainly weren't enemies, I wasn't ready to label Mark as a Bosom Buddy or Confidant.

"The job *does* have its drawbacks," he said, eyeing me.

I fought to keep my face from flooding with color. "Either of your brothers ring?" I figured I could safely ask the question, since I'd been involved last month in a case featuring his family.

Mark shook his head. "No tower around our patch of earth. I never got a chance to hear bells as I grew up. And then, when I went to a few of the sessions with my mate, my interests were turning toward police work. So," he said, smiling and stretching out his arms, "you see why I am the way I am today. The product of a bell-deprived youth."

The person must have exited the tower because the breeze had ceased, along with the faint aroma of crushed pine needles. The bell ropes stood still again. I wished Graham would arrive so we could proceed. "Well, I hope this isn't going to take forever to sort out."

"Yeh. Like I said, one bloke hitting his head, dying alone...suspicious, sure, but not necessarily murder. His Highness coming, then?"

"More than suspicious, Mark. I heard that the head wound doesn't match the angles of the ladder or the hatchway opening in the ceiling. And yes, Graham's on his way. Why?"

"Just wondering if I have time for a leisurely kiss, Brenna. It's Valentine's Day, you know."

"I don't need reminding, thanks."

"This call-out put the brakes on a hot date?"

"Keep your mind on the job, Mark. You'll be a happier lad in the long run."

"I can tear out a heart from one of my notebook pages and hold it over your head, Bren. Just a quick kiss?"

"You're confusing paper hearts with mistletoe," I said, annoyance creeping into my voice. I mentally counted to ten before continuing, not wanting Mark to see he was affecting me. "Anyway, you know the rules about torn-out or missing notebook pages. If you ever need to produce your notes, and a page is missing—"

"Just a figure of speech, Bren. I'd never do it. God, you're getting grumpy."

"Grumpy!" I exploded, then, noticing some of the lads looking my way, said more softly, "Why do you say that?"

Mark pointed to my gauze-wrapped right hand and wrist. "Must hurt."

"Not particularly," I lied.

"Frankly, Brenna, I thought you'd be on the disabled list. With a burn like that—"

"It's nothing I can't work through. I feel fine. Anyway, we need to move. They're about to measure the rope."

"Ta. I'm all for progress."

We moved to the corner and watched as two scientific officers set up a ladder to measure the length of the bell rope. Mark said it looked to be the usual type of rope used in change ringing—a cream-colored flax. The sally—a fluff of maroon and white worsted wool woven into a striped spiral near the rope's end—looked more like a giant drop of blood than the convenient hand grip for the bell ringers. The rope undulated slightly as an officer on the top rung of the ladder lay the tip of his tape measure at the small ceiling hole. He pulled out the end of the tape, keeping it taut. The SO on the floor, holding the other end of the tape at the end of the rope, called out "Seven feet." When he'd reeled in the measure, he noted the length of the sally. Three feet. The two SOs then ascended the vertical ladder on the tower wall and they disappeared into the room overhead, probably to measure that area and get dimensions of the bells.

I had yet to see this, just taking Constable Byrd's word for it right now. The scientific officers did not need another person tramping through the crime scene and muddying the waters. Lord knows I could get into enough trouble on duty without trying. And I had no intension of having Graham come down on me for that.

Graham, properly known as Detective-Chief Inspector Geoffrey Graham, is part of our police team from Buxton investigating this suspicious death—and my superior officer. And I was waiting for him to arrive and take charge. When I had rung him up to inform him of this death, he had been at home, fixing his tea. I had hesitated momentarily before I gave him the news, for I could hear some bit of music playing in the background. No doubt Handel or Bach or one of those early composers, complementing his dinner, mood and fireside read.

PEARLS BEFORE SWINE

I had heard the resignation in his voice when I finally told him; the loud clatter as though he dropped a spoon onto the work top. I could imagine the clenched jaw, the closed eyes as he silently cursed the situation. I could nearly smell the baked salmon, which was of course conjecture on my part, but Graham wouldn't be eating baked beans on toast. He liked to cook. Too bad this had to ruin his evening.

It was only marginally better when he appeared. If not smiling, at least he wasn't cursing.

"So," Graham said, walking over to me. Mark had chosen Discretion over Ardor and gone to look at the blood splattering at the base of the wall ladder. "You have a name for me?" He was wearing the white paper suit we dress in when we enter a crime scene. It preserved the evidence—if there was any—and controlled cross-contamination from any bits we might inadvertently bring in with us. He stood beside me, overwhelming me with his intelligence and masculinity, watching as the chamber exploded with light from the photographer's lamps, towering above me, making me feel small and insignificant, and strangely protected. Both his presence and voice seemed to fill the small space.

"Mind the bits of glass, sir," I said, pointing to a patch of brown glass fragments near the body and around the base of the ladder.

"Right." Graham carefully stepped around them as a SO snapped a photo. "So, who is our deceased?"

"Roger, Lord Swinbrook. Succeeded to the peerage on the death of his father ten years ago. Age 46. Married but no children. Owner of Swinton Hall. Just home from an evening's valentine celebration with his wife." I glanced at Graham and saw that he was gazing at the body. A fragment of valentine verse, long slumbering in the depths of my mind, dislodged itself and mentally echoed again from my childhood. The poem had been printed on red paper, the lettering crude and black, looking like they had been formed from dried streaks of blood. Now, twenty years later, the scene before me forced the embarrassment of my teen years into my consciousness.

Roses are red,
Violets are blue,
I'd kill myself
If I looked like you.

The rhyme had been illustrated with a cartoon of a fat girl lying on her back, a knife sticking out of her chest. The poem was signed with a smear of dried snot.

I recall standing at the letterbox, the valentine in my hand, tears streaming down my cheeks, and my brother asking me if I was all right. I had jammed the filth into my jeans pocket, wiped my eyes and forced myself to smile. Of course I lied, telling him it was a funny valentine and I had laughed so hard I was crying. Either believing me or not really caring,

Samuel had said something about girls being too weird to understand, took a bite of his apple, and returned to banging out a Mozart rondo on the piano.

Now, in the stark surroundings of the bell tower, I must have looked odd, or said something without realizing it. Graham tilted his head, his eyebrow raised, as he always did when intensely interested in something. He said rather softly, "Brenna? You all right? You've gone sort of all greenish. You need to step outside? I know we've a bit of blood strewn about here, but—"

"No, sir," I replied quickly, feeling my face flush. I shook off the childhood mockery as the police photographer stepped around the inert body on the floor. "And yes, sir," I said, anticipating his question. "That's the way DC Byrd found him. With the spilled beer all over him and the floor, and the pearl necklace on his chest."

CHAPTER TWO

"WHAT'S HE DOING with a pearl necklace?" Graham said. Then, without waiting for an answer, asked a scientific officer to bag it and hand it to him if the photographer was finished.

He was, and after a few minutes, Graham held the plastic evidence bag containing the pearls.

Holding it up at eye level, Graham peered at it, turning the bag so he could see the necklace from every angle. It was an 18- or 20-inch strand, with the pearls graduating in size from the silver clasp at the back to the largest pearl in the center. A tennis ball. The Hope diamond. A rugby ball. Might just as well have been. I'd never seen such a huge pearl. My only acquaintance with pearls was the acrylic strand I'd bought to wear for my brother's first piano recital. Since then, I'd relegated all real pearls to Something Unattainable, like diamonds or world peace or Detective Mark Salt's transfer. These pearls, however, were obviously real, lacking the round perfection of culturing, yet still beautifully spherical, with a brilliant white luster that would light up any evening dress. They must have cost my entire career's wage.

"It'll be printed, of course," Graham was saying, "but it's just captured my curiosity, Taylor. Why a pearl necklace? Surely he didn't drag it out of his pocket, or wherever it was, and plop it on his chest in his death throes. Why not keep it in his hand, for example, if it meant something to him—something to hold as he died?"

I murmured my agreement and looked again at the body. Roger Swinbrook looked to be about two stone overweight for his height, which was about five foot eight or ten. He was balding, and what hair was left—beside his ears and around the back of his head—was thin and brown. He was dressed well in gray woolen slacks, a maroon-colored pullover of fine wool or cashmere, gray socks and black casuals. The only mismatch to this finery was the holey, felted blue cardigan. A gray suede peaked cap and black leather jacket lay atop the coiled cast-off rope in the corner. The pearls, while not incongruous with his dressy attire, were an odd bit of feminism. I wondered if they were a Valentine's Day gift for his wife, which might explain why he had dragged them out of his pocket. One last gesture of his love. "Could someone have laid them there?" I said finally.

Graham sighed. "Anything's possible, Taylor. At least until we get confirmation otherwise."

I nodded. Of course it was a stupid question at this time in the investigation. The lads hadn't even finished with the scene, and we had yet to question Roger's family and friends, so we had no idea if anyone else had been here.

"The blood's frightful," I said, looking at the splatters that adorned the base of the ladder, wall and parts of the ceiling. "What was he hit with?"

"We'll find it. But you're right. It looks as though someone struck him more than once. I don't see all this blood coming from a fall. Not the way the blood patterns are."

The pattern of blood was one of the many aids we had in processing a crime scene. From the shape of the blood drops, we could ascertain the direction of the blows. As Graham and I looked at the immediate area we noticed star-shaped droplets nearest the body. Graham mused aloud, as if to aid his thought process. "When you've got a smooth surface and blood hits it directly, the drop will be circular. But it becomes star-shaped, as we have here, if the texture is rough, like these stone walls. If it strikes the wall at an angle, the drop becomes oval with a sort of 'tail' that indicates the direction of flight of the blood."

"Oval spots with long tails," I said, recalling other crime scenes of parallel nature, "indicate that the blood struck the surface at an acute angle and was traveling at a higher rate of speed compared to round spots that have a slight dot of a tail. I'm sorry for the victim, of course, but bloody scenes like this are a super aid for the detective."

"A case where some good comes out of destruction, yes. We've both types of blood patterns here," he said, getting up and walking over to the farther side of the wall. "See this area where we've large drops and then consecutive smaller drops? That's caused by any blood ricocheting, if you will, and the fragments becoming smaller as they hit."

"His lordship's head was struck repeatedly, I think," I said, indicating the wall just above the body. "This can only come when the weapon was raised for a blow. As it was raised, it flung off blood."

"Centrifugal force, yes," Graham said, nodding.

"With each blow, the weapon flung more blood about. We've a few nice trails across the wall, here, and some patterns of blood splashing on the ceiling."

"Had to have been struck with great force, I think, to fling blood up there. What is it—twelve, fifteen feet?"

"Fifteen, I believe. Yes, sir."

"I will be very shocked, Taylor, if this isn't murder. I can't believe a mere fall would produce these hosts of blood spotting. Still, I keep an open mind."

"Even though we've seen similar scenes before, sir, we've not seen *this* scene."

PEARLS BEFORE SWINE

Graham nodded. "Very true, Taylor. Each one is unique and tells its own story. So. Do we know anything yet about the beer?" Graham said as we watched a scientific officer bag the broken bottle and pieces of glass. "I know it's a common combination, drinking and bell ringing..." His sentence trailed off, and I turned to see what had captured his attention. He was looking at the wooden plaque on the wall and reading its verse aloud.

> *Ye Ringers all assembled here*
> *Take Rope in Hand and ring with Cheer;*
> *From Minim Anne to Jotun bell*
> *Strike right on Time and Strike ye well.*
> *Hunt Up and Down, but do not Fail*
> *Or Thee must pay for our Good Ale.*
> *And if Thee does nae buy the Round*
> *Then off with Thee from this our Ground.*

Graham turned to me. "Simple, unmistakable and to the point. Pity our drink-and-drive campaign blokes can't come up with something as stimulating for our present-day masses."

"Maybe we're a different breed from these ringers. Anyway, just because it's posted, who says the poem actually worked?"

"There you've got me, Taylor." Graham smiled, the first time since he'd arrived, and I hoped it meant he had forgotten about his interrupted tea. Or valentine's date.

Without wishing to, I started wondering about him as I frequently did. That he had been a Methodist minister was no secret around B Division, or around our specific piece of it, the town of Buxton. That he played the harpsichord, loved the music of Handel and Bach and the baroque composers, loved excellence on the job and hated ineptness, treated everyone—probationary constables, the chief constable, victim and criminal, believer and atheist—alike was also no secret. But his personal life was. I knew only that he had been engaged to a woman called Rachel, that she had broken it off and that he had been devastated. But beyond that—loves, courting, desires—I hadn't a clue. And that *I* wanted to be the one whom he loved, courted and desired *was* a secret.

"It's evident from that keg over there," he said, "that Lord Swinbrook was not the one to break tradition, assuming it contains beer. Wonder when that was delivered? That's a job for Lynch. Beer in a keg like that should sit for a week to let it settle to proper drinking standards, then it should last seven to ten days."

"So some of these footprints," I said, noticing a muddle of shoe tracks near the dusty corner where the ropes lay, "could be from the lad who set up the keg."

"A good bet, yes. Did you know that ringer's rules were mostly written to upgrade behavior among the band?" Graham said, cutting into my contemplation. I must have looked blank, for he said, "Band. That's what a group of bell ringers is called."

Of course he'd know that. He'd been a minister. And while Methodists weren't as keen on bell ringing as C of E members were, it wasn't unheard of. At least I knew that much!

"Some ringing towers had rules about the band members' attire, such as not wearing a hat or spurs."

We both inadvertently looked at the suede cap lying on the coil of disused rope. "Anyway," Graham continued, "I haven't come here to reminisce. We've a job of work to get at. Pity all this waste." He gestured toward the broken beer bottle, the spilled amber-colored liquid puddled on the floor and flocking the walls. "What's the brand?"

A scientific officer called out that it was Duvel.

"Unusual, that," Graham replied. "Premium, Belgian ale. Expensive as hell—at least on my salary. Didn't know you could get it over here. Well."

"What's a Jotun bell, sir?" I said, pointing to the plaque we'd just read. "I've heard of tenors and trebles, but this jotun is new to me. And that Minim thing."

"Bells have names, Taylor. 'Jotun' no doubt refers to the tenor, or largest, bell. Jotun was a Norwegian giant, if I remember correctly. And 'Minim' means tiny, so I assume that's the smallest, highest sounding bell, Minim Anne. The poet's just confirming that every band member better do his damnedest to pull a good peal."

"And that bit about hunting—the 'up and down'?" I said.

"Well, not criminals, if that's what you're thinking," Graham said. "Without going into the grand and glorious technique of change ringing, you are aware, aren't you, that in change ringing the bells don't play a tune, but play intricate, numerical patterns?"

I said yes and that I had heard peals of bells even in my disadvantaged youth.

"Sounds like a jumble of noise to the untrained ear," Graham said. "No matter which pattern is rung, all these patterns begin with a scale, from highest sounding bell to the lowest. Most bell towers have six, eight or ten, even twelve, bells. At the beginning of the scale all the bells follow in sequence. It's easy to hear one specific note, for instance. But this gets boring—to the ringer and to the listener—so the bells are then mixed into patterns. It may start off one, two, three, four, five, six, seven, eight, but after a bit, pairs of bells will change places in the musical scale. You may then hear two, one, four, three, six, five, seven, eight. Then two, four, one, three and so on. Then four, two, three, one and the rest. The number one bell is traveling from its first place at the beginning of the scale to ringing in the last, number eight, spot. That's called hunting up. Hunting down refers to the same thing in reverse—the last bell rung moving so it can ring first. Think of playing a scale on the piano keyboard, if you can picture that easier. You have the eight notes that you usually play from middle C to high

PEARLS BEFORE SWINE

C. Only instead of playing C, D, E, F, G, A, B, C, the second time you play it, you play D, C, F, E, A, G, B, C. Then you mix the notes up again: D, F, C, E and the rest, interchanging neighboring notes. Plain as a pikestaff?"

"So, pairs of bells are just musically changing places with each other in the ringing order," I reiterated, hoping I had understood it correctly.

He nodded. "Of course there are hundreds of these patterns—a mathematician's delight. A lot of people ring for the joy of making music; some ring because it's like a team sport—everyone pulling together, no pun intended, for a common goal; still others ring because it's great aerobic exercise."

"And you, sir?" I couldn't help asking.

"A busman's holiday, I'm afraid. I like the twists and turns, the knotty problem of the tangle all coming out right."

"And the beer at the end?"

"Work does have its rewards, Taylor." He smiled again. "So, back to the present beer and the ringer's rules. We can't suppose Lord Swinbrook brought the bottle, and we can't even suppose he came here to ring. We'll have to ask around, determine if anyone knew what he was doing in the tower. I suspect, though, he was either here to ring or to do some work on the bell. That cardigan he's wearing doesn't exactly go with the rest of his attire. His ringing garb, then?"

I had thought the same thing, thinking the old blue cardigan an odd accompaniment to his cashmere pullover and wool slacks. The bell tower was cold, and even though Roger might have normally worked up a sweat when ringing, we had no idea that's why he was here. Perhaps, as Graham had suggested, he was here to work on the bells, farther up in the tower and much colder, with the sharp winter wind seeping in through the bell louvers. And the bronze bells colder than a brass toilet seat in Siberia. I shivered.

"Any idea when Faye and Jens will be finished with the scene?" Graham asked, turning to look at the two medical experts.

Home Office forensic biologist Faye Usher squatted alongside the body, looking up periodically to confer with her colleague in the case. A short, petite brunette, Faye held her own, whether it was giving her opinion in court to a detective-superintendent, or to her colleague. Perhaps being small and female contributed to her spirit, but I had my suspicions that she was naturally strong-willed. She'd graduated at the top of her class and landed a job when women in the forensic biologist field were uncommon.

Faye pointed to something, and her colleague, Jens Nielsen, bent over to peer at the area in question.

I said, "Doesn't look like any time soon, sir. They've just begun, actually. Only been here little more than an hour."

"It will be a while yet, then." Graham consulted his watch. It was nearly half past nine. He'd been late in arriving at the scene. "I'll go with them to the postmortem, which, with any luck, will be finished up around four or five o'clock this morning."

Jo A. Hiestand

"Yes, sir." I didn't know how he and the detective-superintendent got through the first forty-eight hours. They worked non-stop, digging at the case while leads were still warm and memories were freshest. Things could turn cold soon enough, Graham always said, without giving clues eight hours to evaporate while the superior officer got his sleep.

"You'll be in charge in the morning," he said, his eyes on Faye and Jens. "I don't have to tell you what to do. Your biggest headache will be the press, I've no doubt."

"Yes, sir." When any celebrity—in this instance, a lord—died, it grabbed media attention. And if it turned out to be murder.... I sighed, envisioning the headlines that would be created and the microphones waved in front of the press officer's face. It would not be easy for Lady Swinbrook, either, dealing with the reporters parked outside her door.

"I assume you can do that," Graham said, his voice shaking the images of tomorrow's hectic morning from my mind.

"Sir?"

"Conduct the briefing session first thing. Get all the teams up and running. I mean, your hand shouldn't impair that part of your work." He touched my jacket sleeve just above my bandaged hand.

I carefully flexed my fingers, testing my pain tolerance.

"You should be home, Taylor, not playing in a bell tower."

"I'm fine, sir," I said, not really feeling it.

"You're fine and I'm the next prime minister. Right." He exhaled loudly, clearly exasperated with me.

"The doctor's cleared me for duty."

"I don't care if the entire staff of St. Thomas' cleared you. I don't think you should be working. Not with your hand still obviously giving you pain. Let me see it."

He grabbed my forearm, carefully avoiding my fingers and back of my hand where the burn was still red and swollen beneath the layers of gauze dressing. The bandaged area looked like an odd boxing glove.

"I soaked it in cold water," I said, breaking the silence.

"There's that to be said for it. As a copper, you should know basic first aid. And what did the doctor say exactly? I know what *you* told me in the office, but what did he *really* say?"

"I should keep it elevated as much as I can and drink water."

"Fine. I have yet to see you do any of that."

I pulled my hand away from Graham's and cradled my elbow in my left hand. Leaning my hand against my chest, I said, "See? I can work and follow doctor's orders at the same time."

"And you can still madden me. When's the magic date of your cure, or hasn't he said?"

"Well, sir," I began before Graham said, "Never mind. Don't tell me. Surprise me one day. It will come about sooner if you'd take a week off, you know."

"I'm fine, sir," I replied, then realized I'd already said that.

PEARLS BEFORE SWINE

He waved off any further statements I might have made and said that as long as we had a few minutes, we might as well earn our wages and talk to her ladyship. I nodded, falling in beside him as we exited the tower. Graham was a master of understatement; we'd certainly have a few minutes. It'd be more like an hour before the medical team would be ready to leave.

I'd thought the bell ringing chamber was cold. It seemed colder outside. A slight breeze ruffled the boughs of the pines and whipped up a handful of snow, throwing it against the sides of the police cars, the tower wall, and my legs. The crystals were ice-hard and stung, sounding like gravel hurled against a sheet of metal. I stomped my feet, shaking off what snow might have wanted to cling to my wool trousers. When we had shed our paper work suits, I handed them to one of the constables near the door, then quickly followed Graham a short distance from the tower.

Near a copse of pines and oaks, the bell tower loomed raven-black against the sky. It was perhaps eighty feet high, a window the size of an arrow slit outwardly marking each of the four storeys. Right now, light from the police work lamps glowed from the windows, casting the structure itself into silhouette. At ground level, a great wooden door studded with iron bolts and a door pull gaped open and allowed the light to cascade across the flagstones. From one side of the tower, the rectangular stately house jutted out rather like the letter L. Dormer windows dotted its slate roof like warts on a scaly skin. With so many eyes on the tower, I was hopeful someone had seen what had transpired here.

Leaving the fantasy to leisure hours, I draped the ends of my woolen scarf over my hand, pretended I wasn't in pain, and walked up to her ladyship.

Geneva, Lady Swinbrook, was sitting on a painted, wooden bench to the left of the tower door. For all the warmth of her fur coat, she still looked cold, for she clutched the collar of the coat to her throat. A damp facial tissue lay unheeded in her hand. She must not have changed from her evening clothes, for I saw a glimpse of her black-and-white dress where the coat gaped open on her lap. Her shoes, high-heeled sandals, seemed more apt for summer than for winter, but they matched the dress, being black with accents of white leather leaves across the toes. A black trilby-style hat with black, gray and white feathers sat precariously on her brunette hair. She didn't seem aware of the drastic angle; she stared ahead of her, crying freely.

A WPC was with her, offering verbal comfort in the way of sympathetic phrases and physical comfort in the way of facial tissue and hot tea.

Graham and I stopped in front of Lady Swinbrook and he introduced us. She seemed not to hear him, for her gaze was fixed on some far object. Or perhaps saw nothing at all but her husband's body in the ringing chamber. Graham remained silent, studying her, perhaps debating how best to begin the questioning. I often wondered during such times if Graham relied more on his ministerial experience than on his police training. Either one would work. For, as he never tired of telling me, he basically had just changed work clothing—the offering of help and comfort were the same in both careers.

Lady Swinbrook balanced the mug of tea on her lap, her fingers interlaced as they encircled the vessel. No steam rose from the mug, so she had probably been sitting like that for a while, lost, perhaps, in images where Roger still lived. A small strangled sob escaped her throat, and when she looked up the glow of the door light splashed across her face. Red eyes, swollen from crying, were barely more than sunken orbs bracketing a red, swollen nose. Streaks of dark mascara, like bird tracks, stained her cheeks.

"I found him about quarter past seven, I should think," Geneva said, then quickly looked away from Graham, perhaps too embarrassed at what she must look like to let him see her. "Or near enough. I wasn't looking at the time."

"No, of course not," Graham said, gently drawing her eyes towards him. Even in the briefest words, he could convey empathy or demand attention. "I should be surprised if you had."

"When I couldn't feel a pulse," she said, blushing slightly from the inference, "I phoned 999, then Roger's brother. I thought, that is, I knew he was—"

"So that explains why *we* are here, then. Why did *you* go into the tower in the first place? I understand you'd been dining together, and that he left you during the meal. Were you supposed to meet him here?"

Geneva shook her head and closed her eyes for a moment before replying. "It was too soon for him to be finished. Ringing the bells, I mean. I wondered why he had stopped. So I went up to look. Up to the ringing chamber. He should've been ringing still."

"Too soon?" Graham glanced at me, his eyebrow raised in confusion. "I'm sorry, Lady Swinbrook, I don't—"

"Of course, you won't know about it, would you? The bet. It was all about the bet. And Roger had stopped too early—" She broke off, the tears spilling again down her cheeks.

We stood silently, waiting for her to recover. When she had taken a fresh tissue from the WPC, she said, "I'm making rather a muddle of it all. I'm sorry. You must be wondering what I'm talking about."

"If you could start at the beginning," Graham suggested.

She nodded, sitting up straight, and practically strangled the tea mug with one hand. The skin of her knuckles blanched with the tension. "You see, Roger had a bet tonight involving the bells. We—" She chocked back a sob, drew in deep breath, and shook her head when Graham asked if she needed to stop. "I'd rather get this over with." She smiled feebly, glanced at me, and continued. "We went out for dinner, it being Valentine's Day. And my birthday." She grabbed the mug with both hands, the tissue forgotten on her lap. "Roger's brother was there—that's Austin. He's several years younger. It's just the two of them. Roger and Austin. Well, we were at

PEARLS BEFORE SWINE

dinner. And my brother and his wife were with us, too. That's Kirk and Noreen Fitzpatrick."

"Sounds a nice gathering," I said.

Geneva smiled, then, perhaps thinking it improper, frowned. "The bet was silly. Well, most of them are, aren't they? Roger and Austin got to talking about marriage. That's about all they talk about lately, marriage. And finances. Budgeting household expenses. Estate tax. Vehicle upkeep. All rather dull, but rather essential at the moment."

"Why is that?"

"Austin is engaged."

"I don't recall you having mentioned her just now," Graham said. "Just Austin, you, your brother and his wife? His fiancée wasn't with you?"

"No. I thought it odd—well, it's Valentine's—a day to celebrate love. But Austin said he'd explain later. I guess he didn't want to spoil the evening."

"You think he broke up with his fiancée?"

"Could be. It's been one of those on-off affairs that's lasted forever."

I don't know why I blushed. Maybe I was hurting for Graham, knowing about his failed engagement and the pain be still lived with. Maybe I was embarrassed that the topic was so personally associated with him, a man I was growing to love. I glanced at Graham's profile. His eyes were steady; there was no hint of blush or agony on his face. But his jaw had tensed, for I could see the vein that ran down his neck throbbing.

Geneva added, "Anyway, Roger bet that he would ring the bells—"

"Pardon," Graham said, holding up his hand. "I'm sorry to interrupt. You keep saying 'bells.' Roger was the only one ringing, correct? So why are you speaking of more than one bell?"

"Part of the bet. The chamber holds six bells, as I'm sure you saw. Roger bet Austin that he could ring two bells alternately."

"Had he done this before?"

"No. That's what made the bet. Roger was a good change ringer, quite outstanding, in fact, but of course, you usually handle only one bell when ringing a peal."

"So this two-bell bet...when did your husband begin ringing?"

"Close to quarter to seven. I think Austin looked at his watch and said 6:40 or 6:45. We could hear him ringing when we left the pub."

"And you say he stopped too early for the bet. What time did the ringing cease?"

"Oh, fifteen, twenty minutes later. Around seven."

"I thought you were dining at the pub," I said. "But you just stated that you heard the bells stop and then discovered him at 7:15. You left during your meal to see why his lordship had stopped ringing?"

Geneva nodded.

"Did any of your other guests accompany you? Did his lordship's brother go too, perhaps?"

Jo A. Hiestand

"We all left the pub," Geneva said, her voice quivering. "But I was the only one who came here, to the hall. The rest went to their own homes."

"And you discovered him at 7:15, give or take a minute," Graham said, making a note of it. He glanced at me but said nothing. I knew he was thinking that if I hadn't burnt my hand, I would be doing this.

"I thought it odd the bells should stop so soon after he had begun. And then when it was silent for so long….well, I thought something might—" She broke off again, grabbed the tissue and stood up suddenly. The mug slipped off her lap and crashed onto the flagstone terrace. The liquid ran and pooled in the lower elevations of the stone slabs and would freeze overnight. The curved shards of pottery rocked gently for several moments, then lay still, forgotten and trod upon as Geneva stepped from the bench. "I—I'm sorry. I thought I could do this. But all this talk about—" She was nearly the same height as Graham, tall and slender with a flawless complexion. Her lips were pressed into a thin, crimson line as she fought to keep from crying.

"Perfectly all right," Graham said, moving back to let her pass. The WPC took a step toward the Swinbrook Hall, then paused as Graham said, "I thought this might be too taxing."

"I just thought that if I could get through it now, I could put it behind me. But obviously—"

"Please think nothing of it, Lady Swinbrook. Perhaps when you're feeling better, later in the day…"

A male vaguely resembling Roger ran up to us, calling Geneva's name in urgent, shrill tones. He was thinner, though, and had a prominent jaw. His hair was thinning, resembling a monk's pate. When Geneva turned toward him, she called out, "Austin!" and held out her arms. Austin grabbed them and crushed her to his chest.

"God, Gen, I can't believe it! When you rang me…"

Geneva sobbed against his chest, the back of her head fitting nicely beneath his chin.

"This bell thing, sir," I said when it was evident Geneva and Austin were going to be consoling each other for several minutes.

Graham answered me but kept his eye on the couple.

"I've never heard of it. Either the one bell ringing or the two bells. Is it a common custom for Valentine's Day in this area?"

"I've never heard of it either, Taylor. And from what Lady Swinbrook said about the bet, *I'll* bet it was just invented this evening."

"But it does seem appropriate, doesn't it? Bells? We associate them with weddings and joyous occasions."

"Funerals, too." He said it so quickly, with such bitterness, that I thought he had a painful association with it. Could his fiancée have left him at the altar? "I *do* know," Graham continued, more calmly, "that there were three different saints named 'Valentine.'"

"*Three?*"

"It would be simpler if there was The One and Only, right?" He smiled, and suddenly I felt my body tingling. But not for Graham, as any of my friends or I might have expected if this had been several months ago. For Erik, another copper in the force. He'd surprised me this morning with a card and stuffed animal—a plush cat looking remarkably like my own moggy. "For my One and Only. Something to hug when I'm not around," Erik had said before giving me a lingering, scorching kiss. I liked him—liked his company and personality. And he certainly made me feel good—physically and emotionally. But we had no future. Our casual relationship soothed my hurt for the moment; I needed someone for the rest of my life. My own One and Only. "Sir?" I said, releasing Erik's image from my mind.

"Only one person who holds the title St. Valentine, so there's no confusion. Like St. Nicholas of Myra."

I glossed over the reference to December's murder case and said, "Who were the men?"

Graham held up his index finger and winked. "There's as much uncertainty over that as there is as to why 14 February is the saint's day."

"Nothing as easy as a birth certificate, I take it.'"

"You've too much 'cop' in you for such a romantic legend, Taylor."

"Someone's grisly death anniversary, then."

"There again, we don't know. But we *do* know that there are eight complete bodies and one head of 'St. Valentine' sitting about at various Roman churches."

"Makes it a bit tough for the pilgrim."

"You'd probably be happier leaving the spurious saints behind and going with the medieval belief, then, Taylor."

"Birds choose their mates on 14 February."

Graham recovered from his astonishment amazingly quickly. "Of course, you'd know that. You being a bird watcher and all."

"We don't recite a pledge before we go out on each sighting."

"No camouflage outfits covered in red feathered hearts, then?"

I was coloring and felt uncomfortable talking about a subject so close to me. Not bird watching—Love. I said rather too quickly, "We didn't do much on the 14th when I was growing up. Just cards exchanged and a decorated cake at home. In school pretty much the same thing. We made valentine boxes during art class so people could slip the cards in without your knowing who they were from." Again the anonymous, hurtful valentine sprang into my mind. I clenched my burnt fingers, distracting myself with the pain.

"You probably had a lot of beaux, TC."

I stared at him, not wanting to admit to my unpopularity or to the cruel jokes I had endured, aware that he had used my nickname for the first time that night. He was relaxing. "You do the same thing, sir?"

Jo A. Hiestand

"I didn't play the field, if that's what you're trying to learn. I had a crush on one red-haired girl, though. Pursued her with youthful ardor throughout our school years. Even tried bribery with ice cream and sweets. She willingly took those and my heart, but gave nothing back." He shrugged. "I learned the hard way that God had other plans for me."

Was he referring to his disastrous engagement or to his police career? "Did you draw lots?" I asked, recalling the easy way in which even the shy boys in class could obtain a valentine. There was no need to ask a girl to be your valentine when Fate handed you a partner via a slip of paper.

"Didn't everyone? But, yes, that was common practice."

"A lot less risky than taking the first person of the opposite gender—outside your family, of course—whom you see on the 14th."

"There are ways around that, too, TC."

I looked at him, trying to discern if he was joking. "Some mate of yours rig up something with your redhead?"

"Never had any mates that clever." He smiled again. "Good thing I didn't live on the Scottish Borders, though. With my luck I'd have ended up married to some crofter's daughter and now be herding cattle."

He referred to the custom of pulling names three times from a box, returning the paper after the first two drawings and ending with a 'future spouse' on the third and final lot. I thought it would be easy to fix such a raffle, and wondered if the result of picking the same name three times affected the suspicious person much as a voodoo or spell would do. Graham did not seem the type to believe in Chance. He trusted in himself, in his own mind. Besides, he still carried his clerical robes and cross in his heart, and there was no room for charms with God in his life.

I was going to inquire what happened to the redhead, but his mobile phone rang. I thought it a little too early for Jens to be ringing up Graham, telling him they were leaving for the postmortem. They were still working the scene in the tower. Still, it seemed rather late for anyone else to be calling him.

I figured it out right away. It wasn't that I was standing there listening; I had nothing else to do—except stare at the moon or scuff the toe of my shoes through the snow.

"Oh," Graham said, obviously startled and looking at his watch. He smiled and closed his eyes momentarily as though he was savoring every second of the conversation—or his mental image. "I didn't know it was so late. But I'm glad you rang me up. *Really!*...No, you're not disrupting anything. I've got a few minutes. Time got away from me, I'm afraid...Yeh, 'what's new' is right...sorry about tonight. I wasn't expecting...yes, it couldn't be avoided, and I'm sorry about all this...I know. I hated to, believe me. It's just that...well, I'd like to reschedule, if you're still up for this...Fine. Okay. Yes, brilliant! What's today? Oh, Wednesday evening. Yes. Well, this mad rush shouldn't tie me up every evening. Cops have to eat, too. Come off it, you don't need to diet. Yes, well, how about...." His voice dropped off at this point and he pulled his engagement diary from his jacket pocket. I walked a few steps away, as though interested in looking at a tree trunk, my face flushed with the hurt that comes from wanting what this person on the other end of Graham's conversation obviously had.

When Graham rang off, he was still smiling. But as he quickly repocketed his diary he glanced toward the hall.

Austin was returning from walking Geneva to her house. Her doctor had arrived, and he and the WPC had taken Geneva inside. Graham introduced us, apologized for the intrusion into his grief, and asked if Austin would mind a few questions. Austin took the seat that his sister-in-law had recently vacated and leaned his head against the cold stonewall. He seemed not to have heard Graham, for he did not immediately reply, but stared at the house. A dog barked somewhere in the blackness, and a car engine started before Austin turned his head toward us and said, "The sooner you get your facts and sort out this accident, the sooner we can put this behind us. Sure. Go ahead."

"You were at the dinner tonight with her ladyship, her brother and his wife, I understand, sir."

"A— A valentine-birthday celebration, yes."

In those clothes? I thought. Pubs tend to be more casual than fine eating establishments, it's true, but for a birthday-Valentine's Day celebration I would have thought Austin Swinbrook would have dressed up a bit more than the torn jeans, jersey and vintage leather RAF jacket he was wearing. Graham's eyes quickly scanned the man's clothing. Good. He's noticing the apparent contradiction.

Giving no hint of his thought, Graham asked, "What time was that?"

Austin sighed and rubbed his forehead. "Around six."

"And it was just the five of you? Your fiancée didn't join you?"

"No. She wasn't feeling well. She cried off. Roger and Geneva didn't mind."

"I understand there was a bet made with his lordship over some tower bells. How did that come about? What was it?"

"Roger tends to get rather sentimental around these holidays—Valentine's, anniversaries, Christmas. You know. He adores—" He colored, realizing he had been speaking in the present tense. He cleared his throat and said, "He adored Geneva. Used every opportunity to tell her so, either physically—as this tower bell bet was going to prove—or with some gift."

"This ringing challenge tonight was a first, I take it."

"Yes. He knew change ringing. Well, we both did. We used to ring regularly in our teens. Great grandfather had the bells added to the clock tower, where you found—well, it was originally a clock tower, as most towers were in previous centuries. Then the ring of six bells was added, and great grandfather retained a bell ringer along with the customary estate workers—gardeners, butlers, farriers and the like—to help ring. That's more or less gone by the wayside now. Roger and I ring, as do two gardeners, a friend of Roger's—Ed Cawley—and either the vicar or chauffeur. It's not a part of anyone's duties, as it was in the 18th or 19th century. Purely voluntary. But you'd be amazed at how may people still love to ring."

"And this bet..."

"I thought it absolutely bonkers and tried to talk him out of it. I was afraid it would kill him."

I stared at Austin and wondered if he had just solved the entire case.

CHAPTER THREE

"Roger was going to use two bells," Austin continued. "One to represent him and one for Geneva. He was to ring them, first the tenor, then a higher-voiced bell for two hundred and eight strokes, then ring the treble bell one thousand times."

"What's the significance of the numbers?" I asked, not really interested in the one- or two-bell combination, but the number of rings was odd.

"He chose two hundred and eight because that's the sum of their ages and the years they've been married—forty-five for him, forty-two for Geneva, seventeen years of marriage—then multiplied by two, which stood for the two of them, their union."

"And when did he start ringing? After his dinner?"

"He didn't even finish his meal, he was so—"

"Which was where?"

"Pardon?"

He blinked wildly, as though such a mundane question was obscene or out of place. He glanced at Graham, then back at me. "Oh, at the pub here. Really decent place. The Cat and Mouse. Awfully good food. You'll have to give it a go. Anyway, Roger got the idea nearly as soon as they'd arrived. I told him it was daft, trying to ring two huge tower bells. But he insisted he could do it. He used the tenor—that's the number six, the largest bell in our ring—and the number five." He stopped, his mouth open, then said, "I'm sorry. I don't mean to insult your intelligence. I just assume you don't know about change ringing. It's a dwindling art. Oh, there are a great many bands in the Kingdom, and a lot of bells and towers were restored to working order to ring in the millennium, but the average bloke has no idea as to how to ring, or even the mathematics of method and pattern. But you've no doubt already seen the bells when you invest—" He stopped again, but this time his face drained of any remaining color and his eyes teared.

Graham said, "I know it's very difficult for you, talking to us just after learning of your brother's passing. And we appreciate your effort."

"As I said, the sooner you get the facts..." He smiled weakly, wiped his eyes with the back of his hand, and continued. "Anyway, he got angrier and angrier as we talked about it, insisting he could do this, that he wanted to do it as a valentine gift for Geneva. I said, half jokingly, that he should just give her a strand of pearls or something and leave it at that. But he insisted that was too easy, to give her something bought. He wanted to do something to demonstrate his love."

"Rather like a white knight," I said, thinking it a romantic and daft gesture at the same time.

"Yes. I'm afraid you're right, luv. So Roger got up from the table, even though we'd just been served our salad, and said he'd show us all. He practically ran out of the pub. We finished our salad and next thing we hear is the two bells."

"And this was..." I prompted.

"I looked at my watch, so I can tell you. Don't look amazed, luv. I wanted to see how long this preposterous thing would take. He left us near enough to quarter past six to call it that. The bells started ringing at 6:35. Then *we* left at quarter to seven. No one was in the mood for dinner after that altercation, even though Geneva wanted us to stay. She felt so bad that Roger had ruined our dinner. But we couldn't go on with our meal as though nothing had happened, could we? I mean, Gen was upset, and Roger....well, we could hear the bells quite distinctly once outside the pub. I walked with Geneva and her brother and his wife to Kirk's car. They said they'd drop Gen at the hall. Roger'd taken their car, you see. I went back into the pub and had a drink. I could stomach *that* even if I couldn't entertain the thought of fish and chips. I needed to get the taste of this idiotic travesty out of my mouth."

"But you'd heard the bells while you were still inside, right?"

"Yes. It wasn't noisy in there. There were a few people, but it wasn't crowded by any stretch."

Graham said, "Your sister-in-law said the bells stopped around seven o'clock. Does that sound about the right time? I ask because, if you were timing this, and didn't hear them for a while as she says happened, I wonder if you'd glanced at your watch."

Austin nodded. "I did hear the pause. I thought perhaps Roger had broken a stay and had to replace it. But when it was quiet for longer, well, I thought perhaps he'd changed his mind or that Geneva had gone up to talk some sense into him. I really didn't think anything was wrong. Just surprised he'd quit after only twenty-five minutes. I'd expected him to be ringing for about an hour."

"Is that how long it takes to pull the bells two hundred and eight times?" I asked.

"Not at all. That would have taken him no time. He was going to ring it *one thousand* two hundred and eight times. The other one thousand times was his silly gesture of their love lasting for all eternity. A thousand years. It would've taken him just under an hour, I suspect."

Graham said, "A peal takes about two and three-fourths hours on a ring of six bells like these, Taylor. Three hours for a ring of eight. A peal is defined as five thousand or more changes on the bells. And a change is the ringing of all the bells in the tower, whether eight or six or twelve. If you have eight, for example, a change would be the ringing of all eight bells. Doesn't matter what order you ring them in."

"So," I said, swiftly calculating the numbers, "if a change is a run through eight bells, we'll say for simplicity, and he was ringing only two bells...it would certainly take less time. So, this was about a third of that. Yes, just less than one hour."

"He was going to do the two hundred and eight," Austin said, "on the two bells, then change to the treble bell for the one thousand strokes. He never got to that, much less finish the duet."

The night suddenly seemed colder. Whether it was Austin's chilling words that caused me to shiver, or the mental image I had of Roger in the tower, determined to ring two bells, and then climbing the ladder to fix something that had gone wrong—a broken stay or a rope—and then dying, knowing he had failed in his gift of love, I don't know. But I pressed my arms closer to my body, pulled the scarf a bit more securely around my neck, and stared at the tower. It had changed somehow. The light gray stones now appeared wrapped in thorns and nettles, as though protecting itself and its secret from our investigation, as though in a grotesque parody of romantic tales, it guarded its sleeping prince from Geneva's awakening kiss of love.

Whatever it was, the structure lurked behind us, losing its roof in the dark sky.

I turned back to the case. Graham was writing something in his notebook. Again I was conscious of my useless right hand and my below-standard help. Determined to contribute, I said, "You mentioned a pearl necklace as a gift, your lordship. Did—"

"Look," Austin said, holding up his hand. "It's going to be damned confusing if you refer to Roger and me as 'your lordship,' or 'Lord Swinbrook.' Yes, by law, I am now Lord Swinbrook, but call me Austin, or Mr. Swinbrook, if that makes you feel better. That'll help us sort out which Lord S you're talking about. Alright?"

Graham said that was very decent of him and continued. "Did your brother have a pearl necklace with him?"

Austin frowned. "I don't know. Shouldn't think so, though. Why do you ask?"

"Had you expected him to give her ladyship one tonight?"

"Well, no. He gave Geneva her birthday gift before they came to dinner."

"You were here, at the hall?"

"No. They mentioned it when I got to the pub. He gave her a Persian lamb coat. Why?"

The coat she'd been wearing this evening, I thought. "So his bell ringing feat wasn't planned, as you said. And he didn't say anything about the necklace."

Jo A. Hiestand

"No. I told you. That was *my* suggestion at dinner. It was a joke, actually, but I meant it. Much safer."

Graham and I exchanged glances. Of course we were thinking the same thing: where did the pearl necklace come from?

I asked about Roger's health. "Any problems, such as his heart?"

"You're thinking he died of a heart attack or stroke?"

"It's not unheard of."

"Right as rain, as far as I know. I suppose you're going to do a post—" He hesitated, looking slightly sick. Graham's nod relieved Austin of finishing his sentence.

"Standard procedure when death occurs in suspicious circumstances."

"You think this is suspicious? I told you, Graham. *Geneva* probably told you. He left the pub to ring bells. What's suspicious in *that*?"

Graham smiled wearily, as though tired of explaining police procedure. "It is suspicious when we don't know how he died—whether he was alone or someone was with him."

"How *could* anyone be with him?" Austin exploded. For all his grief, he was apprehensive about the next few days and funeral arrangements. And probably aggravated that we were probing into his family's lives. He shook his head. "I refuse to believe something untoward happened. Because that's what you're implying, isn't it? Someone was with him and struck him, maybe fought with him, made him fall? Who the hell would have been with him? We were all at the pub, for God's sake!"

"That's what we'd like to find out," I said. "That's why we need to learn of the evening's events, the times you heard the bells begin and end, the people in his life. As you said, Mr. Swinbrook, the sooner we get the facts—"

"Yes. Of course. Go to it. Dig up whatever you want—floor boards, family secrets, the garden…"

I was glad we wouldn't have to do that. Even if I never saw another decomposed body, I'd seen enough of them to fill the remaining years of my career. "You mentioned you and your brother had done change ringing. You were familiar with bells, then? The physical mechanics of them as well as the patterns you ring?"

"Ringers have to be adept at both, luv. The music bit as well as the mechanics. Things go wrong with bells. A stay will break and you have to go into the bell room to replace it before you can continue. You also have to know how to muffle your bell, perhaps attach new bell ropes. Things like that." His face softened, as though he were recalling memories of those occasions with Roger.

I had stood one Sunday, when I was seven or eight, outside a church. It had been early evening in June, and the summer air seemed full of bird song and lilac scent and fiery colors splashed against the western horizon. We had made a day of touring the Blue John mine at Castleton, then a picnic, and the well dressing at Youlgreave, it being midsummer. I'd wanted to stay up that evening, lie on my back in the wilder regions of Derbyshire, feel at one with the ancient earth and her spirits, commune with the Divine. I'd wanted to stare at the stars, picking out constellations or search for heaven, dance around a bonfire in our back garden, flowers plaited in my long hair. But mother thought it heathen and dad wanted to drive to Pendle Hill in Lancashire for the evening, so I was outvoted. But I still recall the sound of those bells floating downwind from that village church, and the slant of golden sun on the stone tower as dusk crept over the land. Its magic still held me.

Austin murmured, "He could have fallen from the ladder on his way to or from the bells, I suppose. If he were in a hurry to get on with his marathon ring..."

"If we find a broken stay, that will at least give us a start to our investigation."

"At least he wasn't daft enough to lean against an upturned bell," Austin added. "Oh, yes, luv," he said, mistaking my confusion for horror. "I've seen it. Beginner ringers, who don't know a thing about bells and how dangerous they can be, lean against them."

Graham turned to me. "At the end of a ringing session, Taylor, bells are often set to rest with the opening, the mouth of the bell, resting upward. The bells are quite safe balanced up like that, but it doesn't take all that much strength to tip them over. I've known of an instance where a bloke leaned against the upturned mouth. The bell knocked into him on its downward swing. Doesn't sound like much, but just imagine getting bashed on your head by the force of a swinging six hundred pound bell."

"Besides," Austin continued, "you said Roger wasn't in the bell chamber. He was in the ringing chamber. He couldn't have fallen into the ringing chamber even if a bell *had* hit him. There's a room between the two chambers. The clock room. Small, I grant you, but it separates the two areas. It houses the mechanical clock works and the chains that run down into the ringing chamber. So you see, if he'd been up with the bells, he'd have been found beneath the bell in the upper storey. Thank God for that, at least," he finished, his voice softer.

"Did your brother drink while he rang?" Graham said.

"What?"

"There is what appears to be spilled ale and a broken bottle in the ringing chamber. It's a usual thing, drinking and ringing."

"If you mean that Roger got slightly smashed from the wine he had before dinner, then completed his drinking spree with an ale or two while ringing, then say it, Graham. It'll all be much more helpful if we don't talk in riddles."

"I am merely asking a question, Mr. Swinbrook. There's a long history of bell ringing and ale drinking. Your own plaque in the bell tower affirms it. Since we found spilled ale and a bottle on the floor—"

Austin waved his hand. His voice was sharp. "Yes, yes, I see your point. No. Roger didn't drink while ringing. If he was thirsty, and Lord knows you get that way after an hour or so of that aerobic exercise, he'd drink water. He knew the risks of mixing swinging bell ropes and hanging and getting drunk. He never touched alcohol during a ring. *Never.*"

"So he wouldn't have opened the bottle, let's say, climbed with it down the ladder, spilled some, slipped."

"He would *not!* Must I repeat it? Roger didn't drink while ringing. That was for berks and beginners who think they can link with the centuries of ringers, form an instant bond. He remained cold stone sober. Oh, we'd have a drink afterwards. He kept a keg for us in the ringing chamber—you've seem that, I assume. But he *never* touched so much as a drop of the beer during ringing. None of us did—neither I nor the others who rang with us."

"Did he ever drink Duvel?" I asked.

Austin stared at the hall, as though trying to recollect its wine cellar and refrigerator contents. Finally, he turned to me and said, "Not usually. Not that I've ever known. That's a Belgian ale. Rather pricy. He could afford it, don't get me wrong. But he liked the local, on-tap stuff. Or bottled Bass. He believed in supporting the economy. No. Afraid I'm no help. I don't know where he got it. Maybe Geneva would know." He glanced again at the hall and said over his shoulder, "Look. I need to see to Gen again. See how she's—well, she needs me. I've got to go."

When he turned back to me, his eyes were filled with tears. Graham said he understood, thanked him again for his help, added that it must not have been easy for him to talk about his brother, then said, "One last thing, if you don't mind, Mr. Swinbrook."

Austin blinked away the tears, glanced at his watch, and sighed.

Ignoring the theatrics, Graham said, "You asked who could have been with your brother while he was in the tower. Though you seemed to ask it sarcastically, it *is* something we need to confirm. It would help us immensely if we knew about friends, enemies, family members…"

The door of the great hall groaned open and the WPC who had been with Geneva hesitated in the doorway. Light from the overhead hallway light fixture spilled onto her head and shoulders, casting her in relief against the bright background. A voice calling from somewhere in the depths of the house thanked her; a strain of some bit of classical music—Chopin or Liszt—floated past her and into the night. She slung her bag over her shoulder, patted her hair into place, put on her police hat, and stepped outside. A decisive clank of a metal spring bolt and the sudden breaking off of Chopin signaled the closing of the door. The constable glanced at the open tower door as she approached us, walking toward the police vehicles clustered on the other side of the structure. Her footsteps rang sharply against the flagstone, crunched across the gravel, then hushed as she encountered the lawn. She turned the corner by the far end of the tower and melted into the night.

During all this, Graham's pen had rested on the blank page of his notebook, waiting for Austin. Now that he no longer had the constable for diversion, Austin sighed heavily, frowned, then said, "Roger was Geneva's second husband. Her marriage to Barry Sykes lasted two years."

"Was it an amicable divorce?"

"Ask her that. I'd just be giving you hearsay, at best, never mind my jaded opinion."

Graham made a note of Barry's name, then asked about children, either from the first or second marriage.

Austin said there were none, and that he was Roger's only sibling. "Geneva has a brother, Kirk Fitzpatrick. He and his wife were with us at dinner tonight. They have one child. Kirk adored Roger, so don't go looking for some angry sister or brother who conked Rog over the head." He stopped and the color suddenly drained from his face. "My God! I just realized..."

"Yes?"

"Oh, God. Rog and Gen have no children. No one to inherit the title. I guess I'm it. *I'm it.*" He made a grimace and gestured toward the black-and-white Tudor Hall. "I mean, I realize I'm now Lord Swinbrook, and all that, but—all that's *mine!* The gardens, the staff, the taxes. Oh, God. I've got to see Gen."

"Geneva may not have an angry sister or brother," I said as we watched Austin march toward the hall, "but *he* could be it."

"Could be a bit of rivalry, younger brother feeling as though he missed out on titled privileges."

"He could also have dashed over here, conked Roger on the head, as he put it, and left in that fifteen minute slot between the bells ringing and Geneva's discovery of the body all so he could inherit the hall, gardens and staff."

"And taxes," Graham sniffed. "Don't forget the taxes. Depending on what the postmortem tells us, we may have to ask around the village about the brothers' inheritance."

"You think Austin wants the hall that desperately, then? He didn't look dressed for such an important dinner—sneakers, jeans, RAF jacket."

"Not my choice of attire, either. So, Taylor, your point is..."

"That he killed Roger, changed his clothes—he saw the blood splatter. He would've got blood on himself. Then he shows up at Geneva's side, playing the part of the supportive, caring brother-in-law."

"You're hinting, not too subtly, that we should check Austin's laundry, then."

"Joke all you want, sir. But we can't rule out anything before we've confirmed it."

Graham shrugged and we gazed at the building. Its ivy-enveloped walls had a romantic tinge when viewed by moonlight, and its furnishings were probably magnificent and dripping with history, but unless Austin could afford taxes and upkeep, it could be out of his reach.

"A good job for Margo," he said, referring to Detective Constable Margo Lynch, my best friend and fellow survivor of male-colleague harassing. "We'll set her among the Exchequer's pigeons."

"She does seem to excel at delving into people's bank accounts," I said.

Actually, Margo itched, as I did, to be in the midst of the action, physically doing something. Not that I abhorred using my brain. I had a very good one, though not to hear my family talk. I liked the puzzle, the sorting of evidence and clues to find the bad guy. But I also liked the hands-on aspect of walking through crime scenes, finding evidence in the earth—except for bodies—and questioning suspects. I would have made a good scientific officer, for I liked the idea of collecting fingerprints, photographing the scene, piecing together fragments. But I liked people contact too much to lean that way in my career. I itched to discern truth from lies by talking to people, learning from body language and voice inflections who was helping and who was hindering our investigation. A good phrenologist, my mom had once joked, laughing about my passion for tactile rather than cerebral data. She was right to a degree, but I liked both. And I think a good detective should have both. That was why I shuddered when put on a task such as sifting through bank statements or household bills or legal documents. Give me a good patch of earth, a spade and a back ache any day.

I was just about to suggest to Graham that PC Fordyce might be better employed than Margo at the will search when an older man hurried up to us. He was panting heavily, clutching his chest, and pointing to the hall. I followed his gesture, wondering if the place were on fire, but could see nothing. Austin had evidently gone inside, for I couldn't see him. As the man came to a stop, peering anxiously from Graham to me, Graham asked if we could help him in any way. That touched off the keg of gunpowder, for the man yelled, "It's about time you lot came."

"Oh yes? Why is that, sir?"

"Because," the man said, pointing a shaking finger at the house. "I want Lord Swinbrook arrested."

CHAPTER FOUR

"Why is that?" I said when I had recovered my composure. Graham was trying to hide his smile, looking away from me so he wouldn't burst into laughter. "This is Detective-Chief Inspector Graham, and I'm Detective-Sergeant Taylor. We're from the Derbyshire Constabulary. And you are...."

"Clarkson. Baxter Clarkson. I live near the hall. Behind, if that's how you want to describe it."

"How would *you* describe it, Mr. Clarkson?"

The man screwed up his face, but it wasn't in puzzlement, for his voice took on an angry edge. "In *front* of it. Along the north road. North being the top, and therefore, the front. Swinton Hall, here, sits on the middle leg of the letter E, if mapping out the village roads that way makes it easier to understand."

"I'm all for understanding, Mr. Clarkson."

I'd seen almost nothing of Oldfield, but the village was probably typical of so many in this area. It lay in a small woodland between Eyam—famous for its battle with the plague in 1665—and Grindleford. The entire area was part of the Peak District National Park and, as such, enjoyed its share of tourists pursuing spectacular scenery, fishing, rock climbing, canoeing, and stately homes. Swinton Hall was easily classified in this last category, and the village was a popular starting point for hikers wanting to traverse a local walk across the dales to Eyam and areas farther west. The village catered to this tourist trade by providing an unusually large selection of bed-and-breakfast establishments, pubs and craft centers. But it also maintained its slow pace of life. The main street, the vertical stroke of the letter E, as Baxter Clarkson referred to it, supported most of the commercial shops, while the upper and lower horizontal roads were residences. Swinton Hall sat at the end of the middle, or shorter, horizontal road. It also sat at the edge of a copse, which might or might not have been original to the hall. In the summer, the hall must enjoy seclusion from the private road via its leafy enclosure. But winter afforded the hall a view of the village, and the villagers a peek at the gentility. And at this moment, I could see the lights go off in the pub, plunging the street into darkness. I turned again to Mr. Clarkson and asked why he wanted Roger Swinbrook arrested.

"You're not here for that?" he said, clearly surprised. He drew his thin, veined hands across his thinning hair, shaking his head. "Don't you lot read your own reports?"

"What report would that be, then?"

"My complaints. I've rung up at least a dozen times, had the constables out about the bloody noise from his bloody bells, *that's* what report!" His voice was growing louder and he gestured toward the hall's tower. "If money or rank or whatever it is has bought him out of a fine or prison term—"

"Wait a minute, Mr. Clarkson. Don't even suggest there has been bribery. You could find yourself facing charges."

"If it's the truth, I don't fear no one or nothing! He rings those bloody bells at all hours, disturbs me and my wife, ruins the nice evenings we've had planned. I don't care if he *is* Lord Almighty High Serene. There ought to be a law about disturbing the peace and neighbors."

"There *is* a law, sir," I said, glancing at Graham, who was still amused, though looking a bit more interested. Either he was mentally grading me on my handling of the situation, or he was memorizing the man's clothing.

"We can't get no rest!"

I could believe that, for the man had thrown a coat over his sleeping attire. They clashed horribly—red plaid pajamas and an orange ski jacket. His feet were probably freezing, thrust into a pair of PVC waterproof boots. He *must* have been angry to come out in such a cold night dressed like that.

"Do you usually come over here when you lodge a complaint about the bells?" I said, ignoring Graham's cough.

"Hell, no. I ring up the police, as you'd expect."

"Then why—"

"Because I saw the bloody lights, that's why! Lit up like a Christmas tree, this tower is. All the cop cars. I was hoping you'd come to cart him off to the nick." Baxter had eased a bit with his volume, but his brows were still lowered. He nodded to a scientific officer who was exiting the tower. Detective-Sergeant Mark Salt, of the Valentine's kiss request, trailed at a leisurely pace but stopped just outside the door when he spotted me. He smiled and waved.

I blushed and hurriedly said, "Don't all these lights and cop cars seem a bit over the top for a routine peace disturbance, Mr. Clarkson?"

Baxter stared at the SO, at the camera equipment and half dozen vehicles, then seemed to realize this was a tad uncommon. He blinked, eyes widening, and stammered, "Wha— what's going on here? What happened? Someone hurt?"

"You seem very concerned all of a sudden, Mr. Clarkson. One minute ago you were ready for us to throw away the key of Lord Swinbrook's jail cell, now you're the caring neighbor."

"I— I'm just wondering what's happened. It's not every day you find the place swarming with cops. Something must have happened. What is it?"

PEARLS BEFORE SWINE

I told him that Roger had been found dead inside the tower, and watched the older man for the effect of the news. Baxter must have slowly comprehended the situation his own behavior had landed him in, for his voice was barely more than a whisper when he spoke. "I didn't know. I swear to God I didn't know!" He looked from me to Graham, perhaps judging our acceptance of his oath. "I hope you don't think I—" He rubbed his forehead. "Do I need a solicitor?"

Graham said, "You think you need one?"

Baxter gestured toward the officers and police vehicles. The activity in the tower would continue for another hour or so while the SOs measured and photographed and probed, but a lot of the personnel were leaving. "All this," Baxter said. "His lordship's death. My anger. You think I did it, don't you?"

"We haven't even determined manner of death yet, Mr. Clarkson, let alone if anyone's responsible for it."

Baxter thrust his hands into his coat pockets and glanced past the hall, perhaps to his own house. "I'm sorry about his death. Truly I am. For all that his damned bells annoyed me, I didn't wish this. It's a hell of a price for quiet."

"How long have you been affected by the bell ringing?"

"Ever since we moved here. Six months. Maybe seven. No, six. I remember because we moved here middle of August, when the village was having its well dressing fete. We lived in Manchester before that. We—that is, my wife and I—were both tired of big city traffic and concrete and neighbors breathing down our necks. We thought a village would be peaceful, easier on our nerves. We're both in our seventies, you see, and I'm recently retired. We wanted some place where we could breathe air instead of car fumes, hear birds instead of car horns."

Graham glanced at me. I knew what he was thinking—a fellow bird lover. Instead of commenting on birds, he said, "You didn't think about church bells and such, then?"

"Not at all. We didn't hear them in Manchester. Nothing large enough nearby. And the church here is small, so we didn't think it'd have any bells. But even if it did, and rang a bell for Sunday service, I had no idea we'd be subjected to the din from bells in a hall next door to us. I had no idea they even had bells!" He looked as though he were going to be sick, for he closed his eyes and swallowed hard.

"So you began lodging complaints ever since you moved in?"

Baxter opened his eyes, stared at the ground as though contemplating how much he should admit, then looked at Graham. "Not right away. It was very sporadic, the bell ringing. No rhyme nor reason, no schedule as to when they sounded."

"But they disturbed your sleep."

"We go to bed early, Chief Inspector. Or try to. It's enough to hear that lot in the daytime, but in the evening—" He snorted, his anger slowly returning through the recital of his months of frustration. "There should be a law about disturbing the peace."

Ignoring the protest, Graham said, "Did you talk to Lord Swinbrook about it? Or to someone else in the hall?"

Baxter exhaled sharply. "To him *and* to his staff. Till I was blue in the face! When we'd just moved in I didn't say anything for a few weeks, partly because I didn't know if the ringing was a usual or unusual occurrence. Partly because I didn't want to establish ill relations at the onset. I'm normally a good neighbor!"

"But that obviously changed."

"I don't know how many times I came over here, rang him up, talked to him in the village. He just said he wasn't doing anything wrong, that it was part of village life and I should have to get used to it. He said he always quit ringing at nine o'clock, that I should have thought about bells and villages before I moved here. Or had the estate agent query."

"But tonight," I said, "the bells only sounded for quarter of an hour, and stopped way before nine o'clock." Roger had even been true to his word tonight, I thought. If the bells had begun at quarter to seven, and it would have taken him just under an hour to ring, he would have still kept to his pledge of quiet at nine. Why was Baxter Clarkson really here? To see if us dumb cops had discovered he'd killed Roger? I ached to ask him, but if Graham could play it cool, so could I. Instead, I asked, "What made you come over here *now*? The bells have been silent—" I glanced at my watch. It was just after half ten. "—for three and a half hours. Since seven."

"I know what you're thinking, luv, but I didn't come here to fight with his lordship. I wanted to see if you lot were finally acting on my complaints and arresting him. God knows he should have been, long before now, making all that noise!" His voice was nearly back to its original volume.

Graham said, "When did you hear the bells start this evening?"

"I can tell you exactly."

"Yes?"

"6:35."

"You always check the time when the bells start?"

"Yes!"

"The reason being..."

"So I can have my facts when I prosecute him. So I know what I'm talking about in court!" His voice thundered, rolling over us. "Way I look at it, God or somebody did me and my wife a favor, taking Lord Swinbrook out of our midst, even if he *was* polite enough to ring us tonight to warn us about the bells! But that was the only time he'd ever been polite!" His finger accented his final sentence, poking Graham in his chest. "Put *that* under your magnifying glass and look at it!" He turned and strode back into the night.

"*Phoned?*" I said, probably staring open-mouthed at Baxter's retreating figure. "That's the first we've heard about that."

"Well, his lordship's not in any position to inform us. Amazing, the things people say under stress." Graham sighed and tilted his head back, gazing at the sky. "Just gone half ten, you said? God, what a long night this is going to be."

"At least it's interesting."

He smiled and stretched. "Our players are certainly making it so."

"What do you make of Baxter's statement about the phone call? You think it's true, or just something thrown at us as a red herring?"

"Isn't it you who said anything associated with the sea—?"

I grimaced, again embarrassed that Graham had remembered something so trivial I'd said months before, yet pleased that he had. I thought I was the only one who retained those little throw-away scraps—phrases, favorite sayings, favorite food, best clothing color, how the sun highlighted the red streaks in his hair, the sound of his laughter. Cherished trifles that meant nothing, yet did mean everything to a lover, for they were the inconsequentials that you held to your heart on dreary, lonely nights, that formed an image of him, that brought him close.

"Well," Graham said, his voice registering Back-to-Business. "Baxter could have been upset enough to deck his lordship in a fight, I suppose. With obvious feelings like that, it's a believable scenario."

"And he came back to see what became of Lord S, if he's hurt, taken to hospital—"

"Dead..."

"Neighbors can have that effect. Close quarters, noise."

"I'd hardly call the hall's grounds 'close,' Taylor. Must be, what? How many acres do you suppose the Swinbrooks have?"

"Her ladyship can tell us, if you really want to know. Or Austin."

"There you go again, TC, bringing up that jealous brother bit."

"Nothing like an inheritance that doesn't go your way to spice the pot of seething emotions."

He'd used my nickname again. TC. The Cop. A name surviving from my police academy days when I'd been the only female in the class, and Mr. Mark Kiss-Me Salt had been the chief harassing male. Mark had mocked me with it, embarrassed me. But it had become my talisman, for I was more determined each time he used it to succeed in the course and in this career. Now TC was used by many of my colleagues—Graham, in particular—as an affectionate title, a badge that said I had indeed become a cop.

"Takes a truly confident man to go after a lord," Graham said. "Wanting to take Lord S to court takes some courage."

"Or stupidity."

"I'm beginning to believe there are more seething emotions around here than were at first evident."

"There usually are, sir, when you start uncovering people's lives."

"If so, perhaps our imagined Baxter-Lord S fisticuffs aren't so fanciful after all."

Jo A. Hiestand

Graham's mobile phone rang and he took the call. He turned slightly away from me, as he usually did when taking calls, still including me in the phone conversation, yet courteous enough not to intrude on anything I might do. I furtively studied his face in the dimness of the moonlight filtering down in shafts between the barren tree boughs. His hair was a dark chestnut, beginning to gray at the temples, but the moonlight silvered the grayness and highlighted the scar on his jaw. Green eyes that could fathom a person's lies or soul now looked at nothing in particular as he listened to the voice on the phone. At 41 years of age, six foot three inches tall, the numbers were still on his side: young enough to work for another decade or two, to attain greater rank if he wished, and to reap the benefits that great height in police officers seemed to produce. Namely, the personification of Authority and the tacit intimidation of suspects. That he kept himself physically fit didn't hinder either his career or looks. But I was drawn more to his intelligence and secretive personal life than by his appearance, which, according to my constable friend, Margo, was hardly believable. Not much to build our relationship on, I admit. But we did have the common bond of love of music. Which wasn't enough, Margo reminded me. I was trying to learn more about Graham, but there was just no opportunity to talk. We always seemed to be exchanging murder theories instead of phone numbers. Or kisses. I touched my lips with the backs of my fingers, for my lips suddenly felt Erik's morning kiss. Yes, it would have to do for now.

Graham closed his mobile and turned back to me. I bent down, pretending to tug at my leather boot, hoping he hadn't noticed my cheeks flooding with color. "That was Jens," he said to my back. I mumbled something he could interpret as an intellectual response, if he wanted, and he continued. "Since he couldn't find me, he rang me up. They're just about ready to leave."

I nodded, glad again that I would not have to attend the postmortem. I could not get used to them. Of course, a police presence was necessary, but I could not yet get beyond thinking of the body as someone's son or daughter. Graham had conquered that. Whether due to his ministerial career and his belief in the soul's heavenly home, or whether he could concentrate on the PM as purely a scientific piece of the forensic puzzle, I didn't know. But I was honestly jealous that he could do that. I'd look at the body and just see a life cut short before its time.

I straightened up. Now, even if I were still blushing, he could attribute that to the blood rushing to my head. I fell in beside him as he started slowly back to the tower. I was glad to be walking, for I'd grown cold just standing around. I jammed my hands into my jacket pockets and hunched my shoulders against the frigid breeze. The sound of our footsteps was lost in the grass beneath us.

"Has he found anything yet?" I asked, my breath exploding in a long, white puff before evaporating into the airy blackness.

"Can't wait for the postmortem?" He smiled, knowing my distaste of the medical examination and amused at my eagerness to know its findings.

"Just a detective's curiosity, sir."

"You know about the obvious bruising to the arms and the impression on the skull. You knew that before we came out here. But he found something suspicious."

"More than the head wound and lack of a witness?"

Graham said something about my being too young to be so cynical, and added, "Suspicious, as in cuts to his hands."

I nodded and pictured Lord Swinbrook's body. It had been on its back. There was no suggestion of him turning himself over. So how does a man fall fifteen feet, land on his back, and sustain cuts and bruises on his hands? I asked Graham.

"I'm thinking, Taylor, it's either murder or some fight ending in a tragic accident. Either way, we're now looking at an official investigation. Especially since the head depression was caused by a rounded object."

"A floor is flat."

"There's always that broken Duvel bottle," Graham said, smiling.

"That would explain the glass pieces, the spilled ale and the blood patterns. But Austin said Roger never drank while ringing. So why should he have that bottle with him when he has a keg of bitter in the room?"

"You're playing devil's advocate tonight, TC. I don't mind. Keeps my brain agile." He laughed, which lightened the mood of the inquiry, but never ridiculed it. "We don't know from what height he fell, if he dropped the bottle as he fell from the lowest rung, if the bottle was even involved in the fall—"

"Is there beer in Roger's hair?"

"Sounds rather like a song lyric, that. Some American country-western thing."

I was tempted to yodel and spin off an improvised verse and chorus. Something like:

'In our long-gone youthful days
You would scorn my dressy ways,
Sayin' workin' duds is good enough for you.
But you've gone and changed your song
Since Meg Trovski's come along.
Now it's ties and tux and salon-chic shampoos.
(chorus) Ohhhhhhh,
Is there beer in Roger's hair?
By his stylist does he swear?
Hair so soft and silky, dyed a golden tan.
Stout or beer—now, which to choose?
Can't go wrong with any brews.
He's the coiffured pride of every pub-li-can.'

It wasn't as irreverent as it sounded. Sometimes in police work you had to joke or you exploded from the grief or tragedy of the crime. Not that we had anything particularly gruesome or heart breaking at this point, but things like this song always seem to be popping up. There was no fear I'd sing this to anyone, especially to Graham. This wasn't the time or place for it. And, as far as I knew, there never would be. "Just asking, sir," I said as I hurried to catch him up. Spinning the song lyrics had slowed me up a bit. "Because if there *is* beer or ale in his hair, well, that might tell us what position he was in relative to when the beer spilled."

"If he was standing on the top rung of the ladder and someone else opened the bottle on the floor, for instance, that wouldn't produce beer in his hair."

"Yes, sir." It was beginning to sound like a comedy team, the repetition of the 'beer in his hair' phrase. I stumbled over a tree root. Graham caught my elbow, steadying me, then dropped his hand quickly. I said, "If Roger was taking off his jacket, or bending over, and someone opened the beer or hit him on the head with the bottle—"

"He *would* have beer in his hair. I see what you're suggesting. Well, Jens will let us know. Oh, Lynch. A moment."

Margo was talking to Mark, leaning against the tower wall, when we came up to them. Even though Margo and Mark both snapped to attention, I knew Margo was the one who meant it out of respect. Mark did it because it was required. He held a mobile phone in a plastic evidence bag, which he offered to Graham. "Found among the coils of old bell rope," Mark said. "Belongs to his lordship. I checked. At first I thought someone might have dropped it there."

"Clue to our pearl-giver, perhaps," I said, catching Mark's eye. He gave me a longing look.

"Could have been the bloke who coshed Roger on the head, if it develops there was a fight. Well, yes, it could belong to him."

"But it's Roger's," Graham said, taking the bag. "Well, still could be fingerprints other than his on it. You must be a mind reader, Salt."

"How's that, sir?"

"We were just talking about the consideration of neighbors and the waning art of manners."

Well, technically we weren't, but that was a typical Graham statement when he was tired or stressed. Exaggeration or understatement.

"Oh yes?" For once, Mark Salt looked confused. Not at all the master of every situation he encountered.

Graham said, "You have a number for me, then?"

Mark flipped open his notebook and read aloud the mobile's number.

"Give that to Lynch, will you? And Lynch..."

"Yes, sir?" Margo said, her face an expression of hope that she was to be given some exciting job. If there was one thing about Margo, it was that hope eternally bubbled within her soul.

"Lynch," Graham said as Mark copied down the phone number on a non-regulation notebook and gave her the slip of paper. "I want you to check out the calls made on this phone this evening. See if there was one made to the Baxter Clarkson residence. He lives here in Oldfield."

"Any time this evening?"

"Yes. But hopefully between, oh, let's make it 5:15 and 7:45. That should cover the time period," he said, smiling at me.

"Yes, sir." Margo took the offered bag, beaming. For once, I thought, she's doing something other than running bank account statements.

"No particular rush but let me know as soon as you find out."

"Right away, sir."

"Oh, and if you're finished with that little job of work quickly, would you check on that pearl necklace? Or Mark. Either one of you. Whoever has some free time, though I'd like Mark to do something else first. Whenever you get around to checking on the necklace, find out the usual—take it around to stores, see if anyone recognizes it or sold it, get name and address of the buyer. That's one of the oddest things I've ever encountered at a crime scene."

"Yes, sir." Mark walked with Margo over to the car park.

"Right." Graham glanced at his watch. "I repeat, this will be a long night. *Now* what?"

The tone of one bell rang into the night, startling us. As Graham looked toward the roof of the tower, he said, "I hope we don't have another death to investigate. Bloody fools, messing about with bells when they don't know what they're doing."

"I suppose someone could have bumped against one. Or pulled the rope to test if it was ringable. You know, sir," I said, envisioning one of the scientific officers conducting an experiment, "finding Roger's cardigan fiber on a sally and wondering if that bell could be rung. To prove it one way or the other."

Graham sighed heavily, rubbing his jaw. "Fine, but just not so close to midnight. And just the one or we'll have people other than Baxter Clarkson complaining. Good evening, Jens."

Now that the medical personnel had finished with the preliminary examination of Lord Swinbrook's body, and the scientific officers had photographed it to Graham's content, Jens Nielsen, the home office forensic pathologist, lingered at the doorway, waiting for Graham. Jens was short. And pudgy. A third as wide as he was tall. Pale blond hair and a fair complexion accentuated his blue eyes.

Graham and I walked up to him as the trolley and body bag were placed into the mortuary van.

"Bloody awful," Jens said, his voice sounding tired.

I murmured that it was, uncertain if he'd meant it as a pun or not.

"We'll know more after the postmortem, of course, but I'll tell you now that Lord Swinbrook has several contusions on both forearms and neck, a deep scrape on his right forearm—"

"As though he got it from defensive wounds—or a deliberate push from a great height?" I said. I remembered the vertical ladder clinging to the wall of the ringing chamber. The ladder stopped just short of the square hatch that opened to the room above. The cover over the opening had looked heavy. I could only surmise what that might do if it crashed onto a skull.

Jens shook his head. "Too soon to say. But it's a good scenario. Especially from the depressions in his head. Judging by the hosts of blood spotting, *someone* certainly hit him," he added before I could suggest it. "There is one depression caused by a ninety-degree angled implement or item, such as the edge of the ceiling hatchway. And two rounder depressions. There may be more, some even layered, but that's all I've got from my cursory examination. I also found a large bruise on his back."

"Kind of underscores the fall—or at least the landing on his back—and makes the mysterious hand cuts all the more significant. So how did he get that?"

Graham glanced at the forensic biologist as she unlocked her car door and said, "The ladder in that ringing chamber certainly seems to be getting the votes for 'cruelty to Roger.' He could have hit his head as he fell from the ladder, which would account for the bruises."

Jens said, "I'd say he's been dead no more than two hours, from all signs, since we arrived. Maybe less. But, as you know, I won't include that in my official report."

"The time fits in with his dinner engagement," I said. "He and his wife dined at 6:00, but he left before the meal finished. I'll question the people he was with to learn when he left…"

"The blood patterns," Jens said, "seem to be consistent with blunt force trauma. You can work on that. You ready for the postmortem, Geoff?"

Graham nodded, turned to me and added, "I'll be at the mortuary, Taylor. I'll have my mobile on in case you need me."

"I hope not, sir," I said.

He agreed, then stopped abruptly as Jens paused. Calling past Graham's tall form, Jens said, "Oh, and Taylor, there's a slight impression on Lord Swinbrook's left wrist. Looks to be from a watch strap. But there's no watch. Do anything for you?" He waved good bye as he walked toward the van.

"Yes," I said to no one in particular, starting toward the tower. "Where's the watch now?"

I cataloged that question with the other one that asked the whereabouts of the pearl necklace's box.

"Taylor. Hold on. Just a minute, Jens." Graham said something to Jens, then walked toward me.

I hurried over, our footsteps—his slow and pronounced as his long legs covered the ground, mine faster and scattering gravel in my haste—echoing off the hard stone walls. We met at the edge of the car park. He was a silhouette against the glare of switched-on car headlights, but I could still feel his eyes on me.

"Make it a short night, Taylor. Because I don't really believe you."

"Sir?" I screwed up the corner of my mouth. What was he on about? Didn't believe I wouldn't need him and ring him up? Didn't believe I'd work for another few hours before going to bed?

Graham gestured at my bandaged hand. "I know you, Taylor, and I don't believe a word of it. Oh, not about your doctor. About your repeated convictions that you can work unimpaired."

"Sir—"

"Is that to assure me or you? Don't bother replying. You'll probably lie. I'll catch you up in the morning after the staff briefing. Oh, and I'll get someone to see about getting an incident room somewhere—either in the pub or the community center. While I'm attending the postmortem, I'd like you and Mark to question Kirk Fitzpatrick."

"Fitzpatrick? Why?"

"Kirk Fitzpatrick is Geneva, Lady Swinbrook's, brother, Taylor. He might know about the inheritance and if wife Geneva was due to come into a fortune on Roger's death."

"Sir, you can't suspect—"

"There are more ways to kill a bell ringer, Taylor, than by hanging. Night."

He lingered for a moment, as though wanting to say something else. But he'd given me his opinion about my returning to duty, and he would not tell me how to run the briefing in the morning. That would be an insult to me, and Graham, of all people, knew I was capable of delegating assignments and giving information. He gave me a nod and a half-hearted smile, then strode back to Jens. He got into his car and slowly followed the mortuary van down the drive, looking for all the world like a paltry funeral procession.

Jo A. Hiestand

CHAPTER FIVE

BEFORE I SET off with Mark, I went back into the ringing chamber to see how the scene processing was getting on. It was half past eleven. We'd been there for nearly four hours. Another thirty to sixty minutes should see them finished.

I lingered in the doorway, letting my eyes adjust to the brilliance of the scene. The police work lamps were especially bright after coming inside from the dark.

"Would you mind, Hargreaves?" I called to Dean, one of the scientific officers who specialized in still photography. A civilian employed by the police force, Dean was in his mid-thirties, with thinning brown hair and a mustache that grew more abundant in direct proportion to his hair loss. "That bit, over there," I said, pointing to the disturbed dusty corner. "The footprints in the dust. Have you got to them yet? Do they look like anything to you?"

"A few good prints," Dean admitted, squatting to look at the area. "No one's swept up here in centuries, I'd say. But they look fresh. Bare floor beneath, if I'm any judge."

"Whether it'll be significant, we'll know later. But preserve that as a Kodak moment, will you?"

Dean nodded, moved his photography lamps, and laid a right-angled ruler beside one print. He called over his shoulder that they seemed to be prints from a leather boot, like a riding boot or men's dress boot.

An image of Lord Swinbrook flashed through my mind. I said softly, "Lord Swinbrook wasn't wearing boots."

"Could he have changed shoes?"

"Might have done. Perhaps one of the lads has found them in the tower someplace."

"You can always check his car," Dean suggested, glancing at his camera before taking another photo.

I agreed, looked around to make sure I wasn't needed, then headed back outside.

The confined space of the steps was cold, with a breath of wind streaming up from the open door at the bottom. I wandered downstairs, recalling various bell-ringing accidents I'd heard, trailing my hand over the cold, rough stones of the tower walls. I wasn't afraid of obliterating prints. The SOs had already been through this section, concentrating on the hand railings. So I let my fingers glide along the rough surface of the stone, as though replaying my own recent tragedy. Had it really been four days ago? My fingertips pressed harder against the stone, the coldness a sharp contrast to the fiery assault my hand had recently withstood. The afternoon had been depressing—a gray sky threatening rain and a series of small, personal disappointments, the least of which was a canceled dinner with a childhood friend. Erik had been in Liverpool, so I was deprived of his companionship. So I had rummaged about in the fridge and had come up with soup, salad and biscuits. They were on the table, waiting for the teakettle to boil. Calhoun, my kitten, lay on a neighboring chair seat, his paws between the back slats and batting at my foot. He had settled in fine, the victim of an arson, and was an amazing comfort to me. A photo of my brother, Samuel, and his current girlfriend grinned up at me from the table. He looked euphoric and handsome, a tan to his skin and a dazzling smile that spoke not only of love but also of his career success. They were leaning against a brick wall, gesturing like game show hostesses at a poster announcing a concert. Sam's concert. In Miami or Johannesburg or Wellington, to judge by their summery attire. He had enclosed a concert itinerary with his note, but I had long ago given up trying to remember dates and cities. They meant nothing to me other than a string of globe-wrapping stepping-stones leading toward the Albert Hall.

I had tossed the note and photo aside, more interested in my quiet evening of reading and a walk around the neighborhood than in Sam's soaring success. And in my tea, for I hadn't had lunch that day. I'd been office-bound, sorting files, finishing reports, meeting with the Police Federation representative about an up-coming fund-raiser. All very tiring and dulling for my mind. Now, at home for tea, the phone had rung as I was igniting a burner on the gas cooker.

There had been no preamble, no inquiry as to my day or health. My sister simply blurted out that Aunt Louisa was dead. Massive heart attack.

For a split second I had been paralyzed, my mind trying to absorb and comprehend my sister's words, my body stone-stiff in shock. It was then that the gas flame had burst into life, burning my right hand.

I had gone to Louisa's house yesterday, the lone representative of her family. My sister was too busy, Sam was wowing crowds in sunny climes, dad had his hands full with mother. Mum had collapsed in grief on hearing of her sister's death, consoling herself with liquor and dad's unaccustomed concern. So I was elected by default.

The house held the barrenness of desertion, of someone never coming home. Even people on holiday left an impression in a house, some lingering warmth—immeasurable but felt—that spoke of their return. Although no furniture had been sold, no personal item removed, an emptiness swelled within the house, as though it knew its owner was forever gone. Grief tore at my heart and stomach with the intensity of vultures ripping apart a carcass. The house and I were emotionally dead.

I stood in the half-light in the hall, listening for the usual sounds of a living house. No clock ticked on the mantle, no kettle whistled on the stove, no music flowed from the radio. Silence and death saturated the air. Down the hallway, in her bedroom, I imagined silence and death to hang heavier. I had no will to venture into that room just yet. The hurt was too fresh, the photos of her with my family still on the bedside cabinet. It was safer here in the hall—safer for my stomach, safer for my sleep, safer for my fragile feelings.

I started to turn on the table lamp, then stopped. Although the brightness would cut the gloom and add some semblance of life, it would destroy the tenuous link I felt with my aunt. So I let the twilight wash over me, and watched and listened with the curious detachment of an observer. Slowly, steadily, the outside traffic noise faded until her voice sang from the kitchen, asking if I wanted plum sponge or apple crackle cake for pudding, if there was enough milk in my tea, if I wanted to play chess or would rather talk. A hint of scent—honeysuckle perfume entwined with the aromas of baked bread and damp geraniums—curled through the room, magnifying the images of her dressing for dinner, cooking in the kitchen, digging in the garden. Through the shadows, I saw her leaning against the mantle, laughing and pushing her hair behind her ear, the smoke from her cigarette curling like question marks above her head until erased with the waving of her hand.

Minutes had ticked by while Aunt Louisa effortlessly became a hundred scenes at once, aged or youthful, serious or funny, as my contemporary or childhood memories materialized.

At the sound of a police siren dashing down the street, I had shaken off the recollections, wiped away the tears, and turned toward the table.

An unfinished letter lay on the table where my aunt had left it days ago. A beige rectangle covered in a half dozen sentences of crisp, dark ink that appeared to hover in their poignancy above the paper. Tissue-thin and wrinkled, the paper mimicked my aunt's hand—mountainous veins pushed upward from cracked-earth skin, dry and sun-baked from fifty-five hard years of life. My fingertips stroked the paper's ridged surface as though it was Braille text and I could discern a deeper message through physical contact. And I did. The words slid razor-sharp and end-of-school-term light against my skin, stirring up memories so rough and warm and prickly and smooth that my flesh tingled at the recollections.

And now I'm reliving that again, I thought, jerking my hand from the bell tower's stone wall. I had enough to think about—like my hand—without dragging Aunt Lou into my working hours.

I pushed open the door of the tower and stepped outside into darkness.

PEARLS BEFORE SWINE

Patches of snow lay deep in the woods to the south and against the northern sides of buildings where the sun could not find them. I shivered, zipping up my jacket.

Just minutes ago, Graham had been with me, standing here hatless, seemingly not feeling the cold. His suede jacket had been open, his cashmere muffler hanging around his neck like a vicar's stole. Exposed earth had crunched beneath his feet as we walked, like black voids alongside the white frosty expanses. As he had strode across the frozen ground, his breath had streamed into the chilled air like clouds that presently cradled the moon.

Now I stood here, waiting for Mark, gazing at the same scene.

The sky was a wash of ebony beyond the feeble glow of the light beside the tower door. Far-off lights from other doorways and windows throughout the village speckled the shadowy landscape to the west and south. In the immediate vicinity, torches sliced through the gloom as police personnel went about their jobs. Footsteps and low-speaking voices and slamming car doors accented the ordinary night sounds of barking dogs and wind whispering through the conifers.

A tranquil scene; I should have found peace from it. But I didn't. I struggled with the opposing emotions of possible murder from rage and St. Valentine's day of love.

"So, what about it?" Mark said, minutes later, on our way to Kirk Fitzpatrick's house.

"What about *what*?" I countered. I'd found him sitting in his car, by the tower, making notes for the necklace inquiry. He seemed relieved to postpone that and drive with me to the Fitzpatrick house.

"Short memory, have we?"

Of course I knew what he was asking about, but I wanted him to sweat a little. I wanted to whittle away at his conceit besides making him work for what he wanted.

He turned the car onto the High Street. The village was quiet, bedded down for the night. A few lights shone from stores, precautions against burglary, and from homes where evening-loving individuals dwelled. But they were merely pinpricks of white in the darkness mantling the village. A splash of ochre light from the street lamp flooded the interior of the car and Mark's face. His normally twinkling eyes were serious, looking at the road instead of at me. I put that down to the fact that he was driving and that he didn't want to do a cock-up with a job of work handed to him by Graham. So, I thought, fighting the urge to sweep Mark's graying curls behind his collar, I'm not the most important thing in your life, as you protest.

"You know what," Mark said, slowing down to consult the sketch PC Byrd had given us. The Fitzpatrick home was on a road branching off the High Street. "The valentine kiss. We're alone. It's dark. No one will see or know if that's got you in a muck sweat. And I don't kiss and tell, Brenna."

"That's reassuring," I said somewhat sarcastically. Not that I had ever kissed Mark, but I still didn't want to be a notch on his bedpost, as I referred to his conquests.

"So?" he said, looking at me, his eyes pressing me to give him an answer. "Your lips aren't particularly busy at the moment."

"But yours are. Stop talking and watch the road. Look out! The litter bin—"

"I see it," he snapped, wrenching the steering wheel to the right to avoid the bin strapped to a street lamp pole.

"You don't drive as though you see it."

"How can I not, with the glare of this bloody street lamp!"

"Right. Just the point. How can you not see it? Then why did you almost run us up on the curb? Graham'll be thrilled when he learns one of the department's vehicles is in repair—"

"Look!" Mark abruptly braked the car in the traffic lane, not bothering to steer over to the curb. He turned off the motor and we sat in the car, the overwhelming quiet of the night, and the nearness of Mark and his anger nearly smothering me. He turned in his seat to half face me, grabbing my hand and squeezing it in a bone-crunching grip. "To hell with Graham, to hell with the department and to hell with Kirk Fitzpatrick! All I want is a simple kiss. A valentine exchange of friendship between two friends—or *colleagues*, if that makes you feel safer. It's *not* a declaration of undying love; it's *not* an engagement or a prelude to a one-night stand. It's a *kiss*, for God's sake! *Just* a kiss. Like in that old song. What the hell is it…in that Humphrey Bogart film…"

"'As Time Goes By,'" I said, recalling the song lyrics about a kiss being just a kiss. He *would* have to think of that, as though it was evidence for his case.

"Yeh." Mark brought my hand up to his chest. His heart was thudding as though he'd just established a new record for the hundred meter dash. "Whatever. So what about it?" Even in the yellowish light I could discern Mark's eyes had darkened, watching me, reading my expressions and body language for what I was really feeling. Damn! Sometimes a cop's skills were definitely out of place.

I must have taken too long trying to hide my emotions, for Mark said, "You're weakening. Are the song lyrics helping?"

In spite of my attempt to remain cool, I laughed.

"What's so funny? I didn't realize the song was so humorous."

Shaking my head, I said, "It's not the song. Well, it *is*. But not *that* song. Not the one you're talking about."

"What the hell *are* you talking about, then?"

I reiterated the beer-in-Roger's-hair episode, but not the lyrics. Mark didn't need to know of my composing attempt. That was opening up my life a bit too much to Mr. Mark Salt.

His grip loosened on my hand, bringing it to his lips and giving it a quick, light kiss before releasing it. As he started the car motor, he said, "We ought to get someone in the department to write that song. Sounds quite funny."

PEARLS BEFORE SWINE

I made a noncommittal remark and Mark added, "Who do we know who's good at that, who's musical? Not the Vic. He'd add harpsichord and oboe and a counter-tenor in a curled wig singing descant. *Now* what's funny?"

Shaking my head, I wiped my eyes. "I can see that whole thing. Not that Graham would do it, but I *can* see it."

"So we get out of the gate first with our own composer and lyricist. Just *no* costumes when we perform, Bren. I don't look good in sequins."

We had approached the BP petrol station at the intersection of the High Street and Victoria Road. Mark consulted the map again, then turned left. The service station was as dark and closed up as the other businesses in Oldfield, the familiar green and white sign nearly obscure against the night sky. As The Golden Sitar Indian Restaurant—fully licensed, live music nightly until 10:30—came into view, Mark muttered that we were nearly there and took the left branch of the road when Dove Street sprouted off Victoria Road.

We were now in the residential area, for a long row of stepped houses sprawled down the road, each nearly identical with its neighbor, baring the front garden or distinctive door color. Not unlike my own place in Buxton, also off the High Street. My front door was a bright, royal blue—police lantern blue, Margo called it—and the front garden was slowly, steadily coming into its own again after the previous owner had religiously ignored it. But I had planted bulbs last autumn, in the universal optimism of gardeners, and was planning on landscaping the tiny plot with hostas, columbine, bluebells and lilac this spring. And pansies. I had to have pansies. They were a tie with my childhood, a cherished piece of my mother before life and my father had disappointed her, so that her joy now came through the liquor bottle. I blinked rapidly, erasing the contemporary mother, and stared at a large willow as we drove past it. The mother of my childhood had taught me to love the earth, its plants and wildlife. She had taught me how to plant flowers, how to care for the vegetables of our garden. She had introduced me to the wonder of plants emerging from winter-freed soil, the detail of the tiny, natural world in the grass beneath our feet—bustling with life and astonishing to those who paused to look. It was probably that delve into the verdant, natural world that hooked me on seeking out details, taking time to explore beneath the surface of the obvious. For all that mother had become, she had instilled this love in me, and I was more grateful than I could ever convey to her.

So now, sitting in the police car with Mark, watching other people's gardens slip past me and merge with the obscurity of night, I mentally made a list of what I would plant this spring. Pansies for my mother. Lady's slipper for mum's sister, Aunt Louisa, a lady who had died too soon. A clump of heather for my dad, loyal Scot that he is. And for me... I stared at a trellis tangled with rose cane, the white, wooden latticework of the structure glaringly bright in the car's headlights. No, not roses. They were too stately, too royal, too prized. And no lilies, either, for the same reason. The safest bet was death cap toadstool. A fitting symbol for me and all the relationships I seemed to poison, whether consciously or not. Mark made a little cough and I glanced at him, then thought of wallflowers. Perhaps I would plant those. That's how I felt most of the time. Like a wallflower.

Mark's voice cut through my emerging self-deprecation. "Bloody hell. Chalk one up for Byrd and his cartography skill. This is it."

He slowed the car and turned into the Fitzpatrick drive. I glimpsed the home before Mark cut off the headlights. It was the same as the others—two storeys with double casement windows, moderately sized front garden, walk curving from the drive to the front door, an ornamental garden statue of a lady with a parasol. At least there were no garden gnomes or ceramic toadstools, I thought, getting out of the car and closing the door. Several lights were on. Perhaps Geneva or Austin had broken the news to the Fitzpatricks. I hoped so. I abhorred having to wake up Kirk with the grim news of his brother-in-law's death. A dog barked somewhere within the house as Mark rang the doorbell.

"Bloody hell," he said, turning to me as I joined him on the front steps. He pointed toward the statue. "Didn't know what it was at first, all white and coming at me out of the dark. Thought I'd have to wrestle it."

"Well, let's be thankful you won't have to," I said. "I think it would have won. What's your level of karate expertise?"

I was spared his comeback when the front porch light flicked on, the door opened, and a dark-haired woman stared at us from within a dimly lit hall. When Mark and I had introduced ourselves and shown our warrant cards, she led us into the room from which the feeble light emanated. As we seated ourselves on the sofa, she turned on two more lamps, then asked if we'd like tea. Mark declined for us and rose as she took a chair opposite us. He reclaimed his seat and did the preliminaries while I took in the room.

It was all glass and chrome, highly modern, done up in tan and black. Accents of orange and yellow in the way of scatter cushions, picture frames and an area rug gave life to the otherwise—in my opinion—dull surroundings. A lamp sporting a stained glass shade reminiscent of the American Mission style sat on a large, black stereo speaker next to the end cabinet of the wall unit. Track lighting flooded a wall of framed posters touting folk music concerts from local gigs to Scotland, Guernsey, Belgium and Denmark. A man playing an acoustic guitar looked at me from one of the frames. Kirk Fitzpatrick's name shone out in silvery letters.

When I refocused on Mark's voice, he was asking if we might speak to Kirk.

The woman, who informed us she was Kirk's wife, Noreen, twisted the facial tissue she had been clutching when she had opened the door. She glanced over her shoulder toward the back of the house, then told Mark that Kirk wasn't there.

"Oh, yes?" I said, glancing at my watch.

PEARLS BEFORE SWINE

"I know it no doubt seems odd to you," Noreen said, a trace of Dublin in her voice. "It being midnight and all." She paused, as though deciding what to tell us.

Mark smiled. It wasn't the come-on that he used with women; it was born of genuine interest, of his desire to make Noreen feel at ease. Police interviews were traumatic enough on people, never mind that a family member's death was involved.

Noreen said, "I know you want to talk to Kirk, to tell him about Roger. Yes, I know why you're here. Austin rang me up a bit ago to tell me what had happened. I—" She paused, her voice quivering. "He thought Kirk needed to know. He needs to be with Geneva. But I didn't want to bother him right now. He...he's on his way to a gig. He needs to be focused on that so he can perform. It's our livelihood, you see. He's a musician. A singer. There's time enough after his tour to tell him of Roger."

I frowned slightly, shocked at Noreen's priorities. I understood about the concerts and the money. That was important. But wasn't supporting his sister, Geneva, important? Wouldn't she want her brother with her? Or maybe, I thought, staring at a photo of Noreen, Kirk and what was probably their son, Kirk and Geneva didn't get on that well. Like my brother and I—sharing a last name and nothing much more. Maybe Geneva would get more support from Roger's brother, Austin, than from her own brother. I exhaled, focusing again on Noreen's delicate face and large, black eyes. Just as in police work, I shouldn't impose my views and opinions on others. It sank many a case.

Noreen excused herself, got up, and went to the stereo speaker. She picked up a sheet of paper that had been lying on it, walked over to Mark, and handed it to him. "That's his schedule," she said, standing alongside Mark as he angled it so I could also see it. She pointed out the top listing—Bolton, February 15—then sat down again. A header announcing Kirk Fitzpatrick's management company ran across the top of the paper. Paddock Productions. A small frog sat beneath the curved part of the capital P. Paddock, or puddock, was the Scottish word for frog. I held it while Mark made a note of the venues and dates, then gave it back to Noreen.

Did Sam, my brother, have similar posters adorning the walls of his flat? Did he stare at himself, approve of his posture at the keyboard, the angle of light that emphasized his smile, the size of the font that spelled out his name? Were concert programs and ticket stubs saved in shadow boxes alongside a pressed rose some ardent fan had given him? I stared at Kirk's wall, at the way the light caught the edge of the metal frames, and knew there were. Most musicians—as well as painters, authors, dancers and singers—had worked too long and hard for their success and public acceptance; they would tack up souvenirs of that winning journey.

"It's nice that he's playing Lancashire and Derbyshire," I said in an awkward moment of silence while Noreen stared at the paper.

Jo A. Hiestand

"What?" She jerked up her head, her eyes staring as though she were unsure of where she was.

"The gigs. The venues," I said, nodding at the paper. "Bolton, Stockport, Buxton. Back home on the 18th. Close by so he can get back here quickly."

"I told you, miss, I'm not disturbing Kirk. He's just made it into the big scene. I don't want to spoil that."

"Looks like he's had some success already by the look of these posters. France, Germany, Canary Islands." The three of us stared at the largest one, a color photo of Kirk, head bent over his guitar, a Martin D-28. I didn't need to read the letters of the logo, 'C.F. Martin & Co,' that arched over 'Established 1833.' I could distinguish the distinctive shapes of guitar's head and pick guard from a million other brands. Turning back to Noreen, I said, "Cracking good poster. His management company do that?"

Noreen nodded. "They've been top line, very energetic about his career. Wanted Kirk with them for ages. But he was tied up with a calendar of dates that he felt he had to fulfill before he signed on with Paddock."

"And when was that?"

"Just over a year, now. First of January last year. They've signed him to a recording contract, so he'll be in the studio in March for that."

"Seems like everything's coming his way," Mark said. "Except his brother-in-law's death. You say Kirk's not here. When did he leave for Bolton?"

"Earlier this evening. We'd been to the local pub, The Cat and Mouse, around six, I think. We attended Geneva's birthday party. For all of her marriage to Roger, Geneva's still Kirk's sister and still regular folk, if you understand me. So is—was—Roger. He never wanted us to call him 'Lord' or anything like that. Just Roger. Real nice man. Sorry he's gone."

Mark exchanged glances with me, then asked Noreen, "Did you both stay for the entire dinner? I understand his lordship left early."

Noreen said they hadn't, that the atmosphere had been spoiled by an argument and the bell bet, but that they'd brought a gift for Geneva. "When Roger left to ring his bells, we finished our salads and then took her home. *We* got home around seven, I believe." She paused to think, staring at the television as if it were a time clock. "Yes. Because I remember thinking Kirk had better get a move on if he wanted to leave for Bolton around half nine. He still had to pack, you see."

Mark scribbled the times into his notebook. "Why did he leave now if he wasn't due to play in Bolton until..." He consulted his notes. "Until tomorrow at 8:00? Seem as though he could have left tomorrow morning, afternoon, early evening, even, and made his gig. It's, what? An hour's drive to Bolton? Why leave now, so late in the evening?"

"He said he wanted the extra day to hit some stores in Chesterfield or Manchester." She smiled sadly, glancing out of the front window. "Oldfield's not exactly London, is it? Or Manchester. Kirk needed a new microphone for his guitar, and he had tomorrow available to find one, so he left early."

Mark glanced at me as though saying he'd heard better excuses from drunk drivers. "Anyone who can confirm that?"

Noreen bristled, her eyes narrowing. "What kind of...what are you getting at? Why does Kirk need to confirm this actions? What's going on? You said Roger was dead. Does that mean—" The last bit of her sentence was too difficult to say, so she sat with her mouth open, breathing quickly, and staring from Mark to me.

"We're not saying anything, Mrs. Fitzpatrick," I said, trying to ease her anxiety. "It's a case of suspicious death. Lord Swinbrook was found in the bell tower. We're merely checking out the movements of those who knew him or were with him right before his death. There's no implication in this. Now, can anyone else corroborate these times you mentioned, the time when you two got home from the pub and when Kirk left for Bolton?"

Noreen glanced again toward the back of the house, then said, "There's Lyndon, our son. He's sleeping now. He was here. He knows when we got back. Unless you think a family member would lie to—"

"Lyndon will do nicely," I said, watching Mark jot down the lad's name. "May we speak with him tomorrow?"

"Suit yourself, I'm sure."

"Right." Mark stood up and tucked his notebook into his jacket pocket. "Thank you, Mrs. Fitzpatrick. We'll try not to make a nuisance of ourselves. See you in the morning. And again, our condolences."

He followed me to the door, but it wasn't until Noreen Kitzpatrick had closed and locked it that Mark said, "Shopping trip, my arse. You can get guitar mics, strings and picks online these days. If you want to go the personal route, Manchester has them. Why would Kirk even consider heading to Chesterfield, the opposite direction from his concert in Bolton? What's going on?"

I pressed my index finger against Mark's lips and winked. "Mustn't tell, must we? That'd clue in the coppers."

"Well," Mark snorted as we got into the car, "we're giving her enough time to rehearse little Lyndon on what to tell us tomorrow. We should have dragged him out of bed tonight and questioned him."

"Oh, fine, and get the child protection services on our backs? No thanks. Besides, what I just told Noreen wasn't a load of rubbish, Mark, and you should know it. We don't know how Roger died, if it was murder or a fight that got out of hand. Let's not get everyone worked up for nothing if it turns out to be an unfortunate accident. You're not thinking right."

We passed the petrol station again before Mark said, "Sorry. It's just happened once too often for me, following the rules, letting someone have a bit of time, and then finding out they've either skipped town or made up a whacking great lie to cover their backside. I just didn't want that happening again."

"Poor Mark. Would a kiss make it better?" I leaned sideways and kissed his cheek.

Mark jammed on the car brake, bringing the car to a stop in the middle of the traffic lane, grabbed my shoulders, and pulled me towards him. It happened so quickly that I had little time to react. But when we parted after that long, strong kiss, I felt less sure of myself and my feelings about Detective-Sergeant Mark Salt than I had before. He let off the parking brake and eased the car down the High Street. "If you're going to apply first aid, Brenna, do it *correctly*."

Ordinarily I would have laughed, but I still felt the pressure of his lips on mine, still remembered Erik's arms around me this morning, and still had to reckon with my racing heart.

"Perhaps it's bad timing," he finally said as he turned into the Swinbrooks' drive, "but that's never stopped me from making an ass of myself before. Would you like to go out with me one night soon? A belated valentine dinner or concert or something? You decide. I'll even sit through the classics if you want to hear Van Cliburn or whoever."

"Van Cliburn doesn't perform anymore."

"Oh, yes? Well, see? I need you to take me out, at least to combat my pitiful education."

This time he kept his eyes on the road. Maybe it was due to the absence of street lamps along the drive; maybe Mark was preparing himself for a disappointment; maybe he couldn't look at me, couldn't stand to see pity instead of friendship in my face. I was just as glad that he looked straight ahead. It gave me time, however little there was, to gather my feelings before I replied.

When he stopped at the tower, the car scattering gravel and swerving slightly to the right, he repeated the question. My heart raced along with the idling motor, for I didn't know what to say. A dinner was really nothing these days, as far as a date went. It could be anything from just a pub meal between friends to a prelude to sleeping with a guy. But as I looked at Mark in the darkness, I knew he would not overstep the line of a meal between friends. He would not force anything on me that I didn't want. Our kiss was something different. It had come from a bit of play that I had instigated.

"I'd love to, Mark," I finally said, patting his arm.

"Really?" He looked so surprised that I smiled. "Honest?"

"Really. Honest. Sounds like a nice evening." I stepped out of the car, then said through the open doorway, "You pick the time, I'll pick the place. Right now, let's call it a night. I'm exhausted."

He said he'd come back to the pub with me but he wanted to question the publican before turning in for the night. "I want to see if Kirk Fitzpatrick and Roger's group were at the pub when they all claimed, and if Austin stayed late for that drink. You wanna tag along?"

"I've had enough adventures for the night. It's been—" I checked my watch and saw that it was just after half past twelve. "Yikes. Our publican isn't going to bless you for waking him."

"He'll just have gone to sleep. It's not a big deal."

I slammed the car door, thinking it may not be a big deal to Mark, but perhaps it was with the landlord. "I wish you luck, Mark. But don't come to me looking for more first aid if he bites off your head."

Jo A. Hiestand

CHAPTER SIX

IN OUR ABSENCE, some enterprising constable had strung up the police tape, a vinyl ribbon of alternating blue and white rhomboids that now quivered in the cold wind. Blue block letters stating POLICE boldly implied Authority, Restricted Access, Security, and Crime Scene. For some, it also implied grief.

One lone constable stood outside the tower door, which was now shut and presumably locked. The tower itself was dark, devoid of police work lamps, telling me the scientific officers had finished their tasks and were hopefully on their way home. I nodded to the bobby before I drove off.

It was a short distance back into the village proper—down the Swinbrook drive again and back up the High Street. The pub where our CID team had its lodgings, Mark had informed me, was on my right. I parked the car, got out, and slowly climbed the stairs to my room.

I'd just tossed my shoulder bag and car keys onto the bed when a knock sounded on my bedroom door. Margo, my confidante and colleague, rushed into the room barely before I had the door open. Flopping down in the chintz-covered armchair, she said, "Well?"

I stood against the door, half amused, half aggravated. One a.m. was not an ideal time in which to giggle about the affairs of the day. "Well what?" I said, rather sharply. The bed looked very comfortable.

"You know what. How'd it go? With Mark?"

"What do you mean?" I walked over to my small overnight bag that I always kept in my car's boot for emergencies and opened it. Margo didn't take the hint.

"I saw you, Bren. Graham sent you and Mark on some fact-finding mission. So?"

"We found facts."

"Come on. You know I don't care about police stuff. You and Mark."

"Well?" I was tired enough to be ornery.

"If you say that one more time—"

"Margo," I said, hugging my pajamas to my chest, "we've had a God-awful, long day, and I'm in no mood to play Animal-Vegetable-Mineral with you. Graham expects us to be awake, dressed and reasonably functioning later this morning. I've got to take charge of a briefing with the various teams, not to mention dealing with the press, and I don't want to spend my precious sleep time confirming or personifying your fantasy. Now, out!" I strode toward the door and opened it, waiting for her to move. She didn't.

"Please, Bren. Just a few quick sentences. You don't have to give me the lurid details—"

"Of which there are none."

"—but I just want to know how you two got on. If he asked you out."

"Why would he?" I said, closing the door. I didn't want the entire populace of the inn knowing about this. Plus, I knew when I was licked.

"You went to dinner with him in January. Remember? When we were investigating that death in his family? I just thought...well, you said it wasn't so bad. And the way Mark looks at you...well...." She flashed her brown eyes and gave me that smile that probably would get her picked up on street corners, if she were the sort of woman who wanted to be picked up on street corners.

I sighed, sat on the edge of the bed, and said, "Okay. But it's nothing, really. We're going for dinner. Nothing romantic. No postponed Valentine's thing." I took a breath, willing my face not to blush as I thought of Graham and his mystery dinner date. I said, "He just wants to go out. So we are."

"So we are," she repeated, getting up. "Where? When? Dressy affair? God, I hope it's not some American burger place."

"Even fish-and-chips would be fine. I like fish-and-chips."

"So do I, Bren, but for a dinner date?"

It was intended as a joke, but I closed my eyes, trying to sort through the evening's events. When I looked at her again, I blurted out, "I don't know what to do, Margo."

She looked at me, probably waiting for something like a case problem, and then smiled when I said, "Mark kissed me in the car tonight."

"Kissed, as in *kissed*?"

I nodded.

"Was it mutual? I mean, did you let him? Did you like it? What about you and Eric? What's that doing to you and Mark? Anyway, I thought you and Mark—"

"I know. That's why I'm confused." I related the incident. In the stillness afterwards, when Margo was taking it all in, I heard the sounds of the night coming in through the closed bedroom window. Gentle, quiet sounds that ordinarily would have been overlooked because they've been heard so often or because they're drowned out by louder noises. Like the Clarksons' big city noises that they never heard. But here, now, a fox barked at the moon, and the pub sign squeaked on its rusty hinges.

"I don't know what I feel about Mark," I said, going to the window and peering outside. Moonlight washed everything under the sky, tinting buildings, roads, terrain and trees in silver. The High Street had frosted over in the frigid temperature and it shone white as it twisted its way north to the deeper dales and mountains of the district. Definitely a Highwayman night, I thought as the moon slid behind a cloud. The landscape suddenly turned dark, opaque except for the spackling of the street lamps' orange lights. I should be reciting the poetry, standing beneath a bare-branched tree, instead of readying myself for sleep.

"When will you know?" Margo asked.

I turned to face her, leaning against the windowsill. The air was cold on my back, but the distraction kept me awake.

"I don't know. Does anyone ever put a time table on things like this?"

"Of course not. I was just curious if you felt yourself falling."

"I'm all in a muddle, Margo. You know what I thought about him when we were in class together."

"First class berk, yes."

"Then he started to change. *Really* change and care about me. That dog incident in December, the dinner last month...oh, little things, but he's changed. He's not showing off for me anymore. I think he's letting me see his real self. And he's gentle and kind."

Margo grimaced and scratched her forehead. "And what about Erik? You can't be void of feelings with a guy who's sleeping with you."

"We've been together for only three weeks, Margo. And anyway, it's not every night."

"Every night, once a week or once a year. Big deal. He's still sleeping with you."

"Only on weekends...when we're both available."

"You've feelings for him, haven't you?"

I stared at my hands, wondering how much I honestly had. The invitation for Erik to move in had been spare of the moment from me. Offered one particularly lonely day. I'd seen his photo in the police newsletter and rang him at his office in Ripley. I don't know what I'd been hoping for—maybe just a rekindling of pleasant memories or a desire to retain a part of my life that I felt slipping away. Whatever the reason, I remember my hand shaking as I closed my mobile phone and the panic that rushed through my body. Had he really remembered me, or was he just being polite? Would he still remember the shared jokes and the confidences shared? I should have known he would; he grinned and kissed me the moment we met, calling me by my nickname, asking after my family. We had talked over a drink in a pub after work, chatting about more than schooling and our jobs, picking up on the same topics on which we'd always conversed. I'd been intoxicated by our renewed friendship, his humor and my vulnerability. So I had hinted, not too obliquely, that I was yearning for companionship. He moved in that weekend. 'Lock, stock and badge,' as Margo had phrased it.

"It's got to be more than solitude," Margo said after we'd been busy with our own thoughts. "You don't invite a guy to live with you—okay, okay, just on weekends—just for the physical relationship. Sure, you can have as many affairs as you wish, and a lot of coppers do. It helps dull the intensity of the job, just as liquor does. But Erik's different. He's—"

"There's no love, Margo," I said, looking at her. "He and I both know that. We've made no pretense about fervor or marriage 'sometime.' Sure, I care deeply about him. I think I always have, since we met at headquarters in Buxton. One of those magnetic moments—God, that sounds so ludicrous! But it happens. There may not have been electricity flowing, but we liked each other instantly."

"Then why didn't you do something about it?"

"I don't know. Job, life, family. Cowardice. Something got in the way."

She didn't say it, but I knew she was thinking about Graham. I'd seen him and felt the electricity.

"Anyway," I said, forcing a carelessness into my voice that I didn't feel, "Erik and I suit each other. I love his company, and we have tremendous fun hanging out together. And we *do* care about each other—maybe not to the degree that demands an engagement, but there's affection. Real warmth."

"So who's 'Porthos' to your 'Aramis' and Eric's 'Athos'?"

I ignored her Three Musketeers jibe. "Yes, we're friends. I think any good, lasting relationship needs that quality. But there's something more with Erik and me. I don't know what. But right now we're together only because we need each other physically. We both need someone in our lives—actual, real, handholding close. We're both sick of just existing and doing our jobs, living with a wish or a fantasy of someday."

The room grew quiet again. I pictured Erik standing on my doorstep, valentine gifts in his hand, his eyes sparkling. It was not love, but it was more than friendship. I didn't know what to call it, but it was fine for the foreseeable future.

"What about..." Margo stopped, afraid to say his name.

"What about..."

"You know. The Vic?"

I reddened and looked down at my hands. "I don't know, Margo. That's the problem. I love Graham."

"That's an awfully strong word, Bren—love. How do you know it's love? Sure, Graham's a hunk. But so is Mark. *And* Erik. All three are handsome and built and brainy in different ways. Whatever's happened to convince you it's love?"

I slumped against the window, trying to ignore the coldness of the glass. "If I don't love Graham, I don't know what I'd call it, Margo. It's more than infatuation. I just like being with him. We don't have to do anything. I just like to sit with him. I like talking to him. I admire him for his morals and his work ethic and his sense of justice and compassion. I like his humor and his intelligence, which I find sexy. As for anything else..." I looked at Margo, afraid what I'd read in her face. It held neither disdain nor mockery, merely concern. "Well, how can I know anything else about him if he never lets me into his life?"

"And from the way things are going, he may never do that. It's rough, Bren. He may always consider you a coworker. One of the boys."

I shifted my gaze to my lap, embarrassed by the intimacy of our conversation. "He's never done anything romantic with me, of course. No flowers or dinner or trips together. Women use such things as a foundation for love. But it's got to be on-going, a history of them. Graham and I haven't done a single thing together. And when we do have dinner, it's at a pub, talking about the case."

"So your feelings for him stem from his personality."

"That's all I have, Margo! I can only go by that and love as much as I can without encouragement."

"But that's going to burn itself out if he never returns it."

"Only so much satisfaction from a one-way affair. Lipstick marks on the photo lose their excitement after a bit." I sniffed and blotted my nose with the back of my hand.

"You're in a bind, like I said."

"What should I do?"

"Go out with Mark, since you're trying to convince me—and yourself—you don't love Erik. Mark's attainable and seems eager to love you. When are you going, by the way? Soon? You need to borrow anything of mine? I've some heels—"

I got up and gently pushed her out of the room, saying, "Nothing decided yet. I'm to pick the place; he's to pick the time."

"Smashing!" Her next sentence was muffled as I closed and locked the door. "I'll clutter his path with hints."

And knowing Margo, she would. I held my pajamas for a minute, thinking that what I had said about fish-and-chips was very true. It wasn't so much the food you had on the date, as it was whom you ate it with. And right now I'd even eat a cold American hamburger if I could eat it with Graham.

TOLLING TOWER BELLS and crumpled Valentine's Day cards plagued my date with Graham. At least, the date in my dream that night. I woke too early and too tired. Standing at the sink, I peered at my eyes, ran my fingers through my hair, and generally wondered who owned the haggard face staring at me. At least my copper-colored hair was shiny even if my eyes weren't. But just so my brain worked, that's all Graham really cared about.

I thought about bells and relationships as I quickly showered and dressed. Graham seemed to have some sort of understanding with his lady friend. He'd been soft-spoken and attentive. Perhaps he'd known her for a long time and was just resurrecting the friendship. Perhaps he'd met her through a dating service or a friend. I stared at my reflection in the mirror and wiped away a tear. It was not the time to feel sorry for myself. I needed to concentrate on the case. But it was hard—all my energy was divided between Graham, Mark's looming date, and Geneva's grief. Why did love have to be so confusing?

The village community hall was on the main road, just up from the pub. It seemed wedged between the chemist's shop and the steeply rising hill on which the church squatted. But perhaps the pre-dawn darkness contributed to that illusion. I could distinguish nothing about the hall except its shape and size, but imagined it was similar to the others in the district: a tan-stone structure with a dark slate roof. Building materials hardly varied in these old villages.

I paused outside the hall's door. No sound other than the creaking of the pub sign could be heard—no conversations, no traffic, no doors slamming. The village appeared to slumber as snugly as a fox in its den. But far colder, for the sun did not yet embrace the cold stones with its golden warmth. Trees, road, and buildings seemed to cower beneath the blanket of frigid air. Patches of snow hunkered tenaciously in the hollows and shadow-filled bases of buildings and trees. Snow lay frozen where it had melted, paper-thin atop the glacial ground. It stretched gingerly across the land, merging its whiteness with the night's coating of frost. Frost glazed the stonewalls of the hall, etched lacy designs on the puddles dotting the pavement, fringed and stiffened the grass blades. Beyond these strangely-visible smears of white, the street, dark and lifeless, lay squeezed between the black bulks of stores running along its sides. Farther north it vanished into the gloom that still enveloped the land. But sunrise would reveal its presence, bring color and definition and texture to the dull shapes hugging it as though for warmth. Sunrise would beckon birds from their nests and fill the still air with song. It would summon people from their homes, people who would soon hear of Roger's death. I blew on my chilled fingers, grasped the cold door handle, and forced myself to face a long day.

Graham was sitting at a metal-legged table when I walked up to him. He smiled and asked if I was as tired as he was.

"Well, sir," I said, moving a folding chair, "I could use a bit more sleep, since you brought up the subject. I'm certain it was ten minutes after my head hit the pillow that the alarm went off." He didn't need to know that my conversation with Margo, and the ensuing thoughts, had robbed me of a precious hour in the arms of Morpheus.

"All in due time, Taylor. What time is it, anyway?" He looked at the electric clock above the door. "Oh, God. Half five. Have you had breakfast? Yes? I'll grab something a bit later. You up to conducting the briefing? I'd do it, but I have to go out again almost immediately."

"Ready as I ever will be, yes, sir."

He handed me the postmortem but gave me the gist of it.

"To begin with," he said, "Jens found extensive bruising on Roger's upper arms and back. These are consistent with a fall, such as he might have sustained from the top of the ladder in the ringing chamber. It's fifteen feet from the ceiling to the floor. More than enough to inflict this damage. But the odd thing, if you remember when he told us last evening, was the cuts on his hands."

"Consistent with defense wounds from a fight?"

"Correct. So whom did he fight with? And how could he have fought with someone and yet have those bruises from a great fall?"

"I suppose," I said as Graham swallowed the last of his tea, "it could have happened if he fought with someone in the room above the ringing chamber where the clock mechanism is, then fallen through that trap door in the ceiling, into the ringing chamber where we found him." I said it slowly, sounding it out as my mind raced ahead, seeing the proposed scenario in my mind. I glanced at Graham, wondering if it sounded like rubbish. He was smiling.

"Fits the evidence, I'd say. Now all we need is Roger's sparing partner. We know he had one. Someone must have smacked him with that bottle."

"Shouldn't be hard to find the person. Take your pick. Angry neighbors, such as Baxter Clarkson. Greedy relatives who can't wait for Roger to die."

"Speaking of your bottle, Jens found several head wounds of a half-moon, crescent shape. He suggested strongly that we might want to pay close attention to that Duvel ale bottle in the ringing room. The indentations are suspiciously of a size that would fit a beer bottle. Plus, the bottle would be heavy enough to inflict several deep wounds—as these are—before breaking, which that bottle did. The nearly superficial blows, which undoubtedly occurred first as the assailant warmed up in his anger, are of that crescent shape. Picture swinging the bottle, Taylor, and the resulting depression from the bottom edge of the bottle imbedded in the scalp. Later depressions are much deeper and accompanied by cuts to the scalp, resulting in bleeding. They would also be responsible for the blood patterns around the victim."

I made a face and thanked Responsible Powers once again that I had escaped attending the postmortem.

Graham ignored my facial comment and continued. "Contusions of the scalp skin are obvious, and he found a palpable skull fracture on the right temporal bone—just above the right ear. Cause of death is cerebral hemorrhage. And, as is frequent with this type of injury, the victim soiled himself due to sphincter relaxation at the moment of head injury.

"Rigor and lividity cannot be relied on to determine if the body had been moved, or even time of death."

"Temperature in the tower was cold," I said, restraining myself from saying it had been bloody freezing in that stone-walled cylinder.

"But we know from talking to the main witnesses that Roger died between quarter after six, when he left the pub, and quarter after seven."

"When Geneva found him."

"One hour. Nice, that. Wish all our cases could be fine tuned like that, instead of Jens handing us 'Ten hours or so.' It's probably closer to seven o'clock, when the bells fell silent and our assumed altercation took place, but I don't want to go with speculation. One hour is close enough."

"Better than we've ever had, yes."

"One of our industrious constables," Graham said, leaning back in his chair, "found a broken piece of wood in the bell chamber. He didn't know the significance of it, but I suspect I do. Of course, it could be nothing, but put with the fact that Roger evidently stopped ringing soon after he began..." He stopped, looked at me, and angled his notebook toward me so that I could read it.

"Broken stay?"

Graham nodded. "A stay is the vertical piece of wood that fits into the metal bell frame to stop the bell from making a continuous, full circle. You've never rung," he said when I frowned.

"No, sir. Never had the chance." Mark's story of his early bell ringing experience popped into my head before I could mimic nearly the same history. Instead, I said, "And you? You referred to your ringing days last night when we were in the tower."

"I can probably still ring, if given a rope, but I'm not up to ringing a peal. The concentration is a bit beyond me. I haven't kept my mind in condition for that. Or remember most of the methods. They're memorized, Taylor. There's no such thing as 'music' for change ringing, just the basic method or pattern. Once you know that, you memorize the path your particular bell makes through the hundreds of positions in the eight-bell—or six or four or however many—pattern."

"Sounds as though it takes a bit of practice."

"Some, yes," he said, smiling. "But that's only half the problem. First you have to learn how to handle the bell. Never forget you've got several hundred pounds of swinging metal over your head. And you're trying to control it. To change the position of your bell in the eight-bell pattern you have to ring your bell either slightly faster or slower that time around so your bell sounds before or after your neighbor."

I must have looked bewildered, for he drew out a succession of numbers, representing eight bells, on a page of his notebook.

"For example, you start ringing a simple scale. Rounds. These are bell numbers, not notes. one-two-three-four-five-six-seven-eight. Fine. But you want to change the pattern so it doesn't become boring, right? So you now ring, say, two-one-three-four-five-seven-six-eight. For number two bell to ring first in sequence this time, the person ringing bell two has to ring slightly faster and the person ringing bell one has to ring slightly slower. Same with people ringing seven and six."

"So," I said, hoping I had it figured out, "if I'm ringing number two bell, and we've just finished ringing that first straight scale of one thru eight, on *this* second time around of ringing eight bells I will ring my bell first instead of second."

"Bang on! Yes!"

"And in order to ring my bell first, I have to pull the rope a fraction faster in order to ring before bell one."

"You've got it. You're pulling faster so your bell doesn't complete its full arc swing. All this pulling the rope faster or slower takes practice, as well as just learning how to pull the ruddy thing in the first place. It's in the feel of the rope and the swinging bell on the other end of the rope that you acquire the skill. There is no muscular strength involved, for the bells, as I said, are mounted on an iron frame with ball bearings that enable them to swing freely."

"So what's to stop them from swinging in a circle and winding up all your rope?"

"That stay we were just talking about. The piece of wood that sticks up vertically from the headstock of the bell. Have you seen a tower bell? No? Lesson one, then. If you're to understand what we're talking about in this case, you need to know about the bells and how they work. Alright?"

I nodded, ready to learn anything that would make sense of all this confusion.

Graham continued. "When the bell's pulled, the wheel revolves so the stay comes in contact with another piece of wood fastened to the foot of the frame. Here. Perhaps this will help." He quickly sketched the bell on its frame.

PEARLS BEFORE SWINE

"Of course," he said, jabbing the pen point at the sketch for emphasis, "this is rough. I've left out parts. But it's just to give you the idea of what the bell looks like. That piece sticking up opposite the wheel is the stay. When the bell rotates around so it's mouth-up, the stay comes in contact with the slider—that horizontal piece of wood beneath the bell's mouth—and keeps the bell from turning in a circle."

"But the stay can break," I said, remembering the earlier conversation in the tower. "And has to be replaced."

Graham nodded. "That's why a ringer not only has to know the physical aspects of ringing, and the patterns or methods to be rung, but also the mechanics of bell maintenance."

"Like Austin said, there *is* a lot to master. How long does all this take?"

"Weeks, months, usually, for most of them. Depending on the number of bells in your ring—that's what a group of bells is called. A ring. Roger's tower, for example, has six bells, so he has a ring of six. Mastering it also depends on the pattern or method you are ringing and the number of times you run through it. A Plain Bob—which is a simple method of changing bell positions—looks like this on five bells."

He jotted down a column of numbers, then drew a line following one bell through the column. The 'path,' he called it.

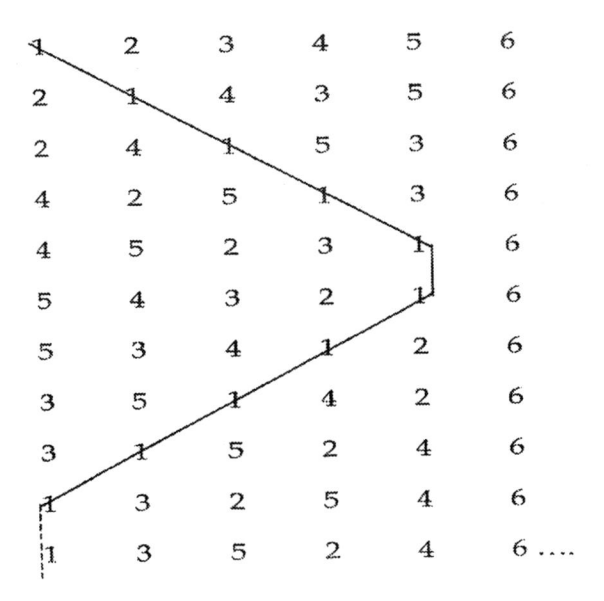

1	2	3	4	5	6
2	1	4	3	5	6
2	4	1	5	3	6
4	2	5	1	3	6
4	5	2	3	1	6
5	4	3	2	1	6
5	3	4	1	2	6
3	5	1	4	2	6
3	1	5	2	4	6
1	3	2	5	4	6
1	3	5	2	4	6 ....

"And so on until all the bells switch back into their original order of one-two-three-four-five-six."

"Takes some memorization, yes," I said, staring at the numbers. It would sound like 'noise,' as Mark had put it, to the untrained ear. But I could understand getting hooked by the fascination of the puzzle, which

Graham said he liked, and the mental gymnastics that a lot of people thrived on. A good hobby, then, for a lot of different reasons. Not the least of which would be the camaraderie of getting through it together, like a team sport.

"It takes perfect manipulation of the bells. I'm rather surprised Roger attempted to ring two bells alternately. Talk about coordination and concentration! I'd have expected to have been called to a hanging if he'd kept it up for the hour."

"Impossible fete, then?"

Graham shrugged. "It's not impossible, Taylor. Jut takes a very experienced ringer. It wasn't accomplished in the UK until the end of the 19th century. Still, there are some who can manage it, though I don't know how. It's beyond me, at any rate."

"So why does the number six bell always play at the end?"

"The highest numberbell, whether you're ringing four or six or eight or twelve bells, is always the largest, heaviest bell in the ring. The tenor bell. It sounds last so that you have an audile anchor for that line of ringing. When you hear the tenor sound, you know you're at the end of that string of switching and you're ready to start the next line of interchanging positions."

I nodded, impressed with the cleverness of those who had invented all this.

"It's the beginning ringer's bane that he sometimes pulls too heavily on the rope, causing the wheel to revolve too far and too swiftly, thereby breaking the stay. When that happens, there's nothing for it but to immediately stop ringing, climb up into the bell chamber, and replace the stay. The job's only a matter of minutes, but it's the aggravation that makes it such a pain. Consequently, towers have a nice store of spare stays."

"And," I said, envisioning Roger climbing up the ladder into the bell room, "since we found a broken stay, that suggests why the bell ringing stopped. But I still don't understand why he placed those two conflicting phone calls. One to his brother saying the bet was off because he wasn't ringing, and one to Ben, apologiz—" I stopped mid-sentence and stared at Graham.

"He could have phoned Austin because he broke the stay. But there are other stays in the bell room. PC Fordyce found them."

"So that doesn't make sense, if that's the reason Roger called off the ringing session. He *would* have if there hadn't been replacement stays, but there were."

"He was certainly dressed for ringing," Graham said. "Similar to what I would have worn. Old natty cardigan. So that, too, seems to fit with his intention to ring. And, speaking of intentions....I think we've had enough bell lessons for the moment and better get on with our next line of inquiry." He stood up, grabbed his jacket, and said he had scheduled the teams briefing for six o'clock. "You better get on with it. I've got a job of work or I'd do it. See you later." He grabbed his car key and strode out the door, leaving me to handle the expressionless faces at the briefing.

CHAPTER SEVEN

By six o'clock, the leaders of the various teams had assembled in the incident room. A dozen officers—press officer, scientific officers, incident team inspector and such—sat at metal tables sipping coffee or tea, talking about the case. They looked as ready for the day as I was. Strained eyes glanced outside at the still-dark morning sky while the smokers in the group sucked on lit cigarettes, needing the nicotine to prod them into their workday. One constable balanced two coffee mugs on his lap and groused to the officer on his left that he'd rushed here without having breakfast. I stepped in front of the group, thanked them for arriving so promptly, and gave them the postmortem findings. Someone whistled softly when I told them we were looking at a murder investigation.

"Kind of hard to give yourself all those head wounds," one of the team leaders said, looking up from his note taking.

I agreed, related the other findings we had, then asked if anyone had any questions.

The leader of the house-to-house team asked, "Are we concentrating on this Ben Griffiths, then? Since he has a history of calling in complaints against Lord Swinbrook..."

"You can talk to him, yes, but it's too early to concentrate on anyone or on any line."

"Am I to let the media know it's murder?" The press officer leaned forward in his chair, resting his elbows on the table top. "Or just say we're still working on manner of death?"

"I don't see any advantage if we keep it a secret. You can announce it's murder."

"It'll bring out the nerks," he said while several officers groaned. "Everyone claiming he did it, or knows who did it. Just to see his name in the papers. Give him celebrity status, it will, knocking off a lord."

"Fifteen minutes of fame."

"Part of you job, mate," one of the men said. "You get the glory, standing in front of the cameras, being quoted in the *Sun*. You've got to take the heartaches that go with it."

A ripple of laughter ran through the room. I said, "We'll deal with the phones when we have to. Anything else?"

"Is her ladyship good looking?"

"If that's it," I said, shaking my head in disbelief, "I'll let you get on with your jobs. We'll meet again tomorrow, same time, for updates. Right."

The scraping of metal chair legs against the linoleum floor ruptured the quiet. I went over to my computer as the group filed past me. One officer reminded the comedian that he wouldn't inherit the title even if he did marry Lady Swinbrook.

"Who's worried about the title?" the man asked, nodding to me. "I need a few hundred quid to get my car repaired. Have you heard that thing squeal when I try to start it?"

His mate's answer was lost in their exit and the ringing of my phone. I answered it quickly, thinking it might be Graham. It was Scott Coral, one of our sections' officers.

"You're up early," he said, a hint of humor in his voice.

"So are you. Don't you have a life other than this one?"

"Not that you'd notice. Graham asked me to ring you up. He wants me to check on something, assuming you have the information I need already."

"We saw each other at the ungodly—"

"Careful, careful. I've delicate ears."

I sighed. "He knows I had a briefing this morning."

"Something about last night. A talk with Kirk Fitzpatrick. That ring a bell?"

"Always the comic. What about a talk with Kirk?" I explained that he had left town. But could Kirk's wife help Scott?

Scott said, "Graham heard Kirk's in Bolton. Or he claims to be."

"How'd Graham learn that?" I asked, interrupting. "Mark and I only found that out last night."

"The man moves in mysterious ways, Brenna. Anyway, you lost eight vital detecting hours sleeping. Graham was still up and working."

"I wouldn't call it eight hours sleeping. More like four."

"Poor darling. You can sleep later."

"You sound like Graham."

"He wants me to corroborate Kirk's concert schedule."

"So he's suspicious of Kirk, then?"

"It's not for me to say. I'm not a detective."

I laughed. "The whole story his wife gave us last night sounded awfully strange. He leaves for his tour a day early, doesn't come back to comfort his sister...yes, I suppose Kirk's whereabouts do need confirmation."

"So where's he supposed to be? Give me some venue dates and names."

I gave Scott the name and time of Thursday's gig. Thank God for my good memory. Mark had the notes.

"Super. Thanks, Bren."

"After you've verified the venue, Scott, perhaps you'd track down Kirk. You can wait around the club to see if he turns up there...that's perfectly fine. But if he doesn't, if he's done a runner, then find him. I'll clear it with Graham. He won't mind."

"He'll give you a pat on the back for thinking of it."

"Just *find* him, Scott. The concert dates may be legitimate, but Kirk might have planned this whole incident as a convenient smoke screen to ease out of town under our noses. We need to know either way what's going on. Got it?"

"I'll find out, or I *will* get it—reprimand, is it?"

I laughed. I could imagine Scott sitting in his patrol car, his left arm draped along the back of the car seat, perhaps, or lying casually over the top of the steering wheel. He would be wearing the white shirt, the combat pants and jacket—the regulation uniform of the response driver. A street cop, to Americans. He'd be lying in wait for a speeder, perhaps, or just finishing a call that had brought him to a fight or vehicle crash or burglary. Any of a myriad of problems that plagued human life. That he was compassionate with people in difficulty was no secret in the department. But that he was wanting something more from his job *was*. And he had confided in me on the strictest level of sworn oaths.

But right now I mentally focused on the conversation and imagined Scott's green eyes alight with pleasure. He was getting some action in this case and he was probably ecstatic.

Which was a far cry from my emotional state at the moment. I wished Scott good luck, rang off, and sat down in the cold metal chair. Was Lady Swinbrook resentful of Austin's succession to Lord Swinbrook? Was she regretting she and Roger had had no children? Would she still live in the hall, albeit in a suite, if Austin moved in? Would she feel out of place, pushed aside? I dropped an ordinance survey map of Oldfield and environs beside Graham's computer and hoped she was the sort of person who could go on with her life. She was far too young to give up.

For perhaps the next half hour I re-read the postmortem notes and tried as best I could to jot down my own thoughts as to motive. A few constables finished connecting a fax machine to a computer printer and stepped back to view their handiwork. I gazed past our small claim of the village community center. Once again we had probably disrupted some event. Or, at the least, the Girl Guides weekly meeting or table tennis matches. I gazed at the folded-up table tennis tables and other sport equipment now shoved into the far corner, the flyers on the walls announcing the championship battle between the Phoenix and the Cerberus teams. Both mythological creatures, one burning itself on a funeral pyre and then rising from the ashes, the other the three-headed dog who guarded the gate to hell. If I were to read anything into these team names, I'd assume Cerberus was the long-undefeated champion and that Phoenix was constantly resurrecting itself as the challenger. But teams don't necessarily take on names that reflect their winning history. Unless they had started out blandly as, perhaps, the Knights and the Gargoyles, and after years of tournaments had decided to change their names. I smiled. Interesting, as Scott would say. I'd have to stop by next winter to find out.

I was just about to wander into the kitchenette to put the kettle on for some tea when Graham came in. He didn't look as tired as other times I'd seen him, but we'd only been on the scene for twelve hours. He would go another day and a half, most likely, before he'd allow himself to sleep.

He came over to the table, took off his jacket, and sat down heavily. He looked up at me, hope in his eyes. "You have a cuppa for me?"

"Sure thing, sir. I was just about to put on the water. I'll not be a minute." I hurried into the kitchen, wondering what Graham had been doing, and turned on the electric kettle. Minutes later, I set the hot liquid in front of him and reclaimed my chair.

"So, anything urgent? Any problems?"

I related Mark's and my conversation with Noreen Fitzpatrick, thinking it a waste of time if Graham already knew that Kirk was out of town. Still, it showed him I had a good memory, if nothing else.

"I don't know if it's a plus for our side that Kirk isn't a bell ringer," he said. "Doesn't preclude him from going over to the tower and hitting Roger alongside the head. Anyone could do that, bell ringer or not."

Before I could answer, Mark walked in. He winked at me, held out his fingers as though to say his hand had been slapped and he needed another application of first aid, and came over to us. Graham shoved aside a stack of paper, turned in his chair, and asked Mark what he had found out.

"Well, sir," Mark said, taking the chair Graham indicated and flipping open his notebook, "I talked to the publican of The Cat and Mouse last night. Howard Milton." Mark gave me a glance and wriggled his fingers. Funny man. He then said, "Luckily, he was still awake. Just closed up the pub, so that's one little scream of police harassment averted."

I smiled and batted my eyelashes. Graham's back was toward me, so he couldn't see my editorial comment.

Mark continued. "I inquired about our principle players, if they were there, when they arrived, departed, if anyone else was with them. The usual."

Graham snorted. "And was there anything *un*usual?"

"Not that Howard recalled. He said it was a bit quieter than many Wednesday evenings. Which surprised him. He thought it being Valentine's Day there would be more couples out for dinner. But he figured they'd gone to fancier spots, in Chesterfield or Manchester or Buxton, or to a film or such."

"So he could easily recall if our players were there."

"Yes, sir. He said they were all at the same table, talking and having dinner. Austin did return a few minutes later, after seeing Geneva out, and Austin was there, drinking scotch, until 8:30. A few tourists were there, at two different tables, who weren't part of Lord Swinbrook's party or with each other. They've been here several days and are staying at two B-and-B's in the village. Here are the addresses."

PEARLS BEFORE SWINE

Mark handed the paper to Graham. It had several names written on it, plus the names and addresses of two bed-and-breakfast accommodations.

Graham asked if the publican knew anything about them. Mark said that they had come into the pub at different times, one group arriving first on Saturday, the other group on Monday. They didn't seem to know each other and there was no reason at this point to suspect they were up to no good. They had not seen the necklace, but he wasn't surprised he hadn't. "Being, as he said, that it was obviously in a league with the crown jewels, and its owner probably wouldn't frequent pubs."

"Not too far of an exaggeration, crown jewels. Only people around here that might fit that category are..." Graham looked at me, waiting for me to fill in the blank.

I supplied it. "Lord and Lady S."

Mark nodded. "I'll tackle people who know them, rather than upset her ladyship. So," he said, closing his notebook, "we seem to be concentrating on our happy pub partiers. Oh, and Ben Griffiths was there—alone, but he had come over to talk to Lord Swinbrook."

"Evidently a very approachable man, Roger, Lord Swinbrook. And Ben Griffiths is..."

"The husband of Mona Griffiths, who is a maid at the hall."

"He doesn't have live-in staff?"

"Yes, sir, he does. Chauffeur, butler, cook, milady's maid. Oh, and head gardener. The other staff live around the area and come in for their shift."

"Things have certainly changed since the good old days."

"Yes, sir. The publican told me that the hall's staff has dwindled over the decades. Said his grandfather still talks about the old times when the earl had dozens employed."

"Was the grandfather one of them?"

Mark nodded. "He and his wife. Under gardener and scullery maid, when they first began employment. Ended up a bit better in the command chain when they retired. But they speak highly of the old earl and the present Lord Swinbrook. Well," Mark said, exhaling deeply, "the recently deceased Lord S. The publican said it's no secret in the village that taxes are the main problem with the family."

"That I can believe. They eat a hefty hole in *my* pay packet and I've not nearly the wealth *they* have. Taxes aside, just the house must demand the Bank of England to keep it in good repair."

"That's the impression I got too, sir. That's one of the reasons for the financial difficulties they're enduring. They've had to sell a bit of the furnishings and family treasures of late. Even sold some of their land, which helped reduce upkeep and brought them a bit of lolly."

"Which is how Baxter Clarkson came to be so neighborly with his lordship, I assume."

Jo A. Hiestand

"They show rooms to the public two days a week, but even so, they aren't the high rollers or the social force they once were, for all the peerage still connected with them."

"A shade of their former selves, then," said Graham. "Sad, in a way."

"Yes, sir. The family used to spell its name with an 'e'. Swinebrook. Back in the 16th century. They deleted the letter—"

"I can just hear the school boys' taunts," Graham said.

"—early in the 18th century."

I thought back to some of the names I'd been called in school. Cruel, hurtful names. Designed to humiliate and outclass me, bring me to tears. Which they did. That malicious valentine had been only a small part of what I had endured through my schooling. By the time I had left school, I had grown a thick shell and perfected an air of indifference and disdain toward my bullies. My true feelings were so deeply buried that I feared I could never trust or love or open up to anyone again. Even with Graham, whom I feared I was falling in love with. Although he liked me beyond the colleague embodiment, having shown concern for me as a person when I broke down in front of him in December, he still had made no overture of friendship outside of our daily grind. Of course, in our current society, the woman could ask the man for a date. But first of all, he was my boss and I didn't think that would look right, never mind it being against Force policy. And second of all, I wanted some sign that he was interested in me, either romantically or cordially. Not only did I not want to make a fool of myself, but I also didn't want to lose my job or get burnt.

So, yes, I could imagine the school bullying the Swinebrooks had had to endure. 'Swinbrook' still carried the implication but was probably a bit less obvious.

"So," Graham said, his palm slapping the table top, "this Ben Griffiths talks to our lately deceased Lord Swinbrook during dinner. Does our helpful publican know the gist of the conversation?"

Mark returned his notebook to his jacket pocket. "Not to say specific phrases. But he *does* know that Ben was angry. He could tell by Ben's expression and gesturing. A few unrestrained words that shouldn't be used in mixed company reached everyone in the room, including Howard at the bar and the tourists in the corner. Everyone was obviously astonished at the word choice and vehemence. Perhaps more so because he was addressing an earl. So, yes, the publican knows Ben was upset."

"Probably putting it delicately."

"After that outburst, Ben quieted down. But his face was still red and he was still irate. Howard said he thought Ben came close to thumping Lord S on the chest, but he didn't."

"Let's applaud Ben's good judgment, then. So how did it end? Did Howard tell you that?"

PEARLS BEFORE SWINE

"Yes, sir. Lord S must have placated Ben, or else Ben had spilled all his anger. It was over in a few minutes. Ben left the pub as he'd come in—alone."

"Did the publican say if he thought it looked as though Ben came there for that purpose? Or was he there, saw Lord S arrive, then go over and accost him?"

"Howard thinks Ben came there solely to talk to Lord S. Ben came in the door, looked around the room, then apparently spotted Lord S and walked straight over to him. He left as soon as he'd emptied both barrels."

Graham sighed and ran his fingers through his hair. "Lovely set-up for death by murder, if Ben Griffiths was as angry as he looked to be."

"Plus," I said, coming around the table to face Graham, "we have the other neighbor, Baxter Clarkson."

"And probably a few more when we start to pick apart this village. Bloody hell, what are we getting into?" He rubbed the back of his neck. I could tell the late hour and the developing inter-neighbor tensions were tiring him. "And all this happened..."

"Soon after Lord S and his party arrived. Near six o'clock."

"And Ben leaves five minutes later. Around 6:05."

"Ten minutes before Lord S leaves the pub," I said. "Time enough for Ben to still be upset about it and be lying in wait for Lord S when he got home. It wouldn't matter that he didn't know about the bet or that Lord S would get home before his wife. If Ben wanted to continue the argument—never mind if he intended murder—he could easily lurk in the shadows and surprise Lord S on his return."

Graham nodded, scribbling something in his notebook. "And what about the dinner party? Everyone come and go as we've been led to believe?"

"Yes, sir," Mark said. "The publican swears that's what he can remember, barring him writing everything down, which of course he didn't. As he said, it wasn't particularly crowded this evening, and he's developed the habit over the years of recalling who stays for how long. So nothing's suspicious—no one obviously exiting at sunset and then claiming he was there till last call, for example."

"At least we don't have to question everyone in the bloody village. So..." He tapped on the side of his mug and stared at the table.

Finally, pushing back the sleeve of his shirt, he said, "Salt, I'd like you and Taylor to root out Ben Griffiths, either at home or at his job. Ask him about his confrontation with Roger, Lord S last evening. See if there's inconsistencies, personal motivation that might have led later to a physical attack—you know the routine."

Mark's 'yes, sir' was not overly enthusiastic. Nor would mine have been if I had answered. Talking to angry neighbors was not my favorite way to start a day. I grabbed my bag as Mark pulled the car keys from his pocket, and we were on our way to question Ben before Graham could thank us.

Jo A. Hiestand

CHAPTER EIGHT

"What the hell do you mean by waking up decent folk at this hour?"

Although it was half past eight, Ben Griffiths had obviously still been in bed. His brunet hair was in disarray, his pajamas rumbled beneath the blue flannel bathrobe that hung open. A reddish blotch, from the pillow perhaps, imprinted his left cheek. He glared at us, his eyes shifting quickly between Mark and me, as though sizing up the situation and deciphering why we were here. When Mark introduced us and explained why we had come, Ben opened the door to allow us to enter, but not without a verbal comment on our manners.

"So," he said, closing the door and leaning against it. "You're checking out my statement like cops in any good crime novel. Check away, if that's how you get your jollies." He turned on the electric fire, indicated a few hard-backed chairs on each side of it, then sat opposite us in an armchair with nearly-flat cushions. He grabbed the packet of Silk Cut and the lighter from the end of the table, lit a cigarette, drew a lungful of smoke and exhaled slowly, watching us through the haze as a felon watches a copper on the beat.

While Mark asked about Ben's altercation with Roger, the man's face turned from registering mere annoyance to anger. He flushed crimson, tinting the black-and-white skull and cross bones tattooed on the left side of his neck blood-red. Probably a relic of his youth, I thought, for the man must be in his mid-forties. Do navy personnel still do that? Or gang members?

"It'll be a let-down for you," Ben said, leaning forward in his chair, his forearms on his thighs. He held the cigarette lightly, his thumb flipping across the filtered end.

"Why's that?" Mark said.

"Because there's nothing in it to get me hauled away to the nick."

"Fine. I wish more people could claim that."

"But I ain't shedding tears over his lordship, if that's what you want to see. I didn't kill him but I can't pretend I'm sad he's dead. Sorry someone beat me to it. You can take that either as a pun or as literal."

He flashed a smile, then stared at us, expressionless. I waited for Mark to reply since he had made the initial contact with Ben Griffiths, and glanced about the room. It was a hodge podge of styles—a contemporary upholstered armchair in a yellow flower print, a Victorian circular ottoman with buttoned blue velvet upholstery, a non-descript 1950s double-door cabinet resting beneath a chrome-framed Monet poster on the wall. The walls were papered in a pastel stripe of blue, yellow and white, and the two front windows sported white organdy curtains. Cast-offs from relatives or bargains at the local flea market? At least the color scheme was harmonious.

Mark took a deep breath before saying, "I repeat. What was your problem last night with Lord Swinbrook?"

"Nothing out of the ordinary. Just the usual."

"Which is...."

Mark's voice was hardening and his eyes were narrowing. Signs that he was getting exasperated. Not good.

I said, "Why were you angry with Lord Swinbrook? Had he done something to you—or your wife? I understand she works at the hall."

He glanced at the photo of a tuxedo-ed Ben and a woman in a wedding dress who smiled out from its ornate silver frame on the coffee table. Either the mention of his wife or the photograph worked. His face blanched and when he spoke, it was in a softer tone, though the anger was still beneath the surface.

"Everything just came to a head last night," Ben said, easing back in his chair. The springs squeaked as he maneuvered to get comfortable. He took another puff before continuing, the smoke drifting into the ceiling fixture. "Same old crap, only I'd had enough of it."

"What's the problem?"

Ben snorted, stared at his clenched fist, then looked again at me. "Mr. Roger Lord High-and-Mighty Swinbrook, that's the problem. Thinks he owns the whole county of Derbyshire—and beyond—*and* the people who work for him."

"Does that include you?" He didn't seem like the sort of person who would work on an estate, pandering—as he put it—to an earl. He seemed more in the category of free-spirited individuals, such as artists or truckers or cops. I knew he wasn't the latter.

Ben smirked. "Not likely to, does it?"

"Then why—"

"Because," he said, his fist smacking the arm of the chair, "I'm sick of the way Lord High Muck treats all his underlings. I'm sick of the once-a-year party that acknowledges their existence. I'm sick of my wife sweatin' away her life for wages little better than a waitress, watching herself drag home each evening, too tired to do anything but take a kip on the sofa. *That's* what!"

His eyes still glared at me, defying me to counter his hurt and the perceived injustice. But he had leaned back, as though spent of all hostility, and concentrated on the wedding photo, his cigarette forgotten for the moment.

"Mona always tells me," Ben continued moments later, still focused on the picture, "that it's good money up at the hall. Especially considering the economy."

"Mona's your wife?" I said, keeping my voice low.

"For twenty years." There was a pride in his voice now. A tinge of love that shoved aside the animosity.

"She's pretty." I nodded toward the photo. "You have any children?"

"Just the girl. Sibyl. She's 16. His lordship treats Mona well, as he does all his staff, I guess. At least Mona never complains about anything up at the hall."

"Would she, if something went on?"

Ben nodded. "She's not one to keep quiet about injustice or ill treatment. For all her saying she's too old to start over in another job, she's not one to hang about taking abuse if there was any. Either from his lordship or from anyone positioned over her in the house."

"And what does your wife do at the hall?"

"Upstairs maid. Cleaning other people's dirt." His voice was taking on an edge again. "Been employed there since she was eighteen. For twenty-two years now."

Mark said, "There are worse jobs, Mr. Griffiths."

"No doubt," Ben said. "But this is *my* wife in Swinbrook's staff. *My wife!* Not some teenager who's going to move on at the end of the summer term break. I just want her to be happy, to get a decent wage for a decent job of work."

"Is she unhappy at the hall?"

Again Ben sniffed and took a drag on the cigarette. "Not particularly. Though I know she'd be happiest if she could stay home and volunteer at the church and such. But she knows we can't afford that. We need the money that two wages bring in."

"You've never worked for Lord Swinbrook, you said. What do you do, then?"

"I do *not* work for the bugger. This ain't the happy old days of yore when whole families were staffed at the hall, thank God. Talk about oppression and mindless obedience to presumed authority!"

Talks like a ruddy communist, I thought.

Ben said, "Roger, Lord Swinbrook got what was coming to him. Lording it over us all, living in luxury while the economy's gone to the dogs. Honest folk can't even live anymore, what with taxes and foreigners taking over our jobs. And Lord Muck and his wife sit in that great big pile, looking down on us poor berks who fetch and carry for them, never knowing what a hungry belly feels like."

"You think he was like that?" I said. It sounded more like 1960s hippy talk.

"Maybe he didn't say it in so many words, but how do you think he was, inbred family and all. Centuries of wealth and privilege. You get that stuff drummed into your head starting when you're just a nipper. Before you really know what it means, before you see the lower classes. So you grow up believing everything's due you and all you have to do is snap your fingers and some maid hurries into the room, bowing, and handing you what you want. Without you ever having to work up a sweat or grow a callus. *'Course* he was like that. They're *all* like that."

"I understood that Lord Swinbrook was very approachable. Anyone could talk to him."

Ben snorted and uncrossed his legs. "If you're in his inner circle, perhaps. But just try to talk to him if you're a garage attendant or sheep farmer. See how often you're asked in for tea—and don't spoil the silk upholstery. No, miss. Class divisions like his highness perpetuated should be abolished. We've no need for them in the 21st century. No one should work as a maid for anyone. Let 'em do their own housework. *We* have to!"

I glanced at Mark, who was jotting all this down in his notebook. "But," I continued, "all these positions—maid, cook, gardener, stable lad and the like—give people jobs. It helps the economy. Your own wife benefits from Lord's Swinbrook's regular pay check. There would be more people dumped on an already-struggling economy if people like his lordship didn't employ so many. What would Mona, and the others of his staff, do if it weren't for the Swinbrooks of this country?"

"Get a regular job like anyone else."

"And do *you* have a regular job?"

Ben smiled. "'Course I do."

"And that is…"

"Chef at Chez Renée."

Mark looked impressed. He ought to be. Chez Renée was a pricey French restaurant in Chesterfield. Winner of various culinary awards. And the funny part to me was that though Ben Griffiths wasn't in service to Lord Swinbrook or other toffs, he was still serving the diners at his establishment. Small difference between that and his lordship's chef. But try to tell him that.

"*Any* kind of regular job Mona could do," Ben added. "Shop clerk, tearoom owner, commercial fisherman, school teacher. *Anything.* I was brought up to make my own way in the world. I can't see why others can't do it, why they have to lean on the poor bloke at the bottom to survive. She shouldn't have to be breaking *her* back for some rich bloke who doesn't know the meaning of manual labor, *that's all I bloody well know!*"

"I'd like to talk to your wife," I said.

"Why?" Ben eyed me as though he expected me to walk off with the family silver—if he had any.

"I'd just like to get her feelings about all this. Perhaps, since she works at the hall, she might know of someone who had a grudge against Lord Swinbrook, who might have fought with him in the tower."

"Besides me, then?"

Jo A. Hiestand

"A lot of people would be part of his lordship's life," I explained. "We're not focusing on you—"

"Not by a bloody long chalk. Not yet—"

"—*and* it's conceivable that someone among his circle of friends or acquaintances might have fallen out with him. Since your wife works at the hall, she might have heard something. Even though she didn't realize it at the time, it may be important now. The staff know a great deal more than their employers would assume," I added, careful not to use the words 'servants' and 'master.' Ben was riled up enough without feudal references.

"She's not here," Ben said, crossing his arms across his chest. He seemed not to notice the cigarette smoke drifting into his eyes. "Hasn't been since eight o'clock or so. She had a bit of a lie-in, complaining of a headache. Got up a bit later than usual. But anyway, she's left for her job. You'll have to talk to her some other time."

I was disappointed that Mark and I would have to postpone our talk with Mona and wondered if I could ask Ben what time Mona would be home. But I thought better of it. It might stir up something about an eight-hour work day or wage slaves meeting at the barricades. Instead, I asked if Ben had heard the bet about the bell ringing being made.

"Yeh," he said, relaxing his arms somewhat. "Daft. But what should I expect?"

"What do you mean?"

Ben sniffed and leaned back in the chair, his right leg starting to bounce. "Well, makes sense, don't it? It's the kind of thing the idle rich do. Waste time, disturb people's sleep. They get some barmy notion and right away trot off to do it. No consideration who might be sleeping. Just haul off and have a go at whatever. What a damned useless lot they are!"

Mark asked if Ben had ever reported the bell noise.

"You think I'm daft?" Ben exploded, jamming his thumb against his chest. "*Me?* Not likely to, am I? For one thing, Mr. My Lord High Muck would wriggle out of any wrist slap any cop would deal him. For another…" Ben leaned forward, his eyes blazing as he focused his wrath on Mark. "Mr Lordly Swinebottom and his lady have dined with the local beak. And *he* and *his* bint have dined at the *hall*. So what does that mean for us poor, bloody peasants? It means they're in each other's pockets like jam's on toast. It means they turn a bloody blind eye to each other's transgressions. So *that's* why I don't ring up the local nick to complain about *anything* Lord Swine does. I'm looking out for my wife and daughter. For my own self. But—" He relaxed, sagged against the back of the armchair and smiled. "I'll say this. Whoever clocked the old boy did us peons a service. *Maybe we can all get our eight hours now!*" His smile broadened, and he shifted his gaze to me, daring us to contradict him.

As his words died, softer, fainter sounds could be heard. A door creaked open, echoing down the hallway; soft-soled shoes—open-toed mules?—slapped toward us; a half-muffled cough on the other side of the wall; then the figure turned the corner and walked into the room, shielding her eyes from the sunlight.

Ben was instantly to his feet, crushing out his cigarette, rushing over to the young girl and putting his arm around her shoulder. His face was all concern now that his daughter had joined us. He held her momentarily, then asked why she was up.

"Can't sleep. I heard—" The girl stopped, staring past her father to Mark and I, then said, "Who are they, Dad? What's going on?"

Mark stood up, introduced us, and said we were merely asking her father some questions.

She frowned, as though processing the bits: two strangers talking to her father, Ben's flushed face and his high-voltage conversation. She looked back at her father, perhaps reading in his face the reason for all this. Sibyl Griffiths was sixteen, brunette, fair complexioned and short. Probably as tall as I, which was five foot. Her slight figure could be discerned even wrapped as it was in a lavender nightdress, which she hugged close in her chill and anxiety, and her painted toenails peaked out from the front of white terrycloth mules. She rubbed the back of her head, disarraying her gelled hair so that the short, dark spikes stood at odd angles like blackened tree trunks after a forest fire.

"I heard you talking about Lord Swinbrook," she said, scrutinizing Mark's face. Probably thinks he's handsome, I thought, watching her obvious, slow mental assessment as her eyes lifted from taking in his collar-length curls to his long eye lashes. If he says anything when we get into the car about her being a babe... I refocused on Sibyl. "I know he—I know what happened. Lyndon rang me up last night."

"That's why she's home," Ben said. "Why she's not at school. She couldn't sleep last night. She's very distraught."

"Lyn rang me up," Sibyl said. "Rather late. Well, actually, early. It was past midnight, I know. He wanted to talk. He was quite upset."

"So Sibyl didn't much sleep. I made her stay home today. She needs her sleep."

I looked at Ben, wondering if that was a subtle hint that Mark and I should leave. We didn't act on it.

"Did you know of any problems his lordship might have?" Mark asked Sibyl. "I know your mum works at the hall. Sometimes the staff talks about things when they are home."

I chimed in quickly when I saw Sibyl take a deep breath. "Not gossip. Detective Salt doesn't mean that. Just if your mother said something in passing, as part of talking about her day, perhaps."

Ben's arms encircled his daughter's waist as he pulled her against him. Their faces stared at us—his, dark and angry; hers, nearly white and fearful. He snapped, "You keep my daughter out of this! She's too young to be involved in your investigation. 'Sides, she doesn't know a thing about Lord High Muck in his ivory tower."

Jo A. Hiestand

"Should we take that as another of your scintillating puns or as literal?" Mark asked. "Lord Swinbrook was found in his bell tower."

Ben blanched and swallowed hard, but then recovered enough to give us some backchat. "It's an adage, or don't you know the word?"

"We know the word," I said, butting in. Mark's eyebrows had lowered again and he was breathing faster. If we didn't wrap up this interview soon, he might resort to more than words. "And we'd like your *daughter* to tell us, in *her* words, if she had heard anything concerning personal problems Lord Swinbrook might have had. And," I added, pointing my index finger at him, "if you say one more thing, we'll haul you in for obstructing a police investigation. Sibyl?"

The girl gripped her father's arm and said in a small voice that she wanted to help us, but that she didn't know of anyone but the Clarksons who were angry. "But they seem to be rowing with everyone, about everything."

"How's that?"

"Well, you know, miss. Them being Mancunians, not used to country life and such. Seems every little bit sets them off."

"Row with neighbors, you mean?"

"No, miss. Just what we all consider normal life, the village and countryside and what goes with it all."

Mark nodded. "Sheep bleating, bell practice, roosters crowing."

"Yes, sir. That's it. Things we take no notice of, don't hear half the time. I guess 'cause we've grown up with it."

"But they didn't because, as you said, they've just moved here from Manchester, and they're used to different noises."

You do get used to sounds, I thought. When my brother became serious about a concert pianist career, he'd practice at every hour of the clock, whenever the mood struck him. I had lain awake night after night as he pounded out a Beethoven sonata or a Bach three-part invention, aware of each note, of each minute ticking away and bringing me closer to morning when I'd have to get up. Eventually, his music became such a common element of evening routine that I didn't hear it. The silence when he was out on a date, forsaking the keyboard, was the startling aspect. Same could be applied to the telly in our home. As my father became one with the couch each evening, the sound of the telly barreled down the hall, slipped under my bedroom door. I'd struggled to concentrate on my school work, distracted by snippets of "Eastenders" and "Keeping Up Appearances" and "Jim'll Fix It." But these, too, faded into the background of home life, and I rarely heard the television anymore. So yes, I *could* understand the Clarksons' frustration with this new sound in their lives. I was surprised, though, that they hadn't become acclimatized before this. Perhaps they wanted to use the bells as an excuse for a fight. But to what purpose?

Sibyl dropped her father's arm and nodded, smiling tentatively now that she was talking. "The Clarksons even got into it on Bonfire Night. Said the fireworks were too loud. Dangerous, too. God, you'd think if they were that unhappy here they'd hop it back to the city. I know a dozen or so who'd be well chuffed to see the back of 'em."

Fireworks on Bonfire Night. Guy Fawkes celebration. My mind went back to this past November and the tragic death in Upper Kingsleigh. The victim had made complaints about fireworks noise, but that was different. That was a residue of war. This situation was mere surliness.

"I didn't hear anything yesterday, either," Sibyl said. "I'd been in my room since after tea, doing my homework. We've got a big test tomorrow in math, and that's not my best subject. And no," she added, a hint of defiance creeping into her voice, "I can't prove it."

"It's a fearful day," Ben said, sliding his arms up to Sibyl's ribcage and squeezing harder, "when sixteen-year-old girls are suspected of murder."

Sixteen-year-old girls do get suspected of murder, I thought. *Maybe more frequently than you know.* I watched as Ben planted a reassuring kiss on the top of Sibyl's head, then said, "No one's said anything about suspects, Mr. Griffiths. But when we do, we'll ask that party to supply us with a statement. At the moment, we're just talking to people whom we believe may have material information. We're trying to discern last night's time table and people connected with Lord Swinbrook. You should want to help with that. The quicker we can establish people's movements and associations, the quicker we'll be out of your hair."

Whether subconsciously or as a subtle understatement, Ben stroked his daughter's hair. "I'm all for that."

"I'm sorry about Lyn's uncle," Sibyl said. "He could be a sod at times—Lord Swinbrook, not Lyndon—but I didn't want him dead. And certainly not in that manner."

Of course. Lyndon. The son of Kirk Fitzpatrick, our guitarist who had hopped it to Bolton. Lyndon was Lord S's nephew. I nodded, encouraging Sibyl to continue.

"Lord Swinbrook was kind to us, letting Lyn and me into the family part of the hall that the public never sees. Well, he would, Lyn being family, even if by marriage. But he didn't have to do it. He took us on fishing trips, had his cook pack us the most elegant picnics." She glanced at her dad, coloring. "Not that he cooked better than you, Dad—"

"But it was fancy food you don't get at home," Ben concluded.

"Well, it *was* fun to eat off Wedgwood and have damask serviettes and stuff ourselves with apple tea and mushroom turnovers instead of Orange Crush and Scotch eggs."

Must take after her mother, I thought. Sibyl certainly wasn't of her father's persuasion about the upper crust's life.

"But more than that," she said. "Lyn's uncle helped the schools round about. He gave us an end-of-year party with a band, and new rugby jerseys for the team. New computers for the library, too. Also some sort of cataloging software to make the librarian's job easier. He was a nice, generous man, and I'm sorry Lyn has to deal with his death." She looked down at her hands and the tip of her thumbnail chipped away at the pink nail polish of her index finger. "He was an uncle to all us kids, really, and I'm sorry for all of it—for Lyn, his aunt, the village, the charities he helped…" She looked at me, her eyes threatening to brim over with tears. "Why would someone have hurt him? I—I can't believe someone would. Not intentionally, anyway. I mean, if you get in a row with someone, and start pushing, well…that's one thing, isn't it? An accident, I mean. From some barmy row that got out of hand. You said he was found in the tower. Couldn't he have fallen against a bell, hit his head that way? I know they're dangerous, bells are."

Mark said Lord Swinbrook was found in the ringing chamber, two stories below the ring of bells.

Sibyl murmured, "Oh," then paused, seeming to think. Moments later, she said, "He must have fallen off the ladder, then. I've nearly done it myself. Misjudged the next rung. It's hard to climb, being vertical, like that. Straight up the wall. He *must* have fallen. *Nobody* I know would have hurt him."

Mark and I left after that. As I slid onto the car's passenger seat, I couldn't help but wonder if somebody Sibyl *didn't* know had hurt Roger, Lord Swinbrook.

CHAPTER NINE

"God, Bren," Mark said, grinning at me once we were seated inside the car. The sounds of morning washed over us—traffic along Victoria Road, a bird chirping on the eave of Ben's house, two women stopping to chat on the pavement. Mark murmured that at least everything else in the village seemed normal, then jammed the key into the ignition. An instant later the engine growled like a pent-up lion. Or an irritated Detective Superintendent.

As Mark backed the car onto Victoria Road, I nodded toward the house. "Nervous curtains."

"What?" He braked the car and glanced toward the front window.

The small opening between the two curtains trembled for a few more seconds, then fell closed as Ben evidently released them.

"Oh. Where's his spyglass, I wonder."

"Didn't have time to grab it," I said. "Our getaway is too quick for him."

"Let's hope we continue our success, then, with the rest of the case." Mark pulled the seat belt smoothly across his chest and said, "You know, Bren, you ought to stand for parliament. I've never heard such oration as you just gave out—outside of Disraeli or Churchill."

"Knew them, did you?"

Mark made a face. "Not outside school texts and telly programs. Did you hear Ben? What's with that bloke? Is he mad at the world?"

"Just the part that's richer than he is."

"Which includes a hell of a big percent."

"How'd he end up with such a gentle soul as Sibyl?"

"Must have her mum's genes," Mark said.

I murmured that that seemed likely and watched the BP petrol sign whiz past us. "But more to the point," I added, "do you think he could be mad enough to act on it?"

"Like getting into a fight with Roger? Can't say right now. But it's a possibility. Do we know he was working last night?"

I sniffed. "Something to have one of the lads on an inquiry team work on."

"If he didn't work, yes, it's a possibility. He'd have the opportunity."

Jo A. Hiestand

"But if he wasn't working, wouldn't Mona or Sybil suspect something if he wasn't home?"

"As in 'He never works Wednesday evenings. Why wasn't he home'?"

I nodded. "It would be kind of obvious, wouldn't it? Maybe it wasn't an argument that got out of hand. Maybe he planned on killing Roger and had the time off already set up. Maybe he didn't say anything to his wife and daughter so they'd assume he was working as usual."

"Could be. Well, we'll tell Graham and he'll have someone look into it."

Mark turned left onto High Street and drove the short distance to the community center while I mulled over the possible scenarios. It wasn't until he had driven into the car park and turned off the engine that I shook myself free from my thoughts.

"Well," Mark said, angling himself in the car seat to look at me, "I won't dash your dreams because odder things have certainly happened in a murder investigation. We'll keep our eyes on Ben, if that will lighten your mental load."

I nodded, got out of the car, and we walked into the center. Graham nodded like an ancient sage when Mark and I related our saga. He nearly echoed Mark's words about keeping an eye on Ben. As he handed out our next assignments, he asked me to talk to Geneva about the phone call Roger might have made last night. He believed that a grieving woman would speak more readily to another woman.

Even though the drive to Swinton Hall was only a matter of five minutes, I was rewarded with sighting a robin. So what if it was a common bird. The orangey-red breast and forehead was a cheering flash of color to brighten my already lethargic day. I stopped the car in the hall's drive, rolled down the car window and listened. The robin's 'tick' call resonated from the edge of the copse. A silence fell between the call and his next phrase, a complex song that rose and fell, varying its speed. I leaned my forearm against the cold metal of the car door, listening, enjoying this bit of commonality in the midst of a murder case. Minutes later, I drove on, sad to leave the bird and its joyful disposition. I was certain Geneva would not greet me so eagerly.

Geneva saw me in the garden room, a pink-and-apple-green affair with bow windows that admitted a flood of sunlight. White wicker furniture, pink flowered wallpaper and green area rugs suggested spring. And, glancing at the white and glass vases hosting hothouse flowers, I imagined the room would overflow with garden blooms and scents in not many more months.

She cradled a cup of tea in her hand and smiled weakly as I sat down opposite her. Her eyes were red and the lids puffy, and she dabbed at her nose with a crumpled facial tissue, but her hair was perfectly brushed and her dark clothes immaculate. I flipped open my notebook, fumbled with the pen as I closed the fingers of my left hand around it, and thanked her for seeing me.

PEARLS BEFORE SWINE

"I really can't imagine who would have been there," she said when I asked about Roger ringing up anyone. Margo had told me earlier that morning that Roger's mobile had been used to place two calls: one to his brother, Austin, and one to Baxter Clarkson, but quickly added that just because Austin and Baxter had been rung up on Roger's phone did not mean Roger had done the ringing. Now Geneva, Lady Swinbrook, was suggesting the same thing. "If, as Baxter and Austin say, my husband called them, then I assume he did. I can't see who else would have done it. Or why. I mean...." She closed her eyes momentarily, as if picturing the group, then opened them and said, "If Roger phoned Austin to cancel the bet, he should have returned home. There would be no reason for him to stay there. Or if he changed his mind, deciding to ring after all, and rang up Baxter to apologize in advance for the 'noise,' as Baxter puts it, well..."

I nodded. "Who would have been with his lordship?"

"So it's definitely..." She avoided my eyes, unable to say it.

"Yes, your ladyship. Someone killed your husband. And intentionally."

"How—" She stared at me with worried eyes.

"By the number of blows to the head. Nearly half a dozen. The postmortem revealed that. A fall from the ladder would result in only one indentation, when his lordship hit the floor."

"I see. Yes. It makes sense."

"I'm sorry to have to tell you, but I thought—"

"Yes, miss. I need to know. It's the uncertainty that's the worst, isn't it?"

I asked what Roger had been wearing when they dined at the pub.

Lady Swinbrook looked at me as if I'd just called her 'Geneva,' then said rather crisply, "You saw him, I assume. You can't remember? Look at your photos."

"Yes, I did see your husband. I recall how he was dressed. I ask because perhaps he had changed his clothes before we found him. And if so, that would give us a better idea of the time sequence of last night."

"Of course. That's very clever." She took a sip of tea before describing the gray woolen slacks, maroon pullover, black casuals, and black leather jacket. The boot prints that we found near Roger's body must have been made at another time—or by another person. I asked if Roger owned boots.

"Several pair. Wellingtons and fleece-lined, soft-soled things."

"Any leather hard-soled boots?"

"Several pair of riding boots. We go riding periodically. The stable, though substantially smaller than in my husband's grandfather's day, still accommodates a half dozen horses. We usually go out on Sunday afternoons. Why?"

Instead of answering, I said, "I understand his lordship gave you a fur coat for your birthday, and that the bell ringing challenge was for

Jo A. Hiestand

Valentine's Day. Was he going to give you a pearl necklace, do you know? Perhaps he had said something. Like as an additional gift, or—"

She shook her head. "I don't recall Roger ever saying anything about pearls, either as a necklace or earrings or anything. I'm not a great lover of pearls. I prefer gemstones. Do you like pearls or gems, Miss Taylor? Jewels fascinate me, utterly attract me, the way the light gets into them and the color mesmerizes...so intense and deep." Her left thumb played with the band of her wedding ring, a crown-jewel-sized diamond surrounded by smaller but no less impressive sapphires. What she had said about the entrapment of light was true; the blaze of color was truly hypnotic.

I was about to ask if she would know about the Duvel ale we had found in the tower when a voice behind us broke into the silence.

"Pardon, Milady." We both turned toward the doorway. The maid who had shown me to her ladyship was now stepping aside to admit a man in his mid-fifties, thick gray hair, tall and well proportioned. The maid announced, "Mr. Sykes," then left in a rustle of starched white apron and stiff-skirted black dress.

The man entered the room, his arms outstretched, calling Geneva's name. Geneva set down her teacup, rose, and leaned into the man's embrace. After a few moments of condoling phrases, hair stroking and cheek kissing, the man released Geneva and guided her back to the wicker love seat, planting himself next to her so he could continue holding her hand. He introduced himself to me, adding he was Geneva's ex-husband. "I heard about Rog," he said in answer to my first question, "from Ed Cawley. He's a friend of Roger's. Me, too, for that matter. Great pals. All three of us. Why?"

"Just wondering. And how did Ed Cawley find out?"

Geneva grimaced and said in a small voice that she had asked Austin to phone Ed last night. "I didn't want Ed to find out from the tabloids or television news. Or through village gossip."

"Perfectly understandable," I said. "And who *is* Ed Cawley? What does he do?"

I sounded rather like my mother, who associated people by their occupation. A dentist gave her a different mental picture of the person's looks, hobbies and education than a ballerina or bus driver did, for instance. And enforced a stereotype that she was happy to live with. Cataloging people made it easier to remember them, and for the times when she was lucid, that was very helpful.

Geneva picked up her teacup again and drained the last of its contents, even though, by now, the tea had to have been cold. She seemed not to mind—or taste it. It was probably just something to do, some normal bit of everyday reality in the nightmare in which she was drowning. "Ed was a business partner of Roger's. As was Barry. They ran package-tours. Ed made a lot of money."

"King and Country Tours," Barry Sykes chimed in, lifting Geneva's free hand and kissing it. "As the name implies, we focused our tour packages on historical sites and countryside attractions. Each package had a theme, whether it was city- or country-oriented. If it was a 'king' tour, we would go to spots associated with that monarch's reign. Like Sheriff Hutton Castle and York for Richard III, or a well-dressing exploration of Derbyshire for the countryside excursion. I thought it brilliant, that idea. I mean, so many sight-seeing packages focus on a city or a circular tour of an area. Sure, they explain the sites, but with our packages the clientele are immersed in that theme so that when they come away from it, they know some real history and can associate Richard III—who was *not* the monster Shakespeare portrayed him, by the way. You know, don't you, that Shakespeare was writing for a Tudor king so Shakespeare had to distort Richard's Plantagenet history to glorify his Tudor boss! Anyway, the tourists going on that tour, for instance, can now associate Richard III, or Cromwell or QEI with having been a real person. They traveled to real places where those monarchs walked and did real things that changed our world. It's a living history book, where the participant walks through time to connect with these people. Absolutely spot-on!"

I said it sounded interesting.

Barry said, "I left after the first few years. I got fed up with some of the clientele. Demanding bunch of—" He shook his head. "Sorry. But some people can really be a pain, you know?"

Geneva continued, "Roger left some time later, when the business got bigger than he felt they could handle. He invested the money—that's what we live off. No, Barry," she said, stopping her ex-husband's protests. "The police will find out. They dig into everything. Why not tell them outright and save all the questioning?" She turned back to me. "Ed still wanted to work. He liked dealing with people and scheduling events, so he became an artist's agent. He handles musicians. King and Country is still under his control as CEO, but he has office staff seeing to the actual tours. He's directly involved in managing musicians."

"Is your brother, Kirk, one of Ed's artists?"

"I don't think so. No, he isn't. It's Paddock something or other, I believe."

"Why is that? Isn't your brother good enough? Not ready to break out nationally?"

"I've not been told. You'll have to ask Kirk. Or Ed. I don't want to guess and have it wrong and give you a false lead."

"Speaking of money and the company," Barry said, "now that Roger is, well, I know it's awfully soon, Gen, but are you alright? Financially, that is? Has Roger left you with enough to live on? This estate must eat up my weight in gold nuggets daily."

Geneva pressed her lips together and withdrew her hand from Barry's grasp. She leaned away from him and said, "That's none of your business. You stopped being my overseer when we got divorced. Roger is still seeing to my welfare even now, with all the money he left me." Barry tried to deny his dishonorable intensions, stating he only cared about her well-being. Geneva said, "I'm very well off, Barry. *Extremely* well off. I won't have to work, so don't go looking for me behind a counter in Boot's or guiding tourists through Blue John caverns. Roger was a shrewd businessman; for all that we show a section of the hall to tourists. That's *entirely* separate. That's English history. People want to see it. We're set for the rest of my life, so don't walk the floor at night. Thank you just the same for your concern."

It took a few seconds for Barry to recover. His eyebrows slowly lowered, his eyes lost the deer-in-the-headlights look, and his upper body muscles relaxed. He cleared his throat and mumbled, "I'm sorry, Gen. I had no intension of insulting you. I was merely concerned for your future. Of course I'm over the moon to hear that you're well off, that Roger was so farsighted. I—" He reddened, the blush even flooding the tips of his ears. He glanced at his hands, as though struggling with a decision to say something, or perhaps having difficulty in finding the right words. He said, more to his lap than to Geneva, "I still love you. I want to marry you. Oh, I know this is bloody bad timing what with...well...I want to let you know how I feel. How I've always felt, actually. Our divorce did nothing for my feelings about you. I want you to take your time. Put all this behind you, and in a few months, when you've recovered and thought about this, perhaps you'll consent to marry me. I only tell you now so that you'll not worry about being alone."

The silence following this extraordinary announcement was abrupt, deep and painful. For a moment, voices of the maid and another woman drifted through the closed door of the garden room. The slow, measured clop of horse hooves, an energetic neigh, and a man's cheerful response flowed past the bow window. A vehicle—most probably a Land Rover or similar estate truck—burst to life and roared away. Ordinary sounds. Ordinary life. Yet so startlingly out of place at this moment.

Geneva pulled her gaze from the window, focused on Barry's face, and said very slowly, "Officer, would you remove this person from my house?"

CHAPTER TEN

Barry was nearly as astonished as I was. I recovered as gracefully as I could, stood up, and asked Barry to walk with me to the front door.

"You can't mean it!" Barry said, looking from me to Geneva, his hands going out as if pleading.

"Officer," Geneva repeated, "if he doesn't go quietly, please arrest him for trespass and harassment."

Barry stood up, the color drained from his face. He stepped sideways as I gestured toward the garden room door. "Gen, what's got into you? Why are you doing this? No!" he said as I walked toward him. "*No!* I want to hear why she's doing this. There's no need for her to be doing this. Gen!"

I put my left hand on his elbow, gesturing again toward the door with my bandaged hand. "Please, Mr. Sykes. Her ladyship wishes you to leave now. She's under a lot of stress. Please don't make this harder on her than it should be. Have some respect for her and for her bereavement."

"*Respect?*" he said, laughing. "God, what did I just show her if it wasn't respect? I've never shown her anything but respect. *And* love. All through our marriage. Ask her! I want to take care of her. I love her enough to want to marry her. What's the harm in that? And because I declare my feelings and my hope, she wants me out of the house, under police escort, even. What a bloody farce!"

I was wondering how I could get Barry into a transport wristlock maneuver with my useless right hand, praying I wouldn't have to, when he said, "All right. If that's what her ladyship wants, *fine*. I'll spare her the further upset of broken Wedgwood and come along peaceably. But—" He turned toward Geneva as I opened the door. "It's no insult to be loved, Geneva. Or wanted. Think about that in your cold lonely bed tonight."

It could have been Mark I was hearing; Mark, who had yelled practically the same words to me not so long ago. Barry's face was crimson from his anger, just as Mark's had been. And mine had been, knowing Mark had spoken very close to the truth. It was no insult to be loved. My problem was the man I loved did not love me in return.

I gripped Barry's elbow tighter, escorted him from the room, and then walked with him to his car.

"I had no idea," he said as he pulled his car keys from his pocket and opened his car door, "that the old boy was that rich. What a surprising world we live in, miss."

"At least her ladyship will be spared that worry," I said as he leaned against his open car door.

"Nice for her and the family, I should think."

"Which? Not worrying, or the money?"

He laughed, a bitter explosion that held anger and resentment and amusement. "*Both*. She's led a charmed life, miss. Got whatever she wants. No reason to think that it would change just because Roger's gone. I should have known that. So the saga continues. Stay tuned for Episode Three."

"You obviously know the family, having been married to her ladyship."

"Before she was her ladyship. Don't forget that, miss. Geneva, Lady Swinbrook, was plain old Geneva Fitzpatrick before donning the crown. And her brother, Kirk, is still of peasant stock and peasant marriage."

"So she gets the lion's share of the inheritance, presuming that's how Lord Swinbrook willed it."

"Look, to make things easier between us let's just refer to him as Roger. I certainly did, being family. And he was that kind of bloke. You know, down to earth. Even though he inherited the title, didn't mean he was all that keen on the family jewels and kowtowing that went with it. He was glad of the money, don't misunderstand, but he used it to better *everyone's* life."

I nodded, recalling Sibyl's statement of Roger's generosity to her school.

"And," Barry went on, "being basically a commoner at heart, he loved working. That's why the King and Country business. He wasn't one to stay shut up in his crenel-edged tower and pine away for serfs and jousting. He liked getting out, staying busy, talking to folk, as I said."

"And the inheritance..." I said, reminding him of my question.

"Ah, yes. Well, Geneva would inherit, wouldn't she? Unless there are relatives buried somewhere, singing in the shrouds, whom I don't know about. New Zealand or Outer Mongolia or Patagonia. Just a figure of speech, miss. My recollection from my short-lived albeit fiery marriage with Gen is that her family consists of her brother, Kirk. No parents either for Gen or Roger. So, presumably Gen and Kirk and Roger's brother, Austin, will get the estate and its accoutrements, in various-sized individual estates. Unless, as I said, there are long-buried relatives who only see fit to rise from their muted coffins and contact the family now, when they can get something. But that's typical, isn't it? Where there's a will there's relatives."

I said that was often the case, then asked about children.

"Nowhere in sight, miss. No offspring of marital bliss—or extramarital embarrassment. But that may change once Rog's death hits the media. Neither did Gen and I produce any carbon copies of ourselves, for that matter."

"And her brother, Kirk, has just the one child, then. Right. How about Roger's brother, Austin? I know he's engaged, but—"

"Yes. You're delicately asking about physical consequences of cohabitation, aren't you? In this so-called modern era, miss, when marriage seems more like something-I'll-get-around-to-if-I-feel-like-it than a societal norm, that might well be expected. After all, you think, Austin has a fiancée, Dulcie Burgess. Why wouldn't they? Ask me again when I'm Geneva's husband and I may know. But right now, being as I am outside the bosom of the family and therefore ignorant of family intimacies, I don't know. Austin had no children when I parted from Geneva. And Austin's engagement has been such an on-off affair, he may have had children by another girlfriend. Though, I doubt it. Austin's a responsible lad. If he had fathered a child, he'd acknowledge it and take it in, caring for it as a father should, whether married to its mother or not. So, if you want my opinion—which is why you asked the question, I know—I do not think Austin has children. Which makes the division of the Glorious Pile so much easier, doesn't it?" He leaned backward, stretched a bit. The car door squeaked as he pushed against it.

"When were you and Geneva married, Mr. Sykes?"

"Call me Barry, please. God, if we peons were allowed to call Lord Swinbrook 'Roger,' I can certainly be called Barry. Lord, when *was* that? We were married for two years, but it ended eight years ago. Geneva had known Roger for the last year of our marriage. Maybe that's what convinced her to marry Roger. His charm, his down-to-earth personality. I'd say his family house, too, because she loves the idea of a dynasty like the Swinbrooks. You know, going on forever since the Conquest."

"Her family —either the maternal or paternal line—had to have come from *somewhere*," I exclaimed. "A last name just doesn't spring into being on a whim. The Fitzpatricks, or her mother's side, had to go back to *some* distant relative."

"Of course! But it was the lineage on *paper*, the ability to see portraits and read stories that captured her imagination and heart."

"Not the title or the wealth?"

"No. She, as I said, was of common stock. But maybe I'm doing her an injustice. She may simply have fallen in love with Roger. And there's no castle or family vault that can lure you away from your lover, if you really are in love. Even if the loved one is a commoner like I." He glanced again at the hall and sighed. "But I wasn't the loved one. Roger was."

"And where do you live, Barry?"

"Next village, Eyam. Ed Cawley, Roger's best mate, lives not too far off—in Hathersage. Said Eyam gave him the creeps. Well, each to his own."

Eyam, forever linked with the plague brought to the tiny Derbyshire village by flea-infested clothing, forever an icon of unselfish sacrifice. Five of every six villagers died within several months. To contain the plague so it wouldn't spread to the other villages, Eyam's inhabitants quarantined themselves within the village rather than running for their lives. The images of these romantic, brave figures had been enough to ease me through many bouts of wintry blues. Oldfield was slightly east of Buxton, our constabulary divisional headquarters. It had always been a quiet place, devoid of police calls. Until last evening.

"Ed rang me up," Barry said, bursting my image of Graham in his ministerial robes tending to the dying plague victims. "This morning. I came right over. Well, I had to, didn't I? I couldn't let Gen go through this alone. I couldn't let her feel unloved." He broke off suddenly, his eyes brimming with tears.

"Don't you think," I said, watching the man wipe his eyes on the back of his jacket sleeve, "that it would be better for Geneva to mourn and for you to wait a respectable length of time before proposing? You're pressuring her right now, and she doesn't need that. She can't think at all straight now, with shock and grief, much less give your offer serious consideration. Wait a bit, and then, when she's getting on with her life, you can ask. She'll appreciate the courtesy, the fact that you thought more of her need to heal than of your own need to get an answer."

"You're right, of course. It's just that—" He took a deep breath, ignoring a tear trickling down his cheek. "God, why does everything have to be so bloody difficult, take so bloody long?"

A white Mercedes Benz zoomed down the drive toward us. As though just realizing we were there, the driver braked and swerved, bringing the car to a stop within a meter of us. Barry frowned, staring at the man who practically leapt from his car and absentmindedly clicked his remote key lock as he turned toward the hall. Barry walked around his car and gestured to the newcomer, Ed Cawley. Short and squarely built with white hair, Ed was dressed as if he was going to church. Or a wedding. Pressed black suit, lemon-yellow waistcoat, and canary-yellow tie served as mere background to show off his pocket watch chain and fob. The heavy gold chain swung as he walked.

"I always said you drove too fast, Ed," Barry said as the man halted on the other side of Barry's car. "Now I've got a copper as a witness."

Ed Cawley seemed not to hear Barry, so transfixed by the hall that he was about to walk past us in silence. When Barry stepped in his way, Ed blinked, apologized, and introduced himself to me. "Are you really a copper?" he said, his voice affected by an expensive public school education. He seemed apparently undisturbed by the fact that he had nearly crashed his Benz into Barry's car. When I nodded, he said, "I suppose you're here about Roger. What a terrible thing! I still can't believe it. Roger, dead. He was so young! And by murder, no less. I can't believe it!" He peeled his eyes from me to look again at the hall.

"Gen ring you up?" Barry asked, leaning against the bonnet of his car. His eyes traveled the length of the man as though discerning the motive behind his arrival.

"What if she did?" Ed replied, staring at Barry with impatience. "*You* didn't."

"Haven't had time, have I? I was going to let you know, but—"

"Yeh. But. But you had to get here first."

"What the hell does *that* mean?" Barry stood up, his hands on his hips. "You sound like I'm trying to hide something. I've no control over Roger's will. I'm not trying to exclude you from anything. As if I could."

I frowned, uncertain as to what the men were talking about. I said, "Is there something in his lordship's will—"

"Look, miss," Ed said, "let's get this understood at the start. I don't know about Roger's will. I'm not interested in Roger's will. I have my own business and am not in need of the Swinbrook millions. For another thing, no matter how Mr. Barry Sykes is trying to make it sound, I just came over to see Geneva. I don't think she should be alone, and servants don't quite cut it on the hand-holding level."

"Very glad to hear it," I said. "She's going through a hard time. She'll be glad of the friendship."

"Just so long as it's friendship," Barry muttered.

Ed glared at him. "Now what's *that* supposed to mean?"

"Just that. You can figure it out."

"Not when it's wrapped in innuendoes, I can't."

"I just think Geneva needs a bit of time to herself. She doesn't need to be bombarded with visitors."

"I notice you didn't waste any time coming over."

"I was in the neighborhood. Anyway, I didn't stay long," Barry added, glancing at me.

"Well, I won't stay long either. I just want to give her my condolences." He pulled a card and a small, unwrapped hinged box from his suit coat pocket. It looked suspiciously like a box that would hold jewelry. I tried to see the logo on the top, but his thumb covered most of it. The scroll was in silver ink, though.

"Condolences come in the form of carats?" Barry said, tapping the card with his index finger.

"What's with you, Sykes?" Ed's voice took on an edge and he stepped closer to Barry. I stiffened, wondering if the man was about to assault Barry. "If I've brought anything for Geneva, that's my business. I didn't ring you up to see if you were going to send flowers."

"Flowers won't fit in that," Barry said, again thumping the card. "Or in there." He tapped the small box.

"Brains don't fit in your head, either. I always wondered about your parentage."

Barry's fist came back, but I stepped between the men, holding up my good arm and turning slightly toward Barry. "I think both of you need to take a deep breath. This conversation is getting nothing accomplished. Barry, maybe you had better be going, as you were about to do. And Mr.

Cawley," I said, looking at Ed, "perhaps it would be best if you went in to see her ladyship. She'll be glad of a friend, I think."

Ed snorted, glared at Barry, and turned abruptly on his heel. He marched toward the hall.

I stepped back from Barry, alleviating any sense of threat I may foster and giving me some breathing room. Barry watched Ed until he had entered the hall, then spoke in a soft voice, his eyes till on the house.

"Funny. Gen wouldn't let me talk to her of love or marriage, yet it's all right for Mr. Ed Cawley to placate her with jewelry. Of all the…" His voice became inaudible as he lowered his head and jammed his hands into his slacks pockets.

"First of all, you don't know if her ladyship will welcome his placating, as you term it. Second, maybe it's for her birthday. Was he in the habit of giving her birthday gifts? I ask because I know he was a business partner with Roger and you."

Barry shook his head. "No formal thing. Never had a party or anything while we had the company going. I suppose he could have given it to her privately." He kicked a lump of frozen snow with the toe of his shoe. "We never did anything as a company. Not official, not even for Roger's birthday. It all seemed kind of…well, we were friends and all that, but we never went down the gift route. Christmas we gave wine or cheese or chocolates. Nothing personal. I never gave her anything like that because I thought that she'd misread it, her being married to Roger then. I would've loved to have given her real gifts, though. Just like when we were married. I still loved her even after our divorce. I still wanted to ply her with jewelry and flowers. Nothing was too good for her." He looked at me, squinting his eyes. "And you know the funny thing? Before I drove over here, I ordered flowers for her. Four dozen roses. Just for her, not for the funeral. She'll probably toss those if she's so dead set against marrying me."

"You can't know that, Barry. As I said a few minutes ago, you need to give her time. She's just lost her husband. She doesn't know what she wants or what she feels—about you or Ed or *anything* right now."

"She'll feel something toward Ed Cawley, the bastard. Him and his diamond brooch. He's got a nerve coming here with that. I love her! Doesn't she understand that? I *love* her! I'd do anything for her! I had first claim on her, I had loved her first. I should be the one now who she turns to. I need to tell her that."

He made a move toward the hall but I stopped him and reiterated the need for time. He muttered that I was sending him to his death if Ed Cawley got in Geneva's good graces, but he got into his car peaceful enough, revved the engine, and shot down the drive.

As I watched him drive off, I wondered if he was jealous of his ex-wife and Ed's friendship or just jealous of Ed's obvious wealth. Whatever the reason, I feared I hadn't seen the last of Barry and Ed's tempers, or the plans to claim the Swinbrook wealth through the widow. The robin, I noticed on my way back, was gone, leaving the drive empty and silent.

PEARLS BEFORE SWINE

I met Margo in the pub for a quick lunch. My stomach told me of the time before my watch did. The Cat and Mouse is the type of establishment tourists associate with Merrie Olde England—dark oak beams, horse brasses, hunting horns and hunting watercolors. A small acknowledgement is given to the 21st century in the way of an area for laptop computer connections, but the modern era was, essentially, held at bay. Perhaps a century from now the computer connections will be looked on as we view horse brasses and copper warming pans.

When I sat down at the table Margo had commandeered, she began immediately to tell me of her morning talk with Mona. I held up a hand. "Can I order something before you delight me with fiction?"

"If you think more of your stomach than of my amazing interview technique, go ahead. There are salads on the menu."

Which was a subtle hint that I should lay off the fish and chips or lasagna and get serious about losing my extra stone of weight. I ignored her, needing something substantial after my emotional morning, and ordered a ploughman's, which wasn't all that caloric compared to the chips. Nice chunk of French bread, slab of Cheddar, pickles. Even a slice of ham, I noted when the waitress brought the plate. Unusual, but very welcome. I took a sip of milk before unleashing Margo.

"Good choice, Bren," Margo said, referring to my lunch. "Calcium helps in the fat fight, did you know? Something about burning it off faster, I think."

"In that case," I said, setting down my half empty glass of milk, "I'll order ice cream. And about milk—I drink it because I like it, Margo, not because—"

"You have only one body, Bren. You need to take care of it. When it wears out, where will you live?" She looked at me with serious, brown eyes, hoping that her message was penetrating my ivory dome.

I reached for the bread and tore off a piece. "Just tell me about you and Mona. I'm doing fine with my diet."

"Sounds like something the Papa Bear might say. Okay, okay. While you were wallowing above stairs in ancient splendor, I was below stairs, in the maid's warren."

"I'd forgotten Mona works at the hall." My head was still buzzing from the earful I'd received when interviewing her husband, Ben-of-the-common-folk. "Cook?"

"*Maid*. Aren't you listening?"

"What?"

"God, Bren. What's your problem?"

I shoved the beer mat around the table top with my finger tip. "Did it ever strike you what a God-awful job we have?"

"Like what? Delving into people's finances, asking them questions?"

"No. Police work. What a bloody-awful career it is."

91

Jo A. Hiestand

Margo stopped with a forkful of salad halfway to her mouth. She set down the fork, frowned and asked, "What's the matter, Bren? I thought you loved police work. Something's bothering you."

I flicked the beer mat across the table. It slammed into the bottle of vinegar. "I hate it."

"You can't mean that. You were so keen on it just out of the training school."

"Things change, Margo. People change."

"But you *love* the job. Just last month..." She angled her head and leaned closer to me. "I can't believe it. Not you, Bren. You love being a cop."

"I don't."

"But why?"

"Did you ever stop to think about it, Margo? *Really* think about it? About what we do? People see us when they are at their *absolute* worse. Think about it. They've just experienced a terrible tragedy—their spouse is killed, their home's been torched, they've been in a bloody fight. And then we show up. These people are still upset, probably the most upset they will ever be. And when they think of this incident years later, who do they associate it with? Us. The cops. The people who saw them when they were hysterical and screaming and pleading. Not at all the face they usually present to the world. But we cops saw them that way, at their very worst. And they think the worst of us for having seen them so raw." I picked up my spoon and traced designs in the wooden tabletop.

Margo shook her head and sighed, probably unsure of how to respond. Not that I wanted her to. Quiet would've been fine. But she took a deep breath and said, "Honestly, Bren. I don't think it's that bad. I know what you mean about the hysterics and the crying. Sure, it's bad for them, but don't you think that if they do remember the incident years later they will be *glad* the cops were there to help? Don't you think we're a calming force?"

I wedged the handle of the spoon into the crack between the table leaves and said, "I don't think so. I don't know. I just think we'll always have a bad image in their minds. A bad memory, like a toothache." I shook my head, trying to sort through my confusion. "Like this morning. I had to escort Barry Sykes, Geneva's ex-husband, from the hall. He was going ballistic. How do you think he'll feel when he remembers that he made a total ass of himself and that *I* was the one who had to get him to leave? And Ben Griffiths? When I questioned him, *he* exploded in my face. He'll remember my presence *years* from now and feel embarrassed I witnessed his anger. Same for Baxter Clarkson. Same for *all* the others who I'll come into contact with. These people are emotional over all this and they erupt into anger. And who's there to witness it or drag them out of houses or jail them for fighting? *Me*. The cop." My fingertip traced the edge of the spoon. "It's worse for Scott. For *all* the response drivers. They respond to calls that we never get. Fist fights, car crashes, robberies, rapes. Scott's right there when

PEARLS BEFORE SWINE

emotions are boiling over. The incident has just happened and the victims are still experiencing it. At least when we detectives arrive, it's usually after the fact—the car's been stolen, the person's been killed. Sure, the victim's still upset, but Scott usually sees them minutes after it's happened—or is *still* happening. How can he stand it?"

Margo sighed slowly. Moments passed and someone on the other side of the room dropped some coins into the juke box. Donna Summer's oldie "She Works Hard for the Money" sprang into the room. Margo said something under her breath and squeezed my hand. "I'm sorry. I don't know what to say, Bren. This came out of the blue. I thought you loved your job. I'm *so* sorry."

I murmured it was all right. Was I merely feeling sorry for myself, feeling unloved and full of low self image? Is that where this came from? Did I want the world to love *me*, or was I concerned with the image of the *police*, which I suspected I really did love.

I yanked the spoon out of the crack and let it fall onto the tabletop. "It's ok, Margo. Don't mind me. I'm just mixed up and tired."

"Mark and Graham will do that to you. Not to mention a murder case."

Nodding, I murmured, "Probably something I ate. Sorry to wax so inelegant. Blame it on the late night and that my hand hurts like hell."

"You're feeling the delayed shock of your aunt's death," Margo said after a pause, during which she picked up the beer mat. "I know you loved her greatly. It's bound to have affected you, her loss and so recent. Honest, you should've taken a week's leave."

"I'm *not* in shock. I'm just—"

"—tired, over-worked, emotionally involved with two men, sustaining an injury to your hand—"

"Fine." I threw up my hands. "So, on with life and on with the job. What were you saying before about somebody?"

"About Mona. She likes working for the family. Likes the family, too, when it comes to that. Especially Roger, who she considered a prince."

"Not far off," I said, referring to his earldom.

"Mona doesn't hold her husband's class views of the rich. She apologized for what he must have sounded like when you and Mark talked to him last night."

"She must know him well." I rubbed my ear.

"Guess so. *Hope* so. If you don't know your spouse after twenty years of marriage...well, Mona mentioned the ongoing feud between the Clarksons and Roger."

"The bell ringing thing?"

"Sounds like a legitimate gripe, Bren."

"I'm not feeling too sorry for the Clarksons, Margo. Bell ringing is a way of life in these villages. Has been for centuries. I'm surprised the Clarksons didn't know that. And anyway, Roger never rang at night. He had a certain time when he didn't ring. He even rang up Baxter last night to apologize for what he was about to do. Don't get much more considerate than that. Especially when bell ringing is as much a part of our heritage as public rights of way through farmers' land."

"Whatever." Margo took a bite of her lettuce-tomato-cucumber salad, glanced at her notebook, and said, "According to Mona, the one-sided feud got nasty at one point, with Baxter threatening Roger with bodily harm or smashed windows. Mona said she never heard anything more after that, so either Roger talked to Baxter or Baxter cooled down of his own accord. Could even have been her daughter, Sibyl, who calmed things down."

"Why would Sibyl, *Mona and Ben's daughter*, get involved with the Baxter Clarkson feud? Baxter's not Sibyl's father."

"Good. Got your families straight. No, she isn't. But at one point, Sibyl was dating Lyn, who is Geneva's nephew."

"*Was* dating? When did they break it off?"

"Around New Year. And no, Mona doesn't know why. Something about her wanting to see other lads. Ask Sibyl. Anyway, maybe Sibyl persuaded Lyn to put in a good word to Uncle Roger and Aunt Geneva, and that stopped the feud. I'm not saying it happened, Bren, just that it could have. You never know about kids, do you?"

"Anyone corroborate this feud? Other household staff?"

"PC Byrd was talking to the head gardener and chauffeur, I know, this morning. He may have heard the same thing from them. Anyway, it's common village knowledge. As was the fact that the Earls of Swinbrook were originally called Swinebrook. Roger's been accosted several times—verbally—in the village. Here, in the pub, at the Greek restaurant, coming out of church Sunday mornings."

"Charming."

"It's never gone beyond verbal threats, but..." She screwed up her mouth, looking sick.

"He may have gone over the edge last night and actually attacked Roger. Yes. It's very possible. Baxter was anxious enough last night at the hall that we arrest Roger."

"It's all conjecture just now, Bren. I'm merely throwing out the info. It's up to you brainy ones to sort it out."

I laughed, soliciting odd looks from those at a nearby table. "Well," I said a bit softer, "all these squabbles certainly give us enough to sort out. Ben hates the aristocracy and anyone earning more than he does. Baxter hates church bells and, by transfer, Roger. The estate and all that go with it may be dolled out to more than Geneva—"

"That's the beauty of wills," Margo said, wiping her mouth and setting down her serviette. "All those underlying, hidden motives of the recipients."

"Maybe the manner of death will clear this up."

Margo leaned over the table and put her hand on top of mine. She said in a low voice, "This case disturbs you, Bren. I could see that last night. Why? Why this one more than others?"

I squeezed her hand in friendship and said, "Because if it's tied to the bell ringing feud it's so senseless. A lot of deaths are, to be sure, but if it's just because some people from the big city come to the country for peace and quiet, and find out they can't get along with their neighbor..." I pushed back my chair and grabbed my purse, leaving half my lunch uneaten. "Let's get back to the incident room. There are a million things we need to be doing, and me wallowing in self pity isn't one."

Jo A. Hiestand

CHAPTER ELEVEN

GRAHAM WAS DEEP into his sandwich when I came over to his table. The computer monitor screen showed the swirl of police cars chasing after a bad guy's car in a realistic screen saver. I walked to the other side of the table so I wouldn't have to watch it. That was the type of thing Scott Coral, a response driver in our constabulary section, thrived on. Excitement, speed, catching the crook. He said he had to have one adrenalin rush each shift or he'd go home feeling like a failure.

I waved at Graham, sat down, and told him of my morning. He finished his sandwich, took a sip of hot tea, and asked, "Anything more on the boot prints the SOs found?"

"Short of pulling a reverse Cinderella stint in the village, we've nothing yet, no."

"That *does* give me an idea, Taylor..." He turned in the metal chair, grasping the back of it as he looked around the room. PC Byrd was standing by the kitchen door, looking like he was going to brew up a cuppa. Graham called to him. "Byrd! If you're not too busy..."

"Yes, sir!" Constable Byrd hurried over to us. "What can I do for you, sir?"

"Trot along to Swinton Hall. Take along any other constable you can find who's not otherwise urgently engaged. Ask Lady Swinbrook if we can have every pair of riding boots in the house. Other hard-soled boots, too, if there are any. I know that will probably entail going through a cavern of closets, but there's nothing for it, Byrd."

"Yes, sir." He turned, then evidently thought of something, and faced Graham once again. "Oh, sir."

"Yes, Byrd?"

"Just thinking, sir—"

"Admirable, Byrd. You should teach a course at the training school."

I sniggered, my bandaged hand over my mouth.

Graham winked at me, then looked at Byrd. "Sorry. Couldn't resist the editorial. Yes?"

"Just wondering, sir, if I'll need a search warrant."

"Oh, hell..." Graham ran his fingers through his hair, giving himself the bed head look. Leaning back in the chair and stretching out his long legs for balance, he said, "Formalities, Byrd, are the pillars of society. And a bloody nuisance at times."

Coming from Graham, the statement was truer than the jest it seemed. I had heard the office buzz that he had left the ministry because he found church rules too restricting. Which I could well believe, learning more about Graham's personality the longer I worked with him. He was impatient with sloppy work or the confines of Procedure, demanded results of his team members, and like a terrier with a bone once he sensed the trail of the crime. He also cared about people and wanted to help, which was a personality trait common both to the ministry and police work. He followed regulations for the most part, but if there was a way to speed things up, he forged ahead when he thought no superior was looking. That was Graham. But there was a personal side to him that he had yet to expose to me. Like this Valentine's Day date. But, I thought as I watched him talking to Byrd, he's not the only dog worrying a bone.

"Okay, Byrd," Graham was saying as I came back to the present. "If she balks, we'll get one. But she probably won't. She wants to get this behind her and show she has nothing to hide. And if she did, she would have hidden it before now. She's a bloody lot of land in which to bury a pair of boots."

Byrd murmured, "Yes, sir," and took two other constables with him as he left.

"Now, TC," Graham said as the door closed behind the constables, "back to the bells and his lordship. You know, the thing that really gets up my nose about this murder is the Duvel bottle. Austin Swinbrook said Roger *never* drank while ringing. What's an ale bottle doing up there, with recently-spilled ale if he was ringing alone, as his bet would indicate? And why would he have that when he has a keg of beer waiting to be consumed? It doesn't add up. Perhaps I should have been an accountant." He didn't laugh, but he winked at me.

"So all we have to do is find out who drinks Duvel, wears boots, was angry with Roger and friendly enough that he'd be permitted up with the bells. Piece of cake. We need suspect only half the village."

"I was thinking more like two-thirds, but if you say half..." He laughed and tossed his pen onto his notebook. "Right. We've done this before, but it won't hurt to reiterate. We may have missed something. First, we have our two angry neighbors—Ben Griffiths, who hates the upper class and the fact that his wife works for Roger, and Baxter Clarkson, who hates bells and loves sleep."

"Staying with love, we may have anxious relations who love Roger's money and hate the fact that he's not in his dotage yet."

"His relations consist of a poor brother-in-law who's desperate to make the big time, a nephew—we don't know anything about how money-hungry he is, do we? No. Thought not. That's something we need to look at."

"Her ladyship may have wanted him out of the way," I said. "Either because she needed to inherit to control the finances or because she thought it easier than a divorce. There may be all sorts of reasons if we focus on her as prime suspect. We've just skimmed the top off her life."

Graham laughed. "Like a good episode for "Coronation Street" or similar telly drama? Well, we'll need to dig deeper into her life as well. I'm not counting anyone out. And, if you like money so much as a motive, TC, it's obvious you don't in your personal life or you wouldn't have chosen the Force for a profession. Money extends beyond family clutches. You mentioned Roger had been in business with two blokes. There could be something going on with them."

"But Ed Cawley and Geneva's ex-husband Barry both made their bundle when Roger did. There's no motive there that I can see."

"Until we check into Ed's and Barry's finances we must consider them as suspects, too. Either of their finances may not be so great. After all, you only have Barry's story on that right now. We cops *have* been lied to before, TC. Barry or Ed could have run into money problems. And while crying into his tea one morning may have remembered his old mate, wealthy Roger, who loved to mess about with bells. What do you think?"

He looked at me wide-eyed, hope on his face, waiting for a verdict.

I said that it was entirely likely, that we didn't know enough about the major players to exclude anyone or any motive.

As always seemed to happen when I was about to turn the conversation to more personal matters, Graham's mobile rang. He grabbed his pen and flipped to a clean page in his notebook and answered the phone. His concentration changed to Work Mode, as I liked to call it. His head was bent, concentrating on what he was writing; his answers were quick and short; his eyes closed momentarily as if picturing the caller's information. When he ended the call and closed his phone, his eyes were humorless, his neck muscles taut. The scar on the right side of his jaw shone vividly.

"That was Geneva, Lady Swinbrook."

I must have looked startled, for he said, "Yes, I know you were just there this morning. But something's happened. You need to go back there. Take Margo or Mark with you. Byrd and the other constables are rooting through her closets, if you recall."

I stood up, grabbing my shoulder bag. "What's happened?"

"A letter just came. She received a less-than-lovely valentine from a less-than-amorous sender. It threatens her life."

CHAPTER TWELVE

VALENTINE'S DAY MEANS KISSES SWEET,
A day of love, a day of hope
To see your face all bloated up,
Your body hanging from a rope.

Margo and I were in Geneva's garden room, where I had left her hours before. The sun had moved in those intervening hours to leave the room cold and dark, a fitting place for Margo and me to read this nasty poem. I looked up from the paper, trying to forget my own brush with cruelty years ago, and asked Geneva how it was delivered.

"Mona Griffiths, one of the housemaids, brought it. It didn't arrive with the regular post delivery, which comes around ten in the morning."

I looked at my watch. It was one o'clock. "So how did it come to the house? Special messenger?" Far fetched, of course, for then we'd have a delivery company, the name of the sender, address. But I could pray. Graham did, and he certainly obtained miracles at times.

"Not according to Mona. She had just come down the stairway from the bedrooms and saw the envelope lying on the floor. She saw it immediately, it being red."

It would be hard to overlook, I thought. *Red envelope, white marble floor.*

Red and white. Valentine's Day colors. I would always associate them, too, with Aunt Louisa. The first decorated cake I can remember was made by Aunt Lou. It was for a Valentine's Day party she had for my siblings and me. The dining room was a sea of red and white streamers, and paper hearts and cupids hung from the chandelier and curtain rods. A lace tablecloth and Aunt Louisa's silver adorned the table, where a bouquet of flowers and a huge cake claimed center attention. I felt grown up, eating from her fine china and silver, and I felt loved because she had done all this for me. But with Erik's gift this morning, I wondered if I would also lodge that in my heart alongside Aunt Lou. Or if the future would bring more memories of Erik.

"It must have been shoved through the letterbox," Geneva said. "How else would it have been sent? No one heard a knock on the door or the door bell sound." She screwed up her face as though she were about to cry. "God, my husband is killed, now I get this! Have people no feelings?"

"Who was working outside?" Margo asked, looking up from her note taking. "The person who delivered this must have been taking a chance at being seen. It's broad daylight. You have outside staff. Perhaps one of them saw someone approaching or leaving the house."

It was inconceivable that the miscreant could slip in and out unnoticed with all the activity of the hall. The paved drive ran like an arrow through the dense copse surrounding the building. When it ended at the double wooden door, it petered out to a gravel lane wrapping around the hall's western and northern sides before enlarging into a car park. A sunken garden, walled by fifteen-foot boxwood hedges, embraced the eastern façade. The lawn rolled down to the fringe of woods and relinquished its claim on the earth to yews and pine, oak, elm and ash. Violets and enchanter's nightshade might fringe the woods in spring. The hall's gardens held the wildness at bay to permit croquet on the lawn, perhaps, and a weed-free lily pond. I abandoned my contemplation of riding trails when Margo repeated her question.

Geneva wiped her hand across her forehead, pushing the strands of brunette hair back and revealing a widow's peak. *Unfortunately appropriate*, I thought. "It's the chauffeur's half day. He wasn't here this morning. Doesn't come back on duty until tea time. The gardener, as far as I know, was with the rest of his staff in a meeting somewhere downstairs. Planning designs of new annual beds for the spring and taking stock of fertilizer and such. I assume the stable hands were in the stable or exercising the horses in the paddock. That's at the back of the hall. As to anyone else..." She let out a deep sigh, clearly upset and wanting an end to her nightmare. "You'll have to ask. Unless someone like Mona happened to be looking out of the front windows..." She tilted her head and shrugged. Yes, it was going to be harder than I had hoped to find the culprit.

"Do you have any dogs?"

"What?" Geneva blinked in apparent confusion, then said, "Oh, yes. Barking dogs that would have alerted the handler that someone was approaching the house. No. I'm afraid we don't fit the customary lord and lady image. Roger's father was allergic, so Roger grew up without dogs. He's actually a bit shy of them, if truth be told. Never fond of them, since he had none in his childhood. Pity, now, in light of what's happened." She crossed her arms on her chest, her fingers gripping her elbows until her knuckles blanched.

Margo jotted down the approximate time of the valentine's delivery and I slipped the card and paper into a plastic evidence bag. Mark, our fellow officer, had just emerged from his own family nightmare last month. The death of one of his sisters-in-law had been horrendous in its own right, but his younger brother's wife had been targeted by poison-pen letters that had sent her into an emotional breakdown. We never had discovered who had sent those. Now Geneva was facing much the same situation. I silently prayed that she wouldn't end up as either of Mark's sisters-in-law had.

I asked if she knew of anyone, aside from her two angry neighbors, who might have had a grudge against her, who might have written it.

She shook her head and vehemently denied having any enemies.

"Do you believe anyone," Margo asked, "might have transferred his anger from your husband to you, now that his lordship is gone?"

Geneva seemed to mentally tick off a list of likely suspects, for her eyes stared toward her right, a bit of involuntary body language that proclaimed her next statement would be true. Her left thumb played again with the back of her wedding ring, as though she needed that physical connection to her husband. Finally, looking at Margo, she said, "No one. There was the squabble with the Clarksons about the bells, as you know. And Mona's husband isn't all that keen about her position here. But for anyone to hate Roger *that much,* that he'd do *this!*" Her tears fell unheeded as she gestured toward the piece of paper. "God! The venom inside some people..."

We assured Geneva that we'd have extra police cars patrolling the area, but also suggested she employ more of her staff as watch dogs. She said she would.

"Do you have a friend?" I said as we lingered in the open doorway. "Someone who could come over, support you through this? There's nothing like a close friend to ease the pain and shock."

"I do, yes. Thank you for suggesting that. I didn't want to be a burden to anyone—"

"Believe me, Lady Swinbrook, a real friend would not consider it a burden to help and support you."

She thanked us and slowly closed the door after us.

"That sort of thing would put me off opening my letters," Margo said as we walked toward the car.

I agreed, then tugged at Margo's sleeve and nodded toward the house before she could say anything.

Mona evidently was on a break, for she stood outside one of the side entrances, a lit cigarette in one hand, gesturing toward the hall with the other. Her daughter, Sibyl, faced her, frowning and crossing her arms on her chest.

"We shouldn't stand here and stare," I whispered to Margo, my eyes on the mother and daughter. "But it's very tempting. What's the argument, do you suppose?"

Margo shrugged and leaned closer to me. "I could always pretend I've lost something. You know—bend down, search the ground, wander about until I'm close enough to hear. That would work."

"Oh, sure. Not at all suspicious."

"It worked in November, at the bonfire."

It had. She'd assumed the role of a tourist in order to eavesdrop on a conversation. I said, "That was a bit different. The blokes didn't see you leaving from questioning someone in the case. And they also hadn't seen you prior to that and know you're a cop."

"Just trying to help." She pouted nearly as forcibly as Sibyl was presently doing.

I nudged Margo's arm. "Now what? Sibyl's jabbing her mother's arm."

In spite of trying to retain anonymity, we both turned toward the girl. I doubt if she or Mona were even aware of Margo and me, so involved was she in her discussion. She poked her index finger into her mother's arm. Mona stepped back, disengaging herself, and again pointed to the hall. Pushing her mother's arm out of the way, Sibyl shook her head and stepped toward her. As she spoke, she gestured wildly. Mona dropped her cigarette, trod on it, and took a step toward the door. Sibyl grabbed her mother's arm, pulling her around. Mona lifted Sibyl's hand from her arm and shook her head. After perhaps thirty seconds of exchanged animated and heated dialogue, Sibyl stomped her foot, yelled one last thing, and marched toward the car park. She got into her car, slammed the door, and zoomed off down the drive. Mona watched her go, lit another cigarette, and slowly walked around to the back of the hall.

"So what was that all about?" I asked when I finally recovered from my astonishment.

"They're upset," Margo said, making for our car.

"Brilliant. But about what? Whom? It could make a difference if it's connected with the case."

"They kept pointing toward the hall. Maybe it's about Roger's death."

"Might be. Or something having to do with Geneva."

"Or Mona's position."

"Or someone else there." I said, opening the car door.

"Or something like a planned trip on Mona's day off, only Mona had to cancel it or it's postponed, and Sibyl's mad because they were going to do something together."

"Well, we've no end of scenarios."

"I just hope," Margo said, starting the engine, "that we're not called back here for an assault. I don't think I could deal with that."

I murmured my agreement, adding that there was enough ill will with Roger's death and Geneva's nasty valentines.

"I'm certain Geneva echoes your sentiments," Margo said as we headed down the drive. The sun had broken through the patch of gray clouds and spotlighted bits of lichen-encrusted dry wall and dried flower stalks. A clump of lingering snow fell onto the car's bonnet, startling us in its icy thud. Margo let out a squeal, belatedly steered the car slightly to the right to dodge any further falling companions. "'Bout time this stuff melts. I'm cold."

"You're always cold."

"What's wrong with that? I'm not a winter person. Give me sun-baked beaches and palm trees swaying in a warm breeze."

"You're in the wrong country and career, then. Anyway, it's only mid-February. We've still got another month of winter to go."

"Well, it can't go any too soon for me." She cheered as another chunk of snow plopped onto the drive ahead of us.

Though I did like winter, I was ready for spring. I loved watching for signs of life emerging from the earth, the tree buds swelling more each day until they exploded from their husks in a riot of color and scent. No matter how many springs I would be privileged to experience, I would never tire of the miracle of tiny green leaves emerging from their hibernation and seeking the sunlight.

"And," I added, "I bet Geneva can beat me in the wish department. I bet this case can't be over any too soon for her."

"It's a ruddy shame, her having to go through this. She seems to be a nice lady. First her husband's murdered, now this horrid note. I hope she doesn't sleep with a gun under her pillow now. She could end up shooting her toe, the state she's in."

"Who can blame her? For all her huge house and staff, she still has to face this. It's a personal intrusion—and a life-threatening one, at that. This is serious, Margo. Anyone who hates as much as that poem indicated—"

"I know. I wasn't making light of it, Bren. I just don't want to be investigating another stupid shooting in which the casualty is the innocent victim. That's all I meant. That's why burglar alarms and pit bulls were invented."

"The hall must be choked with weapons," I said, imagining some of the stately homes I'd toured as a child. Homes that had pistols, rapiers, broadswords, and dirks fanned out and swirled in fantastic geometric designs on the walls of the great hall. I snorted, picturing Geneva taking a mace and chain to bed with her. "She has ready access to someone if she wanted."

"Try finding gunpowder for some of those old horse pistols. I'd bet my pay packet that none of them would fire."

"The home's no doubt got a nice array of knives and swords. There are always those."

"She wouldn't do," Margo said, pausing at the end of the drive and looking before she edged into the High Street. "A knife or sword calls for a close encounter. She'd have to be within a foot or so of the bad guy. A gun's a lot less personal. You can shoot someone from yards away, avoid hand contact. Which," she said, shivering, "would personally creep me. Ugh. Think of it, Bren. *Touching* some nerd like that. Enough to give you nightmares for months. Bloody hell."

Like what rape victims must experience. Only, I didn't say it. The trauma must indeed be hell to live with. How any of those women got a semblance of normal life back was beyond me. It certainly would take a strong personality to vow that the berk would not destroy her quality of life.

Margo parked the car in the community center car park and we went into the building. Byrd and his team had not returned from Swinton Hall, so

Jo A. Hiestand

I gave the envelope and paper to WPC MacMillian and asked her to have it tested for DNA saliva and traces from the fingers. She nodded and left.

When I got Graham up to speed on the valentine, he sighed, then said, "If it eventually comes to taking prints, the only prints on it will be Mona's and Geneva's, but we'll make a show of doing our job. It will impress Simcock, if no one else."

I asked if the superintendent had rung up, asking about the case. Graham said no, and not to wish that on him right now. "I think you and I need to talk to Lyndon Kirkpatrick. See what he knows about his uncle's death. Or the bell feud, if he defused the row between his uncle and Baxter Clarkson. Even a seventeen-year-old lad ought to be awake and lolling about the house by now."

Lyndon was indeed up, had been for several hours, from the look of the front room. It was strewn with used coffee mugs, newspapers, a dressing gown, an open phone directory, an ashtray filled with cigarette ends, and dirty breakfast dishes. The air smelled of cigarette smoke and fried eggs, and the television whispered its way through an old black-and-white movie. *More of a distraction than as a serious form of entertainment*, I thought as Lyn clicked the remote control. The screen crackled into blackness.

"I don't know how I can help," Lyndon said as Graham and I took the offered seats. The lad was tall and muscular, as I assumed his father was, if the concert posters on their living room wall were a true likeness of Kirk Fitzpatrick. Lyndon remained standing, seemingly undecided if he should first clean the breakfast things off the coffee table or talk to us. He picked up a section of the newspaper from a chair, laid it on top of one of the stereo speakers, and asked if we wanted coffee or tea.

Graham declined, as did I, and asked after Lyn's mother. "We talked to her last night. A rather indecent hour, I'm afraid, but there was nothing for it but to get on with our job. I hope she's recovering from the shock of his lordship's death." Graham's raised eyebrows implied he wanted an answer.

Lyndon glanced toward the kitchen. Was he wishing mum would appear, or was he anxious about the washing up? "I suppose so. That is, I don't really know. When I got up this morning, she'd already breakfasted. Not that she could eat all that much, but it was just toast and tea. She told me about my uncle's—well, she was still in shock. I don't think it's quite sunk in yet. She phoned a few people, tried to get hold of my dad. He's playing some gigs in Bolton and such. But he didn't have his mobile on, I guess, for she never got through to him. She left over an hour ago. Said she wanted to order flowers, see Aunt Gen. She'll be back soon. I don't know when, exactly. She's got a lot of running around to do. But if you want to wait—" He stood on the other side of the coffee table, shifting his weight from foot to foot and glancing out of the windows. *Wanting mummy to be home and take charge*, I thought. Well, at his age and in the present circumstance, why not? Not many seventeen-year-olds would want to be closeted with police detectives, talking about his uncle's death.

PEARLS BEFORE SWINE

"Actually," Graham said, moving a Swinton Hall coffee mug aside and laying his notebook on the table, "we want to talk to you, if that's alright."

Lyn nodded. "I don't know that I know all that much. About his death, I mean. But I don't mind. I want to help." He pulled at the long sleeve of his jersey as though it were bothering him.

The sound of a car braking in the drive pulled our attention to the front window. Noreen Fitzpatrick got out, opened the back door, gathered up a grocery bag, and slammed both doors shut. She locked the car, and gave Graham's red Insight a careful stare as she walked up to the front door. A few patches of snow clung to the sides of the concrete step and encircled a clump of dried ferns nodding in the breeze. There was a stamping of feet on something thick—perhaps the doormat, zippers presumably being unzipped, and a rattle of metal coat hangers knocking against the wooden coat stand.

"Lyn?" Her voice and the rustle of the grocery bag as she set it down on the hall table drifted into the living room.

"In here, mum," Lyndon called, making toward the door. "Two detectives are here. They want to ask me some questions about Uncle Rog." He followed his mother into the room, towering over her smaller, slighter figure, and waited to see if she would give her consent.

For all of Noreen's careful morning grooming, the strain of Roger's death had marked her. Dark-rimmed eyes stared cautiously at us, emphasizing her sallow complexion. A general listlessness claimed her, stooping her shoulders, slowing her walk, draining her voice. She clutched Lyndon's hand as though holding onto a life preserver.

Graham repeated the phrases I'd heard many times before, saying Lyndon could stop whenever he wanted, cautioning him about incriminating himself. "You understand, Lyndon, that we're merely interested in learning if you knew of the bell feud. And if so, if you have any idea either who cooled it down or if Baxter would have been angry enough to confront Lord Swinbrook last night."

Lyndon said he'd like to help, and sat beside his mum on the sofa. You couldn't have slipped a knife blade between them.

Seeing that Noreen intended to stay, Graham stood up. Since Lyndon was seventeen, and therefore an adult, he could be interviewed without his parents present. And the presence of a parent might even compromise the inquiry if that parent was a witness or suspect. He asked Noreen if he could speak to her alone. She blinked, obviously surprised at the request, patted Lyndon's hand, then walked into the kitchen.

I waited until I heard the teakettle being filled with water and Graham's soft voice asking her a question before I started my interview.

I nodded at the large poster of Kirk and said, "Smashing graphic, that. I play guitar, too. Took me ages to get calluses on my fingertips. It took a lot longer than I had thought."

Lyndon nodded, saying something about the vicious circle of painful fingers pressing down on the steel guitar strings, stopping for a few days until your fingers quit hurting, going back to playing again...

"It's awful. You need the calluses so your fingers don't hurt, but you can't develop calluses because your fingers hurt!"

"Yeh," Lyndon said, nodding. "Like I said—vicious."

"Do you like your dad's music?"

Lyndon shrugged, saying it was pretty good.

"I understand your dad's doing some gigs in Bolton. Do you miss him when he's gone? You two close?"

"Yeh, I miss him. Sometimes he's gone a week, two, maybe, at a time. Sometimes it's only a day. But mum's here. And I've my mates from school. Plus Sibyl. Her mum works for Uncle Rog up at the hall."

"And Sibyl...did you meet at school?"

"Yeh. She's a year behind me. Sixteen. We were going out fairly steady, but she...well, we still see each other at times, if not so regular now. We're just mates. Nothing special anymore."

"You have any thoughts about after school, what you want to do with your life? Perhaps go into music like your dad?"

"Don't know yet, do I? Haven't thought all that much on it. I like music, sure, but I see how hard it is to get anywhere in the biz. Like my dad. Struggling these past ten years or so, trying to make it big, get out of the folk club circuit and into the main concert halls." He glanced at the poster as though hearing his father's conversations or advice. Lyndon said, "I'd like to go into music—I'm thinking about it. I've got several part-time jobs so I can earn enough for a good guitar and amp. It's hard, making enough money, but I'll do it—maybe another couple of years. I want mum to be proud of me."

"I can't believe she's not proud of you now, Lyn. Just for you being you."

Lyndon sniffed. "Ta, but there's not much for her to be proud of. I've not done much. Except, maybe, stay out of trouble when some of my mates got nicked for pinching CDs in Chesterfield. Petty stuff like that."

"It sounds like she'd be proud of you for that, certainly, but she probably loves you just for you being yourself, for your personality, your morals, honesty—"

"Yeh, well, that's not as important as money and fame." Lyndon sniffed again and bounced his right leg. "Cheerfulness won't bring in the admirers."

I said, "Speaking of admirers, Lyndon, do you know anyone besides Baxter Clarkson who wasn't an admirer of your uncle's bell ringing? Anyone who might be angry enough to confront him physically, perhaps hit him—not intentionally, but doing so in the heat of the argument, say?"

"You think that's what happened? He was in a fight and someone hit him?"

"We know Baxter Clarkson had lodged several complaints with the police about the bells ringing in the evening. He was very angry last night when he came over to the hall. Do you know of anyone else who was angry with your uncle—either about the bell ringing or something else? Something they viewed as a last straw in a line of privilege, perhaps? People's emotional fuses can be short sometimes. We all have a breaking point at which we can't tolerate any more abuse. Do you know if that happened to anyone associated with your uncle?"

Lyndon screwed up his mouth as he glanced out of the window. He obviously was thinking of all the quarrels and snippets of gossip he'd heard in the family and from friends. Finally, shaking his head, he said, "No one. Sorry, miss. Sibyl's dad, of course. He's always rabbiting on about the upper classes. But I don't think he'd follow through with a fight. It has to be someone else who hated Uncle Rog."

A silence as thick as the family's bereavement hung in the air. A car horn sounded farther down the street and the radiator in the hallway gurgled into life. I asked Lyndon if Noreen was affected by Kirk's absence from home.

"She misses him, sure, and wishes at times he had a different job that would keep him home at nights. I know it's not how she dreamed married life would be. She talked about it a lot at nights when we were alone in the house. She thought her husband would be in every evening. Ensconced around the fireplace. That sort of thing. Instead, she—and I—find ourselves gazing at dad's concert posters when we want to see him, putting on a CD if we miss the sound of his voice. No, it's not what she thought it'd be, being married to dad. It's no secret, miss, because she's told me during her weepy spells. But then, you put up with that sort of thing, the absences, if you love someone, don't you? You want them to succeed and find their happiness."

As if mentally connected, Graham and I happened to glance at each other through the open kitchen door. I quickly averted my eyes to Kirk's poster. That had been the grounds for ending Graham's engagement. The strange hours, the evenings vacant from home and hearth. Rachel, Graham's fiancée, had wanted a nine-to-five man, and wanted him firmly under her control, accessible to her social calendar. Graham couldn't promise that. It was impossible in our job. I could feel my face burning under the intensity of my blush and got up, walking over to a photo of the Fitzpatrick family. If the miracle ever happened that Graham would ask me to spend my life with him, the crazy hours would not be a problem. We both were used to that aspect of the job, just as we both were in love with our police work. Or, as near as I could be right now.

"It must be hard," I said, finally turning around. "Does your mum work?"

"She's a typist. She works from home. She types manuscripts for an author in Chesterfield. He's not a name—that is, he's not generally known to the public. But she enjoys reading his work as she types. She also types papers for some of the professors and researchers at Manchester University. And there's a writer in Buxton, and a handful of students at the university she also does work for. I don't know their names, but mum will tell you.

She makes a nice bob or two, and I know she likes it. She can set her own hours, works more or less to her own pace, though there are deadlines, of course."

"I envy people who can work from their homes," I said, picking up a small pottery jug. "No fortune spent on office attire, no sitting in traffic. Nice."

"That could be the best part, yes. It depends on the client as to whether mum picks up the typing or they drop it off. But she can always plan around rush hour, so there's that to be said for it."

"So both your mum and your dad have talented fingers."

"Mum not only types fast but she's accurate. As I said, she makes a good living with her computer."

I said, "Working at home like she does, is she—or you, while doing your homework—ever annoyed by his lordship's bell ringing? I assume you both have to concentrate, with all those papers and deadlines to meet. Do the bells ever bother either of you?"

"I don't think they bother mum. And me...no. I don't hear them most of the time. Well, you know how it is. People say the same thing about the grandfather clocks they have in their homes, don't they? You're so used to hearing them that you *don't* half the time. Same here in the village. I've grown up here. I'm used to the bell practice and hearing the peals. The Clarksons are newcomers to village life. Of course the bells will bother them for a bit. But they'll soon get like the rest of us—not even hearing them."

"Do you know where Baxter Clarkson worked in Manchester? I wonder if he's ever mentioned it to you in passing, or perhaps to Lady Swinton."

"I don't recall anything specific. Just that he was a casualty department doctor. I don't know what hospital."

I could believe it. The high stress of the emergency cases, the life-or-death situations, the stream of human tragedy, perhaps even working on a relative. No wonder the Baxters had hoped for a quiet country existence.

Graham and Noreen slowly came into the front room. Graham stopped in front of the large concert poster, drank the last of his tea in one long gulp, and asked Noreen if she thought Geneva would remarry. "I know it's too soon, with her recent bereavement, but a bit later? I only ask because Barry Sykes came to see her this morning."

Noreen sat down beside Lyndon and nodded her head. "Well, he would ask, wouldn't he? No. I don't think Geneva will make the mistake of marrying Barry."

"Why do you call it a mistake? I got the impression that he was still madly in love with her."

"That's as may be. On *his* part, perhaps, but not on hers. Their marriage didn't last long. It was in trouble before Roger and his wealth intruded into her life. I was sorry to see it break up. There's too much divorce these days. But she seemed to know it was unsalvageable. And frankly, I'm surprised you're asking me."

I said so, too, when we were driving back to the incident room. He had turned on the car heater and although it blew onto my feet, I still snuggled back into the car seat, my arms clasped firmly across my chest, my body and soul chilled. I wiped my gloved hand across my passenger-side window, clearing off the fog so Graham could see. He murmured his thanks and turned the car onto the High Street. Vehicles and pedestrians seemed to sense a change in the weather, for everything seemed to be hurrying toward some destination. I would have been happier if I had been warmer, but I was content to sit beside Graham, enveloped by the scent of his aftershave, and watch the world slip by.

At the community hall car park, Graham slid his Insight into the spot alongside my blue Corsa, turned off the motor, and got out. A mantle of gray clouds had replaced the late morning sun and stretched unbroken across the sky. The steeple of the church vanished against its somber backdrop, its ashen-colored stones becoming one with the leaden sky. The shops along the High Street were alive with shoppers, and store windows glowed from yellow or white lights that cut through the darkening sky. A strand of bright red lights that outlined a window in the community hall advertised the Valentine's Day event. I opened the car door and drew in a lungful of the crisp air. It smelled of a burgeoning snowstorm, and already the pedestrians along the pavement were pulling their scarves closer to their necks. Even a toy poodle trotting beside her owner sported a tartan coat. I grabbed my bag and closed the door as he continued. "Not only do many villagers know people well enough to fathom motives behind actions, TC—thereby giving us another lead—but I also wanted to know if it was assumed that Barry might want Geneva back."

"Because she'll come into a hefty inheritance?"

"What's so surprising about that?"

"Other than the fact that Geneva was clearly upset by Barry's proposal, nothing." I hurried up to him, my breath exploding into huge, white clouds. The temperature seemed to have fallen since earlier this morning. Graham opened the door to the community center and I trotted inside.

"A good motive for murder, then, wouldn't you say?" Graham said, throwing his car keys onto the table top and removing his suede jacket. "As we've said before, *Cui bono*—to whose benefit? Kill the husband who just happened to stand between you and the nice, juicy bundle of cash, get to live out your days in royal splendor in Swinton Hall, command servants about. Nice bit of fairy tale come to life." He hung his jacket on the back of the metal chair. "We've known motives that weren't half so good. And that's not even considering the rest of the family, which includes Lyndon and Sibyl."

"They're children, sir! You can't believe they—"

"Perhaps on the periphery of our suspects, but by a roundabout measure they would benefit. Lyn is Roger's nephew. So, if his aunt, Geneva, spreads a bit of the lolly about, Lyn benefits. Sibyl is a bit of an outsider, I admit. But if her mother gets anything because she's been a loyal employee, she may get something in the trickle-down effect. Or if she marries Lyndon, she may benefit. Don't scoff at this, TC. People have committed murder for much less substantial benefits. Remember last month? Mark's nephew?"

I nodded, recalling the incident.

Graham flashed a smile. "I rest my case. Don't take off your coat. I want you and Margo to pay a social visit to Austin and his girlfriend. If you're any good at this, maybe you'll return with more inheritance motives." He smiled as I grabbed my purse again and called across the room to Margo, who looked like she'd rather sun bathe in ten feet of snow than to return outside.

CHAPTER THIRTEEN

Dulcie Burgess spared Margo and me the extra job of locating her, for she was at Austin's, plying him with cups of whiskey-laced tea and hugs when we arrived. She was nothing as I had pictured the girlfriend of a peer to be—having the stereotype of a high fashioned, long-legged model entrenched in my mind. Dulcie was slender, but short. And with red, curly hair and freckles that would be a cosmetologist's headache to conceal from the camera lens. But she *was* dressed to fulfill my ideal: turquoise wool slacks, cream-colored Aran knit jersey, turquoise, green and black print silk scarf around her neck. And while her earrings were not ostentatious, they certainly murmured 'wealth'—small clusters of jade and silver flowers perched around a large silver bangle.

When we, too, had our tea in our hands—without the whiskey—I asked Austin what Roger had been wearing at the dinner last night.

After getting the same answer as I'd received from everyone else, I answered Austin's question. "Because he was wearing an old cardigan when we found him, which didn't exactly compliment the cashmere and wool. Have you any idea why the cardigan?"

"I assume because he was going to ring. That's what he always wore. So he wouldn't sweat on his good clothes. But if he rang me up to say he was canceling the ring..." He frowned and set the teacup—without a coaster—on the pie-crust Georgian table. "Perhaps he hadn't taken it off yet. After ringing me up, I mean. Perhaps he—he died before he could remove it. Makes sense, doesn't it?"

I agreed. An awkward silence filled the room as I decided what next to ask. Dulcie went back to stroking Austin's hair. I finally said, somewhat clumsily, "Nice place, sir."

"What?" Austin blinked wildly, looking rather like an ostrich, and disentangled his hand from Dulcie's clasp. He looked around the room as thought it were the first time he'd seen it, then nodded, and said, "Oh, yes. Thank you. Nothing special. Just some castoffs from the hall, you know."

If this Elizabethan carved oak table, William-and-Mary winged settee, and Charles II walnut chair were castoffs, I'll be the first person in line come next jumble sale day.

Jo A. Hiestand

Austin's house was a large Tudor-style dwelling, rather big by village standards, but enforcing the sense of wealth and lineage that the Swinbrook name suggested. It had originally been part of the estate, but nearly a century ago, when the family's troubles had forced the selling off of land, the house had relinquished its association with the grounds and been engulfed in the growing village. Now it practically wallowed in commonality, sitting on the corner of the High Street and East Brook Lane, cattycorner to the local butcher's.

How the mighty have fallen, I thought, but felt no pity for the weakening of the once-regal link. Austin wasn't suffering, and the house embraced enough fine furniture, porcelain and silver to make any museum drool in envy. Or consider hiring a burglar.

Which wasn't a bad idea, I thought, glancing around the drawing room. With peach-colored plaster walls, wooden rafters and floors, oriental area rugs and diamond-paned windows, the room was my ideal of medieval perfection.

"I see you're assessing the pile," Austin said, noting my gaze. "No need to blush, miss. It's a bit over the top for most of us, isn't it? But, then, it *is* part of the family inheritance, and the rent is reasonable..." He grinned, showing a mouthful of teeth that would shame a film star. "Which is why I have no intention of moving into the hall. I like it here—it's modest, easy to care for. And, besides not being under the crush of a huge estate tax, I don't need a staff of hundreds to maintain it. I just have a maid who comes in daily. She and a gardener are it."

I said that seemed an easier life, and quite affordable.

"You're right about that," he said. "I can't see giving the government all that tax money. God, it eats up any savings you're trying to establish, doesn't it? Besides, I want to use my money for the greater good. Not that taxes don't help. I mean, that's why we have them, isn't it? But something direct, something I can see immediate results of."

"Like your brother's philanthropy to the school?" I said.

"Exactly! I want to direct what institution or project gets my help, talk to the people it concerns."

Dulcie ceased her fascination with Austin's hair, laid her hands in her lap, and said, "Austin's very conscientious about that, miss. It's not just a load of rubbish. I know first-hand how large his heart is—we met through one of the agencies he helped."

"How interesting! Which one is that, if you don't mind my asking?"

"PAC." I must have looked blank, for she added, "Patient-Animal Connection. We bring dogs, cats, rabbits—basically, anything warm and furry—into hospitals, nursing homes, retirement homes for the patients and residents to hold and pet. It's incredible therapy, connecting people who are otherwise alone or overcome with mental or emotional problems to life once again. The animal represents something helpless, something outside of the patient's own problematic world and helps draw him back to his surroundings. It's amazing how these animals help people. They've been responsible for remarkable turnarounds in some patients' emotional states. One of our Rag Dolls—the cat breed, not a toy—was credited with saving a suicidal woman's life. She can't wait for the cat's weekly visit, when she feeds him table scraps saved from her meals."

I said that I had heard of animals doing wonders such as this.

Dulcie said, "PAC is only one agency that's benefited from Austin's generosity. He's helped a bunch of people in the past, and he's going to help a lot more, now that he'll come into the inheritance."

"And what other sorts of things would you like to do, sir?"

"Environmental projects, mainly. I've been labeled a tree-hugger, which is not too far off the mark, actually. I'm concerned with what we're doing to our natural resources. If we pollute and take from the land, sea and air, there will be nothing left for our children, and we'll be risking human as well as animal life. You only have to read the paper or listen to the news on the telly to know what we've done through strip mining, over-fishing and deforestation. It doesn't need a rocket scientist to announce that the destruction of the rain forest is destroying our own valuable source for medicines."

His voice had increased in volume during his oration, and his neck muscles had tightened. Now that he had given me his sermon, he seemed to relax. The flush drained from his face, and as he relaxed his grip on Dulcie's hands, he said, "Sorry about the lecture. But it angers me to see what human beings are doing to our planet. They're destroying the very ground under our feet. What will happen to us when the seas are all polluted, the air too dirty to breathe?"

"It's greed," Dulcie said, her quiet voice somehow more ominous than Austin's formerly angry one. "Tank-like, petrol-guzzling cars where hybrid, smaller models would do; holiday resorts that clear away rain forests and natural habitat of animals; industries manufacturing on the cheap, belching fumes into the air, instead of developing cleaner ways to produce their items. It all adds up. Austin's not exaggerating. We're destroying our planet —and at an alarming rate."

I said I agreed with everything they had said, then asked if he'd heard about the local crisis. "Your sister-in-law's recent post delivery," I said, referring to Geneva's cruel valentine.

"I have," Austin said, exhaling loudly. "She rang me up, quite annoyed. I'm afraid I can't offer a solution as to the sender. I have no idea who would do such a vile thing. But I tell you, miss, that I'm of a good mind to camp out on the door step, gun in hand, and catch the bloody beggar in the act."

"That's commendable, sir, but hardly advisable." I paused, envisioning the array of weapons the hall had. The wall above the fireplace in the great hall was tattooed with guns, mainly of the highwayman era. With assorted pikes, rapiers, broadswords and dirks, Geneva was well defended, if she went that route. "But maybe you could help in a different way." He looked interested, so I quickly said, "Do you know of anyone angry enough to kill your brother?"

"*Kill* Roger? I—" He fumbled for the word, perhaps through shock or mentally denying the truth. He glanced at Dulcie, brought her hand to his chest and held it there. "That *can't* be! I—I thought he fell from the top of the ladder! Every indication tells us that. Are you saying—"

"We've established it's murder, sir. The postmortem leaves no doubt. I'm sorry."

Austin slowly shook his head, the color gone from his face. He brushed his lips against Dulcie's hand, released it. Dulcie released a giant sob and buried her head on Austin's shoulder. After Austin kissed her head, he said, "But that's *insane! Roger?* Everyone loved him. His charities, his personality—everything he was and would *continue* to be and *did* spoke of love. *No one* would hurt him, would do that to him."

"Really, sir? I understood Ben Griffiths and Baxter Clarkson—"

Austin underlined my statement with a few curse words. "Just because some *berk's* all for the eradication of the monarchy and equal wages across the board for ditch diggers on up to brain surgeons, and the *other* idiot is upset about bell ringing—well, I can't see *any* degree of anger turning physical like that! My God, what a thought!" He slipped an arm around Dulcie and blotted her wet cheeks with his handkerchief.

A loving gesture, conveying care and protection. As a parent to his child. Yet it also carried the unspoken agreement of 'for better, for worse, in sickness and in health.' I thought, for perhaps the thousandth time, of Graham and I ached that our relationship seemed doomed to be boss and coworker. I let Austin kiss Dulcie's cheek, then asked, "How about former staff at the hall? Perhaps someone who was fired. Other family members—that sort of thing."

Austin folded his damp handkerchief and shook his head almost before I'd finished speaking. "No. Way wrong. Nothing like that. Roger was well liked by *everyone*. Well, that is...."

"Excepting the berk and the idiot," I said.

Austin smiled. "Excepting them, yes. But seriously, miss, I can't think of anyone. There could be, of course, someone I don't know about. I didn't know all of Roger's friends or business concerns. There could be something bubbling beneath the surface of a calm exterior, couldn't there? How often have seemingly calm people just snapped under the proverbial last straw and exploded in some deadly action? You read about it all the time in America—post office shootings, school children murdering their class mates..."

"Anyone poking about the village lately? Someone you don't know, someone who seemed suspicious? I don't mean to put too fine a point on this, sir, but if some stranger seemed unduly interested in Roger or the hall..."

PEARLS BEFORE SWINE

"Come to think of it..." Austin's voice trailed off as he stared at the carpet, perhaps calling an inconsequential event from his mind. He held up his finger, as though directing us to remain silent, then looked up and said, "Yes, there was someone! I paid it no mind at the time—the village gets lots of tourists. But I do remember this one bloke—"

"What makes him stand out?"

"His actions. Well, to be precise, his questions."

"*Questions?* Like what? Where to find a B-and-B or something?"

Austin shook his head, his eyes now wide in his excitement. "No. Nothing so mundane or I would've forgotten him. No. He stopped me on the street. I was just about to get into my car—I'd just left the pub—and he calls out and comes up to me."

"And what did he ask you?"

"If I knew of any homes for sale in the village."

"*Homes?* Why didn't he get an estate agent?"

"That's what I was wondering, too."

Dulcie leaned forward, her voice tinged with excitement. "I met him, too, Austin. He asked me the same thing. Wanted to know about a place to live, either in the village or nearby. I told him I didn't know of anything. Then he asked if the hall had any cottage he could have on a weekly basis."

We stared at her, suddenly extremely interested.

I wondered if the question had been a ploy, a mere excuse to talk to residents in order to get information for some forthcoming crime. Like burglars who ring doorbells do to see if anyone is home, then asking if 'Paul Myrtle' lives there when someone comes to the door.

I felt my stomach tightening. "What did he look like? Is he still here?"

Dulcie glanced at Austin, then said slowly, as though seeing the man in her mind's eye, "He was medium height and build, with dark hair. I don't know if it was black—we were standing in the shade, but it was very dark. He was a light-skinned male, perhaps in his thirties, don't you think so, Austin?" She looked at him, wanting his help with the description.

Austin nodded. "Couldn't have been much older. Nice looking chap. Dark eyes. I couldn't place his accent, though. Could you?"

Dulcie shook her head. "It wasn't local. Nor anything readily identifiable. You know..." She looked from Austin to me. "Obvious. Like Cockney or Geordie or Somerset. I haven't seen him since that one time."

"And when was this?" I asked.

"Oh, very recently. Monday, I think. Or Tuesday. This week, anyway."

"Day before Roger died," Austin said. "*Tuesday.* I remember because I was going to ask Rog about the bloke when we dined Wednesday evening. But then that ridiculous bet came up and I completely forgot. Just saw him the one time. Sorry."

I sighed. Maybe Scott had seen our stranger during his round. I'd ask.

Jo A. Hiestand

Margo seemed disappointed in the dead end, too, for she chewed on the end of her pen and stared at her notebook. I asked Austin if he could think of anyone else who seemed suspicious or who might have a grudge against Roger.

"No, no one comes to mind. Unless it's Barry Sykes."

"Lady Swinbrook's ex-husband? Why would Barry kill your brother?

Austin snorted. "Obvious, isn't it? Because he wants Geneva back—in his arms, in his bed, and in his bank account. She'll inherit most of Roger's estate, I assume. That's a lot of money. Barry has always been a schemer—in the nicest sense of the word, miss. Business ideas and so on. Barry can always do with a cash injection. Killing Roger is easier than getting a bank loan. No, miss. Barry isn't such a daft suspect after all. He very well might be scheming on changing Gen's name back to Mrs. Sykes. I revise my list of berks and idiots."

Margo, who had been busy scratching notes all this time, asked Austin why he thought that.

"Because," Austin said, leaning forward, staring at her. "I recently saw an envelope addressed to Geneva, with Barry's return address on it. Oh, it was in a waste bin by her desk, so don't accuse me of snooping among her personal things even if she *is* my sister-in-law. I just happened to see it. Couldn't miss it, actually."

"And when was this, sir?"

"The 13th. The thing was red and white, so I thought it a valentine instead of a birthday card. Rather odd thing to send the wife of another man, don't you think?"

"Knowing your sister-in-law as you do, do you believe she welcomed the attention—either before or after your brother's death?"

Would I enjoy that sort of attention—two men declaring their love? Would it make me feel desirable, make me conceited? I have a girlfriend who's on husband number three. She seems to have no difficulty finding love, while I, to the contrary, have never been asked. Am I giving some unconscious signal that I am a workaholic or am afraid of intimacy? And, though Mark was certainly attentive at the moment, I can only surmise what I would feel like if Graham showed interest other than that of a cohort. Would I be flattered with two males vying for my heart, or would I find it annoying, perhaps confusing? I glanced at Dulcie, who was leaning against Austin's shoulder, her eyes wide and taking in his features. She was a strong, single-minded woman. I doubted if she would enjoy simultaneous wooing. It took a lot of energy and, if you had a goal in mind, took a lot of your time.

"No," Austin said, smiling at Dulcie. "I don't believe she'd like that sort of attention. Geneva was going to leave Barry long before Roger came along"

"So she wouldn't marry Barry now. I mean, companionship with her willing ex means nothing to her."

PEARLS BEFORE SWINE

"That's it. Geneva divorced *him*, miss. She's made no effort to socialize with Barry during her marriage to Roger, not even having him over for drinks or Christmas open house—which is as close to a sardine can as the hall can be, what with all Roger's friends and people from his charities and what have you. Barry could have certainly been accommodated and slipped in, but he was never invited. So his valentine, if that's what it was, or his presence on her doorstep won't persuade her to slip on his ring. And it's not as though Barry's income can complete with Roger's inheritance, either."

Dulcie wiped the back of her hand across her cheeks, then blotted her hand on her wool slacks before murmuring her agreement.

"I'm *not* saying, however," Austin continued, patting Dulcie's hand, "that the inheritance won't be welcome. I'd be a liar—*and* a hypocrite—if I pretended otherwise!"

"Welcome to..." Margo said.

"Me. *And* Geneva. There's always *something* one needs money for, isn't there? That's the bane of life, I think. University tuition, home repairs, car payments. Just daily living dumps its load of bills. No, miss, Roger's money will be welcome, no matter how tragic the circumstance that necessitated the payment."

Of course, every person alive knew what Austin was talking about. And had some story to emphasize his sentiment. As Austin talked, I tried to concentrate, but my mind wandered back to my own recent inheritance. Oh, not that it was huge. It certainly wouldn't excite Austin. But for all the pain of Aunt Louisa's death, the blessing from that tragedy would be my bit of her estate. She'd told me years ago to tell her what I would like. Getting over the astonishment of the early arrangement had taken me a while, and feeling like a vulture—grabbing at bits of her estate—took even longer. But she'd convinced me over a shandy one day, saying it was sensible. I'd be sure to have the items of hers that meant the most to me, and it would be one less bit of trauma to survive. So, succumbing to the sensibility of it, and to Aunt Louisa's insistence, I acquiesced: Two rings—one garnet and silver, one plain band; a shelf's length of books—assorted, but heavy on detective fiction and British wildlife; an upholstered chair. She threw in a lump of cash. The plain silver ring now adorned my right-hand ring finger; the books would soon snuggle up to other novels she and mother had given me through the years; the chair would claim a corner of my front room; and I would use a bit of the money to buy a Tiffany-style table lamp. These things were little replacement for my aunt's life, but every time I would read one of her books, or sit in her chair, or see her lamp, a flood of memories will warm me and I will feel close to her, almost as if I had never lost her.

That was how I felt now, as my thumb stroked the back of her silver ring. Her everyday ring, she called it. The garnet and silver one was for special occasions, and I had always delighted in its appearance at Christmas. Once Aunt Louisa and I had joked about its significance if she ever wore it other than for family holiday gatherings. The 'hot date' never seemed to happen, although Aunt Louisa was only fifty-five. Twenty years older than I. But we had shared a sister-like relationship, giggling about boys during back-garden sleep outs, planning my future before a wintry fire, healing skinned knees and broken heart over cups of hot tea and lemon scones. She had the nurturing gene my own mother, her sister, lacked, and I snuggled up to Aunt Louisa and her wisdom like a newborn kitten to its mother's milk and warmth. So the special ring would stay closeted in the plastic jewelry box, waiting for a trip to the Albert Hall or for a frog to turn into a prince.

"I'm thinking of expanding, too." Austin's voice pulled me back to the present.

I twisted the silver band on my finger, reluctantly leaving her in the shadows for now, and asked his meaning.

"Recording company. I want to create a new label, sign up talent who narrowly miss the big boys contract."

"Like Kirk Fitzpatrick?" I asked.

"Exactly. Yes, Kirk. I've heard him several times at various clubs and pubs. I think he's got a great future, and I'd like to help him toward that end. A recording studio and contract may not guarantee it, but it should get him noticed, expand his audience."

Evidently Austin didn't know about Kirk being signed by Paddock Productions, with a recording session shining in the very near future. Or maybe Austin did know and was putting on a good show for our benefit. But to what purpose?

"That takes a lot of money," Austin said, "setting up a recording company. Money that I haven't got right now, due to my other environmental concerns. I won't lie, miss—Roger's gift will be *very* welcome and benefit a lot of people. I hope," he added, abandoning Dulcie's hand and pointing toward his chest, "that doesn't place me under your interrogation lights. No amount of money can make up for my brother's death, believe me! But it will certainly aid a great many people. Both with the establishment of my environmental charities and the recording label."

"Not that he's idle now," Dulcie said, smiling into his eyes. "He's not just the younger brother romping through his family fortune, yachting around the Mediterranean. He works. And quite hard, too. No, you *do*, Austin. Don't hide your lamp! Miss Taylor should hear it, so she doesn't label you as one of the Idle Rich."

"I don't think I'll do that," I said, glancing at Margo, who was trying not to cough.

"Austin is the estate manager of Swinton Hall. He draws a regular salary, which is what he lives off—."

"And," Austin said, butting into Dulcie's remarks, "I don't mind admitting that I hate it! Chained to ledgers and nice columns of figures and tax calculations and the fax and phone. I want to do something *useful*, something *creative*. That's where my environmental charities and recording studio come in. I need to do something for the greater good before I pass!"

"He wants to get out," Dulcie said. "Be on the road. Not only enjoying the world, but also discovering talent. Which, in turn, will make people happy when they listen to this new music. It will benefit everyone."

"Kirk would be a smashing start to my label, get it off the ground in great fashion. Dulcie and I have talked this over and she's in favor of it," he said, squeezing her hand. "She'll be a big part of it all, too. And I see no potential problem with our finances once we're married, so..." He shrugged, suggesting 'why not take the plunge'?

I asked Dulcie what big part she would be in Austin's Grand Scheme. "I'm a graphic artist. I work in Manchester."

"Perfect, isn't it?" Austin said, his enthusiasm beginning to bubble again. "I can take care of the business books—and talent management—and Dulcie can design the business logo and such. The CD covers, concert posters...we've got it taken care of!"

"Except for the recording engineers," Dulcie said.

Austin nodded, screwing up his mouth. "Too bad I don't know anyone. Oh well. We'll find someone, I've no doubt. Pull some poor bloke off the dole. See? Another advantage to this project."

"We're getting married this December."

"But maybe we can move up the date. Now that there's the inheritance, we can afford to kick things into high gear and get on with our plans. Would you like to hear the wedding bells sooner, luv?"

Dulcie leaned sideways and planted a swift kiss on Austin's cheek.

"Bells are nice," Margo said, tapping her pen against her notebook, "but we've got a bit of bell mystery to solve right now, sir. What were you and Miss Burgess doing last night around the time Lord Swinbrook rang the bells?"

Jo A. Hiestand

CHAPTER FOURTEEN

"WE WERE AT my house," Dulcie said. Her voice had an edge that challenged Margo's inference. "Working out logistics for the recording company. And no, we can't prove it. No e-mails sent, no phone calls made, no take-away from the local Indian. Nothing that will give you a time." Her lips pressed together in a thin, hard line, mutely speaking her defiance that we disprove her statement.

"Did anyone see you? Perhaps when you, sir, arrived?" Margo looked at Austin. She stopped short of saying 'when you left,' for he might have stayed the night.

"Could be. I haven't a clue. Dulcie lives in Buxton."

"Oh, yes?" I said, wondering if I had a neighbor whom I didn't know. "Where?"

"Green Lane, between College and London Roads. Why? You going to interrogate everyone?"

"Nice spot," I said, envisioning the older, multi-storied homes, the large front gardens and giant trees. The street was quiet, home to several bed-and-breakfast establishments, and footed Grin Low Woods, a country park and nature trail. Solomon's Temple, a century-plus-old tower built on a Neolithic burial mound, shot out of the park's woodland and afforded dramatic views of Buxton and the area. Pooles Cavern burrowed into the earth of this one-hundred acre wood. Besides offering the summer visitor a view of the source of the river that threads its way through Buxton, the cave also fuels the legends of the robber purported to have lived within it in the 1440s.

Austin added, "We did do some work on the Internet. Looking up prices of recording equipment, office furniture and such. Any good?"

"If you printed something out, yes. That would give the time and date."

Austin shook his head and glanced at Dulcie. "I'm afraid I'll get the rocket for this, but no, we didn't print anything out." He forced a half-hearted smile.

"Hard cheese," Margo murmured, returning to her note taking.

"I suppose so, if my life depends on this. But we *did* bookmark them, if that proves anything."

PEARLS BEFORE SWINE

"We can always confiscate Dulcie's computer," I said when Margo and I were driving back to the incident room. The clouds had broken up along the west and sunlight, even if it was a tad feeble, dappled the landscape. The darker, snow-laden clouds, however, were advancing steadily, and I wondered if we'd have snow tonight. But for now, the birds were enjoying the respite from the gray weather, for sparrows chirped around a puddle of melting snow at the base of a stonewall.

"The lads at the lab can prove what times they visited those websites," Margo said, nodding. "God, *nothing's* private anymore, is it? Mobile phone calls you make, Internet purchases, bank withdrawals, hospital records. What have we come to?"

"A society of voyeurs," I said, turning into the community hall car park.

"Nosy Parkers is more like it."

"I don't know about that, Margo. It's an unfortunate side effect of the information age we're in. Or fortunate, if you're a cop needing that information."

"And the tabloids fan it," Margo continued, ignoring me. "They practically shove it down your throat with their headlines and photos. 'Read what Miss So-and-So did on holiday, see who she holidayed with—and it wasn't her husband! Read what our secret microphones caught on tape...' God, it's enough to make me sick. I repeat, Bren, there's no such thing as privacy or respect of the individual anymore."

"Practicing for your corner in Hyde Park?" I said, braking the car.

Margo angled toward me. "So you think I'm preaching. Over-reacting? Fine. But I'm not far from the truth, and you know it."

"I agree the tabloid press at times makes a shark feeding frenzy look like a church tea, but you can't make a blanket statement like that, Margo. There are a lot of ethical journalists. Those are the ones who get Nobels and Pulitzers and such. How'd we get into this, anyway? What's wrong? You're supposed to be on the cops' side."

"I know. I'm sorry. It's just that...well, stuff like this makes me crazy. Hits awfully close to the mark."

"Something personal, then? Okay." I turned off the motor and turned to face her. The silence as I waited for her to speak was surprisingly suffocating, as though I were back in school, waiting to be picked for a sports team, wishing in vain not to be the last one standing. "I've bared my soul to you many times, Margo," I finally said when I'd watched Mark take off his jacket, unlock and get into his car. "You can bare yours to me. A good talk does wonders, as you keep reminding me."

I was afraid she wasn't going to speak, and I'd just about decided to grab the car keys and open the door when she said, "Don't tell your boyfriend everything, Bren. Not until the ring's on your finger. And even then it's fine to have secrets."

Jo A. Hiestand

"What are you talking about?" For some reason my heart started beating faster and my throat tightened. I searched her brown eyes, trying to discern the story behind her words. All I saw was hurt. I said gently, "Did something happen with you and Angus?"

"Besides him leaving, you mean?" She snorted and lowered her head, talking to her lap. "Things happen when you're in love, Bren. And I don't just mean sex. I mean talking, baring your soul, as you put it. You're so anxious to be intimate with this person that you talk about everything—your life, your dreams, your desires."

"What's wrong with that? It's part of building the relationship."

"Yes, but it should wait. Don't bare your soul within the first month of your euphoria. The relationship might not last. And then where are you?"

I took a chance. "Alone, crying at the kitchen table with the bloke in Australia, knowing something about you that you wish he didn't."

"Houdini." She raised her head, eyed me, and gave me a tired smile. "A girlfriend of mine was in a pub one night. Angus was there, at another table, with a bunch of his mates. As usual, he'd been drinking too much. My friend told me later that the great joke of the evening's drinking session was that I slept with—" She gulped, as though choking back a hurt. "With a teddy bear." She tapped on the window as Mark drove out of the car park and turned onto the High Street. "You can tell yourself lies, Bren. It's so easy when you're deeply in love. But put a brake on the first throes of euphoria and remember that it mightn't be forever. He might not be the one for you after all. And then you'll feel like shit when he leaves in the morning, still laughing and calling you names."

The tail lights of Mark's car disappeared around the corner of East Brook Lane. Mark was probably making for Buxton, either on a lab run or to get some equipment. Or perhaps Scott Coral, our division's eager constable, had located Kirk Fitzpatrick and Mark had to question him. I busied myself with inconsequential things—watching a sparrow drink from a pool of melted snow, counting the number of blue cars stopping at the petrol station, watching people entering Boot's—before I had enough nerve to reply to Margo. Of course my speech was nothing that would jeopardize either Churchill's or MLK's thrones, but it broke the awkwardness and offered what poor balm I had. "It's not a crime to love, Margo. Or to give your heart and want to be close. But what Angus did was close to a crime, in my opinion. A crime against decency and against you. You did nothing wrong. *He* was the one who took something private, something intimate that you had shared, and dragged it through the mud, joking about it with his mates and cheapening it. Of course it hurts! Of course he's a bastard for doing that to you! You have every reason to be cheesed off! But at least he's out of your life before you got married to the git. *That* would've been a double disaster! Just think of *that*, count how lucky you are not to be legally tied to him, and learn from it. You're always telling *me* to live and learn! I can't be the only reformed dunce around here!" I probably looked anxious, but I ventured a smile, squeezed her hand, and held my breath.

When she finally nodded and returned my smile, I gave her a hug. "We need a night out, Margo. Just us. Girl talk. I'll gripe about my job and you can unload about Angus. Things always look better over a plate of fish and chips."

"Or a glass of beer. You're on, doc. This is one therapy session I'm looking forward to."

"Look, Graham's back from *his* session." I nodded toward his car as I opened my car door.

"I didn't know he'd gone anywhere." Margo jogged up to fall in step beside me. "Session with who? The super?"

"*His* therapist. I'm *joking*, Margo. Don't look so shocked. He had to ring up Simcock and give him the details of the case so far."

Margo shuddered, following me into the incident room. Graham was talking on his mobile, which ordinarily wouldn't have told me anything one way or the other, but his long legs were propped up on the table top, his chair was tilted back, and he was smiling. No Simcock on the other end of his chat. Most likely his postponed date.

Margo caught the significance of Graham's posture too, for she murmured, "At least Love makes for nice working conditions. When are you and Mark—"

"I don't know," I snapped, suddenly overwhelmed with jealousy. I wanted to be the recipient of Graham's smile and soft voice. I wanted to know what he was telling her. I apologized to Margo and wondered, as we approached Graham, if Margo was right about our current society.

After we'd brought Graham up to speed on the morning's interview, I said, "Even if we check out Dulcie's computer and there is evidence of Internet activity, that doesn't prove they were both there."

He agreed. "One might have slipped out, then, fought with Roger, and used the Internet work as an alibi for both of them? Why not? They'll soon be married physically. Might as well be married in lies and conspiracy. It tends to strengthen the union."

I wondered if he were talking from experience or just jesting. That was the trouble—I hadn't been working with him long enough to know many times when he joked. I said, "You know, sir, for all of Austin's denial that Geneva wouldn't marry her ex-husband, still, the open arms of someone who purports to love you is awfully comforting and enticing—especially when you're grieving and seek solace."

"You think Barry's a good candidate, then, for prime suspect?"

"As far as motive, perhaps. We don't know about his financial state, if inheritance would make him want to get rid of Roger. And we certainly haven't checked on his whereabouts. He could have an alibi that eliminates him."

"Like, an audience with the Queen?"

"That would tend to erase him from our list, yes."

"So, let's do some checking with all our players. I've got Mark doing that with the Griffiths and the Clarksons. The financial problem may have been a thorn in Roger's side, too. Since he was selling off furnishings, land and whatnot just to live, might not he have taken that strand of pearls from the vault to sell? They would've fetched a nice price. And about this other. Margo—"

"Sir, I have the information you wanted about the keg delivery. From The Cat and Mouse, the local pub."

Graham nodded. "I assume it was fairly recent, if Roger was a ringer and drinker. So, when was the beer delivered to the tower?"

"One week prior to the murder. The delivery chap picked up the empty keg when he brought the new one."

"One week is time enough for the beer to settle to drinking standards, so that doesn't particularly tell us anything one way or the other."

"But," I said, "it tells us that Roger didn't need the Duvel ale. He had an entire keg of beer that was available."

"So we're back to the question of who brought the Duvel. Thank you, Margo. Now that you're rid of that little task, would you ask around the village about the pearls? Take a photo of the necklace with you and see if anyone identifies its owner. Ask the usual people—merchants, Swinbrook's neighbors and family. That's good for a start. I don't want to make an appeal on the telly. We'll have every nut case in the Kingdom ringing us up. Hopefully we'll get an owner this way. And as for ex-hubbie Barry Sykes..." He motioned to PC Fordyce, who was just getting up with an empty coffee mug. The constable set down the mug and hurried over to us. He asked if he could do anything, and Graham nodded. "I've a bit of work for you," Graham said as he stood up.

Graham was tall, over six feet, but at this moment, when he emanated Authority and Direction, he seemed nearer ten. His eyes, which I usually could read so well, were devoid of expression. The only thing that hinted at his emotional—or perhaps mental—struggle was the manner in which he scratched his jaw. It was slow, deliberate, his fingers lingering beneath his ear and pressing into his skin before traveling slowly back to the scar near his chin. It had the sheen of newness and suggested physical police action. Yet, in the few months I'd been assigned as his partner, I'd only seen him engaged in such activity a few times. Which didn't preclude a fight before that, of course. But I thought the scar too recent to be from his beat-walking days. It was just something else I didn't know about him, and it ate at me like a piece that didn't fit in a murder case. Graham picked up his car keys and said, "I'm sorry to lay this at your door, Fordyce, but would you mind delving into Barry Syke's financial statement? Might as well nose about in everyone else's while you're pestering the bank people."

"*Everyone?*" The constable's eyes widened. I didn't blame him. It sounded tantamount to trimming a golf course with a pair of nail scissors.

PEARLS BEFORE SWINE

I felt self-conscious that I had got off so easily, and glanced at my finger nails as Graham said, "Shouldn't take you two minutes. But get someone to help you, if you wish. Byrd or MacMillan, perhaps. We need to know if someone's in financial trouble, making money a motive, and if so, who's got the strongest motive. Right." He picked up his suede jacket and asked me to accompany him to Geneva's.

I could feel Fordyce's eyes following us from the room.

GENEVA, THE DOWAGER Swinbrook, we were informed after our brief heels-cooling in the Hall's foyer, would be glad to receive us in the drawing room. I don't know if she was particularly glad, but she did see us, welcoming us with an offer of coffee or tea and motioning us to two damask-upholstered ladderback chairs. I felt elegant sitting in mine, transported back to the Regency period, but Graham looked decidedly uncomfortable in his. Whether due to the chair's straight, carved wooden back or to the purpose of our visit, I didn't know. But he was all official, unlike his previous—and usual—easy-going, friendly self.

A woman was seated on the settee next to Geneva, a plumb blonde with a starlet's complexion. She took a glass from Geneva when she'd finished drinking, setting it on the table next to her, and introduced herself as Sharon Seddon, a friend of Geneva's.

"I came over to help," Sharon explained, putting the cap on a bottle of prescription medicine and then settling back in the couch. "We've been friends for...how long, Gen? Well, probably twenty years or so, anyway. I used to date Ed Cawley. Do you know him? Roger's former business partner? Yes?" Her eyes widened as her eyebrows shot up. "Oh! Well, anyway, since Ed is Roger's friend, I naturally got to know Roger that way. But I've known Gen before that. Back to our carefree, single days."

I wondered if the 'carefree' reference was merely a phrase, or if there was a history we had yet to uncover. "And are you still courting," I asked.

"No," Sharon said, glancing at Geneva, then back to me. "I liked him and all that, but there were too many differences between us that we couldn't straighten out. Like children. I don't want any, and Ed did. And where to live. I'm a city dweller, and he likes the country. Antique furnishings vs. modern. You've probably heard it all before. It may seem petty, these differences. But when they define who you are and what makes you truly happy, well, it's not so petty. You can't live untrue to yourself, can you, and be content? It will lead to problems later." She grimaced and blushed, staring momentarily at her hands, perhaps embarrassed at talking so openly or recalling painful memories. When she again looked at me, her eyes were moist. "Anyway, Ed wanted a wife with all the traditional trimmings—cook, housekeeper, mother to his kids. I told him he was reared on fairy tales and that I could recite Gloria Steinem by heart. So we parted. Rather amicably, I suppose, if a broken heart is termed 'amicable.' Anyway, we see each other off and on, at Geneva's dinners, parties, what have you. We're friendly, just not married." She said the last sentence in a lowering of her voice, the breath escaping from her as though she were a deflating balloon.

Geneva cut into the silence. "I'm sure the detectives didn't come to hear about our miserable lives, Sharon. Other than what's pertinent to their investigation. Is it, by the way, Inspector? Pertinent, I mean." She tilted up her head, stretching her neck muscles taut as she looked at Graham from her half-reclined position. The skin of her neck was white, smooth and firm, more like a teenager's than a woman in her forties. I was envious—mine didn't look that good now, and I was only thirty-five.

Graham said that we were here again because it was definite that Roger had been murdered. He paused as Geneva blanched, grabbed Sharon's hand, and buried her face into the pillow. He again offered his condolences, then turned slightly in his chair to look at a photo on the table. "This looks like it was taken recently. What a nice remembrance you have of his lordship." He angled the photo toward Geneva.

She raised her head, dabbing her tears on a facial tissue Sharon handed her. She stared at the photo and said that yes, it was. "Taken this previous Christmas. That's Roger and me, of course, and my brother and his wife—Kirk and Noreen. I—I'm glad I have it." She dug her elbow into the settee's armrest and raised herself to a sitting position. As Sharon tucked the duvet about her, Geneva said, "You said Roger was...that he was killed? Why? What suggests that?"

"I don't think you want to hear about that, do you, Lady Swinbrook? Not just now, at any rate. Just know that we are certain. Had his lordship any enemies, any problems with people—either here in Oldfield or elsewhere, through his business dealings, perhaps?"

Geneva reiterated the ill feelings harbored by Ben Griffiths and Baxter Clarkson. She added nothing new to what Graham and I had already heard. "But," Geneva said, "I can't believe they hated my husband. Not really *hated!* They may have been angry—Baxter about the bells and Ben about rich people in general. But to be so angry as to kill someone..."

"So other than these on-going problems, there was no one else. No one from business, another woman—I'm sorry, your ladyship, I have to ask. If you want us to find Lord Swinbrook's killer, and I believe you do, then we need to know everything about his life, no matter if it's painful or embarrassing for you to relate."

"Of course," Geneva said, forcing a smile, though her eyes stared emotionless at Graham. "You have to ask. I know. It's unexpected, that's all—the question, his death. All this. But no, I can't think of anyone he had business dealings with who was upset with him. He and Ed parted ways, but that was years ago—and mutually friendly. And as for the other..." She paused as if she didn't know how to phrase it, or was trying to come to the possibility that it was true. During the silence, I could hear a hushed conversation beyond the drawing room door, the sounds of footsteps—a hard-soled shoe and a rubber boot—retreating until another door opened and closed and the hard-soled shoe alone tracked across marble flooring and faded into stillness. A squeaky-wheeled cart rumbled down the gravel path outside. Perhaps it was that sound that finally prodded Geneva from her reverie. Her eyes flashed life and she said, "The other woman, now..." She squeezed Sharon's hand and glanced down at her wedding ring before saying, "No. I know there wasn't. A wife knows, doesn't she? Well, most of the time. There are always little signs from the husband, if the wife's attuned and watching. But no, I can't believe there was. Roger would have given it away."

"Roger," Sharon said, "was a saint! A hard worker who helped *anyone* who asked for a helping hand. He fought for what he had. Oh, I know he came into the earldom through heredity, but the family has seen some hard times. Roger's struggled to keep the estate solvent and to keep his charities going. He valued anyone who was working toward a dream and he wanted to give them a boost if it was needed. And as for Geneva..." Sharon pulled Geneva's hands onto her lap. "Roger *adored* Geneva. He married rather late in life, Inspector, and knew what he wanted in a wife. He *worshiped* her. I know he'd never cheat on her. It wasn't in his nature."

Graham said he was glad to hear that, then asked Geneva if she concurred with her friend's statement.

Geneva blinked several times, shifted her gaze from Sharon to Graham, and said, "Yes. Absolutely. Roger was a faithful husband. He—and I—took our marriage vows seriously. He took his business concerns seriously, too. More interested in that, at times, than in the two of us. I knew before I married him that his work necessitated long hours, sometimes days, away from home. But it didn't bother me. I knew where his heart really lay. And other than with me, it lay with wanting to help people."

"Which included Gen and I," Sharon said.

"Oh?" Graham said. "In what way?"

"We were thinking of opening a greeting card company. I'd write the verse and Gen would do the photography. She does such clever set-ups for her photos. Antiques and homey things that create nostalgia and moody sets."

"You're very good yourself, Sharon," Geneva said. "You're just a born writer, that's all."

Sharon shook her head, as though the praise bothered her. "I know we couldn't help but make a go of it. Gen's very clever. Yes, you *are*, darling! Don't deny it! Thank you for those kind words just now, but it's your images that will sell the ruddy things. People are drawn to images. Anyway, Roger...he thought we'd do well and was set to divert part of his money from another company into ours."

"I was already talking to various boutiques," Sharon said. "Places in tourist centers and small shops in towns like Buxton, Bakewell, Chesterfield and the like. The shop owners liked our cards and were willing to carry them."

"And are you working on that now?" Graham asked. "Will that be a full-time job when it gets off the ground—presuming you and her ladyship are still going ahead with your company—or is it just a supplement to a job you already have?"

"I work in a pub. The Winnats Pass in town, here. Why?"

"Have either of you seen this before?" He took a photograph of the pearl necklace from his jacket pocket and handed it to Sharon. The women stared at it and Graham, I knew, stared at them for signs of recognition. There was no eye widening, no intake of breath, no shout of ownership. Merely blank stares and questions as to where it had been found, what length was the strand, why was he asking. Graham took the photo, put it back in his pocket and withdrew two business cards. After writing his mobile number on them, he handed one to each of the women and asked them to ring him up if they remembered whose necklace it was. They nodded and assured Graham they would.

Graham thanked them, stood up and moved the chair to one side. As I stood up, he again offered Geneva his condolences, then added, "If you think of anyone who might have had a grudge against his lordship, please let me know."

It wasn't until we were in his car that he spoke again. "I believe they'd no idea whose necklace it is. No facial or voice betrayal gave the secret away, at any rate."

"You can usually tell, sir." So could Scott Coral. Which was one reason he was so good at the poker table.

"That pretty little speech Geneva gave us about understanding the long hours needed away from home. Very stiff-upper-lip and all that, but what wife would honestly say that?"

"Besides a martyr?"

"I believe she couldn't help but be jealous of his time away on business. It's only normal if you love someone." He paused, as though remembering his work-related verbal battles with his fiancée, Rachel. He continued hurriedly. "And if she was jealous, then I think the mistress in this instance, Taylor, might not be a woman but his work."

"Do wives ever kill husbands over that?"

CHAPTER FIFTEEN

"Isn't that rather like asking if the sun rises in the east?" Graham said, laughing.

"I wonder," I said, staring at the house as Graham started the car, "if Sharon regrets her decision about not marrying the wealthy Ed Cawley. He made a fortune with that company he had with Roger, and he's doing very well now, from what I understand."

"Maybe she could escape the drudgeries of housework by hiring a maid, you mean. Ah, what distasteful things become palatable with the right amount of money."

"I'm serious, sir. Sharon may be jealous of Geneva's lifestyle."

"By that, I take it you mean she's so envious that she did something about it. Like what? Murder Roger?"

"Not so far-fetched," I said, somewhat hurt by his light attitude. "People kill for money all the time."

"Only, in this instance, the gain is a bit roundabout. It's filtered down through Geneva."

"Doesn't mean it won't happen. If they really are such friends, Sharon and Geneva, Sharon may be expecting something from the estate. Maybe she's been told." In spite of my dialogue, the estate planning with Aunt Louisa flashed through my brain. Families did things like this. I added, "Maybe Sharon's only hoping, but Geneva will inherit much if not all of the wealth. And even if she gives something to her brother, Kirk, she could still settle some on Sharon to help them finance their card company."

"Why would Sharon—or Geneva, if you picture her as the killer—need to bump off Roger to do this? We just heard her say that Roger helped everyone, that he was going to finance their dream. Unless—" He braked the car so suddenly I had to brace my hand against the dashboard to keep from going through the windscreen. "Sorry, TC. But that's where you're leading me, isn't it? We've only their word for it. Roger may have laughed in their collective face. Denied them the money. So to get money into their bank account and get their business off the ground, they needed Roger out of the way." He eased off the brake and I settled back into the car seat. "Either one could have done it, if we go by motive. We'll have to check time tables for that evening. Where, oh where, was Sharon?"

"In her pub, filling drinks?"

"A good job for someone. I daren't give it to Fordyce. He's already smoldering about the bank bit of work. And Margo has her hands full of pearl necklace interviewees."

I hummed a snatch of a Gilbert and Sullivan song. Graham said, "Yes?"

"I wouldn't mind doing that, sir. I'll go to the pub, ask if Sharon was on duty that night."

Graham smiled, his face suddenly alive as the car passed by the green grocer's on the High Street. "Going incognito and downing a few pints to make it look real?"

"I could have dinner there. Take someone along to make it more incognito." I held my breath, hoping he would take the hint. He didn't.

"Fine. You can drink your way through the interview this evening. Just don't overdo it and be off tomorrow due to a hangover. I need you."

But not like I want you to, I thought, turning my face toward the window, afraid my expression would give away my hurt.

"I wouldn't be surprised if Sharon or Geneva did it," Graham said, stopping his car beside mine at the community center. "This whole damned place seems to be one nest of dreamers and schemers."

"Yes, sir," I replied, following him meekly into the building.

"So, HE DIDN'T take you up on your dinner suggestion," Margo said that evening. We were in the pub on the western side of the village, the Winnats Pass, named after the road cutting through the mountain range near the Derbyshire village of Castleton. The Winnats had probably once been a cavern, but eons of wind and rain had reduced the towering mountain to today's gorge. It was a desolate spot, made seemingly lonelier by the fierce winds that howled through the twisting pass. Grasses and sheep clung to its nearly vertical sides, while hawks and kestrels soared overhead. They were the lucky ones, able to maneuver easily across the rocky landscape. Humankind, being earthbound, relied on the good graces of good weather for its travel, for the Winnats was only suitable for light traffic. Even that was at times blocked during a bad winter.

"I don't know why not. We all get meal breaks. He could have got the information first-hand."

"You didn't exactly invite him."

"I don't need to! He's the senior investigating officer. He can come here if he wants."

"And he didn't. He took you up on your suggestion to find out about Sharon's work hours. You should be glad he trusts you. It's a compliment. Just leave it, Bren. Besides, he's probably working late. You know him. All work and no play."

"I'm not so sure," I said, spearing a chip with my fork. "He seems to have some kind of hot date on."

"You know who the bird is, where they're going, when?"

PEARLS BEFORE SWINE

"Did you have any luck with the pearl necklace inquiry?"

"Stop changing the subject, Bren."

"I'm interested. Sounds like it would be more fascinating than the time I had talking again to Geneva."

"You were with Graham. That should've made it *more* than fascinating."

"It would have been, but she was sniffling. And had a friend with her. Two on-lookers kind of take the romance out of the moment."

"I asked the Clarksons and the Griffiths. No one ever saw it, or claimed to have seen it. I believed them."

"Anyone else?"

Margo sighed, seeing I was determined to keep on the subject. "I started asking here in Oldfield. They've no jeweler's, so I'll have to go into Chesterfield or Bakewell or Buxton, I guess. Hit the closest big centers first. I even asked our friendly pub personnel just before you came in. I figured they would see a lot of people, perhaps remember it."

"Having seen something like that once," I said, "who can forget it? So what was the answer?"

"They passed the photo around, even to the people at the bar and the tables. No one remembers it. I think this is a washout. God," she sighed, running her fingers through her hair, "I thought sifting through financial statements was bad. If I have to track this thing down with every jeweler in Buxton or Manchester or London..." She grimaced. "And what's wrong with Mark doing it? Graham originally said either of us would do it, whoever wasn't busy."

"I guess Mark's busy."

"Bloody hell. What a damned job of work this whole thing's turning out to be."

"Might not have to ask around Manchester et al. You've still Ed Cawley and Geneva's ex, Barry Sykes."

"Seems like something he'd give her, does it?"

"I don't know. Off hand I wouldn't think he's got the money, but you never know."

"Seems more like Roger gave it to her. But if Graham believes she was telling the truth when he asked her..."

I nodded. "Anyway, there are other family members Roger may have been planning on giving the pearls to."

"His sister?"

"Seems a good bet, doesn't it?"

"Unless we find out he's got a bit of fluff on the side and was intending to give her the necklace. Wonder if he had a date planned with her, she met him in the tower, conked him on the head—"

"Roger didn't have a mistress. Or a date. He loved Geneva, and that's why he was in the tower. Stop trying to make it lurid."

"At least he's got something in common with you," Margo said.

"Oh yes? What?"

"No date. But Graham does. I repeat. Who with? You know her name?"

I shook my head and laid down the fork. I knew when I was defeated. Margo always got the information she wanted, no matter how I tried to side step the topic. "Just something I surmise. I overhead part of his phone conversation. I think he had to put it off from Valentine's evening."

"Work spoils a lot of stuff," Margo said, staring into her beer mug.

I raised my glass and we saluted her statement.

"It also helps a lot of stuff," she added after setting the mug back onto the beer mat. "Keeps your mind off things. You don't feel the hurt so much when your mind's occupied. It's when you're alone, quiet, that you have time to feel."

"Well, I don't intend to spend every waking moment working just so I can ignore my feelings. I want a life outside the job. I'm tired of being emotionally cloistered."

"You sound like a monk."

"Monks are men."

"I don't know the female equivalent," Margo said, sniffing. "Anyway, why so down and out all of a sudden? You've got Erik's arms to run to. He's more than happy to provide solace from your emotions. Isn't that why you invited him to live with you?"

"You just said it might not last, Margo. Erik and I are fine for the moment, but..." I brought the glass up to my lips. "Other women have survived being a spinster. What's so bad about that?" I drained my glass and looked around for our waitress. She wasn't in sight.

Margo said, "Nothing, as long as you're happy. And you aren't. Why you don't date is beyond me. I *know* about you and Erik! But you said yourself that it's nothing long term, and that's what you want. I'm not bad-mouthing Eric—he's great for right now. But you need the reassurance of someone being there for your future. There are a lot of lads who'd be thrilled to go out with you."

"Right."

"Do I have to name them?"

"Alphabetical will do. You don't have to list them by age or height or one-to-ten rating."

"I can't stop laughing. If you don't want my help—"

"Yeh, I do, but I don't think even you, Mistress of Feminine Wiles, can snare Graham for me."

"God, Bren, there are other guys in this world than Detective-Chief Inspector Geoffrey Graham! And, from your suspicions, he's tied up at the moment. Not that ties can't be untied..." She paused. I knew she was thinking of her and Angus, but I didn't say anything. Instead, I got up, took my mug to the bar, and returned moments later with a refill. She said, "You might stand a better chance of untying those present ties if you knew more about his ex-fiancée. So you don't make the same mistakes. Do you know anything?" She picked up her mug, took a long sip and eyed me from over the rim of her glass.

"Her name is Rachel."

Margo's mug thudded onto the beer mat, threatening to slosh its contents onto the table top. "Great. You're practically walking down the aisle with him."

"So don't book the honeymoon yet. I can't help it! He's a very private person. He doesn't talk about his life. What am I supposed to do, run an inquiry on him?"

"How about seduction?"

I poked my finger into my hip. "Do you need a prescription for eyeglasses or are you being kind? In case you haven't looked at me lately, I'm about one and a half stone overweight."

"So? Mae West always got her man, and she wasn't even a Mountie."

"That's smashing, but the female ideal of beauty has changed a bit since her day. You need to get out more, Margo."

"Not every man thinks a bean pole is sexy, Bren. Lots of guys like curves."

"And I've got well padded curves, is that it?"

"You don't have to lure him into bed to get him to love you. Despite the blare of the media, lots of couples remain chaste until their wedding night. Sexual attraction may be there, sure, but not everyone jumps right into bed on the first date. There is such a thing as personality, humor, intelligence. There are plenty of men who value that. Looks and the body beautiful fade. But intelligence and humor endure."

This was sounding awfully like the talk I'd given myself last November when I first suspected I was falling in love with Graham. I shoved my plate away and said, "I don't think Graham's one of them. He's been subjected to my humor and so-called intelligence every workday and he's never asked me out. He's obviously got different values for a companion."

"Well," Margo said, sighing and picking up her fork, "you really can't say that with any certainty until you start going out with him. And from your attitude at the moment, that won't be for a bit, yet. He may be shy about asking, thinking that you'd *have* to say yes because he's your boss and you fear you'll get fired if you refuse. Sexual harassment stuff. Or he could be waiting for the right moment. Standing over a bloody corpse isn't exactly like a moonlit stroll in the park. Concentrate on Mark. You *know* he's wanting to get together with you."

"An octopus is not my first choice as a steady guy."

"So, go out fishing. You know, Bren, this may be just the thing to nudge Graham into action. If he sees you going out with Mark, he might get jealous and ask you for a date. Worth a try, isn't it?"

It was developing into the familiar ring of Geneva's two-men attraction. I sighed.

"You're not exactly a stranger to this, Bren," Margo continued. "Remember when you completed initial training?"

"Very well. What are you—"

"When you were a probationary constable?"

"Where is this leading?"

"Your first year at Buxton. The lads you were with."

"The lads—"

"Chad Hughes? Kirk Fowler? Adam—"

"Okay."

"You say that as if you'd forgotten them."

"I had. Why bring up the past?"

"To remind you that you have had dates, that you had confidence then, that *you* were the aggressor with Adam—"

"I *did* like him, didn't I? Where is he, do you know? Transferred to Cambridge, isn't he?"

"—that lads *do* find you attractive, that—"

"Fine. You've made your point."

"Glad you recognize that. Now, go with that and reconnect with your old self. Or become serious about Erik. You've got the foundation of a serious relationship there. You know, Bren, most female colleagues would be all over Graham or Mark, never mind if they're superior in rank or not. You need to assert yourself."

"I don't want to trick him into anything. If he doesn't have deep feelings for me—"

"Like I said," Margo whispered, holding out her mug for a toast, "seduction works every time."

SCOTT CORAL WAS talking to Graham as I got out of my car at the community center. Graham asked me to join them, saying it would save time if he didn't have to reiterate everything.

"Scott was just telling me about his adventure in finding Kirk Fitzpatrick," Graham said, making room for me in the group.

"I also will tell you," Scott said, turning slightly toward me, "that I never saw the Mysterious Stranger who talked to Austin Swinbrook. I could ask around the area, if you think it's important."

We glanced at Graham, waiting to see if he thought so. Graham said Scott could ask about in the course of his shift, but not to do anything special.

Scott nodded. "As to what I found out about Kirk Fitzpatrick. I caught up with him at his first gig in Bolton. He was right where he was supposed to be. No trail of red herrings, no smoke screen or attempt to flee the country."

"Not disappointed, are you?" I said, knowing Scott loved action and craved involvement in anything that would feed him an adrenaline rush. Which was why he liked being a field training officer. But even that was getting old, so he recently had applied for a position in the armed unit.

Tactical, gun-carrying Scott. Perhaps he should have been an American street cop.

"Not in the least," Scott said. "I don't mind playing the Mountie. Gives me something with which to impress the wife and kids."

"The more so if it's embellished a bit. How will this one grow? Captured in a helicopter sweep of the town?"

"You can chin wag later," Graham said, glancing at his watch in the light from the street lamp. "Right now I'd like to get on with this. I've yet to have dinner."

"Sorry, sir," I said, feeling my face grow warm.

"Go on, Coral." Graham leaned against the door of his car, waiting patiently.

"Well, sir," Scott continued, "Kirk was shocked to hear of Roger's death. I don't think it was play acting. I think he hadn't a clue. He'd no mobile phone with him, so he couldn't have heard from his wife, unless he rang her up. And he had no need to do that."

"He doesn't usually check in with her when he's on the road?"

"Evidently not. I got the impression it wasn't something he usually did. I suppose Noreen looks on his silence as part of his job and only talks to him when he's home."

Another wife separated from her husband by business, I thought. Was this the standard in marriage these days? Spouses catching up with their marriages after long absences? Did it prove to be healthier for the marriage, making them cherish each precious moment when they were together, or was it detrimental, giving them time to think about grievances and giving them a long lead so they could stray?

"Kirk's on his way back," Scott said, his eyes focused on me. Had he devised my thoughts? If so, he ignored them. "He's going to finish the Bolton concert and cancel the remainder of his gigs. I checked out the venues on his tour. They're all legitimate. Each concert or pub date had had him booked for months."

"He could have planned this," Graham said, crossing his ankles. "What better alibi than to have a genuine reason to leave town. Only he quietly slips away somewhere between venues, perhaps. It'd be days before we got wind of it. And that'd give him enough time to go anywhere in the world."

"I thought of that, too, sir. I suppose he could still bale out, but that would surely point to him as being the murderer. And I think he's too smart for that, even if he is guilty of Roger's murder."

"Did you ask him why he left last night?"

"Pardon?"

"Bolton's not halfway around the world. It's only a few hours' drive from here. Why did he leave nearly twenty-four hours early for his gig?" We waited and I found myself crossing my fingers, wishing for some strange, inexplicable reason that we'd hear the same reason that Noreen, his wife, had given us. I don't know why I wanted Kirk to be innocent. Was it the face, or that he was a singer, a guitarist, and that I identified with him, even if it was just slightly?

"I thought that odd, too, sir. And I asked. He said he wanted to detour to Chesterfield to pick up a new microphone for his guitar. The one he has is giving him problems."

"And did he detour? Did he get his mic?"

"According to Kirk, the store didn't have the model he wanted. So he left."

"So, no new mic. Why didn't he return home, then, and leave for Bolton this afternoon?"

"I asked the same thing, sir. Kirk said he thought a larger city might have it—Sheffield or Manchester. So he drove to Manchester, stayed the night in a car park, and hit the stores early today before his venue."

"Dangerous way to sleep, in a car park. He could wake up dead."

"I agree. But Kirk has the microphone. Got it at Strings 'n Things, on Oxford Road. I checked the store. It was purchased when Kirk claims."

"Good for him. It establishes some sort of reasoning behind his early departure from Oldfield."

"Maybe," I said, "he went through all this for a reason, giving him another alibi that we don't yet know about."

"Meaning?"

"He could have ordered the mic online, couldn't he? Right from the manufacturer. Or from the store. He could have had it with him and left the village later, as you suggested."

"Maybe he's been burnt."

"Victim of identity theft or credit card fraud? I suppose."

"Not everyone is computer savvy, TC. Or even if they are, want to order online. For those very reasons. Still, it *does* add another layer to any suspicions we may have."

"Did you find out," I asked Scott, "when Kirk was at the Chesterfield store?"

"He didn't have time to double back here and kill Roger, if that's what you're hinting at," Scott said. "But I guess he could have killed him before he left. Do you have time of death established?"

"He could have set all this up," I said, thinking out loud, "the gigs supplying his alibi. He kills Roger, acts the innocent mic buyer in Chesterfield, all the time knowing the store doesn't carry that brand but going through the motions to establish alibi. Then he drives to Manchester, again purporting to look for the mic. You know, sir," I said, running with my thought, "do we even know if Kirk *needed* a mic? Might this not be a convenient smoke screen to institute a reason for his departure from the village?"

"So he'd sneak out of the country, as we just surmised? Sounds plausible."

"He leaves early, on the supposed buying trip, but all along is planning on ditching the tour somewhere between Bolton and his return home. The microphone hunt buys him a few hours alone so his wife—or us, as it turns out—won't suspect anything."

"And why does he need this extra time, Taylor?"

I shrugged. "Maybe we'll find out as we dig a bit deeper."

Graham smiled and shoved his hands into his jacket pockets. "And his motive in all this racing about?"

"Same as everyone else's. Roger's wealth. Maybe a good chunk of cash will get him marketing and promo materials, buy adverts on the radio, help get his name out there. Fordyce may unearth financial problems he's trying to hide. Or debt. It doesn't take money troubles to make people greedy for a bank account."

"Couldn't agree more. And is wife Noreen a dupe in his operation, or an accomplice?"

I said I didn't know yet, then told him I'd learned that Sharon, Geneva's friend, had been working at the Winnats Pass during the time of Roger's death. "So she couldn't have murdered Roger."

"But that doesn't preclude her from being an accomplice, before or after the fact, if Geneva killed Roger."

"No, sir."

"Gives you something else to work on, TC. Well..." Graham stood up and dusted off his jacket where the frost had clung to it. "I'll have Byrd and Mark ask about the village tomorrow to see if anyone remembers seeing Kirk or his car after the time he says he left last night. And right now," he stretched, making his silhouetted, slender form appear taller against the background lights. "*I'm* going to leave. I suggest you both get some sleep."

Scott and I watched as Graham got into his car, turned left onto the High Street, and disappeared into the darkness. I turned to Scott. "I thought he was going to sleep. He missed the turn to the pub. It's just next door but one."

"He didn't say *where* he was going to sleep."

I colored, suspicion burgeoning in my mind like a cancer. Would a former minister overstep God's morality and sleep with his date? "He didn't exactly say he was going to *sleep*, either. Not just yet. He just said he was leaving."

"But he implied it. He said that we should both get some sleep, *too*. That's the operative word, Brenna. Maybe he's going home. Maybe he's going to get a drink at a pub where he's not known. Maybe he's reporting to the station. What's the difference, anyway? What do you care?" He paused, open-mouthed, realization creeping into his eyes as he stared at me. "That's the trouble, isn't it? You *do* care. I'm sorry."

I forced a lightness into my voice that I certainly didn't feel. "You've got it wrong, Scott. I don't care. Not like you think. I'm just curious. It's the damned detective part of me, I guess. I always seem to be hunting for motivation and truth."

"It's not that late, Bren. It's just gone nine o'clock."

"Oh?" I stared into the night, in the direction Graham had driven. "It's probably his date, then."

"Pardon?"

I told him about overhearing Graham's phone conversation. "So that's probably where he's off to. Not that it matters..."

"No, it doesn't. Not for you, at any rate. And, if you'll listen to a friend, I think you should start dating someone, set your sights on someone attainable."

I was glad of the darkness, glad he couldn't see my face, for I knew I was blushing. I'd never spoken with Scott about this. If he had guessed, it must be more obvious than I had thought. I said a quick prayer that it hadn't been obvious to Graham.

Scott said, "Dating your boss is a bad idea, Bren. Not only can it hurt your career, but it also can hurt emotionally. And you'll have a hard time getting shut of it, for you see the guy every day on the job. So you either end up transferring out of a division that you really love or you end up in the mental ward. Or sealing yourself off from life and potential happiness. Any option is bad."

"I don't need a doctor, Scott, to tell me about the bumps of life or love."

"Well, fine. Then grow up and— what?"

He stopped, staring at me. I snapped my fingers. "I just remembered! Baxter Clarkson is a retired surgeon."

"Kudos. I don't see—"

"I do! If he really got mad at Roger and went to the tower to kill him, he would know where best to strike a man and make it look like an accident. All those years of anatomy courses and traumas in the hospital must have taught him something!"

"Presuming he was calm and collected enough in the heat of an argument to remember that."

"I think I'll do a bit of sleuthing myself tomorrow. Thanks for the tip." Scott's 'don't mention it' was barely audible as I hurried to the pub.

BEN, SIBYL, LYNDON and another teenager were standing in the car park of the Cat and Mouse pub, dressed nearly alike. All wore faded jeans and dark colored jackets, though Ben's was a ski jacket, Lyndon's was a denim jacket, and Sibyl's was a voluptuous poncho-style coat. The teenagers held glasses of Coke with lemon slices, and Ben was holding a cigarette, periodically pausing in his conversation to take a puff. The evening's chill didn't seem to bother them, and there were two other small groups of people standing near the building, drinking and talking. I slowed my gait, hoping I could overhear some bit of Ben's speech before I entered the pub. Dawdling was entirely out of the question; it would be too obvious.

As I approached, Ben's raspy voice rose over the less vociferous tones of the nearby groups. He held his cigarette between his thumb and index

PEARLS BEFORE SWINE

finger and waved it about as he spoke. "And for another thing, I don't want you mixing with that crowd. You understand?"

I inwardly groaned. It sounded like a typical parent-teenager speech. I didn't know who to feel sorry for.

Sibyl gripped Lyndon's hand and said, "I told you, Dad, that Lyn's not like that. You know his mum and dad. You know Geneva, too. Coming from family like that, do you really think Lyn is one of 'that crowd,' as you call them?"

"The apple may not roll far from the tree," Ben said, glaring at Lyndon, "but there's other influences in a person's life."

"*Influences?* Like what?"

"Power. Peerage. Money."

Sibyl stared, mouth open. "All of which haven't a thing to do with Lyn. Or me. We're just friends. That's all, dad. We're not talking marriage."

"Yeh, well, things lead to other things, missy. And in this instance, I don't want it leading to His Mighty Highness Lord Swinbrook. Understood?"

"Why? What is so wrong with Roger?"

"Oh, it's 'Roger,' is it? How chummy we've got all of a sudden. Why? What's going on? Something I need to know about?"

"He asked me to call him 'Roger,' Dad. He's Lyn's uncle. I see him when we're up at the hall. We've all been there. Boyd, too." She grabbed the other teenager's hand as though she was leading him through fire. "Boyd and I have been there often. What's wrong with that? What are you so afraid of?"

"I'm *afraid*," Ben said, pointing at Lyndon, the smoke from his cigarette blowing into the boy's eyes, "that he's gonna turn out to be one of them rich bastards who never do a day's work and never help anyone but themselves. That's what I'm afraid of. And I'm afraid of it corrupting *you*, too, if you keep hanging about him."

Lyndon held up his free hand as if it would stop the barrage of words. His voice was so calm and low that I hardly heard him, even though I was passing within two meters of them. "There's nothing wrong with my uncle or his money, Mr. Griffiths. He's well known for his benevolence throughout the area."

"Have you forgotten the school computers?" Sibyl said.

"I've forgotten nothing," Ben snapped. "And I haven't time to stand here and listen to you, lad." He took a step toward Lyndon and dropped his voice. "I work for my living, so I have to get home and to bed now. But I'm not letting this drop. I don't want you pestering my daughter, hear?"

"Dad," Sibyl said, "nobody's pestering anybody. Except you, pestering Lyn. I told you—we're just friends! I'm seeing Boyd, if that makes any difference to you. What's wrong—"

"I told you what's wrong. He's one of *them*, one of the Swinbrooks. Not born to the velvet, but associated by his aunt. And that's as close as I want *you* to get to them, too! If I had my way, there'd be no more lords and barons and those with and those without. And I'm gonna do my damnedest in my own way in my own patch to make that a reality."

"What's *that* mean?" Sibyl struggled to break Ben's hold on her hand.

"Whatever you think."

Boyd set his glass on one of the massive oak tables and stepped closer to Ben. "Mr. Griffiths, I wish you wouldn't do this. Sibyl's done nothing wrong. Lyn asked us if we'd like to see the hall, and we said yes. Your daughter hasn't done—"

Ben laid his open palm against Boyd's chest. "I don't care if she swung from the chandelier or rode to hounds or scrubbed the floor. I don't want her up at the hall. And I don't want *you* leading her there. Either of you." He glared at the two boys. "Got it? Now, *enough* of this. Sibyl, you're coming home right now."

"You think so?" She stood straight, her mouth pressed together in a thin line, her eyes daring her father to do something physical.

I glanced at them, ready to lend assistance should anyone ask, but they ignored me. Perhaps no one wanted to make a scene. Perhaps Sibyl knew her father well enough not to resist him at this moment. Whatever the reason, I entered the pub, leaving the four of them to sort out the situation. But I felt unusually uneasy as I undressed, and wondered if Ben had already instigated part of his plan.

CHAPTER SIXTEEN

It was 7:00, later than normal, when I woke the following morning. Usually I would have had a proper breakfast—eggs, toast, bacon and grilled tomato, for I had learned early in my career that lunchtime hardly ever comes when my stomach needs it. But since I was late this morning, I bought a coffee-to-go and a scone at the bakery three shops down. I headed for a park bench across the street and sat in the village green while I ate, needing the brisk air to wake me up and needing to feed the sparrows.

The pavement along the High Street was beginning to fill with people grabbing breakfast as I had or hurrying to open their shops for the day's business. I huddled in the weak sunlight, cold but happy to be outside. My coffee sat on the bench beside me while I balanced a large fruit scone on my lap, alternately breaking off chunks for the sparrows and mouthfuls for me. I had just thrown a large raisin to a cheeky sparrow when two voices rose over the noise of traffic. Ordinarily, I wouldn't have paid any attention to the disruption, but the voices were familiar. I tossed another chunk of scone onto the ground and looked up. Sharon Seddon, Geneva's friend, and Ed Cawley were standing on the pavement just up from my bench. I watched as Sharon gestured toward the hall.

"You can't let him bully you, Ed. You've got as much right to see her as he does."

Ed Cawley stood in profile to me, his white hair all the more brilliant backlit by the early sunlight. "I agree with every word you say, Sharon. But I don't like confrontations. Lord knows the world has problems enough."

"So, you're going to stand by and watch him bulldoze over you? Is that any way to win?"

"Winning by driving a wedge between family members isn't my idea of a victory. They don't benefit and I certainly will come out a loser. Besides, I don't want her to remember me like that."

Sharon made a face. "She won't have to remember you at all if you succeed. You'll be right there. Every minute of every day."

Ed rubbed his chin. "I don't know, Sharon. It's risky."

"Life is risky! Is this how you and Roger started King and Country Tours? Is this how you started your current company, by playing it safe and not taking a risk? You don't sound like the entrepreneur I once knew."

Jo A. Hiestand

"I would hardly classify her as a case for my entrepreneurial skills."

"Fine. Watch it all slip away. But don't come crying to me when she's up and flown away."

"You're talking like there's no other way to accomplish this, Sharon. God, she's a human being whom I care about!"

"If so, think longer and harder about the situation. Something will present itself."

"And that's all you have to offer? No inside information?"

Sharon reached into her purse, brought out a small spiral notebook, jotted down something on a page and tore it off. Handing the paper to Ed, she said, "If you can tear yourself away from your board meeting or whatever you've got going on, be there at this time. It's not a guarantee, but I'll do my best."

Ed glanced at the paper, folded it and shoved it into his coat pocket. "I'll ring you up if I can't make it. Your mobile or at the hall?"

"Better make it my mobile. I don't want a maid running around trying to find me, yelling that I've got a phone call. You set, then?"

Ed nodded, patted her on the back, and they walked down the street.

I finished my coffee in a few large gulps, stuffed the better part of the scone into my mouth, shook out the paper bag to scatter the crumbs and last bits to the birds, and stood up. I watched them walk as far as the end of the block, where they turned right. From this angle I couldn't tell if they entered Austin's house or if they headed down East Brook Lane. It had certainly been an odd conversation, but I couldn't put off beginning my day any longer. Besides, I was in a hurry to talk to Graham about my Baxter Clarkson theory.

He listened intently, making little notes on the paper in front of him as we sat in the incident room. He didn't look tired, as a late-night date might have suggested. He didn't look particularly exultant, either. Perhaps it had not gone well. Or it had again been postponed. But he had probably allowed himself to sleep last night. Having followed his rule of working forty-eight hours non-stop, he could now fall back into an easier schedule. I shoved the speculation of his date to the back of my mind and concentrated on the case. The snow had never materialized, and the morning was sunny and warmer, bringing the birds to the trees and the snowdrops bursting into bloom. It was a day to be savored.

"That's an intriguing idea, Taylor," Graham said, tapping his pen against the sheet of paper. "But we're kind of up the spout at the moment. We can assume a fight, certainly, that Roger defended himself. But I don't see that Baxter's medical knowledge was particularly needed as a red herring. Still," he said, his voice brightening, "you never know. Early days yet. Yes, Mark?"

"Just reporting on pearl necklaces and guitarist sightings," Mark said, coming up to our table. He looked especially neat this morning—maroon tie, gray shirt and V-neck pullover, a splash of after-shave. I wondered what he was up to—impressing me so that I'd set a date for our dinner? I flashed

PEARLS BEFORE SWINE

him a smile, then pretended to search my shoulder bag for something. It didn't pay to let Mark know that I noticed.

"Pearl necklace? Margo's handling that."

"Yes, sir. But while I was talking to people about possibly seeing Kirk, I asked about the necklace. Showed them the photo. Two birds with the one stone, as they say."

"And their responses..."

"Blank. Well, except for the occasional drool or emphatic oath when they estimated the cost of the bloody thing. No one recognized it, a few wanted to know where it was so they could try their hand at burglary—"

"Why is everyone a comedian?"

"—and a few wanted to know what store would carry that type of thing. Presumably for gift-giving in the future."

"So it's a brick wall. Lovely. And the guitarist?"

"No one remembered seeing him or his car after the time he said he left."

"Why am I not surprised? He's a common sight around Oldfield. Even if he was here thirty minutes later, for instance, I doubt it would register with anyone. Besides, it's dark, despite the street lamps. Oh well, nice try."

"Kirk's home, sir. Arrived a few minutes ago. I saw him turn into his drive."

"Good." Graham got up and picked up his jacket. "I'll tackle him before he gets away. Ah, Fordyce. Everyone's bright and early this morning. We may get shut of this case before I'm another year older. What's going on?"

Fordyce bid us good morning, thumbed to a page in his notebook, and said, "I've gone through Ed Cawley's financial statements."

Graham grinned. "I know the suspense has been overbearing, Taylor, but you'll soon be out of your misery. Go on, constable."

"Well, sir, while not in Roger's league financially, Ed is solvent, a bit in credit card debt, but he's paid it off every time in a few months." He showed Graham and me Ed's current balance.

"So," Graham said, "that knocks him farther down the list of suspects, if we go for money as the motive for killing Roger."

"Sir?"

"I was just thinking that if Geneva will inherit Roger's vast sum—as it seems likely she will—well, then, Ed might marry her and profit that way. Or he might be mentioned in the will since he was Roger's friend. Even if he's not included as a beneficiary and has killed Roger for nothing, he's not lost out on anything."

"Except a friend."

"Yes, well, Roger would agree with you there."

"No one else connected with Roger has money problems. I checked everyone's credit card statements, bank drafts. Everything."

Jo A. Hiestand

"Which still doesn't eliminate pure greed as a motive, I know. Well, at least we know this much. Thanks, Fordyce."

"I also discovered," Fordyce said, taking back his notebook, "that Austin, Roger's brother, is paying child support."

"*What?*" Graham nearly dropped his jacket. "I didn't know he had a child. By Dulcie?"

"Evidently not. It comes to a hefty monthly payment, see?" He flipped to the next page and again showed us the notebook. "I'm thinking, sir, that Austin might want his inheritance to help him through his monthly expenditure. He had to borrow a bit to help the mother with hospital costs. Maybe this bit of money he'll get from Roger's estate will go toward paying back his loan plus going toward his child's care. What do you think, sir?"

"I think things are getting very interesting, Fordyce. And I think I need to ask brother Austin that same question. But he'll have to wait for a bit. Why don't you and Mark inspect Kirk's car for anything suspicious while Taylor and I keep Kirk busy with questions. Do you prefer camouflage or the direct attack?" He was halfway across the floor before I caught him up.

Kirk Fitzpatrick reiterated the microphone story, even digging an old mic out of a cardboard box in the garage. Of course he had a sales receipt. He'd buy a new mic if he needed it or not. But, as Graham and I had commented back in the incident room, there was no way to verify when that old mic became 'old,' nor if it were really bad—the idea being that Kirk pitched it as another piece to his elaborate alibi. Bad mic = shop for new one = take off early for Manchester = skip the country…I saw it all coming, but we acted like True Believers and listened to Kirk's fable.

But what I didn't see coming was the epilogue to Kirk's tale. He flushed slightly, then said in a strained voice, "I could have ordered it over the internet, sure, but I wanted an excuse to leave early, to get away from Noreen. We—" He paused, his eyes fixed on the doorway to the hall, as though judging if she would overhear him, then quickly said, "We're having trouble. It's been brewing for months, but lately it's…" He shrugged. "I know I'm gone a lot. I know that makes for a hell of a family life, trying to rear a child when one parent's gone half the time. But I don't know what else to do! I have to travel! I have to follow the money. God, what does she want? At least I'm holding down a job. And I've not done too badly, either. We've got a good house, food, clothes, a car. What am I supposed to do?"

Graham agreed it was difficult.

"Understatement, that," Kirk sniffed. "I know you're here about my brother-in-law's death, that you need to check out stuff. If you want to ask Noreen about my schedule, anything at all about the valentine dinner at the pub, go ahead. She's in the back bedroom, I think. Noreen!" He called but there was no response. He got up, but I said quickly, "Don't bother, sir. I'll just go and find her, shall I? Mr. Graham can ask you what he needs to know while I'm gone. That'll make it faster, and we'll be out of your hair that much sooner. All right?" Before he could respond, I'd opened the door to the living room and stepped into the hall.

PEARLS BEFORE SWINE

I closed the door and stood for a moment, listening for a sound that would indicate where Noreen was. I didn't want to go yelling through the house, and I didn't want to just barge into any rooms. A blast of music from a radio or CD player came from the back bedroom, so I made for that room.

I tapped several times on the bedroom door but the music drowned my knocking. I finally called Noreen's name and slowly opened the door, not wishing to surprise her.

She was struggling with a pullover, yanking it over her head and singing along to the song. There were bruises on her stomach, as though she'd fallen down basement steps. I immediately thought of Roger and the bruising on his arms and back, and for one swift instant wondered if Noreen had tangled with him. I called her name again, and as her head popped through the garment's neckline, she blushed and yanked it down around her hips.

"I'm sorry," I said, acutely aware of her shock. "I called and knocked, but with the music..."

She hurried over to the radio and turned it off. Smoothing her hair, she said, "Of course. Sorry. I didn't hear you. It was one of my favorites. I always listen to it too loud. You come to talk to Kirk?"

"Actually, I wanted to ask you a question, if you don't mind."

"Yes?" She leaned against her dresser, offering no sign of welcome or cordiality.

I repeated what Kirk had said about their marriage and asked if that were true. She glanced from me to her wedding photo that sat on her bedside cabinet, and said, "It's true. We haven't said anything to Lyn. Not yet. It's too early. We're not talking divorce. Not yet. We may not. God, I hope we can work through this! I—I'm Catholic, you see. I don't believe in divorce. It's not that we've ceased to love each other. On the contrary, we love each other very much! But with him gone so much of the time, and Lyn needing his dad..." She raised her head and looked at me. Her eyes were tearing up but her voice was still strong and steady. "We can get through this. It just takes a bit more effort to make it work than if he were home with a normal job. Thank God Roger was there for a lot of Lyn's growing up."

"Roger helped out with parental bits, did he?"

"Not to say like a real father, no. But if I had any problems, I'd go see him, talk to him. He hadn't any children of his own, but he offered a lot of support and advice. I don't know what I would've done without him sometimes. Kirk was so far away..."

I said I was sorry she and Kirk were going through such rough times, especially with Roger's death.

"I know he just came back. I know he's not had time to talk to me about things—and I don't want to talk about our problems right now. There'll be time enough for that when we've waited a decent length of time after the burial."

I wished her luck and went back to the living room.

Jo A. Hiestand

Kirk was just bringing Graham a cup of coffee when I entered. He asked if I wanted one, assured me it was no trouble, then reclaimed his chair when I declined his offer.

"Sure, I'm mad about the money I'm losing," he said as I sat next to Graham. "Who wouldn't be? I finally start to make some headway in this business, and I have to cancel almost every venue. What kind of an image am I giving the club owners if I pull out like this? Are they going to trust me again when I want a booking?"

"And you saw no one or nothing odd prior to Roger's death Wednesday evening," Graham continued, no doubt thinking it wiser to pass on mind reading. "No one followed Roger from the pub, you saw no car turning into the Hall's drive?"

"'Fraid not. Wish I had."

"Do you know if Roger had any enemies? Someone angry at him, not just over a business venture, but something personal, perhaps?"

"There I'd be speculating if I said so. I wasn't Roger's bosom buddy, so I hardly knew what went on in his life. He may have problems with people that I don't know about. Other than the obvious two, Baxter and Ben, I've not heard of anyone who'd be considered an enemy—and I don't really think of them as such. Just angry. They'd not physically harm him."

"So Roger—"

"Would help anyone. They just needed to ask. He'd a generous heart."

"And was kind and generous to all," Graham muttered when we had thanked Kirk and were outside. "A saint on earth. Which is fine, but his halo was either slipping or he had done something unsaintly to provoke anger in someone."

"Austin's looking a bit less saintly, too. A child he neglected to mention isn't exactly up there with rule number one about telling the truth."

"We'll hear his story in a moment. Well, Fordyce and Mark seem to have finished. They've left a cryptic message, no doubt." He grabbed the scrap of paper that lay beneath one of his windscreen wipers. It was a page ripped from a small notebook, the paper torn diagonally from the lower corner to about two inches up to the other side. Graham smiled, said something about heightened police security, and read, "'Pub car park.' Good thing he spent the time to put it into code. This'll fool anyone who happens to lift it." He laughed, folded the paper and stuck it into his slacks pocket. "Well, I didn't think they'd stand around here to tell us, but this works. Mark's choice of rendezvous spot seems appropriate, don't you think, TC?"

I commented that it seemed never too early for Mark to want a drink, and remained silent until we met him and Fordyce in the car park.

"Nothing much," Mark said as he and Fordyce walked up to us. He had a polystyrene cup in his hand. And from the aroma that came to me, I assumed it was coffee. As to whether it was straight or whiskey-tinged was another assumption. But at least it explained the reason for the choice of rendezvous. He paused to take a sip, and I was overwhelmed by a desire to

PEARLS BEFORE SWINE

hold the cup—my hands were cold. Graham listened to Mark's report through the open window, remaining seated, the car engine idling. Fordyce stood by his side, adding an element of solidarity that I wondered if Mark needed. Had he done a cock-up of searching Kirk's car? Perhaps there was more whiskey than coffee in that cup. Mark said, "Without doing a complete vacuum job and proper dismantling of the car, I can't be dead cert there's anything in the car that shouldn't be there."

"No bloody boots, for example." Graham sighed.

"Or poetic valentines. Nothing suggesting the murder weapon, either."

"I didn't think there would be, but we go through the motions. It contributes to Simcock's good night's sleep. And, speaking of our good superintendent..."

I braced myself for a directive, but Graham said, "Simcock wants us, which includes me, to keep our eyes open for any suspicious activity in the area."

"What does he term 'suspicious'? Our strange tourist or a spaceship landing?"

"I wasn't told. But probably something in between. You're all good coppers. You'll now when something doesn't smell right."

We mumbled 'yes, sir' and I could tell by my co-workers' frowns that the directive didn't smell right. Something, as they say, was afoot.

"Well..." Graham said after a slight pause. He pressed his lips together, perhaps wondering what could be more suspicious than Roger's death, then said, "Join Margo in the necklace inquiry, if you will, Mark. And Fordyce, I'd like you to work with them, too. I need to know whose pearls those are. Thanks. Taylor and I will visit Austin and learn more about family secrets."

AUSTIN OBVIOUSLY DIDN'T want to talk about his 'indiscretion,' as he labeled it, but offered us the story, along with coffee and cream.

"It didn't mean a thing," he said, leaning against the marble mantelpiece, looking like a tour guide talking about Adam architecture. "It was a brief fling. No more than a week. I can't believe you're asking me about this! Is nothing private anymore?"

Margo's tirade from last night rolled through my mind as Graham replied, "And I can't believe you didn't mention it. You very conveniently overlooked it, giving us the details of your forthcoming recording business but forgetting about something that may be linked to this case."

"How can something like a child be of any concern to finding my brother's killer? It's ludicrous!" He ran his fingers through his hair, causing what little he had left to stand out, as though he'd received an electrical shock. Well, "shock" was the right word, for all the color had drained from his face. His eyes bulged as he stared at Graham. "You—you've not told Dulcie, have you?"

"No. Why?"

"Well, think about it." Now that the shock was over, he was becoming angry. His voice built in volume. "*Why?* God, I'd have thought that obvious! Because we're engaged, that's why. And I can't think of a woman alive, about to be married or not, who'd enjoy hearing about her husband's illegitimate child."

"And you think that's a good idea, do you, hiding something like that, so major, from your fiancée?"

"It's not your decision, is it? It's not your life. I'll tell her. I'm not keeping secrets. It's just that, well, the right time hasn't presented itself, that's all."

Graham shrugged. I knew he wanted to go into his "church mode," as Margo called it, to speak about morals and responsibility. But, as Austin had stated in so many words, the right time was not now. "How old is your child?"

"Eleven months, if you need to know. The mother and I had a short fling, which neither of us took seriously. The affair was over a year ago. The mother moved before my son's birth, so I couldn't find her. She had the baby and now is back in touch with me for child support. Which, I might add, I pay willingly. Only it's hard to always get the money, despite what you think about my family, wealth and estate."

I suppose I blinked, for the home obviously *did* speak of money. But even with Chippendale furniture, ready money might not be abundant. There were such things as household bills, church pledges and such. And auctioning off property took longer than you think it should.

"I've never missed a payment," Austin continued, his voice softening as his anger abated. "You can check my bank statements."

"Where are the mother and your son now?"

"Lincoln. You want to check up on me—or them?" He walked over to the desk, scribbled a name and address on a sheet of paper that he tore from a notepad, and handed it to Graham. "I know what you're thinking," he continued when Graham had pocketed the paper.

"Really? And what is it?"

"That I killed my brother in order to get money for child support."

"What a novel idea."

"Well, I didn't. Not for child support or to launch the recording company or *anything*! I loved my brother. I didn't even hit him for a loan, which he would have given me. He was the most generous—"

"I suppose," I said, cutting in on the now-familiar pronouncement, "you are certain the child *is* yours. There is no doubt of paternity, I mean."

Austin looked at me as though I'd just told him Julia Roberts wanted to date him. "*What?*" His hand went to his head and rested on his bald spot. "You think she's telling me that to get money from me?"

"It's been known to happen. Especially if you didn't know the woman very well before all this happened. Isn't it just a bit odd that she leaves town without telling you or mentioning her pregnancy, doesn't tell you where she is, and the next thing you hear is, 'Hey, I've had your kid; I want money for upkeep befitting its lineage, no matter if its born on the wrong side of the blanket.' That doesn't strike you as odd? Maybe more so because your child is a son, and may be in line to be addressed as The Right Honorable the Earl of Swinbrook?"

"But that—that's *unethical!*"

"So is murder," I said, somewhat amused at his indignation. "Along with blackmail, extortion, cheating, lying, money laundering, bearing false witness..." I stopped, suddenly feeling I was quoting Moses' tablets. "Have you asked for a paternity test? It'll save you money in the long run if the child isn't yours. You won't be responsible for university tuition, medical bills—"

"That's a hell of a way to look at the world, miss. Awfully cynical."

"A career of dealing with devious criminals and murder cases tends to color my outlook," I said.

Graham wrote a phone number on the back of one of his business cards and handed it to Austin. "It's the number of a solicitor, should you decide to look into this. He's very ethical." He caught my eye and flashed a quick smile. "Just in case. You never know when you'll need legal advice."

The door to the living room opened, admitting Dulcie. She caught the exchange of paper, the fleeting smile and the conversation. As she stood against the closed door, she gave Austin an icy stare and demanded, "*Why* do you need a solicitor? Did you murder Roger?"

Jo A. Hiestand

CHAPTER SEVENTEEN

AUSTIN TURNED SO many colors, I was thinking he had chameleon blood in him. He stammered a bit, looked from Graham to me, then fell silent. I fought my desire to save him, to jump into the stillness with some explanation. But it was Austin's show; he had dug his own grave, as they say, and he needed to do the talking. The right time, as he had said not ten minutes ago, had just presented itself.

"Wha—*What* paper, luv?" Austin slowly wrapped his fingers around the slip of paper, trying to hide it.

Dulcie strode across the room, grabbed his hand and brought it to eye level, and said in a clipped voice, "*This* paper. The one you're trying to reduce to pulp. Now, what is it? And what the hell is going on? You look like you've been caught with your hand in the biscuit tin. Come on. Explain."

Austin wrenched his hand free, jammed his fist into his pants pocket and said it was none of her business.

"Great! Thank you very much. Smashing way to talk to your future wife. Or maybe not. If this is how you're going to treat me—"

"Don't go that way," Austin barked. "Threats are kind of childish, don't you think?"

"*Childish! You* should talk! 'What paper...' God, of all the childish—" She stopped, clenching her fists, her chest rapidly rising and falling. As though needing a comforting hug, she folded her arms across her chest, her fingers digging into the soft flesh of her upper arms. Finally, she took a deep breath, and said, "Don't lie to me, Austin. I can't stand a liar. If you want this marriage to go on, tell me what's happening. No, don't look to your mates for help," she said as Austin glanced at me. "Tell *me*. Now!"

When Austin had repeated nearly verbatim what he'd told Graham and me, Dulcie remained quiet for several seconds. Her fingers whitened as they pressed into her arms. In the stillness, I could hear the ring of the front door bell, the click of the maid's shoes as she crossed the floor, the sounds of traffic and bird song and children singing when the door opened. The sounds vanished, relegated to that other, ordinary world, when the door closed once more. Such simple things, traffic, birds and children, but oddly out of place among extortion. Dulcie walked over to the far end of the mantle, lay the framed photo of her and Austin face down, then slipped off her engagement ring. She turned, jammed it into Austin's hand, and said, "I don't know if it's too late, Austin, but you should have told me about this a long time ago. You should have been man enough to own up to it—"

"I *have* owned up to it!" Austin yapped. "God, aren't I making those damned child support payments—"

"I'm not talking about that. I'm talking about us. *Our* relationship. I don't know if it's over between us. I can't think right now." She took a few steps from him. Austin reached out for her and grabbed her left hand. He pulled her around to face him.

"Dulcie! *Please!* Can't we talk about this? Can't you listen to me for ten minutes? That's all I want. Ten minutes. I have to tell you—"

"You've *told* me, Austin. But you've told me too late." She tried to wrench her hand free, but Austin's grip remained strong.

"Dulcie, please let me explain. *Please.* Can't I still see you?"

"You're seeing me. You're seeing me walking out the door, out of your life. Now, leave me alone!" She pulled her hand from his grasp, then swung and slapped his face. The retort was not so much the surprise as was the action. Austin stood still, his hand against his cheek, his eyes staring at her. His lips trembled and called after her as she slammed the door behind her.

The silence threatened to smother us once again, only this time it was tinged with a layer of great sadness. I spoke quickly, not wanting the gloom to take hold. "Maybe it would be for the best if you insisted on a paternity test. In light of the circumstances..."

Austin seemed not to be hearing me, perhaps focused on Dulcie or the returned engagement ring or his child. When he did look at me, his eyes were void of expression, as though he were sleep walking through this nightmare. He said quietly, "What? Oh, yes. I—I'll think about it. Perhaps when I've seen him, if the baby doesn't look like me..."

"You've not seen it, then," Graham said.

"No. But even a blond wouldn't rule out my fathering the child. My grandmother was blonde."

"Heredity does show itself at the oddest times. Were your parents both brunets? I know you and your brother are—"

"Look. If this is your subtle way of gleaning info, it's not working. I own up to my parental responsibility, but that's *all.* I did *not* kill my brother! Now, I've just about had it. I'd appreciate it if you'd both leave." He picked up the photograph so slowly and gently it could have been his infant son he held. He was still gazing at it as Graham and I left the room.

Graham stopped by the side of his car, his car keys in his hand, and stared back at the house. "Have you noticed that people say one thing, TC, and do another?"

"Sir?"

"The paternity test. He won't do it. He's neither the money nor the temperament."

"Too trusting, you mean?"

"He's of the old-fashioned, romantic ilk. Help the damsel in distress and all that."

"Well," I said, readjusting my bag on my shoulder, "there's one damsel who's in distress that he's barred from helping. I don't think Dulcie would have him on a silver platter. Or on a credit card."

"From the sound of his finances, she may not get either. Poor little rich boy. Too bad. I rather like him. And her. It's sad when love dies and the relationship breaks. Like a physical death, with the same need to mourn."

I nodded and gazed at the ground, afraid the images of previous boyfriends would merge with Graham's face. But he was right about the need to mourn. The loss of love was a physical sensation, boring a canker into your soul, destroying your sleep and appetite, tinting not just your world but also your whole outlook on life a dismal gray. It was a thief, a murderer, a bully, robbing you of happiness, killing your trust in future relationships, dictating your seclusion and loss of personal contacts. It embittered you, forced you into an existence permeated with the monotony of merely breathing. It *was* a physical thing. Anyone who had endured such bitterness knew that.

Graham pulled out his mobile, punched in a number, and seconds later was telling PC Byrd to run a check on the mother of Austin's child. "In particular, see if she's a history of this sort of thing. All right, 'career,' if that makes you happy. Is Mark there? Good. Let me talk to him. He's going to love this." He smiled at me as he waited for Mark to come to the phone. Margo's lecture rumbled in my brain and I took a deep breath.

"Sir?"

Graham tilted his head, looking at me with large, dark eyes. "Yes, Taylor?"

Great. Not even calling me by my nickname. This just oozes romance.

A car horn honked at a pedestrian who was about to cross the street and a shopkeeper stepped outside to bang her dusty mop against the edge of the building. I frowned.

Graham cocked his eyebrow. "Taylor? You want to ask me something?"

I nodded, took a deep breath, mentally crossed my fingers, and opened my mouth.

Graham held up his hand. "Hello, Mark? Yes. I want you to see Lady Swinbrook, find out the terms of Roger's will. It's no good trying the solicitor—he won't divulge that. If her ladyship won't tell you, get the information another way. Also, ask MacMillan and Fordyce to check around the village to see if anyone saw anything suspicious last night. We need to get to the bottom of those hate valentines Lady Swinbrook has been getting. Might as well do that while you're asking about the necklace. It'll save time. No one will have seen a thing, but we have to start somewhere.

Thanks." He flipped the phone closed and repocketed it. "If you don't mind, TC, would you mind lending your feet and mind to that task, too? I feel that the more people we have on that inquiry, the sooner we may solve this thing and relieve her ladyship of any alarm she may be feeling. Now. You wanted to ask me something?"

His mobile rang, cutting off my response. He talked for thirty seconds, wrote something down on his notebook, said he'd be right there, then rang off. "Sorry, Taylor. I'm a popular fellow at the moment. What did you want? Can you make it quick?"

This obviously wasn't the best time to ask him out to dinner, and as I watched his fingers tapping impatiently on the steering wheel, I wondered when I would ever catch a 'best time.' So instead of inviting him to my place for grilled salmon, Caesar salad and chocolate mousse, I said it wasn't urgent and that I'd love to walk around, especially as it was a nice day.

"Good." He opened his car door. "I'm off, then. We can talk later. If you need me, I'm just a phone call away." He waved to me as he steered the car onto the High Street.

It was easy to imagine him rushing off for his Valentine's Day date, taking a long tea break with her, making up for their lost time by cooing in her ear. Only trouble was, Graham was not the cooing type. At least, I couldn't envision him whispering sweet nothings into an ear, however well-built or gorgeous its owner was. Still, I admitted, I'd never been in a position for him to coo into my ear. He could very well be a great cooer.

The only things I gained from my two hours of walking and talking were a pair of sore feet and a new admiration for the English language. I'd never heard the definition of 'saw nothing suspicious' expressed in so many different ways. It was truly astounding.

I'D JUST MADE myself a cuppa when Graham and Mark came into the incident room. They filled their mugs, took off their jackets and draped them on the backs of the metal chairs at my table. Graham sat down, not looking particularly happy—date problems?—and waited rather impatiently while Mark loosened his tie and then opened his notebook.

"Her ladyship very graciously read me the terms of Lord Swinbrook's will," Mark said, taking a chair next to me.

"She *read* it? She could have been lying, Salt."

"I know, sir, but when she went to her bedroom, I read the will."

"And why," I asked, "was she going to her bedroom?"

"To fetch a photo of her and Kirk when they were children. We'd been talking about that, and I asked if she had any childhood photos. She obliged me by getting it. I thought it a good way to be alone with the will."

I had nearly expected Mark to say 'alone with the woman,' but he was putting those days behind him.

Graham congratulated him. "And who are the beneficiaries?"

Jo A. Hiestand

Mark glanced at his notebook. "The will dictates the division of the estate as follows: some minor bequests to the staff—£3,000 to £5,000 pounds per person, dictated by length of service to the family—provisions to the village in the form of a grant to oversee repairs to the town hall, when needed; some smaller, miscellaneous items such as specific books and original oils, a horse, and a Land Rover to various friends. And, much to a certain someone's surprise, I'm sure, the establishment of a fund to pay the annual salary of one person—selected by job application—to daily ring the hour on the estate's tower bell at noon and at six o'clock."

Graham blinked, caught off guard by the request. "That *will* make for on-going niceties between her ladyship and the Clarksons." He snorted. "And the bulk of the estate—unless there are any more bomb shells?"

"Not really, sir. Pretty smooth sailing. As expected, her ladyship and Austin split it equally. House, land, holdings. The solicitor estimates each one will get approximately £14,000,000 after taxes. What's that do for you?" He smiled and closed his notebook.

"Nothing for me," Graham said, recovering his composure, "although don't think I'm not jealous. That's a hell of a lot of money, even if the family considers itself sunk in their fortunes."

"Poor little rich boy," I murmured again.

"But I'm sure it will presently do something for *someone*."

"Enough to make that a motive."

"Feuding Clarksons and Ben Griffiths aside, anyone would kill for that much, provided they are included in the will, or *think* they are included."

"Even the minor bequests," I said, "aren't so minor if you're flat broke. £3,000 is nothing to sneeze at. And you can always sell books, oil paintings, the horse and Land Rover and get your ready cash that way."

"Even the mayor gains," Mark said, picking up his mug. "Sure, the money is supposed to go to town hall repairs, but what's to stop him from diverting funds or cooking the books? He wouldn't be the first government official to find a bit of the public's funds in his pocket."

"There *are* taxes," I reminded them. "That's bound to cut into their inheritance."

Graham sighed and stretched. "The field's just opened up for our suspects, I'm afraid. No wonder they classify greed as a deadly sin. If that's the motive in Roger's death, it certainly proved deadly for him."

I said, "About Geneva's valentine, sir..."

"Oh, yes?"

"I was just thinking about it. We keep focusing on Ben Griffiths or Baxter Clarkson as major players in this."

"I get the feeling you're about to demote them."

"Well, yes, sir, I am."

"Why?" He looked at me, his eyes serious and wide open, waiting for my opinion.

PEARLS BEFORE SWINE

"Well, sir, Mona brings the post to her ladyship. What's to prevent *her* from slipping in the valentine and then that second cruel piece of trash into the stack of letters, making it look as though it was delivered by the postman?"

Graham rubbed his chin, his fingers lingering on the scar on his jaw. I'd always wondered how he'd come by that. The fight must have been intense, the cut deep, for him to sustain that scar. He scratched his ear lobe, then said, "I'll put someone on checking out her background. See if she's in credit card debt. You know the drill. Anything that might provide a motive for Roger's murder. Good job, Taylor."

I was about to thank him when his mobile rang. He sat up straight, indicating it was something serious. A few sentences were exchanged, he assured the caller I would leave immediately, and he hung up. As his fingers closed around the phone, he said, "Taylor, that was her ladyship. The post was just delivered. In the mail there was a packet. When she opened it she found a stack of photocopied pound notes."

"*Money!*" I said, trying to understand. "Why? And why are the notes photocopied? What's going on? Who's it from?"

"There *was* a typed note among all this. It said she'd get the real equivalent when she moved out of the hall."

Mark whistled, a slow, low tone that conveyed the gravity of the situation. "What's next, I wonder. A 'To Let' sign posted in her front garden?"

"More likely a forced vacancy, with the removal men in black ski masks, toting guns, and removing her bodily from the hall." He turned to me. "I told her ladyship that you'd be right over. Here's also your chance to question Mona, if you've a mind to."

I said at least Fortune was smiling on me, if not Geneva, stood up, grabbed my bag and jacket, and made for Swinton Hall.

GENEVA HAD TAKEN refuge in prescription drugs and in her bed by the time I'd arrived. Which didn't surprise me. Three intimidating, if not terrorizing, incidents in three days would have sent me scurrying for my darkest closet and a handgun. Not that I'm making light of the subject, because I'm not. I'd be quite frightened, never mind my police training. Knowing the mechanics of how to deal with a reported burglary was one thing, but becoming the victim and protecting yourself and your property against such invasion was another. I hoped I'd never have to deal with it.

But Geneva was dealing with it, I thought, as Mona Griffiths watched me bag the box, outer wrapping paper, photocopied notes and typed message. I worked at a small marble-topped table in the hallway, almost surrounded by masses of flowers, part of the outpouring of condolence from Roger's and Geneva's friends. The air was heavy with the scents of freesia and lilies and roses. I understood why they occupied this high-ceilinged area for the air was sickly sweet and hard to breathe after too many minutes. When I'd finished with the evidence collection, I asked Mona if the box had been with the post proper or sitting alone on the doorstep. She said it had been with the post, part of the day's delivery, and that she had not even thought it suspicious so hadn't glanced at the postmark. I asked if she knew of any other such deliveries, whether by post, delivery van, or just appearing on the doorstep. She said no, that Geneva would have said something, asked who had delivered it.

A maid rushed down the main staircase, her mouth open, her eyes staring, her white starched apron flapping. She saw Mona and asked her to phone the police.

"Why?" I asked, identifying myself as I met the maid on the stairs. "What's the matter?"

"It's her ladyship," she said, trying to talk and calm her racing heart at the same time. She took another deep breath, then said, "She's in her bedroom. Her brother's with her. They—they're having a dreadful row. It's awful! I think he's going to hit her!"

She hurried up the stairs again, with me following, and led me to Geneva's bedroom. I could hear the raised voices in the hallway. I thanked the maid, assured her I could take care of the matter, then tapped on the door. The knock passed unnoticed in the verbal melee in the room. I knocked harder, received no answer, so opened the door and stepped inside.

Holding a bouquet of flowers, Kirk Fitzpatrick was standing beside Geneva's bed, his face a violent shade of fuchsia. He seemed more interested in his sister than in presenting her with the flowers, for he held them at his side, the flowers pointed toward the carpet. Geneva reclined on several pillows, the duvet clutched at her throat, and stared at her brother with large, frightened eyes. I apologized for intruding, then asked if I could help.

"The only help we need," Kirk said, throwing the flowers onto the bed, "is common sense. I suppose you haven't any to spare. It seems in rather short supply—here and worldwide."

Her right elbow propping her up to a half sitting position, Geneva said, "I'll pay whatever it costs. He needs more common sense than I fear can be found anywhere. You'll probably have to requisition a special order."

"*Me?*" Kirk said. "I'm talking about you!"

"How like a man. Nothing's ever wrong with them. It's always the woman's fault."

I stepped closer, stopping at the foot of the bed. It was a woman's room, done up with ruffled white curtains and bedspread, white furniture with delicate painted flowers flowing over the top and sides. Huge sprays of flowers and dozens of energetic potted plants took over the two far corners of the room, some of the remnants, perhaps, from the floral tributes in the entryway downstairs. Geneva watched me, rather less queenly than she had seemed on previous visits, and waited for me to take charge. I did. "Now what precisely is the problem? How can I help?"

Geneva opened her mouth but Kirk rushed ahead. "Her. She's the problem. Her and her stupidity. And I don't think there's a cure for that. Other than a good sock in the mouth."

"You wouldn't dare!" Geneva said, sitting up. "I'll have you up on assault. I don't care if you are my brother. You can't hit me and get away with it!"

I held out my hand, rather like I was stopping traffic. "No one's going to hit anyone. And no one's going to get away with anything. I repeat. What's the problem?"

Kirk sniffed and said, "I just came over here to see how she was. I mean, after all, I'd been out of town, and this is the first opportunity I've had. So I came over, offering—" He stared down at his handful of flowers, then glanced at the roomful of gigantic bouquets, and said, "Well, I thought she'd like some company, like a bit of cheer. So I came over."

"Seems very brotherly. So what's the problem?"

He shrugged, as though he had no idea. I asked again. He exhaled loudly and said, "All I did was ask if she was going to come home when this is all...when Roger is...well, I didn't know if she was going to stay here or if she was going to come home. I thought she'd come home, since Austin and Dulcie will probably be moving in, him having inherited the title and all. That's all I wanted to know. So we could clean out the guest room for her, or help her house hunt. Whatever she wanted. What's wrong with that?"

"Simple question. Why did that get everyone riled up?"

"It wasn't the question," Geneva said, pulling the cover up to her chin. The white duvet reflected the light of the overhead light fixture onto her face, accenting the hollows of her eyes, the red of her nose. Her hair was disarrayed and unwashed. She could have doubled for any of the Weird Sisters. "It was the way he asked it, the tone in his voice."

"And how did he ask it?"

Geneva wrinkled up her nose. "He asked if I was going to stay here or come back to my family—'turn common,' is what he actually said. Yes, 'turn common.' He said that I should be true to myself and our parents and come back to being Geneva Fitzpatrick. He'd found my whole marriage a bit ludicrous anyway, and now was my chance to 'fix it,' I believe he said."

I turned to Kirk. "Is that correct? Were those the words you used?"

Kirk snorted. "Stick and stones—"

"I asked if that was what you said. Please don't waste my time."

"Yes. That's what I said. Near enough. So, what's wrong with that? Is it a crime to want her back with her family? Lyn would love to see more of you, sis, and I know Noreen would, too. We hardly ever see you. Why don't you stay with us? Or I'll find you a nice cottage somewhere. Maybe one of those nice houses in Castleton. You like it there. Or you could trade places with Austin. He won't need his home if he moves into the hall."

Geneva said, "You have absolutely no feelings at all, Kirk! I haven't even had Roger's funeral, and you're worried about me moving back into the bosom of the family and relinquishing my title and such. My God, what is wrong with you? You come in here, give me a minute of your precious time, and right away start badgering me. Give me a chance to get over this, a chance to think!" She shook out the duvet, sending Kirk's bouquet onto the carpet. "Now, out of here. Right now! I don't want you ringing me up or writing to me or appearing on my doorstep until I ask you to. I'll tell you what I'm going to do when I figure it out—not that it's any business of yours." She sniffed and wriggled down into the bedding. "I don't want to talk about it anymore. My head's about to split. All I want is to be left alone! Now! Out, Kirk!" She rolled over, her back toward us, and pulled the cover over her head.

I prodded Kirk out of the room, turned off the light, and closed the door. At the landing, the maid approached me, clasping her hands and looking like she'd just discovered a dead body. I watched Kirk descend the stairs and leave by the front door, then asked the maid what she wanted. She glanced over her shoulder, as if expecting Geneva to be eavesdropping. When she was assured we were alone, she said, "I hope I did nothing wrong, miss."

"On the contrary. You did well to think of ringing up the police."

I started toward the stairs, but she called after me. I stopped and turned toward her. She said in a small voice, "Thank you, miss, but I meant I hope I did right about letting her ladyship's brother into the house."

"I don't see why not. You had no way of knowing he and her ladyship would argue."

"Yes, miss, but I meant earlier. When he first came here."

"Pardon?" This was getting confusing. "When Kirk *first* came? You mean you let him in twice?"

"No, miss, but I let him in nearly an hour ago. I thought he'd go straight up to see her ladyship. He had those flowers, you see, and I thought he'd come specifically to see her. When I told him where he could find her, he thanked me and went upstairs. I didn't watch him after that. It's not my place to, is it? Besides, he's family. But I was that surprised when I heard them yelling at each other, and him standing there with the flowers in his hand, like he just got here. So you see what I'm saying, miss, don't you?"

She curtsied and I thanked her, then walked slowly down the stairs. If Kirk had arrived some time before the maid heard their argument, where had he gone? What had he done in the intervening time? Geneva had said Kirk had given her a minute of his precious time, that he came right into her room and started badgering her. That implied he had arrived merely minutes before the maid had come downstairs and taken me to Geneva's room. Kirk's own stance by her bed also implied that. You don't stand by a person's bed and hold a bouquet for nearly an hour. I looked back at the house, glancing at the row of windows running the width of the first story.

I dug the car key out of my pocket. Kirk wanted Geneva to move out. So did Baxter Clarkson. And Ben Griffiths would be thrilled if Geneva relinquished her title, being one less 'idle rich' in his vicinity. So was this concern with Geneva's immediate future more than just friendly nosiness? And what had he been doing during that unaccounted for chunk of time?

CHAPTER EIGHTEEN

AT THE INCIDENT room, Graham looked at Geneva's latest valentine package. The photocopies of the notes looked to be life-size, as though the person had placed them on the bed of the photocopier and run off dozens of pages. He'd taken the time to cut them, evenly trimming around each note, then rubber-banding them together into neat bundles that he stacked inside the cardboard shoebox. Just out of curiosity, I wanted to count them, to see if our prankster had given Geneva a fair market price. But that wasn't necessary. It was the implied threat behind the paper money that was important. And frightening.

Graham said that the postmark on the box wrapping was Chesterfield, adding that it meant nothing, as it was a large town and anyone could have driven there—even from John O'Groats or Lands End—and posted it from there. He looked around the room, saw Byrd coming in the door, and called to him. The constable walked quickly over to us.

"I was just going to find you, sir," PC Byrd said, standing behind my chair. "Those items you gave me to get fingerprinted—the valentine and envelope and that poem. Nothing definite, sir. A sea of smudges, I'm afraid. Sorry."

"Gone through too many hands on its journey to Lady Swinbrook," Graham said, sighing. "Well, I didn't really expect otherwise. We've got a few people between the person who posted it and Geneva."

"Makes for a bit of a muddle with prints, yes, sir."

"Well, perhaps you can do better with this one, Byrd." Graham handed him the box and its contents. "Would you mind? I'm sorry to send you back to Buxton, but this just happened. The usual, if you'd be so kind."

"Certainly, Mr. Graham." Byrd took the package.

"He probably wore gloves. The git who did this, not the postman."

"Yes, sir."

"But we may get lucky. He had to hold the paper when he cut apart the photocopied notes."

Byrd nodded without really understanding what it was about, turned, and left the building.

"Now, then." Graham stood up, stretched, and said, "It's just gone five o'clock. I know we usually work another hour or so, but let's call it a day.

We've been going at it steadily, we've put in some long hours, and I, for one, think we need a bit of a break. You have plans for dinner, TC?" He smiled as he looked at me, folding his suede jacket over his arm.

I could feel the heat building in my neck and cheeks, and I lowered my head, afraid he'd see the excitement in my eyes and know this is what I'd wanted for several months. I pressed the end of the sticking plaster onto my gauze-wrapped hand and mumbled that I hadn't yet thought of where I'd like to eat this evening.

"Well, if you don't mind me offering..."

I held my breath, afraid to pray, afraid to hope or listen. I shut my eyes quickly, wishing he'd just say it.

He did. It was short and sweet. "Why don't you get something from the pub? You can take it up to your room, perhaps relax in a hot bath, then eat in bed, in front of the telly. An early night will do you good. You need to relax, Taylor. You seemed tired today. See you in the morning. Night."

He slipped on his jacket and dug his car keys out of his pocket as he headed for the door.

I slowly raised my head, blinking. Had I really heard him correctly? Had he left without me? Mark turned a chair around, straddled it and leaned his forearms against the chair's back. His hand lifted my chin and he peered into my eyes. "What's going on, Bren? You look like you're about to cry." He glanced at the swinging door, then back to me. "That's—the bastard. You thought he was going to ask you out. *That's* it! God, Bren, I'm sorry."

I shoved his hand away and fumbled for my bag. "I was not! How can you think...where do you even get such an idea? Of all the—"

Mark held up his hands as in surrender. "Okay. Fine. I had it wrong, then. But you're giving the best imitation I've ever seen of a bride left at the altar without the benefit of an altar—"

"Funny, Mark. You do stand-up comedy during your off hours?" I jammed my arms into my jacket, zipped it up, and shouldered my bag. "Get a good night's sleep. I have a feeling we'll be running through hoops tomorrow. And in the words of our fearless leader, 'night.'"

The door banged behind me as I strode outside and stopped several feet from my car. To my right, the church loomed like a black shell on its mound of earth. Quiet, peaceful. Offering solace from worldly care. Opposite it, the BP garage across the street was alive with white and green lights. To my left, the street continued its dark-bright alternation, businesses either closed or open, geometric masses pitch black or gleaming white. Next to me, the chemist's sat dark and empty, its northern wall washed in the glow from the pub's lights. Neighboring the pub, the green grocer's exuded the same empty darkness of the chemist's, but the Greek restaurant glittered beneath its rows of blinking lights. It was nearly the same beyond the village center; houses glistened with light or merged with the night. Beyond the confines of earth, the sky stretched in an unbroken black band from horizon to horizon. Tree boughs, normally silhouetted against the gray backdrop, disappeared into the darkness. There was no hint of the moon. Perhaps it would break later from its opaque prison. I hoped so. I needed something to cheer me.

My cheer came from a human quarter: Scott Coral's car was headed toward me. I ran to the pavement along the High Street and waved. His car, a newer model Morris Mini, immediately turned into the car park. As he stopped beside me, he lowered his window. His face peered at me from the darkness of the car's interior.

"I hardly recognized you without your green glow," I said, bending forward and gazing into the car's interior. "Good thing you drive the Bumble Bee or I'd never spot you." His car was black with two wide yellow stripes running from bonnet to boot. He hated the nickname I'd christened his car.

Ignoring the jest, he said, "I'm just off duty and dying for a pub crawl. As much as you may think I live and breathe police work, I leave that behind at the end of the shift. Along with the computer," he added, referring to the laptop computer that sits in every response driver's car. They were a definite boon to the cop, providing information about the call to which they responded, but the green light thrown out from the screen was as good as a spotlight, announcing to passing motorists that this driver was a cop. Again, we struggled with the extremes of technology. Scott, now in his personal car, was temporarily free from the computer's blessing and curse. "So, what's up?"

"You in a rush to get home?"

"Not particularly. I'm a grass widower this week. The wife's off visiting her mum in London. The kids are at the sitter's till I pick them up."

"So you're the happy bachelor, then."

"Not to say happy. I'm already tired of pub grub and take-aways."

"If you've not got to rush home," I said, "feel like combining a bit of detective work at a restaurant?"

"You're muddled," Scott said, opening the passenger door. "I've not put in for a transfer to the C.I.D. I've applied for the Force Tactical Unit."

"Well, you won't have to move, at any rate." I got into the car, closed the door, and smiled at him. "You live near Ripley, don't you?"

"Funny how that worked out, isn't it?" He laughed.

One of the qualifications of that position was that the firearms officer could live no more than a twenty-minute drive from headquarters. At least Scott had successfully completed that requirement—and without trying.

"So," he said, turning the car around. The car's headlights panned across the side of the community hall, pulling details from the white-washed bricks, exaggerating the pits and crevices of the mortar. The glare of the chalky colored wall contrasted painfully with the black night. He seemed not to notice, for he was starting to his right, looking for traffic along the High Street. He eased the car into the street and said, "Where are we sleuthing? And whom are we sleuthing? You have a lead on that stranger? Is it connected to the case?"

"It's a case, all right," I said, indicating that Scott should turn right. I told him of Graham's suggestion, adding that I wanted to know where he was going.

"I know you won't listen to me when I suggest you drop this," he said, slowing for a traffic light. "You're going to keep at this and drive yourself into the psych ward, aren't you?"

"Just shut up and drive."

"Okay. Ignore the best medical advice, then."

"You're not a physician, or doesn't your job suggest that?"

"Metaphorically speaking, Brenna. You ought to put in for a holiday. I've got mine inked in and approved. It's already helping, just thinking about my to month away from here."

"*A month!* I know you've been saving up the weeks, but I never dreamed it was a month. Where you going to again?"

"Las Vegas."

"Say no more. Poker tournament, right?"

Even in the relative darkness of the car, I could see Scott's grin. I was surprised his jaw didn't break. "Best relaxation and fun in the world. Nothing to do but play day and night."

"Sounds like an addiction. What got you hooked on gambling?"

"It's *not* gambling!" he said, forced horror in his voice. "Gambling is the slots or blackjack or baccarat, which the house can control and therefore make their money from. To win any of those, it's pure luck, for it's 51-85% stacked *against* the player. The house doesn't control poker—that's pure talent. Gambling..." He snorted, glancing at me. "I can't believe you said that. Poker is *skill*. It's reading people, and that's *incredible* fun."

"Sounds like what you do all day long on the job."

"That's why I'm so damned good at poker!" He laughed, turning his face toward me, his eyes alight.

"Well, just so you don't bet the homestead and lose, Scott."

"No chance of that."

"The bet or the losing?"

"What do you think?"

He hardly ever lost. It was that ability to read people, to remember the cards the players had bet and their histories of betting in each game that made Scott a winner. He was incredibly formidable at the table.

"So," he said, breaking the silence, "where are we going? Would you give me a hint? I assume Graham said something so we don't have to drive around Derbyshire. It's a rather large place."

"He didn't say," I admitted, silently cursing Graham. "But I've a good hunch."

"Oh, yes? Where?"

"One of three places, I think."

"Only three? That shouldn't take us past midnight."

"What a wag you are. I'd have been better off with Margo."

"Margo hasn't my tailing technique."

"What 'tailing' are we doing? I don't even see Graham's car!"

Scott raised his index finger. "Ah, but we may. And that's where I shine. Tailing the suspect, keeping observation while blending unnoticed into the background."

"Yeh, well, you may have to practice some other time. He's nowhere in sight."

"So, where am I headed? What three likely spots are contenders for the scene of your crime?"

"If he's hurried off for his postponed date, he'll either be at that chic-chic restaurant Bovary's, or at his place—" I swallowed, turning my head toward the window so Scott wouldn't see me closing my eyes in a swift prayer. *He wouldn't do that, would he? They weren't that far along in their relationship that he would cook dinner for her...* I turned back to Scott, pretending to cough, and said rather quickly, "or The Pearl Onion."

"That pub in Bakewell? Hardly. He'd do it up proper if he's trying to impress her. Why not dinner at *her* place, while you're tossing out Places of Interest? What's wrong if she cooks for him?"

"Nothing," I muttered, sagging into the corner between the front seat and the door and silently prayed for a well-lit, public place as their dating objective. Houses slipped past, giving way to the grandeur of the dales and mountains of the Peak district while I sat mute, my mind supplying vivid details of my rival. I'd just progressed to the good night kiss when Scott cooed, "Coral, you may now go to the head of the class."

"What?"

He smiled, tapping on the windscreen. "Two cars up ahead. Your heart's desire."

I sat up, leaning forward. All I could see was the car immediately in front of us, and the dark mountains flitting by. "Are you sure? How do you know?"

"When we came up to the traffic lights in Bakewell, we were right behind Graham's car."

"We're not now," I said. "What happened?"

"O-level Tailing, Brenna. You can't successfully shadow your person if you stick to him like a tattoo to an arm. You've got to give him some space. Otherwise, he'll spot you and change course, and you'll have lost your objective target plus shown yourself to him. When we turned onto the A619 I let a few cars pass me."

"You know for sure it's him?"

"How many red Insights *are* there around here? Besides, it's his number plate. I know it. So..." he said, patting my hand, "you get top marks for Deduction. Looks like it's Bovary's. You ever been there?"

I shook my head. "On *my* wage? You've got to be joking."

"Granted. But that doesn't preclude a date of your own."

I let the silence fall between us as I remembered a postponed date from my probationary days. It had been with Erik. He had made reservations at

Jo A. Hiestand

Bovary's. Only it had never materialized. A string of late evening call-outs, a bout of flu and his subsequent transfer had ended our brief fling. Maybe we could take up where we'd left off, have our missed date. Nothing romantic; just a very nice evening to cement our friendship. I leaned forward and peered through the windscreen, afraid Graham would turn off and Scott wouldn't notice.

Or, worse. What would Graham do if he spotted us on his tail? Would we receive a verbal reprimand, a written report on our conduct—'misconduct to a member of the Force'— or worse? Would I lose what I could loosely call a friendship? Friendship...could the relationship with him now be called a friendship?

I was about to tell Scott to turn around, that I was afraid what would happen if Graham recognized us. But Scott's tailing skills were excellent, and Graham had no idea we had followed him. We were only five cars behind Graham as he parked outside Bovary's restaurant. I sank down in the car seat, shading my face, and watched Graham slam his car door, lock it and run across the street.

CHAPTER NINETEEN

"You want to continue surveillance, I take it," Scott said, looking for a parking place near the restaurant.

I pointed to a vacant spot a few cars ahead of Graham's and said, "I have to know, Scott. I know it's snooping and digging into his private life, everything I detest, but—"

"But you're dying to know. Right. Give me a minute to park this baby."

My heart beat faster than I had ever felt it, threatening to explode if we sat here a minute longer. As soon as Scott had shoved the gear lever into first and set the hand brake, I was out of the car and dodging traffic in my rush across the street. Scott jogged up to me a few seconds later, commenting on my death wish.

"Chesterfield isn't Oldfield," he said. "Traffic fatalities are higher here, I suspect."

"Come on." I had my hand on the restaurant's door handle when Scott said, "You're about to get Lesson Two in O-level Tailing, Bren. Once your quarry has arrived, don't blunder in on him. Survey the terrain, decide what cover is available, still maintain your camouflage, then sidle inside. Any potted palms in there?" He leaned his forehead against the glass in the door, shielding his eyes from the street lamp, and looked inside. "Never a potted palm or shrub or elephant to hide behind when you need one."

"There's a coat rack in the foyer," I said, joining him in his surveillance. "Complete with coats. Any good?"

"Not unless you want us arrested on suspicion of theft. The maitre d' will think we're suspicious characters if we stand among the coats—especially if there are any furs—for any length of time."

"A stretch in the nick might do you good. Give you some sympathy for the bloke who's been charged."

"The only sympathy I have right now is with *me*. It's damned cold out here, or are you too flushed with victory to feel anything?"

I *was* warm, and I could feel the heat in my cheeks, but I wasn't going to admit it. I was embarrassed enough by this entire incident, but sometimes a woman's got to plow ahead, regardless of what others think. Besides, Scott wasn't going to tell anyone. My emotions and secret were as secure as if lodged inside the Bank of England.

"So," Scott said, clearing his throat. "Shall we sidle? Wait!" He grabbed my jacket sleeve as I was about to open the door. "A good tailer knows what he's walking into before he walks. As I said, case the joint before you blunder in. What do you prefer as cover—the wine bottle, the skinny hostess, or the table leg?"

I sniffed. "Doesn't seem to be a lot to choose from, does there? I suppose if we went in with our jackets pulled over our heads...no. It'd look too much like a hold-up. Then Graham *really* would notice us when the panda cars arrive. And if we get into line pretending to wait for a table..." I could feel my pulse racing. I tilted back my head, looking into Scott's eyes. "You can't see anything, I suppose, you being taller..."

"By 'anything,' you mean Graham and Co. Nary a recognizable face. Without that potted palm—"

I turned to leave. "Maybe this isn't such a good idea. Sorry I wasted your time, Scott."

"Never give up, Bren. Look."

As the hostess returned from seating a family, Graham and a woman stepped into view. They had been obscured from our vision by the L-shaped wall at right angles to the door. Now that the family had been shown to their table, Graham and his date were next in line. I know I clutched Scott's arm in a near-death grip, but he didn't yell out. He had no desire to blow our cover now that the quarry was sighted.

Graham was the gentleman I had occasionally glimpsed during our working lunches and dinners. He held the chair for her and draped her coat over the chair back before taking his own seat. His smile was as good as any fashion model's—perhaps better. He must have said something witty, for the blonde laughed, throwing her head back so that her long hair swung over her shoulders.

Yes, she was a blonde. Need I say more? Drop-dead gorgeous, long legs, thin.

I have no idea how long I stood staring at them. Scott, perhaps being a friend and not wanting to punctuate my jealousy, later told me it had been one minute. Good thing he hadn't been under oath. I couldn't have run through my feelings of envy and resentment and spite and despair in only one minute. I do remember, however, my peripheral vision darkening and shutting down, and Graham and Miss Gorgeous shimmering as though spotlighted or seen at the end of a long, dark tunnel. I heard nothing but the frequent, silvery tones of her laugh and the occasional response of Graham's deep chuckle. I know I shouldn't have been there, but I felt incapable of moving. I was like a druggie, craving another fix, knowing that it was killing me, yet unable to abstain. Eventually, Scott's voice filtered in through Graham's and Miss G's imagined conversation, and I blinked wildly at him, not knowing what he had said. He repeated it.

"I said, let's go. This isn't doing anything for you but making you miserable."

"I'm not—"

"Miserable? Then why the tears?" He tracked down my cheek with his index finger, then held it out for me to see. It was wet. He took my hand and blotted my fingers against my skin. As I stared at my damp fingertips, he said, "Evidence. Indisputable. As I said—miserable. Now, let's go." He turned, pulling my arm, and led me to his car.

He must have opened the car door, seated me, and buckled my seat belt. I remember very little of the return trip to Oldfield except my anguish and breaking heart. A thousand scenes kaleidoscoped through my imagination, a thousand laughs thundered in my ears. When Scott patted my hand, I awoke to the present. We were in the pub's car park.

I turned to him, thanked him and opened the door. His hand shot out, grabbing mine, and halted my departure. When I met his gaze, his eyes flashed in anger.

"Don't do anything," he said, his low voice matching his irritation.

"Don't *do* anything..." I repeated, confused.

"Just what I said. *Don't do anything.* Don't resign, don't ask for a transfer, don't take too many sleeping tablets, don't swear off men, don't put in for sick leave, don't forget meals, don't lose sleep. He isn't worth it."

I opened my mouth, wanting to respond, but my astonishment at how exactly Scott had read my emotions stopped me. I closed it again and glanced out the window, my lips quivering. I fought back the tears I knew would soon break forth. The warmth from Scott's hand flowed into mine, making me feel at least partly alive.

He said, "I mean it, Bren. Don't do anything stupid. If you do, by God I'll track you down in your miserable hole and drag you out by your hair and force you to sit in the sunshine."

"Bully," I said, trying to lighten the atmosphere. But Scott's lowered eyebrows and set jaw conveyed the promise behind his words. He would do it. He might joke about police problems, his receding hairline and a recent incarceration of an old age pensioner, but he was serious about this. I shook off his hand and got out. Before I closed the car door, I said, "You needn't waste your O-level skills on me, Scott. I'm fine."

"You're fine and tomorrow I'm being promoted to Divisional Commander." He tilted his head and eyed me. The lights from the pub must have illuminated my face, for he said, "You look like you're ready for a good cry. If that'll get him out of your system, fine. Go at it. But don't do anything else."

I slammed the door, waved over my shoulder, and walked toward the pub. I barely heard the car tires turning on the gravel.

MY LUCK WAS still running to bad as I met Margo upstairs in the hallway. She shoved her room key into her slacks pocket and hurried over as I unlocked my door. "So," she said, following me inside my room and closing the door, "where have you been? I was waiting up to have a nightcap with you, but I couldn't find you. Did you and Mark have your date?"

"I wish I had," I said, tossing the room key and my shoulder bag onto the bed. "The whole evening might have turned out better. I'd definitely be feeling better, at any rate."

It was the wrong thing to say, for Margo pushed aside my nightgown and sat down on the edge of the bed. She leaned forward, her eyes bright with interest. "Why? What happened? Where were you? Interviewing someone?"

"The only 'someone' I interviewed was myself," I said, taking off my jacket and dropping it on top of the dresser. "And that was a fiasco."

"What *are* you talking about?"

"Oh, nothing. It's not important. The world still revolves. The birds still sing. The flowers still bloom."

"I'm not leaving until you tell me, Bren, so open up. Give."

I sank into the chair opposite the bed and studied my hand. The red mark from Scott's fingers was still visible. At least that was a reality in my nightmare. "Okay," I finally said, looking up at Margo. Her face was alive with interest. I took a deep breath, then told her of the restaurant episode, finishing with my confusion of emotions.

Margo was silent for so long that I thought she'd not been listening. When I started to get up, she murmured, "You know, Bren, you've just been given a gift."

I stopped, frowning. "How the hell do you figure that? I've just been kicked in the stomach, slapped in the face, strong-armed in public, and forced to view a nauseous spectacle. If that's your idea of a gift, take me off your Christmas list."

"You know what I mean, Bren. Stop feeling sorry for yourself and look at tonight's little play."

"I've a right to feel sorry for myself, Margo. My heart's just broken. Or have you forgotten about you and Angus so quickly?"

"I haven't forgotten. He rears his ugly head sporadically in my nightmares. But this is about *you*. And Graham. *Your* hurt. And how you're going to deal with it. You can't let it possess you, Bren. You've got a smashing career ahead of you. You can't jeopardize that because your boss had supper with some trollop."

"She wasn't a trollop. Just drop-dead gorgeous."

"Whatever. You don't know who she was, or why she was with Graham. She could've been a friend or a business connection."

"Friends don't look like that," I muttered, remembering her slinky dress and bare shoulders. "And don't give me the sister routine. No one has such a sister."

"Someone might. At least she's a daughter. God, you're thick as two planks. Give me some slack!"

I leaned forward, my heart pounding. "Give *me* some, then! *I'm* the one who's been slapped. *I'm* the one whose soul is dying. *I'm* the one whose dreams have just been dragged through the mud and destroyed. Or don't I rank as a human being or deserve any consideration?"

"You know you do. And when you stop feeling like 'poor me' you'll realize this is not the mountain you're creating. So he had dinner with someone. So it wasn't you. Maybe next time it *will* be you. Maybe Miss Epitome of Grace and Loveliness is a friend of a friend. Maybe she's some colleague he's talking to concerning this case. You don't know."

"Not from the way they laughed, she wasn't."

"Okay. Fine. Build it into the romance of the century. But you've either got to put this behind you or act on it."

"I thought I was acting on it. I'm angry and hurt and—"

"God, Bren. I mean 'act' as in take action. Either shove this to the back of your mind, steel your back and stiffen your upper lip—you know, suffer silently until you can get over it. Or you do something about it."

"Like murder?"

"I won't ask who the victim will be."

"Either guess will get you a prize."

"So, channel your anger and hurt into action. That's a lot of energy you're wasting. Change it into motivation for a different combat. You'll feel better because you're doing something positive."

"Like what?"

"Well," she said, lifting the hem of my nightgown, "the old stand-by."

"You're serious?" I said, not knowing if Margo were ridiculing me or the situation.

"If you want to fight for him..."

I stood up and yanked the garment away from her. Holding it to my chest, I said, "You *aren't* serious. You have only to look at me and then look at Miss Perfect. I haven't a chance! We're complete opposites. I'm short, she's tall; I'm fat, she's thin; I'm a redhead, she's a blonde; I'm old, she's—"

"So he's robbing the cradle, which I doubt. All that's just an outward shell, Bren. No person 'is' her body. That's not what makes an individual the person she is. It's the being within the skin, the soul and goodness and humor and personality and intellect and morals that combine to make you who you are. And for all her—or any other woman's—outward beauty, *your* soul and talent and intellect and humor shine through your eyes and speech and actions. People see that. They sense the affections that make you who you are. And that's no small thing in this world crammed with greedy, selfish nerks."

"You forgot 'kindness,'" I said, remembering Mark's harassment during our training school days. "I'm very kind to animals."

Margo stood up. "I know you're hurting. It's fine to wallow in grief for a day or two, but don't you dare drown in it or I'll kick your backside so hard you'll plead to be Scott's sparing partner next self-defense training session. Got it?" She glared at me, defying me to contradict her.

I nodded, not trusting my voice. I hugged the nightgown, then murmured, "But no one gets to know you that way, Margo. Not at first. Guys are attracted to beauty. How will anyone ever know me if he's stopped by my body?"

"Mark knows you and likes you. So does Scott."

"Mark likes me as a possible bed partner. Scott's married."

"So? That doesn't deter Scott from caring about you, liking you as a very good friend. And Mark has definitely changed in the past two months, Bren. You've got to admit that."

Margo was right. He had changed. I recalled the dog incident in December, the concern he'd expressed about my safety, the talks we'd had last month at his parents' home. I dropped my head, letting the tears fall. They dripped onto my shirt and the pajamas I still clutched.

"I know you want someone in your life," Margo said, handing me a facial tissue. "Everyone does. You want to feel special and loved. You want to give the love *you* have. I know how it feels—it's bottled within you, about to burst if you can't shower it on someone. It'll come, Bren. You just haven't found the right bloke yet. Erik might be it, he might not. Hang on a bit longer. It'll come."

Margo slipped out of the room as I sank onto the bed, wishing Calhoun, my cat, was purring on my lap. I needed something warm and loving to cling to. So, when did admiration become love? Was I merely respecting Graham for those qualities that I valued so highly? Was I just clinging to him because I was feeling lonely? Surely there were other fellows who had those attributes. Why was I so desperately pursuing Graham?

SOMETIME LATER, WHEN I had wakened in the darkness, curled into a fetal position and still clutching my night clothes, I stared out of the window. The moon had risen and broken through the bank of clouds. Stars, tossed like a handful of confetti, winked between the tangle of tree branches. Two cats vocalized their grievances before a yelping dog broke it up. Beyond the village, perhaps on Piebold Tor, a heavy lorry groaned its way up a mountainous road. I listened for several minutes until the engine's noise faded into the quiet. The world outside seemed normal. I fixed my eyes on the moon and wished with all my heart that I could feel normal. That I could take Margo's advice and drop my pursuit of Graham. But the heart did not obey the mind. And until I could talk some sense into myself, I was afraid it would be a while until I could function normally. I was also afraid Graham would 'read' me next morning and learn my secret.

CHAPTER TWENTY

IF IT WEREN'T so serious, the phrase 'saved by the bell' would come to mind. I was saved my fear of Graham reading the emotions surely etched on my face when the phone in the incident room rang first thing the next morning. I was holding my cup of tea when Graham walked into the room and mouthed 'good morning' as I answered the phone. It was Scott. I braced myself for a barrage of friendly advice that never came. Instead, he managed in two words to turn my focus from my heart to my job.

"Sibyl's dead," he said. Short. Succinct. No preliminary to soften the blow. Like my sister announcing our aunt's death. Waste no time, for time was precious. But only for the living. And the grieving.

I gulped in a lungful of air, then stammered, "Wh—how? When? Where are you?"

Scott's voice bore into my ear, giving me the skeletal details. "Swinton Hall. The bell tower. Time of death et al are up to you and Jens Nielsen. I'm just the uniformed informant."

At the mention of the Home Office pathologist's name, I stopped envisioning Sibyl's face.

"Bren?" Scott said, his voice insistent, drawing me back mentally to the incident room. "You all right? You've gone all silent—"

"Yes," I lied. "I'm fine. It's just—"

"A shock. Yes. I've got the tower secure. I'm standing guard, as it were, with Fordyce. Nothing else I can do until you and the Vic get here." At least he didn't refer to Graham as Lover Boy.

"Right." I paused, glancing at the clock above the door. There wasn't much else for Scott to do. The tower was still cordoned off due to Roger's death. All Scott could do was secure the scene inside and wait for help. I turned to Graham, who was leafing through his case notes. He looked like the by-product of a super evening—well-groomed hair, smoothly shaved, after-shave lotion, smiling and humming a snatch of Gilbert and Sullivan's "When a Felon's Not Engaged in his Employment." At least it wasn't Mendelssohn's "Wedding March." His left hand toyed with his mobile phone on the table, spinning it idly as he read. Was he waiting for a phone call from Miss Gorgeous? I angled my body, leaning on the edge of the table so I couldn't see him, and spoke to Scott. "Any hint of a weapon? Anyone know what happened? Is she alone?"

"Good. You're back to normal."

I was going to say something rather rude when he added, "You better see for yourself. I'm not a tec. Not that I can't tell someone's dead. A headless torso is a dead giveaway, but..." There was silence. I could almost see him shrugging. He said, "Not that Sibyl is. Just an example. Not a good thing to say. Sorry." I could hear the blush in his words of apology. "I hope Graham includes me on the team. It's too damned quiet. I want something to do."

"That's good. Quiet means no one's in trouble, Scott. You want your day filled with chasing after bad guys?"

"I only meant that I hate Saturday mornings. All the troublemakers from Friday nights' drinking binges are quietly sleeping it off. Nothing's happening. Dull...beyond boredom. When are you coming over?"

"How does 'immediately' sound?"

He was still chuckling as I hung up.

Graham did not look up from his notes but said, "Who was that? It sounded official, from the questions you asked."

I was past being astonished. I'd learned months ago that Graham could simultaneously read and listen to a conversation while garnering the information from both. I pocketed my phone and said, "It was Scott Coral."

"He's out early. What's happening?"

As I related the information, Graham closed his case folder and stood up. "*Another* death? That makes two in three days. At the same location." He stopped short of saying it was fishy. He didn't need to. His eyes said it. Glancing at his watch, he said, "Right. So much for a leisurely morning. Who have we got?" He looked around the room, saw Mark, Byrd and a few other constables, and ordered them to Swinton Hall. He asked me to phone up Jens Nielsen and the scientific officers, and grabbed his mobile to request the video team stationed at Ripley. Then he called our office and talked to Simcock. As detective superintendent, it officially was Simcock's case. But as senior investigating officer at the scene, as it were, Graham was already here. Besides, Simcock rarely showed up, preferring to view the video and still camera photographs. He symbolically held the reins, but Graham wielded the shovel.

When he'd finished, he said, "Simcock turned it over to me. Why are we not surprised?" He flashed a smile before turning serious. "What else? Oh, Lynch!" Graham called to Margo as she came into the room.

"Yes, sir?" Margo walked over to us, avoiding looking at me.

When Graham had relayed the information, he said, "I'd like you to work on Geneva's valentine's case. Would you mind? We can't let that fall by the wayside. Not because she's Lady Swinbrook. Because she's a woman being harassed and stalked." He meant it. Rank did not impress him. He would treat Geneva and a derelict equally, polite and patient with each.

PEARLS BEFORE SWINE

She nodded, stepped aside to let him pass, and winked at me as I fell in beside him. At least she refrained from speaking about our late night chat.

SIBYL GRIFFITHS WAS lying on the ringing chamber floor at the foot of the ladder that led upwards to the clock and bell rooms. Exactly where Roger had been found Wednesday evening. I stood beside the doorway leading down to the ground floor, hugging the stonewall, needing its massive support to hold me up. The scene played out in that odd déjà vu I'd witnessed many times but that was now beginning to haunt me. Hadn't we just done this very thing three days ago? Hadn't Roger, Lord Swinbrook, been in exactly this same place and position? I glanced at the white paper work suits that the crime team wore, the photographic lamps, the officers measuring and photographing and noting. It was too eerie for me to take comfort in the words I always whispered to myself—we would find her killer, we would bring her justice. But as I stared at her, I couldn't help but think that Roger's death had been a rehearsal for this one, that perhaps the murderer had got the wrong victim at first.

I was spared further ghoulish speculation when Graham called me over to the ladder. I slowly approached, stopping about a meter from the body.

"Remind you of anything?" he asked. He had donned the work suit, shoe covers and latex gloves and squatted beside Sibyl, who was clothed in jeans, Manchester United football jersey, denim jacket and once-white trainers.

My voice spoke from somewhere far away. "His lordship."

"Jens will confirm all this, of course…" His voice trailed off.

If it had been a death that hadn't looked at all suspicious, our police surgeon, Karol Mattox, would have been called in. But because Sibyl was found in the same spot as we had found Roger and under similar circumstances as Roger, Graham called for Jens, the Home Office pathologist, to take charge of the body and the subsequent postmortem examination. I murmured Graham's statement.

He sighed and added, "By the position of Sibyl's body—the sprawled arms and legs, the neck and head at this obtuse angle, and the blood pooled beneath her nose—" At least there wasn't the large splatter of blood as we'd seen with Roger's murder.

"She fell."

Graham looked up at me, no trace of last night's lightness in his face. "Two deaths by falling?"

"Roger's was murder. I don't want to think that Sibyl—"

Graham stood up and stared at the teenager. "What a waste. What a damned waste of a young life." He swore silently, expressing grief more than anger. "Why the hell was she here? We've got the tower cordoned off, a constable at the outside door…" He stepped back and angled his head slightly to look at the trap door in the ceiling. It was open. Occasional flashes of light from police lamps spilled onto the top rungs of the ladder.

Graham talked to the structure. "How'd she get in? If that constable was asleep or off to get a beer—"

"I expect there's some other explanation, sir," I said, drawing Graham's gaze back to me. "Peters is reliable."

"He *has* been, yes. So that leaves some other explanation as to Sibyl's presence."

"I'd like to investigate. Yes, sir. I don't mean the death proper, but the tower. As you said, she has to have got here somehow. And if we take Peters on past performance, with never a black mark against him, well, we're stuck with discovering how Sibyl got here."

"We are indeed, Taylor. So, if the outside door was locked and our vigilant bobby was vigilant, there's another access to this area. I don't suppose she could have sneaked a key from her mum." He cocked an eyebrow, asking for my vote.

"Well, sir, Mona *does* work here, being a maid at the hall. But would she have a key to the bell tower?"

"Maybe not, but she knows where all the household keys are." He bent over the girl, gingerly felt her clothes, then straightened up. "No key. Nothing in her pockets and no string around her neck. Perhaps it's in her back pocket. Hell. It'll have to wait. I don't like to shift the body before Jens seen it."

I nodded. "Shift in lividity."

Graham smiled. "We may have hard enough work on this without deliberately doing a cock-up. So, no key. I repeat—how'd she get in?"

We shed our paper suits outside the tower door and stuffed them into a bin placed there specifically for that. Graham called Peters over from his station just outside the police tape and asked about his shift.

Peters, a youngster in police experience but seasoned in human emotions, was a walking bear—tall, hefty and purposeful. He emphatically swore that he had never left his post. "Not for a second, sir. I walked about a bit. You know, to warm up and keep the circulation in my feet going. But I never had the front door out of my sight. I was either walking parallel to the door, standing with my back at the door, or standing watching the door. There is no way on God's green earth that that young lady could have slipped into the tower by this door without me knowing."

I could believe that. The gravel car park on the west side of the tower dwindled to a three-person wide pathway that wound past the tower and up to the hall. Even if Sibyl had hugged the tower's wall and come on tiptoes, the gravel would have announced her approach. Coming by way of the grass was not realistic for, to get to the tower door, she would have had to jump the six-foot wide gravel path. Which, while not impossible, was slightly ludicrous, for Constable Peters would have seen her. No. There had to be another means of tower entry.

I was just about to go over to Scott, who was leaning against his police car and making a note of who entered at what time, when PC Peters said, "I let PC Coral into the tower, though, this morning, if that means anything, sir."

Graham's eyebrow raised in interest. "Oh? When was this?"

"Eight o'clock, sir. I know because I was looking for my relief. I thought Fordyce was coming over for that, but Coral showed up instead. He walked up to the front door of the hall, went inside for a moment, then returned here and entered the tower by this door. I don't know why he went inside, but it wasn't five minutes later when he came out, his face gone all white. I thought he was gonna puke, but he didn't. He recovered quickly, walked over to that bench—" He indicated the wooden bench that Geneva had sat on after finding Roger's body. "—Took out his mobile, and rang up someone. I assume it was you, sir, since you're here." Having finished his account, he waited at ease, arms clasped behind his back, feet apart, and waited for Graham's verdict.

"Thank you, constable. Very succinct account." Graham turned around, saw Scott next to his car, and motioned me to join him.

Scott stood up as we approached and waited for Graham to speak.

"Would you tell me about discovering the body this morning, Coral? I understand you went to the tower after visiting the hall."

"Yes, sir," Scott said, abandoning his note-taking. "I was called to the hall by Lady Swinbrook. I wasn't inside more than two minutes. She wanted me to go into the tower's ringing chamber and look for his lordship's Rolex."

"His *watch*?" Graham said, clearly surprised. "Why? The crime scene lads have already been through it, anyhow. Why did she think it was there?"

"She thought Roger had removed it prior to ringing Wednesday evening. She wants it for the funeral, to bury with him. She can't find it, so she thought I—"

"Didn't you tell her the room, the whole ruddy tower, in fact, had already been searched and that we didn't find it?"

"Yes, sir." Scott had lost a bit of his color, whether from Graham's questions or from remembering Sibyl's body. But he didn't look as hearty as he usually did. He said, "But her ladyship was so insistent and was crying...well, I didn't see what harm it would do. Not if I or another officer went in. I mean, well, since the SOs have already been through it..." He broke off, looking at Graham for sentencing.

Graham exhaled deeply, seeming to consider Scott's statement and, perhaps, Geneva's request. To anyone outside the job, it might have looked bad for Scott, perhaps even put him on the suspect list if it turned out Sibyl was murdered. But police officers know each other. They work together daily, under intense pressure—a recipe for thoroughly knowing a person. Scott would no more have killed Sibyl than the sun would rise in the west.

Graham must have thought so too, for he said rather slowly, "Right. A bit out of the ordinary lines of procedure, but no harm done. I'm glad you looked for the watch. Not that the SOs would have overlooked it

Wednesday evening, but because Geneva can now hunt somewhere else." He shook his head as though trying to understand the murders, the missing watch, the feuding neighbors and the hateful valentines. "What a bloody mess this all is. Well, thank you, Coral. I'm sure Geneva appreciates your effort. So do I, on or off the record."

I gave Scott a wink, then waited with him as Graham answered his ringing mobile. I watched another group of scientific officers search the perimeter of the tower both inside and outside the crime scene tape, afraid to talk to Scott in case he mentioned my reaction to Graham's date. I watched a squirrel scamper up to an oak bough, sit, position his stolen acorn at just the right angle, and begin eating. His tail, fluffed up from the cold, twitched and jerked as he ate, perhaps staking his claim to this prized possession.

When Graham had rung off from his call, he said, "For what it's worth, Ben's coworkers have been questioned and each one swears Ben was working the night of Roger's murder. The owner of the restaurant and the waiters were also questioned, and while they weren't in the kitchen every moment, they also agree Ben was there. So that eliminates him from our suspect list, doesn't it?"

I said that, short of bribing everyone to give him an alibi, it looked like it. "But someone doesn't have an alibi," I added.

"We'll find it. Just as we'll find out who killed Sibyl. Good, here's Jens. You certainly got here quickly." Graham stepped forward, welcoming Jens Nielsen with an eagerness I rarely saw.

"Believe it or don't," he said, shifting his work case to his left hand, "I was in the area. So I put my Saturday morning chores on hold and trotted on over. What have we got, then—*exactly*, I mean?"

When Graham told him of the suspicions we had about Sibyl's death and the location of the body, Jens blinked rapidly and said, "You've got to be joking."

"Wish I were. Whether we've assumed incorrectly and it turns out *not* to be murder doesn't lighten the fact that she's dead. It's a tragedy whatever it turns out to be."

"Well, let's see, shall we? At least you can get on with your case, if it becomes one." He nodded to Scott, suited up in a paper work suit, and disappeared into the tower. Graham and I followed more leisurely and stayed just outside the doorway to the ringing chamber.

Jens did his usual stuff—preliminary physical examination, sketches made, and notes and photos taken of the body's position and its environs. He took his own photographs merely as a job aid, not because it implied he thought Dean's photos weren't up to his standard. Graham and I watched from the sidelines, having seen it already and also wanting to give Jens room to work. But Graham *did* ask Jen if Sibyl's shoelaces were tied.

"Yes," Jens said, turning around and looking at Graham. "Why?"

"Just wondering."

PEARLS BEFORE SWINE

"I can be more accurate at the PM, but I'd say off hand she's been dead eight to ten hours."

"Thanks, Jens," Graham said. "She's all yours. I'd like the report as soon as possible, if it's not an imposition."

"Anything else you want? £10,000 raise, holiday in New Zealand, date with Gwyneth Paltrow..."

Which he already had done—or nearly so. Last night's Miss Amazing looked enough like any star or fashion model to satisfy that dream. Did Jens know about Graham's girlfriend? Was that a shared, coded joke that the lads would laugh about in the men's loo? I'd have to ask somehow without appearing interested.

Graham said something I couldn't catch, turned around and asked a scientific officer if she'd mind climbing the ladder.

"No, sir," Beth said, obviously surprised. She was of average build, a brunette who wouldn't stand out in a crowd. But her observation skills *were* outstanding, as she had previously proved. I doubted if any atom of evidence ever escaped her examination. She paused at the foot of the ladder, glanced toward the hatchway in the ceiling, and said, "What am I looking for?"

"Cause of an accident. Uneven floorboard above. Loose ladder rung, perhaps."

"Right, sir." Beth carefully, slowly ascended the ladder, her hand gripping, yanking, twisting each rung in turn as she climbed. At the top, though, she stopped and appeared to be studying something minutely. When she eventually turned to Graham, her face had darkened and her neck muscles had tightened. It did not look good.

"You've found something, then," Graham said.

"Yes, sir. At least, it screams of suspicious circumstances, I'll say."

"Your ears are as good as anyone's. Let's have it."

"Well, sir, there are remnants of what may be a nylon fishing line. There's a tiny bit tied around a screw head on the ladder uprights next to the ceiling opening, and opposite that..." Her voice faded for a moment while she turned to inspect the other piece of lumber. Roger had installed two wooden posts on either side of the ceiling opening to function as handrails, making ascending or descending the ladder easier. Though I had yet to climb the ladder or see the bell chamber above, PC Byrd had told me it was a simple matter to grab a post and pull himself up as he left the ladder and stepped onto the floor. Same thing would prove true as one climbed down, grabbing the post to steady oneself as you left the floor and placed your foot on the ladder's top rung. So now, as the scientific officer explained, it appeared to have been booby-trapped. She continued. "This opposite upright has what looks like fresh tool marks gouged into the wood. I'll know more when I've looked at it properly. That what you want, sir?"

"As though a screwdriver missed the screw head in the rush to raise the screw," Graham mused aloud. He nodded, perhaps seeing the scenario play out in his mind. "To affix the nylon line to it. Nice way to trip someone up. Literally. Thank you."

Beth pulled an evidence bag from her worksuit pocket and started the process of bagging the fishing line.

"Well," Graham said, taking a deep breath and gazing at the entrance into the ceiling. "It's a bit surprising, but it did the job."

"You talking about the line, sir?"

"Yes. A bit of a risk, rigging that up. It wasn't there for Roger's death. The lads combed these two rooms. They would have found it."

"So someone sneaked in here—probably the same way Sibyl got in—and ran the line across the uprights. Yes, it's murder, then."

Graham looked like he was about to be sick. His thumb and forefinger massaged the corners of his mouth while he stared at the ladder. He seemed to be considering something, for he was silent for perhaps a minute. When he spoke, his voice was very soft. "As risky as it was for the killer to sneak in here and string up that line, he probably felt it less a risk than pushing Sibyl off the ladder. He might have worried about postmortem findings such as a hand imprint or indications of a kick, suggesting Sibyl had been pushed."

"The nylon line's a safer weapon, I agree. After all, we can match a bruise to a specific shoe or boot."

"Plus," Graham went on, "maybe the killer didn't want to get that close to Sibyl. He might have deliberately stayed several feet from her, giving her a sense of security, perhaps, or perhaps he was afraid that if he did push her, she may have grabbed his leg in her attempt to keep from falling. He could have run the risk of being pulled down with her or been left with damning scratch marks. The ceiling hole is quite large. Big enough for two people, I should think, to fit through."

"Even in a fall, with arms and legs outstretched, it would still accommodate them. It wouldn't matter if an arm or head hit the edge of the opening before slipping through. What's a bruised arm or head when you're sprawled dead on the floor beneath?"

Graham shifted his gaze from the ceiling opening to the foot of the ladder, nodding at the possibility. Even if someone had been desperate or angry enough to kill, he may have still been wary or cowardly enough to avoid the physical contact of murder. A booby-trap was so much more impersonal.

"As much as I'd like to indulge right now in my boyhood fantasy of exploring castles, we first need to contact Sibyl's parents." He shook his head and glanced at his watch. "God, what a way to start their day. What a damned tragedy. Bloody hell." His eyes seemed to reach into my soul and reveal his pain, his belief of duty, his fear of injustice, his concern for the parents. I wanted to assure him it would work out well, with the killer behind bars, but I couldn't. I knew Graham's sense of righteousness and his apprehension of a botched case or jury acquittal. There was a lot that could go wrong with a case prior to and during a trial: local lawyers who excelled at courtroom antics and procuring bail; judges who were too old to sit on the bench and who mediated the trial on their personal life experiences of fifty years ago, not on the case evidence; evidence that got contaminated or incorrectly processed; police officers who lied or distorted the evidence to obtain convictions for the suspect. Graham, as the idealistic, former minister, had a hard time under such conditions accepting releases of accused suspects from custody.

"I could do it," I said, unable to break the gaze of his eyes. They flashed his anger and irritation. "I—I wouldn't mind. If you'd rather do something else…" I trailed off, suddenly embarrassed. I shouldn't be saying this. As the senior investigating officer, he should be directing the personnel. The room felt very confining and hot as I wondered what to say next.

"We'll both do it," he said, motioning toward the door. "Each time's as difficult as the last, and I'm never used to it, but I won't say no to your company. Since you offered."

I murmured that I wouldn't have suggested it if I hadn't wanted to, and preceded him from the tower.

BREAKFAST WAS ON the table but soon was forgotten as Graham told Sibyl's parents about their daughter's death. Mona collapsed on the couch, crying hysterically, while Ben pointed toward their front door and yelled for us to get out.

"Our leaving won't erase your daughter's death," Graham said, his low voice filling the room with a tone of concern and authority.

Ben closed his eyes, perhaps squeezing the sight of Sibyl's crumpled body from his mind. When he looked at us, his eyes held the wildness of a hunted stag. He motioned us to the couch but remained standing by the telly. A framed photo of Sibyl sat on top.

"When did you last see her?" Graham said, his pen ready for note taking.

I tried nonchalantly to lay my left hand on top of my right hand, to hide the white bandaging from sight. He was well aware of my burned, useless hand, just as he was well aware of my action. I gave it up and draped my left arm across the back of the couch, laying the bandage in plain view.

Mona was still crying, albeit more softly, so Ben answered. "Last night. When she went to bed. I heard her tell her mum good night at ten. That was when she came out of the bathroom. I'd seen her minutes before that, when she went in to brush her teeth. She wasn't in her pajamas, but many evenings she didn't change until after she'd finished in the bathroom. Friday and Saturday nights, she usually changed later—she liked to read a bit before getting into bed. I didn't see her this morning, but being Saturday, she sometimes sleeps late. I assumed she was still in bed or had already dressed and breakfasted and was out with friends."

"She have a particular friend she hangs out with, or did she have a date with someone?"

"How the hell do I know? I'm not her diary."

"No, but you're her father. I'd have thought that you'd know your daughter's friends, maybe what she had planned for the day."

"Well, think again." His neck muscles tightened, causing the tattoo to bulge. "I didn't see her all that much. If she wasn't in school or playing hockey or studying in her room, I was at work. Not that I wanted to be. But we've kinda got used to eating and having a home. *Someone* has to support the family."

"Your wife works."

"Aye, she does. But it takes the both of us to keep this house standing. Life isn't easy, despite so-called conveniences. You still have to do the bloody laundry, mow the lawn, wash the car, stop at the grocers..." His hand hovered above Sibyl's photo as though he were going to pick it up. Instead, he pushed it farther back.

"Do you mind if Sergeant Taylor looks in your daughter's room?"

"Why?"

"To see if anything's disturbed, missing. Signs of a break-in."

"You think someone broke the window and snatched her, like a kidnapping? You're daft, man! I've no money for a ransom payment. Everyone in Oldfield knows that. And what would be missing?"

"That's what I'd like Sergeant Taylor to discover, if you don't mind."

Ben sighed and waved me to the hallway. "Go on. First bedroom."

"I'd like you or your wife," I said, "to accompany me."

"Why? You gonna steal something?"

"You would know if something's not there. A purse, piggy bank, suitcase..."

"She wouldn't run away. She wasn't the sort. She had no reason to."

"We need to know, sir. Teenagers can be very secretive. Something may have been bothering her. She may have left to spend the night with a girlfriend to talk about something. Girls do that, confide in a best friend."

I'd never skipped out at night, but I'd bent many a friend's ear with boyfriend problems and in discussions of the future. And, if I admitted it, I was doing the same thing now with Margo. It was good therapy, as long as you didn't pick the wrong friend. "If Sibyl's nightgown is gone—"

"Right." Ben angled the photo toward the wall. "Let's get it over with, then."

"If you'll just give me a moment to get some worksuits..." His verbal disbelief followed me from the house.

When we had suited up, we entered Sibyl's room. It smelled of lavender potpourri. Her likes were evident in the pastel color scheme and the animal posters plastering the walls. It was also evident that she was very neat, for everything was folded in dresser drawers or on shelves, or hung up in the wardrobe. Ben made a search, though I could tell he had little idea of what might be missing. His daughter's room obviously was not familiar territory.

"Does she keep a suitcase in her wardrobe?" I said, shoving aside dresses to peer at the floor.

PEARLS BEFORE SWINE

"She's not the sort to run away," he repeated, his voice quiet and heavy with sadness now that he was in her room.

"Doesn't have to be. She could have been at a friend's, like I said. Any clothes missing? Anything obvious, such as a favorite jacket you've seen her in?"

Ben searched methodically, pausing at each piece of clothing in the wardrobe. But when he'd examined the entire closet and the chest of drawers, he admitted he didn't know. "I gave her this for her last birthday," he said, picking up a silver necklace. It was nestled in a shallow ceramic bowl on her dresser, a square chain of delicate filigree work. A turquoise stone hung from the center of the necklace.

"Her birthstone, that," Ben said, fingering the pendant. "Twenty-fourth of December was her birthday. Right before Christmas. There's some as would combine Christmas with birthday celebration, but we never did. Mona was determined Sibyl should have two parties, just as any child would who had a birthday any other day of the year. She said it was worthy of a festivity in its own right. So we shoved aside Christmas Eve and had Sibyl's birthday party. I know Sibyl loved her mum all the more for that, for Mona loves Christmas Eve. But she loves her child more. She put Sibyl before her own feelings." He carefully coiled the necklace back into the bowl, taking his time, as though he were loath to break the tactile connection with his daughter. As he stared at it, I wondered if Sibyl's death would bring him and Mona closer together. A child's death should be the time to bond parents to each other, to give them someone to cling to. But so many times it drove them apart. Was it guilt or blame or inconsolable grief that led them to divorce?

I abandoned my speculation and returned with Ben to the living room. Mona was sitting up, drinking coffee and talking to Graham about Sibyl's childhood. I assumed he had played Mother and had got the coffee. Not that it mattered, but he was good at these soothing gestures.

As he drove us back to the incident room, I wished he would make a gesture and soothe *my* aching heart.

Jo A. Hiestand

CHAPTER TWENTY-ONE

"Hard to see clear fishing line at night," Graham said, when he had poured us both a cup of coffee.

We were seated at the table that held his laptop computer and printer, talking about Sibyl's death. The room buzzed with conversations and ringing phones. Outside, noises of passing cars and pedestrian traffic seeped in through the windows. An ordinary Saturday morning filled with an extraordinary occurrence.

"Yes, sir. Undoubtedly why the killer used it."

"If you're doing something nefarious such as burglary, and don't want to get caught, you don't turn on the overhead fixture and you don't shine your electric torch around."

Again I agreed and took a sip of coffee. What was coming next? "You think Sibyl was up there at night poking around? Why? Why not wait until the investigation is over and look at the scene of the crime, if that's what you're suggesting."

"Because someone coaxed her up there, TC. Someone who is frightened and needed to rid himself of possible threats from real or imagined quarters. Like a trusted confidant or a person he believes might figure out that he—or she—is our killer."

"And his name?"

"If I knew that, I'd be at his house right now. Any ideas?"

"I'd be able to tackle this a lot more logically and get better results, sir, if I knew how Sibyl got into the tower."

"And that, oddly enough, is the number one item on our list after the scientific officers leave. Great minds, TC. Were you any good at hide and seek as a child?"

"I believe they're still seeking me, sir."

Graham grinned and said, "We can start our investigation by concentrating on who might want Sibyl out of the way. Probably in conjunction with Roger's murder, since they share murder scenes and method."

"She and Roger had a lot of mutual friends and acquaintances. This isn't going to be so easy."

"First and most obvious, unfortunately, is her parents. Sibyl's mother works for Roger. Mona's a link between Roger and Sibyl."

"I don't know that Mona would kill her daughter, sir. I have the feeling that she really loved Sibyl."

"I don't doubt it. But there could be some reason we've yet to unearth that would drive her to kill Roger."

"And she'd then have to get rid of Sibyl if Sibyl found out. Okay. I don't really believe it, but it makes sense."

"Mona might not have wanted to murder Sibyl—remember the idea of the non-personal booby-trap—but the desire to save her own neck may have been stronger than paternal love."

I shrugged. "I grant you self preservation as a viable motive. Next?"

"Every member of Geneva's family." Graham laughed at my astonishment and jotted down their names. "I know. Brother Kirk, sister-in-law Noreen, nephew Lynn, her brother-in-law—Roger's brother—Austin..."

"They're all familiar with Roger and his daily routine. And with Sibyl, being Lynn's girlfriend..."

"Let's not forget either Geneva's ex, or her friend, Sharon. Being family friends, they could know what's going on within the hall."

I said, "And Roger's former business partner, Ed. Although he's more of a long shot, I think. Still, if he's kept up his friendship and knows Sibyl through seeing Mona at the hall..."

"Even in Geneva's immediate family," Graham said, "that's four people: Geneva and her direct kin. Plus Roger's brother and his fiancée, whom Sibyl knew." He shoved the notebook against the computer monitor. "Damn. We can't really eliminate anyone until we establish alibis and, perhaps more importantly, discover how Sibyl got into the tower, and learn who else knew about it."

"Obvious people would be the staff."

"Of which her mother, Mona, is one."

"So we're back to self preservation winning out over mother love as motive."

"Don't let it disillusion you, TC," Graham said, squeezing my good hand. "Not every female harbors that tender affection in her bosom."

I didn't say it, but I agreed. I'd seen too many women who had gone down for child abuse. "I'm wondering, sir, if Kirk knows about a passage."

"Why? Just throwing out family names?"

"No, sir. Not exactly." I told him about the time discrepancy when he had visited Geneva, then added, "I wonder if he could have been poking about, looking for a false panel or some such access to a hidden passage. It was a fairly safe thing to do. Roger's gone, so he wouldn't run into him. Geneva, he finds out from the maid who let him into the hall, was in her bed. There's no one else to discover his snooping. And even if a member of the household staff did see him wandering about, she wouldn't say anything.

It's not her place to." I echoed the maid's words, realizing how damning this looked.

"Where was he, indeed. I can't think of a plausible reason for his delinquency at his sister's side. I wonder if he kept to the first floor."

"There are probably back steps to the second floor. He could have rooted among the empty rooms up there, too. It doesn't take all that much time to knock on panels and poke at plaster fireplace decorations."

"It does, with the number of rooms the hall has. *And* if he wants to be sneaky about it, TC. He won't go stomping about on the floors or banging on the walls. That would make noise, and that would attract attention. And along with that, Geneva. Then he'd have to explain himself and give away his game."

I murmured that he'd probably be back and that we should plant Scott or Byrd around the estate to spy on him.

Graham's phone rang before he could comment, which was probably just as well. He grabbed his notebook, wrote down a few words, thanked the caller, and rang off. He stared at the paper before him as though thinking through his conversation, then looked at me. His light-hearted demeanor had vanished in that brief moment. "It's happened again."

"*What's* happened? Another death?"

"No, thank God. Sorry, TC. Didn't mean to frighten you. No. That was Geneva. She's received another valentine."

"*Another* one?"

"It came in this morning's post. It's a paper heart with a crude pen drawing of a woman hanging by a bell rope."

The sounds in the room evaporated as I imagined Geneva sorting through the letters, opening the envelope while perhaps talking to her friend, Sharon, then glancing at the paper heart and the drawing, letting it fall to the floor as she cried out. Sharon would have picked it up to see what had caused Geneva's agitation. Then she, too, would have dropped it or thrown it in the waste bin, wanting nothing to do with the filth. As Graham's voice slowly pulled me back to the incident room, the two women faded into blackness.

"Can you do that?"

I blinked at him, unaware of what he was asking me to do.

He said, "I want you to take care of this latest occurrence at the hall. I'll get someone else to question some of Sibyl's friends. They could have heard about an appointment she had, or a dare to sneak into the tower. Daft teenage stuff. Something. We've ruffled someone's feathers while investigating Roger's death. This second murder has the stench of fear and cover-up. I'd like *you* to see Geneva, explore this current valentine prank. Can you do that?" He looked at me, his head slightly tilted as he stood up, waiting for my reply.

Of course it was just a formality. He was really ordering me to Geneva's. But Graham was gracious enough to phrase it as though I were doing him a great kindness. I nodded and stood up.

"You'll probably have as much luck with this valentine as we have with the others," he said, digging into his pocket for his car keys. "But we'll make a show of working on it. I don't know how far Margo's got with it, if anywhere. Perhaps you can ask her when you get back." He toyed with his keys, thinking about something, then said, "I wish to hell we could clear this up. I know it's got to be terrifying for Geneva. Plus, I don't like the idea that someone's laughing at us. All right? I'm off to Sibyl's postmortem. When will it ever end? Thanks, TC." He strode out of the room, putting on his jacket as he reached the door.

IF I EVER left the force, I'd give serious thought to giving psychic reading. Sharon Seddon, Geneva's friend, was indeed there, comforting Geneva and demanding that I put an end to this harassment.

"She can't even open her post," Sharon said, first eyeing Geneva and then me. "She's afraid to go outside, walk around her estate or take a horse out. Someone's watching her, perhaps lying in wait for her. She's not safe! Can't you do something? Station a cop at her door, give her a bodyguard—"

I had slipped the envelope and valentine into a plastic evidence bag and sealed it, and now stared at it. The drawing looked like something a five-year-old might draw. Hardly more than an oval for the body, a circle for the head, and lines representing arms and legs, it nevertheless held a surreal reality in the way the tongue protruded from the head and the rope circled the neck, connecting it to the tower bell. There was no doubt that the figure was meant to be Geneva, for a triangle of a skirt turned the figure feminine. I said, "Believe me, there is nothing that the chief inspector or I would like more than to catch this perpetrator. But posting a constable at the door is rather impractical, even if we could spare someone. These have come, by the most part, through the post. There have been no physical attacks, no phone calls, no attempt to run her off the road. So I can't see where a bodyguard is needed. Perhaps you or another friend could open her mail for her. That would alleviate some of the stress until we discover who—"

"And how long is this going to take? This is the third day she's received these things. You knew about them from day one and you haven't stopped it. How many more is she supposed to receive before you catch this creep? She's scared out of her wits."

Geneva did look scared. She sat on the settee, silent and staring ahead of her, her eyes red from crying. The veins in her hands protruded like the embossed lettering around the mouth of a bell. Was she lost in memories of peaceful days with Roger, or was she emotionally shutting down, cocooning herself from further attacks?

I said, "I will ask for increased patrols in this area—"

"A hell of a lot of good that'll do," Sharon sniffed. "So a cop drives by every five hours instead of every eight. Big bloody help. The berk will just wait in the shadows until it's safe to come out."

"—and ask again that you or some friends screen her post. Perhaps you would consider ringing up some of them and asking them to take turns staying overnight here. That would ease Lady Swinbrook's anxiety by placing a friend by her side." *Plus,* I thought, *put a few people inside to catch Kirk at his wall pounding, if he were indeed coming back to search for the secret passage.*

"How long are we to camp out here?"

"As long as you wish, as long as her ladyship feels she needs it. I should think that wouldn't be too much of an imposition for a friend."

Sharon patted her friend's hand, suddenly losing steam. She said in a more restrained tone, "Of course. I apologize for exploding. It's just so *awful.* I feel so *helpless.* This beast is out there, lurking behind every bush, watching the hall...."

"Speaking of which," I said, "do you recall a man, a stranger, calling at the hall several days ago? He may have been asking about a cottage to let on the estate, or wanting to know if there were any houses for sale in the area." I held my breath, hoping the man had stopped here, that we could get a lead on him.

She glanced at Geneva, then back at me. "I haven't come into contact with such a person, no. Have you, Gen?"

Geneva shook her head, her handkerchief still pressed against her eyes.

"If you should remember this person," I said, "or if you know of anyone who has seen him, please contact me."

"Why? You think he killed Roger? Is that why you're asking?"

"Just please ring me up."

"He's not dangerous, I hope. God! That's all we need."

"Perhaps you will see to having someone stay with Lady Swinbrook," I prodded.

"I'll ring up a few people and get this organized today. She won't be alone again. Ever."

"We appreciate any help you can give *us,* too," I added, standing up. "If you suspect you know who it is, or something else arrives—"

"It's got to be Baxter Clarkson."

"Because he's had a row with Lord Swinbrook?"

"This thing that was delivered today—" She gestured toward the valentine. "It had a...there was a drawing of a bell. Baxter *hates* the bells. He's threatened Roger before, you know. Civil action, police action. Now he's just continuing in a different vein. He's probably heard about the bell bequest in Roger's will and is trying to scare Gen out of carrying on with ringing the bells. It's like something he'd do. Anonymous, bullying, cowardly."

"Baxter Clarkson. Right. We know about his feud. I'll look into it."

Sharon walked me to the door and stood with her hand on the doorjamb. A biting wind had sprung up since I'd arrived, and it carried dead leaves into the hallway. They scurried across the marble floor, coming to rest against the base of the umbrella stand at the far wall. Some soared, swooped and looped through the air, finally settling among the baskets and containers of condolence flowers. "This isn't a threat, Sergeant. Don't take it wrong. It's just a warning. We've weapons in this house. I'm not afraid to use them to protect Geneva. Nor will any of her other friends. You catch this bastard and lock him up, or you may have a bloody corpse on your hands."

Only, the way she said it, I knew she meant it literally, not euphemistically. I nodded and hoped that they wouldn't shoot Kirk, should he reappear in the dark of night. I gave her my card and phone number, and drove over to question Baxter Clarkson.

BAXTER DIDN'T SURPRISE me. Nor did his wife, Eileen. They vehemently denied sending valentines—threatening or amorous—to Geneva. They also weren't overly concerned about her welfare.

"I'm not saying I condone it," Baxter said, removing the pipe from his mouth and knocking its bowl into the ashtray. I sat in their front room, a collection of mementoes from trips abroad and kudos from his medical colleagues. The walls bracketing the front window were coated with photos, sketches, decorative plates, framed menus from foreign restaurants, and travel posters. A travel agent would feel at home here. Baxter dug the last of the ash from his pipe with a straightened paper clip and studied the ashes before he continued. "I don't like scary stuff like that. If you're going to have an argument, do it in the open. Be an adult about it. Don't go sneaking around in the dark." He reached for his tobacco pouch and flipped it open. "But I don't know who'd do it. And I didn't!"

"Your fight with Lord Swinbrook—"

"Has been settled, hasn't it? I mean, the lad's dead. Why hassle his widow? She's not ringing the damned bells."

"But she will."

"You're talking about the stipulation in his will, are you?"

"So you know about it."

"Of course, I know about it. Everyone in this village knows about it. Hard to keep anything private."

"So if the bells will keep ringing as before—"

"I'll deal with it when they start. But for now, as I said—" He stopped, filled the pipe, lit it and took a few puffs. Satisfied, he said, "I don't terrorize innocent parties. And I don't know who did!"

"You're not angry because the bells will continue, then."

"Sure I'm angry! But, like I said, there are other ways of silencing a tolling bell. I've been looking into the law, missy, and I think I've got 'er stopped. Nice and legal. No need for valentines to do my talking."

I asked him to ring me up if he found out anything about the pranks, and returned to the relative sanity of the incident room.

Jo A. Hiestand

I looked around for Margo, wanting to talk over the Valentine Case, as I was calling it, but she wasn't there. I tried ringing her on her mobile, but she didn't answer. So, instead of our felonious tête-à-tête, I tried to fly solo through motive and opportunity, but after five minutes, gave it up. I wasn't able to concentrate. Sibyl's body kept intruding into my thoughts and I was feeling sick. And, rather than sit there waiting for Graham to return, I decided to square my shoulders and inform Lyndon about his friend.

Late morning traffic congregated around the BP garage and a stalled car at the intersection of Victoria Road and Dove Street. I radioed in the incident and sat with the other drivers in traffic. It gave me time to practice introductory phrases to the Fitzpatricks. I jotted down several sentences, scratched out some words, rearranged words, and memorized the final version. When the traffic sorted itself out and I was heading down Victoria Road, I wondered if I should have rung up for an appointment. But that would have necessitated telling them my purpose for the visit. Best to catch them at home, I thought.

My word crafting had been a futile exercise, for the news had beaten my arrival at the Fitzpatrick house. Ben had rung up, telling Noreen about Sibyl's death. By the time I saw Lyndon, he was in bed, his face white, the CD player on his dresser churning out Pachelbel's Canon. Odd choice for this teenager, I thought, but perhaps the ethereal quality of the violins and harpsichord helped with his mourning.

I didn't stay long. I really had nothing to do but ask the usual questions about Sibyl's movements last evening, if Lyndon knew of any plans she'd had—the routine stuff that hardly ever garners useful information. He answered in a monotone, gazing past my left shoulder to the poster above the dresser. Swinton Hall, washed by golden light from a setting sun, peeked out from a bracketing of trees and a curved title across the top of the poster. Hours of entrance, accommodating bus lines, and a phone number spread across the bottom. Felt pendants of the hall and Manchester United were stuck like preserved dead insects into the wall, the edges of the cloth curling and dusty. Clothes, a book bag and a nylon camera bag transformed his deck chair into a miniature Materhorn.

As he struggled into a sitting position, his leather bracelet slipped down his forearm, revealing red marks on his wrists that nearly matched the indentations on his cheek. I felt suddenly guilty for disturbing his sleep. Noreen stood beside the bed, smoothing the wrinkled pillowslip and his rumpled hair, repositioning his twisted t-shirt. Beethoven in sunglasses. Only, the wrinkled shirt made him looked more than usually unkempt.

Lyndon pushed his mother's hand away and said no, he hadn't seen Sibyl last night. He'd understood she had had plans. No, he didn't know what those where. He hadn't asked. They weren't bosom pals since he wasn't really dating her anymore—not since she had broken it off and insisted they go out with others. No, he didn't know how she got into the tower and was surprised she had sneaked in. Wasn't there a bobby standing guard?

PEARLS BEFORE SWINE

Noreen echoed her son, adding she was certain her husband, Kirk, didn't know anything, either. "He may be Geneva's brother," she said, "but he doesn't know a thing about the hall. Structurally, I mean. We don't, either. So I can't see how Sibyl could have got in. It's unbelievable. Your bobby couldn't have dozed off, I suppose..."

"Anything is possible," I said, trying to master my rising anger. "But I tend to discount that possibility. Constable Peters has an impeccable record."

"Perhaps on his walk about...Sibyl could have sneaked past him—"

"I'm not here to debate the constable's manner of watch, Mrs. Fitzpatrick. I just came to inform you of Sibyl and ask if Lyndon, or you, knew anything of her plans last night. I thought that if she was going out to some party, perhaps Lyndon would've been included or had heard about it."

Noreen tugged at the bottom edge of her blue corduroy shirt. It was unbuttoned, revealing a green t-shirt beneath. The slogan "Save the Whales" curved above a whale fluke.

I smiled and asked Lyndon to let me know if he thought of anything. A mumble replied from the bed. I coughed, rubbed my throat, and said, "Could I trouble you, Mrs. Fitzpatrick, for a glass of water? I guess I've been in the tower too often. All that dust—"

"Certainly, dear. I'll just be a moment." She left and I turned back to Lyndon. He was a shapeless lump of covers and pillows.

"Lyndon," I said, walking back to his bed.

The mass stirred and he poked his head out of the mess. "Yeh?"

"I'm sorry, but I just have a question. Do you know anything about Sibyl's home life?"

Lyndon's black eyes darkened. "What? 'Course I do. I've been over there. Her dad's Ben. He's a chef. Her mum works at the hall—"

"Right. I meant personal bits about Sibyl and her parents, how she got along with them. They seemed broken-hearted this morning, but you can't always go by outward signs. Not if someone's a good actor and has something to hide."

"They wouldn't have harmed her."

"Maybe not intentionally, Lyn, but sometimes emotions flare, we lose control and we do things we later regret. What about her and her dad, or her and her mum? Any problems?"

"None. A happy family. They all loved each other. I know. She couldn't have hidden anger or hurt from me. I would've known. I would've sensed it. She would've told me, besides."

"She was close to her parents, then?"

"Yeh. She was lucky that way. Lots of my mates haven't the support and love she had."

"Or that you have, either, from what I can see."

He sniffed. "I look out for my mum. I have to, you see. My dad's on the road a lot. He can't be here for her as he'd like, so I'm the man. I'd do it anyway, 'cause I love her. But it makes me feel good, valued. I need to be here for her."

"And they love you, no doubt," I said, ending it quickly as I heard the slap of Noreen's slippers. I walked toward the door. "Well, Lyn, thanks for the chat. I'm very sorry about Sibyl."

He mumbled something and slid back beneath the blankets.

"He's going through a lot," I said, walking up to Noreen. "I believe he'll be fine. He has to work through the shock and the grief, and the only cure for that is time. Thanks for the water." I reached for the glass and bent my knee, lunging forward as I approached her. My hand hit her forearm, forcing it upward as I fell, spilling the water over her t-shirt. She gasped more from surprise, I suspect, than from the temperature of the water. It seeped immediately into the cotton fabric and clung to her abdomen. I got to my feet, retrieved the plastic glass from the floor and apologized profusely.

Noreen pulled the sodden shirt away from her skin, staring at her chest. She said she was fine, that it had been an accident and was I all right, had I hurt my knee when I fell?

"I'm fine," I said, lifting the edge of her corduroy shirt. "But you need to change. You'll catch your death if you stay in this wet shirt."

"I won't be a minute." She took the glass and walked down the hall to her room.

I moved outside Lyndon's doorway and bent over, massaging my knee. Lyndon had again become a lump beneath the covers. I counted to ten, then tiptoed down the hall and cautiously peaked into Noreen's room. The corduroy shirt lay on top of the bed and she was pulling off the wet t-shirt. Her back was toward me and I thought I'd gone through all these shenanigans for nothing. The bruises on her arms I'd seen before, and I was hoping to see something else. The shirt finally off, she reached for the polo-neck pullover. As she slipped her arms into the sleeves, she turned around. I thought I was about to be caught, but the garment slid over her head, blocking me from her view. Then I saw what I had hoped, yet dreaded, to see. Severe trauma marks to her right shoulder and upper arms. I fought my training instinct to offer her aid and protection and eased out of the doorway as she pulled the garment over her head.

I hurried back down the hall and yelled my thanks and goodbye as I opened the front door. Outside, I sagged against the door, my chest heaving and stomach knotting, not knowing whether to congratulate myself or ring up a social worker.

AT THE END of Victoria Road, as I stopped for the traffic lights, I glanced at the Indian restaurant. A large heart-shaped, pink poster advertising Sunday's Valentine's Day dance was cello-taped inside the front window. Sunday. Tomorrow. I mentally ran through everything we had accomplished and had still to accomplish before we could leave the village, and wondered how many of our star players would attend the dance. With the rush and stress of daily life, a romantic interlude such as this Valentine's

Day dance promised to be would be restorative as well as a nudge to Love. And heaven knows we all needed that.

I needed it, if I were honest with myself. Hard detective exterior didn't fool many people, most of all Mark and Margo. They were too well trained to read body language and voice inflections. But as good as they were, I wondered if Graham knew what was happening with my emotions. I worked with him, was partnered with him. Surely by now, he had realized my emotional state. Or had he? Perhaps he was too smitten with Miss Perfect to see the ardor flitting across my heart.

I stared at my naked left ring finger. Well, why shouldn't Graham be happy if Miss Knockout could do it? He deserved it. Of course it hurt that he didn't seek affection from me, but I was forcing my conception of what made him happy upon him. I obviously wasn't his type. Love didn't have to be reciprocated.

The lights changed to green and as I drove to the incident room I thought of giving Mark a chance. A *real* chance. Not just a dinner because I was sorry for him, as I had been in January. A real date, a real look at him and an honest consideration. He had certainly changed, no longer the git who just wanted a romp between the sheets. He seemed genuinely caring. Perhaps it would work out between us, and years from now I would wonder why Graham had ever interested me.

Many of my girlfriends had experienced that. Butting their heads against a brick wall to get Mr. Hot Stuff to see them, then falling deeply in love with Mr. Average. It happened frequently. Was that how it had been with Roger and Geneva? He had certainly loved her, wanting to declare that love through a risky bell ringing stunt. And Barry Sykes still harbored a passion for Geneva, or he would not have approached her with the remarriage proposition.

I turned into the car park by the community hall and parked in the rear, away from everyone. I sat there for several minutes as Graham's and Mark's faces welled up in my mind's eye, their voices whispering in my ear. The last three days had seen duels of love and hate, good vs. evil. From the Swinbrooks' affections to their neighbors' enmity, from Mona's loyalty to her employer to Geneva's detestable mail, from St. Valentine's day of love to an evening of murder. I stared again at my ringless finger, and wondered how the juxtaposition of such fervency and hatred could possess so many people in a mere three days.

And now Sibyl was part of this vehemence. Sixteen years old, time when her life was really starting, and taken from those who loved her. I felt my stomach tighten again and knew I had to get out of the car.

As I headed for the village green across the High Street, Scott's patrol car barreled down the road. I turned to wave at him but he yelled, "On my way to a call. We'll talk later." He closed his car window before I could find out anything more.

Some might label it a hunch. Others might call it police training. I think of it as woman's intuition, which I strongly believe in, having experienced it.

Jo A. Hiestand

I grabbed my mobile from my shoulder bag, rang up the station, and asked to what call Scott Coral had been summoned. It was as I had suspected: Ben Griffiths. I ran back to my car and practically burned rubber as I peeled out of the car park.

BEN WAS TALKING to Scott when I arrived. I stayed on the far side of Scott's car, for it wasn't my call and I had no wish to complicate matters by intruding. Besides, Scott was a veteran cop; he could certainly handle a complaint, if that's what it was. Even though I was several meters from the men, I could plainly hear the conversation, for Ben was hollering.

"I've got her dead to rights, officer," Ben said, gesturing toward the hall. He was dressed in a rumpled, oversized T-shirt, nylon jogging bottoms and black trainers. Perhaps he didn't work today. Or maybe he reported later, for the dinner shift. He said, "My wife saw her. So did the neighbor across the road. You've got to arrest her. I don't care what title she uses, she's plain old Geneva Fitzpatrick to me and she's trespassed on my property and slandered me."

"What exactly is this slander, sir?" Scott had opened his notebook and waited for Ben's story. The sunlight highlighted the brown flecks in his green eyes.

"What do you think it is? Those damned valentines. *She* accused *me* of sending them."

"Which, I take it, you deny."

"Of course! If I was going to scare her, I wouldn't do it with any bloody valentines. Or a drawing. And don't take that as meaning I intend to scare her! I'm just saying that's not my style. I don't do that sort of thing."

"Why would Lady Swinbrook assume you sent those valentines? She must have had some reason."

"Besides her bein' a vengeful, bloody-minded, megalomaniac bitch?"

"Besides that."

"Besides her thinkin' she's still a toff and better than us so-called serfs?"

"Besides that, yes."

"Besides her bein' mad that I broke up her nephew and my daughter?"

"Besides that, too."

"Besides her havin' too much money—"

"I know your views on the Swinbrooks, Mr. Griffiths. But I don't know why you believe her ladyship would think you are responsible for those valentines. Now, if you don't mind not wasting any more of my time..." His voice was firm, implying penalties if Ben did not cooperate.

Ben heaved his chest, screwed up his mouth, and gestured with his lit cigarette toward the hall. He said, "I want her arrested. She can't go around harassing me, threatening me with God knows what kind of retaliation, as she put it, and getting away with it."

"No one's going to get away with anything, Mr. Griffiths. I have to sort through this."

"Sure. Fine. Take her side."

"I'm *not* taking anyone's side! I've listened to your side, now I'll go over to get hers. The law will decide who's guilty, not you nor I."

"The law! Hah! That's choice. You seriously think I stand a snowball's chance in hell of comin' out of this without time in the nick, or whatever penalty I'll get? She's upper crust. I'm shit beneath her feet, a commoner whose wife works for her. You think any judge will look at the two of us and not side with her? You've got to be jokin', lad, if you believe it. The beak'll side with her. He knows where the lolly comes from."

Scott's lips compressed and he pocketed his notebook and pen. I knew his tactic to remain calm. He said, "I'll let you know about this when I've made my report. In the meantime—"

"In the meantime? Bloody hell. In the meantime I sit back and wait for another attack, eh?"

"What attack? You said she came over here to talk to you about the valentines. You never mentioned an assault."

"Make a difference, does it? Now are you taking her to jail?"

"Mr. Griffiths, I have to first ascertain—"

"I want Geneva arrested, thrown in jail. *You!*" He pointed to me and yelled across the distance. "You know what I'm talkin' about. You know my version of events. You know what she's done afore today. Now..." He turned back to Scott, his eyes flashing fire. "*You* take her to jail or by God I'll have your job for dereliction of duty or insubordination or whatever the bloody hell you call it."

Jo A. Hiestand

CHAPTER TWENTY-TWO

"All I can do right now," Scott said, his voice even, "is talk to Lady Swinbrook. I'll get back to you."

"Well, talkin' won't be enough, will it? Not when she's done *this!*" Ben pointed to the side of the house and asked Scott to look at something. I followed, since I was drawn into the complaint. I was also curious.

Someone had egged the windows. Egg yolk had dried in long, thin ribbons running the length of the panes. Broken eggshells lay on the window ledges or on the ground beneath. I pitied Mona, for I would have bet my pay packet that she'd be the one to clean it. Ben would continue his tirade, act the injured party, but leave it to his wife, labeling it "woman's work."

He paced adjacent to the "crime scene," as he referred to it, babbling about not getting any sleep and trespassers and moral breakdown of society and damages for emotional trauma—short, quick steps in a short, ten-foot long area. A cigarette was tucked behind his right ear. He seemed content to jabber to the air, as though lecturing to unseen hundreds. But he focused his irritation on Scott again when the moment presented itself.

"Did you see her ladyship actually throw the eggs?" Scott said, returning from his car with a digital camera. He took several photos to record the incident.

"No. But I didn't have to. I saw her walking from my front garden into the street. So if she wasn't egging my windows, why the hell was she leaving my garden? Like I said, trespass." He smiled, looking smug, confident he'd closed loopholes in his case.

"Was this after or before she'd talked to you about the valentines?"

"Before. She probably sneaked in here, did her dirty work, then was hoping to get away, only I saw her leaving. That's when I came to the door and asked what she wanted."

"You don't think there's a possibility you didn't hear her ring the door bell at first, and that you were aware of her presence after, say, the second or third ring? That you saw her leaving your property *after* she had waited on your front step?"

"If she was waiting on my front step, why the hell did I catch her in my garden? The doorbell ain't over there by the willow."

PEARLS BEFORE SWINE

We looked to the garden, as though expecting a large X to mark the spot on which Geneva had stood. A tall willow cast a gray shadow that spread across the lawn and onto the front window. An abandoned squirrel nest balanced itself near the end of a branch.

"No, it isn't," Scott said, catching my eye, "but perhaps she was admiring the layout, or looking at the bird house. I have no real evidence—"

"You want evidence? How's *this* for evidence?" Ben led Scott to the window closest to the front of the house and pointed to the ground. I joined them. A depression about five inches by three inches was clearly visible on a barren patch of earth near the window. I stooped down to look at it while Ben asked if that was Geneva's footprint.

"I don't know," Scott said, bending over to examine it. "Could be almost anything. What makes you think it's a partial footprint?"

"Because it wasn't there yesterday!" Ben yelled.

Scott opened his mouth, probably about to remark on Ben's knowledge of his ground, then closed it as I grabbed Scott's camera. We were just play-acting, of course. But I wanted to placate Ben and get out of there. I also didn't want Graham coming down on me or Scott if it later turned out that something was going on at Ben's and this was the case-breaking clue. So I snapped it from several angles—with and without the right-angle measure—and stood up. By then Scott had Ben calmed down and was talking criminal scene investigation as portrayed on the telly vs. real life. Ben, praise the Lord, seemed actually to be listening. Probably memorizing some of the bits to use later on.

"And," Ben added as I picked up the measure, "I've no complaints ordinarily with the police. They've a hard job and get little enough reward for doing it."

I held my breath, ready for just about anything.

He said, "I know you're working through a lot, but me and my wife'd appreciate it if you could coordinate your questions."

"Pardon?" I hadn't a clue what he was on about.

"This morning. First you and your inspector turn up, asking a load of questions about Sibyl. Then your woman PC turns up, asking about a pearl necklace. As I said, ordinarily I wouldn't mind. You've got to ask your questions, but with the situation today about Sibyl..." He swallowed and jammed his hands into his pockets.

I apologized for the various intrusions and said I hoped we wouldn't be bothering him and Mona again.

Scott took the camera and led the way back to the front garden. He tucked the camera into his trousers pocket, grabbed his car keys and said, "I'll talk to her ladyship and see if I can discover who egged your windows. But in the meantime, *don't* retaliate if the person comes back. Ring up 999. Got it?"

"I *did* that!" Ben snapped, watching me and Scott get into our cars. "That's why you're *here*, ain't it? And *you*, miss—" He pointed at me from the other side of Scott's car. "You're a detective, right? *You* take over this case. I got nothing against a bobby, but if there's detective work to be done, might as well have a detective do it."

"I gave you my card," Scott said, exhaling sharply. "Ring me if you think of anything pertinent I can use. Otherwise, you'll hear from me when I've concluded the investigation." He revved the car's engine and was down the street before I could ease away from the curb.

My mobile rang not a second later. It was Scott, fuming at the stupidity of the so-called case and giving me his opinion about Ben.

"Geneva *is* upset," I said, "so she might have gone to Ben's place. I don't mean to egg his windows—that's pretty childish. But to confront him about the valentines. She's scared and wants it to stop."

"If she's so scared, why confront her suspect? That calls for courage."

"There comes a point when even frightened people bring up their resolve so they can end a nightmare. Besides, she may be feeling somewhat more bold. She's got a legion of friends lined up to stay with her during the nights."

"Bully for her."

"You think that soil depression is anything?"

"It's got to be *something*, Bren."

"Something connected with Ben's allegation? A shoe print?"

I could almost see him shrug as he said, "Who knows? You want to grab Geneva's shoe collection and do match-ups?"

"I'd rather grab lunch," I said. "You have time for a bite? I'm thinking about the pub. It's cheap and quick."

"Not a chance. I just got another call."

"Not Ben—"

"Hell no. I would've made up some story that I was sick on the side of the road. No. Car crash—no injuries.

"Maybe your next call will be something nice and quiet, Scott."

"Like a pub brawl? I'll take it. Ta." His phone went silent and I rang off, heading for the pub nearest the incident room.

I THOUGHT BETTER of going straight to the pub, however. I wanted to see if Margo was back and to talk to her about the valentines. She wasn't in the incident room, so I spent a few minutes typing up Ben's story even though Scott had the official notes. I didn't want to forget the incident—it could prove important.

About thirty minutes later, I walked to the pub. It was on the other side of the chemist's, which neighbored the village community hall where we'd established the incident room. It was fairly crowded for Saturday lunch, I thought, but I found a table in the corner close to the bar and ordered a ploughman's. Fast, nothing to fry up, cheap. The harried cop's ideal meal.

As I waited for my order, I pulled out my wallet and flipped through the photos until I got to the one of my mother. She hadn't always been a

PEARLS BEFORE SWINE

drunk. Nor had she always distanced herself from me. Marriage disappointments had contributed to her downfall. As she grew weaker, I grew stronger, determined to use my life as a good example and to help others. She had loved me greatly in my childhood, perhaps even still did. But between her periods of insensibility, my unorthodox work schedule, and my father's obvious negative opinion of my career choice, I hadn't been home for months and had not been able to show my love to her.

How strange that seemed now, in light of the two teenagers connected with our cases. They were both loved and returned that love. I stared at my mother's face, a reminder of easier times nearly fifteen years ago, before life's stress and time had etched their cares into her skin. She was smiling in the photo. These days I rarely saw her smile.

My lunch arrived and I put away the photo. With my left hand, I began making notes on motives for Sibyl's murder. My 'famous list,' as Graham termed it. I couldn't help it. It was a great tool for sorting through these tangles. I drew a vertical line down the center of the paper. In the left column I jotted down names of people associated with the case. In the right column I listed motive. *Cui bono*, as Graham never tired of preaching. To whose profit? Every crime benefited someone. If not, the crime would never have occurred. It didn't matter if it was murder or arson or burglary or something else. Every crime rendered a gift, whether it was the death of a hated person, money from insurance, drugs from a robbery, or a television lifted from a residence. Every crime gave the criminal something.

I was just starting to scribble down possible motive opposite Geneva's name when I heard raised voices. At first I thought it was two football fans arguing—one of the usual fight topics—and expected to hear Manchester United statistics bellowed out. As long as I would live, I would never understand how grown men could get so passionate about a game. Certainly, they obviously identified with their teams. But it was something more—a linking of personalities to where the fan imagined team player qualities as his. A form of self improvement or ego building. My team is number one; therefore I am, too, by transfer of hanger-on status. I'd seen it with fans of rock stars. To belittle the idol or the team was to belittle the fan.

But this was no football argument. No Derby County vs. Nottingham Forest. As I listened, the voices and subject grew familiar. Uneasily so. I stood up, trying to see over the towering heads surrounding the two combatants. It was no good; I was too short. I sat down, listening, hoping the roar wouldn't translate into something physical.

It did. Not one minute later. The familiar thud of a fist connecting with flesh brought me to my feet and onto the seat of my chair.

Barry Sykes, Geneva's ex-husband, was backing away from Ben, yelling that he had better stop sending valentines to Geneva. Fear filled his eyes, but there was also anger, for he yelled again that he was going to sit in his car by Ben's house and make certain he didn't go over to the hall.

Ben hollered that he hadn't sent the bloody things and that he would sue both Barry and Geneva for slander. I shut my eyes, tired of hearing the phrase, and opened them in time to see Ben grab the collar of Barry's jacket. The area around the two men had enlarged, as though the spectators knew what was coming and wanted to give the men space in which to fight. I sighed and let them maneuver like wild animals during the vocal preliminary. I got off the chair and pushed through the crowd to the bar. As I flashed my warrant card at the barkeeper, I told him I'd handle it. He nodded, probably glad of Official Intervention, and retreated to the far end of the bar. I went back to my table and pulled out my mobile, turning my back to the noise and calling in for back-up. When I pocketed my phone, I walked around the group, telling the bystanders who I was, to move farther back, and not to get involved. As I gently pulled one eager onlooker away from the bar area, Ben lunged for Barry and pulled him to the floor. Though Ben was of smaller build than Barry, he was ten years his junior. He rolled on top of Barry, grabbing the man's collar and pulling his shoulders forward. As chairs fell and beer glasses were knocked over, I knew the fight wouldn't last long. Unlike the telly's fictionalization of anything for dramatic suspense, real fights rarely last longer than thirty seconds before complete exhaustion overtakes the combatants. Ben was straddling Barry's midriff, throwing his fists in apparent slow motion, missing Barry's face more times than connecting. But one well-placed smash to the face brought an immediate splatter of blood that mottled Ben's face and shirt and Barry's jacket front. He delivered one final blow to the jaw and stood up—momentarily. He blinked several times, gazed down at Barry, then fell to the floor, vomiting all the way. Barry struggled to his knees, wiped the blood from his nose, and slowly stood up. As they say, if he was the winner, I'd hate to see the loser.

Several uniformed constables entered the pub. They would escort Barry and Ben outside and then home after cleaning them up a bit. There would be no arrest unless Barry pressed charges for assault. Property damage was non-existent—just some spilled beer when tables had been bumped. All in all, it had ended as hundreds of other fights I'd seen, with two drunks exhausted and battered. Ben had sustained several cuts to his lips and jaw. Barry, however, would have a large welt below his left eye for several days.

I grabbed what was left of my lunch, wrapped it in several paper serviettes, paid my tab and munched on the apple as I walked back to the incident room. So much for a leisurely break.

GRAHAM HAD NOT returned from the postmortem, so I rang up the various team leaders, getting updated on their progress. It was slow going as I typed with my left hand, taking notes. Several times I had to ask the leader to stop for a moment as I hunted and pecked at the computer keyboard. But by the end of my calls, I had probably increased my typing skill to ten words per minute.

An hour or so later, Graham came in. He pulled out a chair and slowly sat down, looking tired and hungry. I looked at the chunks of bread and cheese that still sat beside the keyboard and wondered if I should offer him food that I had chewed on. Thinking better of the suggestion, I asked if he'd like the pickle.

"As much as I appreciate your offer," he said, eyeing the damp paper as I peeled it from the pickle, "I decline. Just this morning my doctor told me I was eating too much fiber."

"I'll pick off the clingy bits," I said, not certain if he was joking.

He shook his head and said he'd make up for his missed lunch by eating dinner. "Why didn't you finish that? I assume you were in the pub."

I told him about the fight, then said, "Those weren't the only bruises I saw today."

"Oh yes? Whose else did you see?"

When I'd recounted Noreen's bruising, Graham said, "I wonder...if it had been on the abdominal area, I would have said that's classic signs of domestic violence. Hit 'em where it won't show and you're not suspected. But bruising on her shoulders..."

"Yes, sir. I just happened to see her arms the other day. That set me thinking in that direction, and today I deliberately fell into her so she'd get wet and have to change. I know it was snooping, sir, but I had to know. It bothers me."

"Unfortunately we can't do anything about it until she registers a complaint against Kirk. We can make a note of it and make discrete inquiries, but that's about it right now."

"Perhaps it's a good thing that he travels."

"The more he's out of the house, the less she's battered? Maybe. But he might be all the angrier when he returns from his road trips, take it out on her in his frustration. His traveling and putting up with small audiences and inadequate star treatment might fuel his temper."

"It's your fault I'm not a star? Like Super Bowl Sunday in the States. I hear it's the number one day for domestic abuse calls."

"Would've thought Christmas might claim top holiday. Well, as you say, 'my team lost, it's your fault.' Lovely."

"I wonder if it's curable, like going to AA meetings."

"Kirk might be nicer if he stayed in Oldfield and tended bar or sold shoes, for instance."

"Not creative enough."

"So he creatively slaps his wife around," Graham said, sighing. He wrinkled his nose and poked the pickle. "You going to eat that thing? It smells terrible."

I looked at the pickle, held it up by the sodden paper serviette, and said, "I guess not." I leaned over the edge of the table and dropped it into the waste bin. "That better?"

Graham rubbed his nose. "Marginally. I can still smell it, though."

I picked up the bin and walked into the ladies.' When I returned with the empty container, Graham said, "I hope I didn't influence you. If you really wanted that pickle..."

"No, sir. It's all right. It's resting where you'll never smell it."

He laughed and patted my hand. "Thanks, TC. I'll put you up for a commendation. Bravery under Untoward Circumstances."

I glanced at his hand on top of mine and wondered if this was a good time to ask him out. As good as any—the room was quiet, no one was standing around to overhear, Graham didn't have to rush out to attend a postmortem or anything equally romantic. As my mind raced to form the correct sentence, I slowly withdrew my hand and pretended to look through my bag for something I couldn't find. It was no good. I couldn't think this quickly. So, instead of asking about dinner, I asked about his morning.

"Nothing useful from anyone. Wesley rang me up to say his team has talked to three of Sibyl's friends. No one admitted knowing her plans for last night or knowing how to get into the tower. They were shocked to hear of her death, and I hated being the one who had to do it."

"Does it get any easier?"

Graham shook his head. "Not really. The words become generalized, an automatic thing. At least when I have to do it. I never feel stilted. I know these people have lost someone they love. I try to remember that."

He would do a better job than most, I thought, watching him tap his pen against his notebook. If he'd learned anything from his ministerial career, it would be that.

"And what about the postmortem, sir? Has Jens Nielsen determined anything?"

Graham nodded, tossed the report on the table, and relayed the gist of the finding.

It held few surprises. Beneath the obvious scrape on Sibyl's forearm, Jens had discovered bruising. She had died of a twisted neck, the striking force coming from behind as her head hit the floor, presumably from the fall. This striking force would have caused hyperextension-flexion movement of the head on the spine. There was a fracture of the cervical spine and compression of the spinal cord, resulting in immediate death.

"Which," Graham said, "would explain the head's loll when we saw it."

"Any broken bones? I know a fifteen foot fall wouldn't necessarily produce a lot of breaking," I said, recalling other scenarios I'd been involved in.

"But there's a lot of bruising as the body hits," Graham finished. "Rigor was well established, Jens says. And livor of the dependent portion of the body. So..."

"At least we know approximately when she would have died. Even if she sneaked into the tower at ten last night, Scott got the call from Geneva around half seven and he found the body at eight. That's ten hours at the most she could have been dead. Ben said Sibyl was seen at ten at home. Even if she sneaked out of the house, drove straight to the hall and died immediately in the tower, that's ten hours. Rigor would be well established in ten hours and wouldn't have yet worn off, particularly in the cold temps of that bell tower."

"Perfect little fridge," Graham said. "Stone walls and wooden floor, open louvered windows letting all that February night air roll in. It's nice that for once we can work with a time slot so easily verified."

I agreed and hit the 'Save' button on the computer. "Just typing up notes from the teams," I said when Graham had asked me what I'd been writing. I printed him a copy.

"And did *you* make any headway with the latest valentine?" he asked, after he'd scanned the report.

I related the bits of my morning, of talking to Sharon at Geneva's and getting involved in Ben's altercation and egged windows.

Graham said, "And you don't believe Ben is our valentine prankster, I take it."

"No, sir. I don't know why exactly, but I can't come up with a motive for him."

"The angry commoner doesn't work for you, then. All right, what motive is behind the valentine attack?"

This time it was my mobile that rang in the middle of our conversation. I excused myself, noted that Margo was the caller, and answered quickly. I probably nodded more than talked during the short exchange, but when I rang off I said, "That was Margo. She having her tea, but just rang up to tell me about the necklace investigation."

"It's gratifying when an officer finds time for duty among the social whirl of her day. I'm *joking*, TC! Don't look like I'm going to line her up against a wall." He smiled and was about to grab my hand when he realized it was the bandaged one. Instead, he leaned back in his chair, but his eyes still shone with amusement. "So, between the pickle and the chips, Margo rings in. Commendable. What's the report?"

"She asked at the Fitzpatricks' this morning. Noreen claims the necklace is hers."

Graham blinked rapidly, clearly not expecting that statement. Neither had I. The necklace was more than a year's wage to the Fitzpatricks. I couldn't see Kirk spending tens of thousands of pounds for a trinket. Especially if he used Noreen as a punching bag. But maybe that's why he would buy it for her—to make amends for his violence?

I continued with Margo's brief report. "Noreen hadn't realized it'd gone missing. She rarely wears the thing. But she looked in her jewelry case and it wasn't there. She can't remember the last time she'd worn it."

"Not an everyday fashion accessory, no. I assume she wouldn't lie about owning the necklace. There'd be no point."

"Margo's going to ask around when she's finished with tea. See if someone other than Kirk knows about it."

"But she asked Geneva and several other people prior to this, and no one said it looked familiar."

"Could just be fear, sir. You know how it is—if it's not yours and you don't want to get involved—"

"Yes. You disown any knowledge. Right. Well, what does that do for us? How did Noreen's necklace end up in Roger's clutches? Or, if you're a stickler for precise facts, on top of Roger's chest?"

"She *is* related to him through marriage. Perhaps she gave it to him to get the clasp fixed."

"No sign of a broken clasp, TC."

"Well, Margo said Noreen's as perplexed about it being in Roger's possession as we are."

"Like the inundation of valentines which we were stumbling through when Margo astounded us with this bit of fun. As I said, what motive could be behind the valentine attacks?"

"Well, it all started after Roger's death, as you know. So, since Geneva's the primary heir to the estate, I think someone's trying to scare her into selling and moving away."

"The lone, defenseless widow, the intimidated female. Yes, I suppose that's possible. So, does your perpetrator want Geneva to sell to *him*? Has she had any offers? If he doesn't want the house, do you see any other motive for chasing her out of town?"

"There's always the old fashioned one, sir."

"Money. Yes. We could all do with a bit more. Who do you see as benefiting from her house sale, if that's the main object?"

"Well, sir..." I paused, my mind sifting through the list of names and motives I'd started writing in the pub. I said, "I guess all of the beneficiaries of Roger's will."

"So, we're back to our original cast, then." He laughed. "At least you're not rushing your fences, trying to cram a favorite suspect down my throat."

"I try to stay objective, sir."

He winked at me and told me not to ever change my style.

I felt uncomfortable with the compliment, so I turned slightly and asked if I could pour him a cup of tea from the flask on the table. As the phone on the table rang, he held up his hand, winked again, and answered the call.

I watched his facial expressions, trying to decipher who was on the other end of the conversation. I didn't get much time to develop my skill on this one, for he rang off within a half minute. As he closed his phone, he said, "That was Geneva. She's seen Roger's body at the morgue prior to claiming it for the funeral."

"So soon? We're not ready to release it."

Graham agreed. "A few days make a big difference."

That was something I'd learned quickly in my short career. Three or four days after death all fluids have settled and marks of violence are much clearer. Straight edges are much more defined. Bruises on the body can be matched to specific objects, such as shoe imprints or tools. We needed to keep Roger's body until we were finished with our investigation.

"Is anything wrong, sir?" I knew there was. A woman didn't ordinarily ring up the senior investigating officer to say thanks.

"She says Roger's watch has definitely gone missing. She thought, as a last resort, some PC might have found it and turned it in. Or that it'd been in Roger's slacks pocket when he was taken away."

"After Scott didn't find it in the tower this morning, she goes to the morgue to hunt for it?"

"Seems like. She's apparently exhausted all other logical places to look—"

"So she now tries the illogical, like Roger's person."

"She swears he was wearing a Rolex that night. I don't remember seeing one on him in the tower, but I do remember Jens mentioning the impressions on his left wrist as he left with his body."

"He took it off," I explained. "You said some bell ringers don't wear watches when they ring because it could get caught in the rope."

"Then where is it? It's not in the tower nor in the clothing he was wearing. He didn't run home and put it on his dresser top or Geneva would have found it. I repeat, where is it?"

"Another odd thing, sir, is the ale in the tower."

"The Duvel, yes."

"Well, Austin swears that Roger wouldn't have been drinking during his bell ringing feat. Yet, we have the bottle of ale. We have witnesses, if you want to call them, who heard the bells ring for nearly thirty minutes before they stopped—which brought Geneva to the tower. If we have an empty ale bottle in the tower, suggesting Roger was the one who drank, and several people swearing they heard the bells ringing—" I paused, thinking it through.

Graham finished my thought. "We're left with either a Roger who drank the ale and tried to ring bells, which is out of character for him and I don't believe he would have done that—not with such a difficult stunt as ringing two bells—"

"Or someone else was there to drink the ale."

"Of course, he might have chosen to forget the bell bet and have the ale himself—"

"But we've got our witnesses who heard the bell, sir. And Roger's got a full keg of beer sitting in the very room he was ringing in. Why bring in a bottle when he's already bought the keg and it's drinkable?"

Graham took a deep breath. "But we're also forgetting Austin's statement that Roger rang him up to say he *wasn't* going to ring. The phone records confirm a phone call at that time."

"So he cancels the bell ringing, downs a Duvel ale, and someone else rings the bells? Why?"

"As we hashed out before, TC. It had to have been Roger's killer who rang the bell. He arrived after Roger's phone call to Austin, so he didn't know the bet was canceled. He rang for a few minutes so Geneva, let's say, wouldn't rush up there to see why he wasn't ringing."

"And another thing, sir. Why did it take Austin nearly an hour and a half to get to the hall after Roger died? Geneva told us she rang up Austin. If she discovers Roger around quarter past seven, and we know Austin was drinking in the pub until eight thirty..." I frowned, gazing at Graham for the answer.

"Sounds fishy, I know. But I can clear that up, at least. Austin didn't have his mobile with him. It wasn't until he'd returned home that he got the message about Roger."

"So he says. Do we know for certain?"

"The publican said Austin was sitting at the bar, drinking. He didn't hear Austin's mobile ring. And Austin never consulted the phone while he was there."

"So he goes home, gets the message about Roger, and rushes over right then. Could've changed clothes, too, before turning up at the hall."

I must have looked disappointed that we had to forfeit a suspect, for Graham smiled and asked if anything else was bothering me.

"The watch...could Roger's killer have taken it?"

"As good as any theory right now. What about those photos of the boot prints? You have them?"

He leafed through the papers in his case file and pulled out the photographs. There were several shoe prints in various sections of the tower—in the ringing chamber, the clock and bell chambers, and in the muddied area just inside the front door. But the prints in the dust attracted Graham's attention. He studied them for minutes, then pointed to the trail of boot prints leading from the spilled ale to the outside doorway. "What was that country song you wanted to sing the other day, TC?"

"Which one, sir? The one about beer in Roger's hair?"

He smiled. "Soon to be a famous ditty, I think. Does this photograph suggest anything to you?"

I took the picture and examined it. "Yes, sir. I think, paired with the broken bottle, no one drank any Duvel that evening. I think, as we also discussed previously, that it was used by the killer, brought by the killer—since Roger did *not* drink while ringing and he had that keg in the ringing chamber—"

"—so he wouldn't have needed to bring a Duvel with him, yes—"

"—whether planned as a murder weapon or not, perhaps just to give the killer Dutch courage to talk to Roger?"

"That's a question for our killer when we find him. We need to get some shoes matched to any prints that may have appeared. That's a good job for—*now* what?" The phone on the desk rang again and he grabbed the receiver. Even I could tell it was Ben Griffiths. The volume and word choice coming over the line left no doubt. I wondered if he was sitting at home, an ice bag on his jaw, but gave up the mental game when Graham hung up minutes later.

"That was some talk you had with Ben," I said as Graham leaned back in his chair.

"Some talk *he* had with *me*, you mean. I barely got to speak."

"And what did our fearless fighter have to say? If it's not personal, that is."

"The only thing personal was my ear, which I'll have to have checked. I hope my hearing is still intact. I'd hate to have to retire and owe it all to Mr. Ben Griffiths." He pulled on his left ear lobe and wiggled his jaw.

"I think hearing damage is caused by long periods of exposure to something louder, sir, like cannon fire or jet plane engines."

Graham patted his ear with the palm of his left hand. "It was long enough and loud enough, believe me." He shook his head, then said, "I think I'm okay. Unless I get another earful from Simcock in the next minute."

"I'll take the call, sir."

"Loyal sidekick."

"So what did Ben say?"

"Ah, yes. Well, Mona went down to collect Sibyl's clothes. She came home without a necklace that she swore Sibyl always wore."

"If it was a silver thing, with a turquoise pendant, I saw it this morning. Ben saw it, too. It was in a ceramic bowl on her dresser."

"This one is a locket. Gold. They gave it to Sibyl for her thirteenth birthday. She never took it off, even when bathing, and wore it with other necklaces. Mona says it wasn't with her returned effects, and there is no mention of it in the police list."

"Could it be in the tower? Perhaps it broke during her fall."

"Of course we'll ask the SO who worked that area," Graham said. "I don't recall seeing it on the body. I hope to hell we find it. I've had enough of Ben Griffiths to last me two lifetimes."

"That's two items missing. Roger's watch and Sibyl's locket."

"But we've gained a pearl necklace, TC! Do we have a pack rat, then? Trading two items for one?"

"He could be a rat, all right. Do we have a murderer who likes to keep souvenirs?" I asked the question in a soft voice, afraid to say it aloud for fear we were getting into serial killer area.

Graham said, "Early days to know that yet. At least he wouldn't wear them. It'd be a dead giveaway. Especially the Rolex."

"So they're just trophies. Lovely."

"Know any pawn shop dealers?"

"No, sir. I had a dull childhood."

"Well, let's remedy that as best we can, shall we?" Graham reached for the phone, punched in the number and winked at me as he waited for the phone to be answered. I was about to say something when Graham said, "Ah, Byrd. Good. Any idea when I can play in the tower? After tea?

Marvelous. Thanks." He smiled at me as he dropped the receiver back onto the cradle. "A good cop never misses an opportunity to sharpen her skills, TC."

"I heard you say tea time. What am I sharpening, sir?"

"Your hide-and-seek ability."

"Who's hiding, besides the killer?"

"A secret entrance into the bell tower. Are you game?"

CHAPTER TWENTY-THREE

"Sounds like a bit of fun, sir. I'm ready. I assume we're doing this on our own. I mean, no bloodhounds."

"And have them win? I've been beaten enough today."

"Speaking of beating, sir..."

"Yes?" He leaned back again, his fingers interlocked behind his head and looked intently at me. I felt like it was oral exam time in front of teacher.

"Well, sir, what you just said about beating."

His right eyebrow raised; his interest was piqued.

I continued. "Those bruises I saw on Noreen today." I took a deep breath and plunged ahead. "I'm beginning to wonder if it really is domestic violence."

"And why do you question it?"

"Well, sir, classic signs, as we've noted, are the abdomen."

"And you don't vote for domestic violence because the bruising was on her shoulder and arms, I take it."

"Yes, sir. I know it still can be that, but I'm wondering if she got those bruises fighting with Roger."

He stared at me, silent, his index finger and thumb stroking the corners of his mouth, as though he was considering the two settings. A constable came into the room, letting in a gust of cold air that traveled over to our table and ruffled a piece of paper. Graham clamped his hand on top of the paper, cleared his throat, and said, "Could very well be, Taylor. In a way, I'd rather that was the reason than having it turn out to be Kirk taking a few swings at her."

"Yes, sir. It seems to make sense. I mean, Noreen hasn't the haunted look of a woman who's being battered. There's nothing in her eyes or in her manner that suggests fright like that. You talked with her in the kitchen. Did she seem like the other battered women you've talked to?"

"I must admit, Taylor, she didn't."

"I can't believe she could be that good of an actress, sir. And her son, Lyndon, didn't seem overly concerned or protective. I think domestic abuse is rather a dim possibility. She either fought with Roger in the bell tower, or she came by those bruises innocently."

"Slipped on ice on the pavement? Yes, she could have done. So, until we know for certain," he said, glancing at his watch, "we can sort through murder motives for a bit, then we assault the tower. *Now* what?" He grabbed his ringing mobile, glanced at the caller ID name, grimaced and turned from me.

It didn't take my detective skills, such as they were, to decipher it was Miss Charisma. Graham's voice had dropped to a breathy murmur and he bent over the phone. I didn't think he was having stomach pains so he had to be masking his conversation from me. Fine. Let him drool over Miss Stunning. Mark, bless him, was obviously more interested in a woman's personality than in her looks.

A few brief exchanges, a barely audible 'good bye,' and he faced me, the phone again put away.

But as determined as I was to cultivate a friendship with Mark, I was still curious about Miss Wonderful. Not her looks, for I'd seen her at the restaurant. But her name, her personality, why she attracted Graham, who had always impressed me as favoring intellect and humor over mere physical attractiveness. I watched him as he gathered the file papers together. He wasn't smiling as I would expect after having just talked to Miss Dazzle, but he wasn't frowning, either. Perhaps he was merely good at hiding his feelings about her. After all, I hid mine from him.

Graham was humming a snatch of Handel's "Hallelujah Chorus." Great. It sounded like he had a date with her after all. And I was determined not to follow him. I was going to focus my emotions on Erik, if he'd have me. Or Mark.

When Graham picked up the photos of Roger's body, the tune died on his lips. He angled one toward me and said, "Why would Roger wear his old cardigan if he weren't going to ring, as he told Austin on the phone?"

"We decided we only have Austin's word that Roger said that when he rang up. Roger could have said something else, which made Austin mad, so Austin comes over and kills Roger."

"Austin has no alibi, except for Dulcie."

"She'd supply his alibi if it meant getting money for their business."

Graham grimaced. "What else have we assumed or overlooked?"

He searched through the stacks of papers on the desk, picked up the PM report and re-read it, then inspected the photo again. "It's perfectly normal, Taylor, to get a scrape and bruises falling like he did, so that's not something set up at the scene. We can take that as read."

"I think, sir, it all hangs on the phone call."

"Go on."

"Well, Roger phoned Austin to say he wasn't going to ring. He had no intention of ringing. He had bumped his hand and it hurt like hell. So he phones Austin to say he'll ring in a week or month or whenever his hand heals. He does this so he won't lose the bet. Fine. The killer arrives *after* the phone call was made—maybe even walked into the chamber as Roger was ringing off—doesn't know Roger had decided not to ring, and kills Roger. He then proceeds to ring the bell to establish that Roger is alive and to establish his own alibi."

"Which is..."

"Obviously he's not in plain sight, like at a table in the pub. He's in a room in a house, let's say, where he *should* be, and everyone *thinks* he is. He sneaks out, kills Roger, rings the bell for thirty minutes, but no more because he can't risk being gone longer. He also is scared that Geneva or Austin might come up there to cheer on his ringing. He has nerves of steel to do this—the sneaking out, the ringing, even staying in the same room where the body is. But he can't do it longer, so he hops it back to home or wherever. Then he probably pops his head out to establish that he's been here all evening."

"And the ale and cardigan?"

"The cardigan is just a bad bit of timing. Roger probably put it on right away, then climbed up to the bell chamber to do something before he was going to descend the ladder to the ringing room. He really did bruise his hand going up or down that ladder. Then he rang up his brother to cancel the ring. He was wearing his cardigan and would have taken it off after the phone call, only he was killed."

"And the Duvel was a fancy touch the killer didn't know about. Most lore connects ale with ringing. I've even read the odd plaque or two in ringing chambers about rules concerning who supplies the beer at the ringing events. Remember the one in Roger's tower, Taylor?"

I nodded while looked at the photos. "I know it's conjecture, sir, and the murderer could have phoned Austin—"

"Providing he was aware that Austin knew about the bet—"

"—and the murderer could have dressed Roger in the cardigan to make it look like Roger rang, but it's awfully hard to dress a dead man, even if it's just a cardigan."

"There, again, only immediate family knew about the cardigan and the drinking rule."

"By immediate family, who are you including?"

"There you've got me. But I don't think the murderer rang up Austin. There was no reason, even if he knew about the bet. Why phone Austin to say Roger wouldn't ring and then proceed to ring? That's idiotic. The phone call *has* to be legitimate. It has to be from Roger."

"So Roger put on the cardigan, intending to ring."

"And the killer brought the Duvel to set the stage."

"Why? Why go to that added bit of trouble?"

"To make it look like Roger drank himself silly and fell by accident in a drunken stupor? I don't believe it. *No* one would believe it. Not in these days of crime TV shows where everyone knows the PM can detect alcohol level in the blood. No, that's not the answer."

"To establish the fact that another person was there?"

"Again, why? That would just kick the investigation up a notch. Instead of having us nosy coppers running about the village trying to establish the accidental death of Roger, we would be poking into villagers' lives to find out alibis for the time of this mysterious visitor and witness to Roger's death. Why would anyone want to subject himself to such questioning? It would be damnably nerve-wracking. We might truly uncover some motive for the crime. No, it's just a piece of stag dressing that was unnecessary but our killer, as many do, went overboard and over-dressed the scene, thinking it was authentic. He may have intended just to leave the bottle in the room, perhaps on the floor near the rope, but grabbed it as a murder weapon when he got angry."

I reached for the PM report and read that the ale bottle held only a partial print of Roger's forefinger. The photo of the scene showed the spilled ale coming from the broken glass bottle. I said, "Wouldn't Roger have at least a thumb print on the bottle, even if he did drop it, as this scene suggests?"

"He would. Have you ever picked up anything with just your forefinger? I think, as they say in the States, 'eureka'!"

"So, aside from the stage dressing, what's it get us?"

Graham picked up the phone and talked to a scientific officer. After hanging up, he said, "Too many cases, Taylor, and too few SOs. He's sending the rest of the crime scene photos over. We should have them in thirty minutes."

"The bottle is the murder weapon. Sure. The rounded depression in Roger's skull. Kind of like Poe's purloined letter, sir, keeping the murder weapon in plain sight. The killer doesn't run the risk of disposing of it or having it found in his possession."

"I think we're beginning to see daylight, Taylor." He grinned and brought me a cup of tea. "How's your hand, by the way?"

I held up my banded hand, rotated it slowly, and said, "Bandages come off tomorrow. I think the air needs to get at it."

"I agree, but how *is* it?"

"Sore. Stiff. Still hurts when I hit it against something."

"Then don't."

"Thanks, sir. As good as a doctor, I'd say, and less expensive."

"You haven't received the bill, yet."

"Then I think I'll skip your advice and take off the bandages tonight."

We were both on our second cup when Scott came in and handed the photos to Graham. The size of Roger's skull wound was indicated on the photo, as were the dimensions of the Duvel ale bottle. "As we said, our murder weapon," I said, still staring at the two pictures.

"The lab found a hair wedged under part of the bottle cap where it's still crimped onto the bottle mouth. It matches Roger's."

"There's that eureka again, sir."

"So we've got our murder weapon, which we suspected all along. We also know the local pubs don't carry Duvel. That was one thing I checked on."

"Nothing like research to help the case along," I said, smiling at Graham.

"It's rough, Taylor, but someone had to do it." He winked.

"Brought to the scene, sir, either with intent to use as a club or to stage dress the scene, then."

Graham nodded, still staring at the photo, then tossed it onto the table top and stood up. "Would you mind hanging around for a few minutes, Scott?" he said as he grabbed his jacket. "I'll phone in and tell division that you're still on this assignment if you like."

"Fine. Thank you, sir," Scott said, leaning against the edge of the table.

Graham handed me my jacket and called to Mark, who had just entered the building and was sliding out of his coat. "Mark. Hold on a minute. Anything pressing?"

Mark shook his head and walked over to us. He glanced at me, then at Scott, his eyes mirroring his confusion. I could imagine his thoughts. What was a response driver, a lowly street cop, doing here, in the realm of detectives, and not out issuing fixed penalty tickets and searching for missing dogs? He kept his mouth shut, however, and looked at Graham as he shrugged back into his coat.

For an answer, Graham grabbed his mobile phone and herded us out of the door. After talking to division, he pocketed the phone and told us we were going to the bell tower. "It's useless to ask anyone in the family about the secret passage," he said as we got into my car. "If one of them is our killer, he'll lie, so that won't get us anywhere. It's best if we find it ourselves."

"YOU DON'T THINK one of the lads working the scene would have found it by now?" I said, getting into the car and snapping the seat belt buckle.

"Don't know why he would have done. It's not particularly a standard item we always look for. And we didn't suspect the passage when the scene was processed that first night when the SOs were there."

"I've always wanted to follow a treasure map," I said. I could hear Mark in the back seat, his breathing raspy from too much time in the cold wind.

We fell into silence as I drove to the hall, each of us busy with our own thoughts. On any other occasion I would have relished having Graham in the front seat with me, but not only was I thinking of the task ahead but I also didn't feel particularly romantic with Mark seated behind me. So I ignored the occasional brush of Graham's jacket sleeve against mine, the warmth of his breath as he turned to glance out my window, and concentrated on my scant knowledge of medieval architecture and priest holes.

Jo A. Hiestand

When we were in the tower, Graham assigned a floor to each of us, the idea being that the search would go quicker that way. Graham remained in the ringing chamber, while Mark and I climbed the ladder. He remained in the small clock area and I continued up to the floor where the bells hung.

It was my first time alone with the huge bells, and I was alternately overwhelmed and alarmed with their monstrous size. The workmanship on the sound bow, that band of raised design encircling the outer edge of the bell's mouth, was beautiful, the metal shining in the sunlight that squeezed through the window's half-opened louvers. The massive wooden wheel onto which the headstock that supported the bell was attached looked to be like a wheel of a carriage. A new rope ran from the wheel spokes, through a small hole in the wheel's rim and then down into a small wooden box before disappearing through a hole in the floor. This, then, was the origination of the bell ropes I'd seen in the ringing chamber below, when the ropes had seemed to vanish into the ceiling and some nebulous hinterland. Graham had called to me when I was halfway up the ladder, warned me not to touch the bells, which were all resting mouth-up, their heavy clappers lying obliquely against their silent, gaping mouths. He had said it was easy to tip over a bell, to cause it to swing and knock against you. Now, looking at their massive weight, I could believe the stories I'd heard of injury and death caused by such an accident. Thousands of pounds of swinging bronze could kill with one blow to the head. They looked peaceful now, in the scattered streams of sunlight and the still air, but their mouths could break into a fearsome clamor of rocking, pent-up energy.

Despite Graham's warning, I gingerly slid my finger along the lip of one bell. The metal was icy cold. I instantly removed my hand, whether from the cold or my over-active imagination, I don't know. But the physical contact with centuries of ringers and the inscription on the body of the bell seemed to speak to me. I jammed my hand into my trousers pocket, suddenly afraid of the intimacy, and read the engraved words.

Though my voice be small,
I sing in pearl-like tones
with power great.
I lead down the true path
to the glory of God, 1654.
Peninah

What was that last word? I stared at it again, thinking I'd misread it in the dim light. But I could read nothing else but those seven letters and get no meaning from them. Perhaps Geneva would know. It was her bell.

Then the other oddity struck me. I stared at the engraving. *Pearl-like tones.* Did that have a link to Roger's death and the pearl necklace? Was this the bell he'd been ringing when he'd died? If so, what did it mean? I slowly moved away from the bell and concentrated on finding the hidden passageway.

PEARLS BEFORE SWINE

The room was nearly square, incredibly cold, with windows on two adjacent walls, and the same type of whitewashed stone blocks as the lower section of the tower. The wooden louvers slanted open, letting in fingers of sunlight and February's cold wind. Six bells, all mouth-up in their metal frames, huddled together in a rectangular shape, some of the frames lined up north-south, others facing east-west. Graham had explained the dynamics of ringing to me, saying this alternating placement of bells literally kept the tower from falling down due to the enormous exertion of thousands of pounds of swinging metal. Frayed bell ropes were coiled and stacked in one corner, while a pile of wooden stays claimed another corner. They were the uprights attached to the bells' headstocks that kept the bell from revolving in a complete circle. They also were easily broken, Graham had told me, and needed to be replaced immediately before ringing could continue. I glanced around the floor for a broken stay, recalling our theory that a broken stay had lured Roger up here, where he'd met his attacker, but I could see nothing. Perhaps Roger had replaced a worn rope; this Peninah bell looked to have a newer rope than the others.

In another corner of the room reposed a wooden cupboard about six feet high. If it had been positioned in the outside corner, I would have considered it easy access to the wooden beams in the ceiling and then out, perhaps, to the roof, but it claimed an interior wall and looked to be as old as the house.

I walked around the room, my hand running along the walls, my torch playing against the seams of the stones. No mortar was loose, suggesting a passageway behind the wall. I stepped heavily on the wooden floor, hoping to detect a hollow sound. There was nothing uneven. When I'd returned to my starting spot, I shone the torch on the ceiling. It was a series of wooden beams supporting a wooden roof, hardly the type of structure to hold a tunnel. Besides, there was no way to gain access. It was at least fifteen feet above the floor, and the window sills were beyond my reach. So there was no way to grab onto the sill and swing up to the roof. Even Tarzan couldn't have accomplished anything.

I was about to admit that the passage, if it existed, must be on the levels Mark or Graham was searching, when I noticed a clean area of floor near the cupboard. I walked over to it and slowly opened the door. Inside was a stack of frayed bell ropes, sections of broken wooden bell wheels and a small wooden shelf that ran the length of the back wall. The shelf held several old hymnals, a battered tin ladle and a sheet of paper with several dates under the heading "Complete Peals." I stared at the ropes and noticed another bit of clean floor. If Roger had broken a rope, he would have thrown it onto the pile. And he certainly wouldn't have rooted among the cast offs for a newer rope. Intrigued, I shone my torch onto the tangle. Nothing looked suspicious, other than the bit of clean floor, but I pulled aside the dozen or so rejects. There was nothing on the floor. I tugged the broken wheels into the room proper and then ran my fingers and torchlight over the cupboard's back wall against which the wheels had leaned. I was rewarded with a hinged door.

On opening the door, I peered into the blackness beyond. The ray of the torch revealed a small wooden tunnel about five feet square that sloped gently downward toward the hall. My heart rate significantly increasing, I ran to the top of the ladder and called down to Graham. Mark was with him, evidently having exhausted his search of the clock room. When they stood beside me, peering into the tunnel, Graham said, "It stands to reason the family and perhaps some of their closest friends would be the only ones who know about this. We've yet to discover where it leads, of course, but why tell the gardener, for example, and be startled one night when he walks into your bedroom?"

"It's not exactly a priest hole, is it?" I said, getting up from peering inside and dusting off my hands.

"Could be on the other side," Graham said. "This could lead to a chamber where the priest hid. Very clever, this. The seam of the door fits flush against the wallboard seams. It's probably nearly imperceptible by candle or lantern light, I'm thinking. Awfully hard to discern. The priest hole on the other end of this passage should prove just as hidden, providing your pursuers didn't find this entrance. I wonder what they covered it with in the good old days. If the king's men were ruthless in their searching, they would've eventually spotted the seam, but it would certainly take them days to hunt over the entire hall."

"A family member could have come into the tower from the ground floor and moved something heavy, like these broken wheels, against the door and then returned to the house."

"Something heavy that wouldn't arouse suspicion." He nodded and stared at the dark tunnel, as though envisioning the scene. "And if those soldiers made as half-hearted searches as some of our lads do today, they wouldn't move a heavy bit of broken bell or wooden beams. They'd do a superficial search, tap on the walls, then leave for the nearest tavern."

"Where they'd complain about their job and their superior officer," Mark said.

"Some things never change, do they?" Graham and Mark exchanged stares, and I wondered if there was something implied by his answer. Mark merely returned Graham's gaze and said at least politics was a bit tamer these days. Which wasn't what Graham had meant, but he let it go.

"This probably dates from the mid 1500s," Graham said, "when Catholic priests were persecuted by Elizabeth I's secret service agents. Elizabeth, being Protestant, devoted a lot of energy to rooting out Catholics and penning strong laws against them. Well-to-do Catholic families employed workers—usually Jesuits skilled in carpentry—to construct hiding places for priests who were smuggled into the country."

"Mass was outlawed, wasn't it?" I said, recalling a bit of school history.

"Punishable by crippling fines, confiscations of property, or death. A captured priest was automatically sentenced to death."

"So these Catholic priests were smuggled into the country to start a revolution against Elizabeth's government, then?"

"Not so much a revolution as we would understand the meaning of the word, but of converting the English back to Catholicism. And to do this, there was a seminary established in Flanders that trained these priests. *They* were the ones who were smuggled into the country and hid in homes. Not only were the priests hidden, but also the altar furnishings of these manor homes' chapels were hidden. If *anything* pertaining to the mass or a priest was found, the house would be searched in frenzy."

"So," Mark said, getting into the adventure, "how were certain homes suspected? People didn't go around saying 'I'm Catholic' and wearing crucifixes, I assume. How did Elizabeth's agents know where to look for renegade priests?"

"World's second oldest profession—spies." Graham smiled and looked from Mark to me.

"Walsingham," I said, amazed I could remember that bit of history.

Graham nodded. "The great spy master. Many times he employed agents as servants to the great houses. These servants were great sources of information, knowing about the guests of the household, who was expected to visit, the times they'd be there. These servants would slip the information to Walsingham's agents outside the house, and a raid would ensue."

"But the hiding place of the priest might not necessarily be known to the servant," Mark said. "Right?"

"Yes. But the knowledge that the family harbored a priest was often enough to yield a hiding chamber if the searchers were thorough enough."

"It must have been terrifying," I said, envisioning the priest crouched in a dark, nearly airless room or coffin-like hole hidden in a wall or beneath a floor, hearing the sound of government troops pounding on walls and shoving aside furniture, smelling burning torches as the troops poked about in the dark recesses. The family must have huddled together in the great hall, silently praying the priest would remain hidden, for the penalties were frightening for everyone.

"The most skillful and famous crafter of priest holes—that we know about, at least—was Nicholas Owen. He was a servant of Father Garnett, who was a Jesuit in England. Owen was incredibly ingenious, never twice constructing the same type of hiding place entry, for once it was discovered, it would be easy to discover the rest in other great houses."

"So not all of them were doors in the backs of cupboards," Mark said. "What else did he construct?"

"False chimneys, usually in attic rooms; false beams in walls of the wooden beam-plaster type you find in Tudor style; false treads in staircases; chimney breasts; spaces between floors. In one stately home, there's a celebrated trapdoor between the floor of a medieval lavatory and the roof of a bread oven. A hole leads from that to a shaft, and from there to the moat.

Jo A. Hiestand

In order to descend the shaft, there's a system of pulleys that works the spit in the kitchen fireplace."

"Ingenious. Incredibly sophisticated engineering."

"They were. They had to be, if the priests, family and carpenters were to stay alive. Other entryways were by false floorboards—"

"The favorite squeaky board of my childhood mysteries," I said.

"—a stone slab in a fireplace hearth, drains, chimney flues, movable sections of wall plaster, and sliding boards in wooden paneling. Sometimes, even if the soldiers couldn't find a priest but had reliable information, they'd camp for weeks inside the house, hoping to force the priest out through starvation. Many priest holes had provisions stocked against these emergencies, but it was a dicey cat-and-mouse game all the same."

"No tinned food or bottled water in those days. It must've been terrifying watching your food dwindle and hearing the soldiers clumping around the house."

"Well," he said, playing the beam of his torch into the passage, "why not bring this bit of history back to life? What say we clump down this passageway and see where it emerges? You game?"

I would've said something like 'does the sun rise in the east' if we weren't on duty, but merely nodded and waited for Graham to take the lead. Mark fell in behind me and we waddled single-file, stooped, our torchlight covering every inch of the floor and walls.

Thinking back on this, I don't know if it was better or worse that I was in the middle. It gave me a secure feeling that nothing could jump out from the blackness and attack me, as it might have done if I'd been lead or end, but it also magnified the rising sense of claustrophobia I was trying to combat. I kept up a running commentary on anything I could think of, noting the unevenness of my voice and the ludicrous topics on which I spoke. Either Graham and Mark knew I was fighting off my fear, or they weren't listening, for no one replied. The stone passage seemed to stretch indefinitely ahead, the blackness broken only by our torchlight. The stones were February-cold and of a light color, harboring the odor of mold and the dampness of seeping water. I tried not to breathe deeply, for the air was stale and probably held bacteria of rat droppings. I could see nothing but the walls and floor, the painfully bright patches of torchlight, and Graham's broad back. The only sounds, once I had ceased my babbling, were our shuffling footsteps and sporadic deep breaths.

When I thought I couldn't stand another minute of my confinement, Graham stopped abruptly, causing me to bump into him. His torch revealed a solid, plaster panel with an iron latch. He turned toward us, his face a dark mask silhouetted by the bright light behind him, which gave him an almost haloed look. "Behold the key to the problem."

He turned toward the panel, focused the beam on the latch, and turned it. It evidently was stiff, for the veins of his thumb and wrist were taut beneath his skin. But several seconds later the distinct 'click' indicated the latch had turned, and Graham slid the panel aside.

PEARLS BEFORE SWINE

CHAPTER TWENTY-FOUR

MARK AND I crowded next to Graham in the small opening, jockeying for best vantage point, and we peered into a bedroom. Graham leaned into the room and angled his torso so he could see the wall behind him. He grinned.

"Perfect! Students, what were we talking about?"

I wedged my head beneath his arm, turned so I could see, and said, "Chimney breastplate."

"Seems to be a guest room," he said.

I agreed, for there were no personal items that would indicate the room of a family member. And, what was more important for us at the moment, there was no fire burning in the grate.

I said as much to Graham, who replied with a laugh.

Our return trip hadn't the same feel as the exploratory trip, for not only did I now know the length of the corridor, but I also knew there was an escape at both ends. It did wonders for my confidence. We had simply reversed our order, and now it was Mark who led. As we searched for doors that might branch off from the passageway, I talked about the bell inscription I'd read in the bell chamber. "Do you think the 'pearl-like tones' inscription on that bell has any relation with Roger's death, sir?"

"I don't know. We'll have to ask Geneva. Could be a coincidence."

"Or," Mark said, his voice vaguely muffled in front of me, "it could be the catalyst for this ridiculous bet. Perhaps it gave Roger the idea to give her ladyship musical, pearly tones instead of a pearl necklace."

"Well," Graham said, his voice loud at my back, "whatever it is, I hope to find out."

"Do you know what that word means?" I asked.

"What was it again?"

"*Peninah.* I think I've got it right. It's so odd. I've not heard it before. Yes, Peninah. I think that's it."

"I'll look at it when we get out of this. God, I can't believe my back hurts already."

"You've been walking like this for a few minutes. It's bound to hurt."

"Maybe this explains Quasimodo's stance," he said, then added "Eureka!" as Mark stepped into the bell chamber. When he'd straightened up and stretched, he said, "I think we've a good case that only a family member could have come in this way with Sibyl. I don't think a family member would show a secret passage to the staff. It's none of their business."

"Not the sort of thing they'd accidentally discover, either," Mark said. "You'd want to get on with your job of work, dust the room, change the bed linens and get on with the rest of your duties, not pound on panels for secret doors. Anyway, why suspect one? It's not common knowledge in the village. I've heard no stories."

"Things like these priest holes and passageways are kept in the family," Graham said, walking over to the bells. "Villagers may know a priest hole exists in the hall, but they don't necessarily know where it is. Anyway, not many people care these days. It takes too much energy keeping a job and paying the bills to worry about finding old passageways. Where's this bell inscription, then?"

I showed the name to Graham, illuminating it with my torch. Graham read the inscription aloud, shook his head and said that he didn't know what it meant. "Peninah. Can't even get a feel for it. Not Latin, I don't suppose." He sighed, rubbing his chin. "Where's my old professor when I need her?"

"Seems like she's kind of superfluous," I said, then mentioned his priest hole knowledge.

"I'm afraid that comes from independent pursuits while in seminary. Nothing at all to do with ministerial studies. Just plain curiosity."

"Well, I'm glad you had it. It's an interesting subject."

We climbed down to the clock room, then paused at the top of the ladder while Graham looked down into the ringing room. He said, "Part of a nylon fishing line was found here, acting as an agent to cause someone to lose her balance."

"You think Sibyl was led up here," Mark said, crouching by the top of the ladder, "through the passageway, which is why Peters didn't see her enter the tower, and then pushed from here."

"The push probably would've been enough to ensure a deadly fall," Graham said, "but we don't know how close the killer was to Sibyl. He could've stayed some feet from her, giving her a sense of security if she was at all nervous about climbing down. It is fairly high—fifteen feet—and perpendicular. Enough to make some people nervous."

Sibyl's conversation rushed back to me. I saw her in her living room, just awakened by our presence. I said, "Sibyl commented that she'd nearly fallen from the ladder. Remember, sir? In her house?"

"Could very well be, but I still think the nylon line helped her to her fall. It doesn't particularly matter if she was tripped or pushed. The point is that it was deliberate."

"Jens didn't find anything to indicate a push. No...."

"I just cannot accept that two people die within three days at the same spot in the same manner—not with that bit of fishing line to suggest murder. It's beyond logic. It has to be a deliberate push or constructed 'accident.'"

"So," Mark said, taking up Graham's line of thought, "if she was sneaked into the tower via the passageway, the only person Sibyl would most likely go with along this creepy route is—"

"A Swinbrook family member and her friend," I said. "Lyndon."

"I can go out now and arrest him," Mark said, pausing with one foot on the ladder's top rung.

"We've no evidence," Graham said. "It's all conjecture."

"Damned good conjecture, all the same."

I said, "So, if Lyndon killed Sibyl—and we'll have to sort out motive—do you think he killed his uncle? You think he got into the tower the same way?"

"Since the two deaths appear nearly identical in manner, I'd say yes, Lyndon's our killer for Roger, too. But I don't think he had to get into the house, sneak along the passageway and into the tower. He would've simply walked into the tower by the ground floor door. There was no reason Roger had to lock it, especially."

"And," Mark said, "if the ground floor door was locked, he could always try another day, assuming he had no key to the hall itself. Geneva was back at the pub, so he couldn't get into the hall without getting the servants to let him in—which would blow his alibi."

"I think," I said, "I understand why Lyn would kill Roger. Lyn's been struggling for everything he wants. Remember him telling us about wanting to get into the music industry and saving every penny he can get from working odd jobs? He never got a thing from his uncle...he was totally ignored. All that charitable giving and such was fine, but Lyn never got anything, no acknowledgement from Roger. If Roger could give away hundreds of thousands of pounds, and Lyn had to work odd jobs to save up a measly couple thousand..."

"What's wrong with this picture, as they say?"

"I think he was pushed over the edge emotionally. He couldn't take the snubs anymore, the flagrant disparity. He was *family!* He should have received *some*thing from Roger! I understand Lyn's hurt. It's a slap in the face. He probably struck out in anger."

"So why kill Sibyl?"

Graham was letting me run with this, and I was glad of the chance to show him I'd thought through the case. I said, "Maybe Sibyl knew Lyn had killed his uncle. They were dating for a bit until she broke it off. Maybe she guessed or overheard some remarks and pieced it together. Lyn discovers she knows and, to keep his secret, he kills her. Maybe she knew about the passageway. Maybe she didn't—not until Lyn showed her in order to lure her into the bell chamber. Perfect alibi, besides. Peters, or whoever's on duty, wouldn't see anyone go into the tower. Therefore, Lyn can claim he's innocent, that he's never been in here. Lyn couldn't know if Mona had ever told Sibyl. He couldn't take a chance that his alibi for killing Roger might be blown, so he kills her. Maybe Mona is next on his list, insurance that Mona wouldn't talk about the passageway if she started thinking about time and motive and opportunity."

"Makes sense," Graham said, climbing down the ladder. "You think Lyndon and Sibyl sneaked into the hall? How'd he get a key?"

"The family probably has one."

"He'd know enough about the hall to know when and where to sneak in. That's not a big concern of mine. But perhaps we'll know more about that when we get back to the incident room. I've put Margo onto sorting through all the bits."

When I had climbed down, I looked up at the ceiling where the bell ropes disappeared. Now I knew where they went, how they operated the swinging bells. I told Graham that it seemed like short people such as I wouldn't be able to control the bells.

"On the contrary," he said. "It's done by the feel of the bell through the rope. Brute force has nothing to do with it. See?" He pulled out his notebook and sketched two ringing stances. "This is the backstroke..." he said, pointing to the first drawing. The ringer's arms were straight over his head.

"This is when the bell is on the backward, or second half, of its cycle," he explained. "This other..."

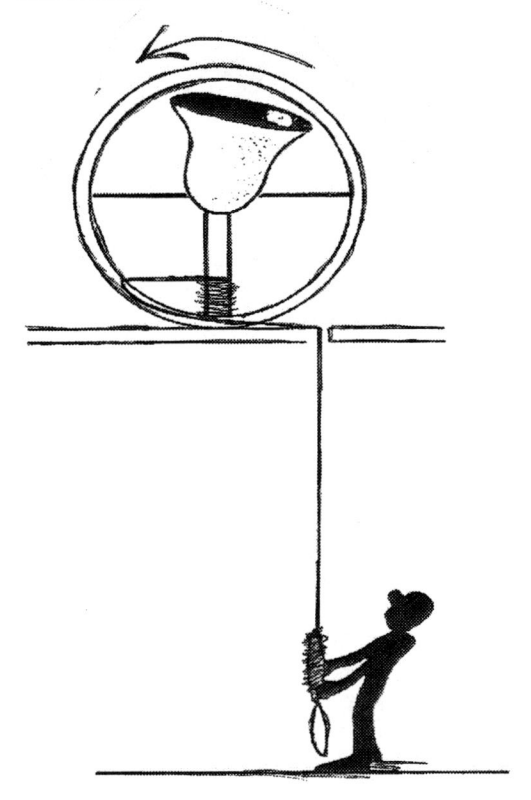

He indicated the second drawing. "This is the hand stroke, the first half of the pull when the bell is tipped downward from its mouth-up resting position. Does that help?"

I stared at the sketches. Though they were clear, I wished I could understand what it felt like. I told him as much.

Reaching for the nearest bell rope he said, "I'll show you. We'll try the backstroke first."

He undid the loose knot that kept the rope coiled and off the floor. When free, the rope was barely long enough to reach to my nose. He showed me how to hold the rope, placing the bottom, tail end, in my hands, my right fist touching on top of my left. He told me to relax, feet slightly apart, and look straight ahead and then talked me through the motions before drawing up one of the large, wooden boxes that was propped against the wall of the ringing room. He placed the box in front of me and promptly stood on it.

"This will put me above your hands and help me keep control when we try it. Are you ok, TC?" His voice was in my ear.

I nodded and mumbled, looking him straight into the chest. I took a deep breath, willing to ignore the pain in my burnt hand so I could be near Graham.

"Right, relax," he said, as he took hold with both hands on the maroon and white woolen sally—the colored, fluffy section of rope. "Look to," he said as he took the strain. "She's going." He pulled gently down on the sally. "She's gone." He said it as he let go of the sally and it started a rapid upward movement, drawing my hands up right above my head.

I felt his hand touching mine and then he said, "Pull, TC—long and gentle all the way down."

A blur went past my face as the sally came down and his arms went out. He took hold of it as it changed direction and brought it to the balance point. "Steady, steady, not so heavy," he said as he pulled down again.

Again my arms rose and I felt him guiding me at the back stroke.

"Right. Now, pull!" he said, and again I pulled and he caught the sally.

As the huge bell found its voice, I could feel the wooden floor tremble, rising through my shoes to my heart, and wondered what it would feel like with all six bells ringing simultaneously. It was the same sensation I felt during church services when the organ rumbled through the floor and into my feet. It was marvelous. Sensual.

It felt really difficult, but the backstroke was only one half of the complete stroke. The backstroke was simply that—the back, or second, half of the complete ring. It occurred after the bell had swung downward and had come briefly to rest upright. The backstroke brought the bell down again and back to its original position. At that time the greater length of the rope was also wrapped around the rim of the bell wheel, which was why I was standing with my arms straight up over my head, grasping on a little bit of rope end. The sally was as close to the hole in the ceiling as it would ever get.

The hand stroke, he said, was even more intricate.

After a while, he stopped the bell by gently letting it ease over on the hand stroke onto the stay.

I could envision it sitting with its great open mouth pointed toward the rafters, its clapper resting against one side. He was fixing the same fancy slipknot around the coiled end of the rope so that it was held off the floor when Geneva stepped into the ringing chamber.

Her face was deathly white, her eyes large and staring. Her hands clung to the door jamb as she took in the scene, then she seemed to collapse against the frame as she stared at Graham and the rope in his hand.

"*What the bloody hell are you doing?*" she demanded, fear and anger tinting her voice. "Who gave you permission to muck about with the bells?"

Graham let go of the rope. The end swayed against my body as though Roger's spirit had taken hold of it.

Graham walked over to Geneva, apologizing for frightening her, explaining he had merely wanted to show me how to ring the bell.

"You damned near scared me to death," Geneva said, her eyes focused on Graham. "It's unforgivable—not only because you're fooling about with my property, but also because you scared the hell out of me. I thought...for one hellish moment..." She swallowed, her neck reddening in her embarrassment. "I thought it was that bastard who's been harassing me with those bloody valentines and poems."

I walked over to her, stopping just behind Graham. "I know. I'm terribly sorry, your Ladyship. We shouldn't have been fooling about with them. I can only imagine the fright you got. It's just that...well, I'd never been up with bells before—we were up in the ringing chamber just now, doing a bit of investigation for the case—and the bells were so incredibly beautiful in the sunlight, and I wanted to know how to ring them..." I stopped, knowing we shouldn't have been touching the bells, knowing we should have asked permission first, understanding her horror at being forced to think about Roger's death.

Geneva stared at Mark, who stood silently by the ladder, unmoving, then at Graham, then back to me. She glanced at the bell ropes, following their lengths up to the ceiling, then nodded. She spoke to them rather than to us. Her voice was little more than a whisper. "I can understand your fascination, miss. They *are* wonderful. I've listened to Roger ring for years, but I've never dared try it myself. I suppose I've always been rather afraid of them, their weight, their ability to injure. That doesn't dilute their glorious music, however, or the skill needed to produce it." Her eyes dwelled on the ringing tablet on the wall. She read it silently, as though needing the assurance of something familiar in this tragic room. Finally, she looked at Graham and said, "I don't mean to sound inhospitable, but I'd rather you didn't ring anymore. It—it's too painful for me right now."

"Of course. I do apologize again, Lady Swinbrook. I offer no explanation other than I was caught up in their beauty and the exciting prospect of ringing again," Graham said.

"You don't ring regularly, then?" She seemed to relax now that Graham was talking about himself and neutral subjects.

"Haven't for some years. I used to ring regularly, but since I joined the force, well..."

"Of course. It's rather difficult, I believe, to make Wednesday evening practices and Sunday morning ringing sessions."

"Work has a nasty habit of getting in the way, yes."

"What's your preference—tenor, treble, something in between?"

"Doesn't really matter, though I do enjoy the lead."

I would have guessed the treble and been correct, I thought, smiling. Perfect for a senior investigating officer. Lead and have others such as Mark, Margo, and me follow in his wake. He told Geneva he had rung since he was twelve, at the village church where he'd grown up, but had had to abandon it when he'd left his ministerial career. He apologized again and motioned for Mark and me to follow him from the tower. We trailed along after him and Geneva, listening to her talking of Roger and some peals he'd rung, then stepped outside where the sunlight warmed our faces.

WHEN WE WERE back at the incident room, Graham asked Scott to hang on for a bit longer, get a cup of tea in the kitchen. I watched Mark as his eyes followed Scott's progress into the kitchen, and felt an anger build within me. Last month I had thought Mark and Scott had sorted out their feelings. Apparently they hadn't. Or at least Mark hadn't. I asked Mark if he'd get me some tea, thereby giving him a chance to talk to Scott in private. Mark smiled, as if glad of a reason to trail Scott, and left quickly. Oblivious to Mark's departure, Graham began discussing the motive of the two murders.

We agreed that Lyndon was the likely suspect in Sibyl's death, but disagreed about Roger's killer and motive. Finally, to give us a break from the solemnity, Graham logged onto the Internet, saying he wanted to find out the meaning of the word "Peninah." Almost immediately the search engine brought up the word and several sites. Graham said something about the meaning of names and double clicked the web address. I looked over his shoulder and discovered we were looking at a page of baby names and their meanings. Graham looked at me, the surprise obvious on his face, and said, "Who would've guessed? Peninah. Israeli. Meaning 'pearl.' Well, what do you know?" He scrolled through the original search list but could find nothing else for Peninah—no company name, no consumer product, nothing else but the feminine name. He logged off and asked if I thought it had some connection with Roger's pearl necklace.

I replied that that was what I was going to ask him, and he grinned, saying I had the makings of a detective.

"Since we're talking about the case again..." I sorted through the papers for the PM report.

"What are you thinking of?"

"The pearl necklace, sir. It's Noreen's. She couldn't understand why it'd gone missing. Well, if we go with Lyndon as Roger's killer, he'd be the likely one to take his mother's necklace, wouldn't he?"

"So he confronts his uncle, fights with him—that's where you're leading?"

"Yes, sir." When I found the report, I read aloud, "Skin under the victim's fingernails does not match the victim's DNA." I looked up and added, "Lyndon has two scratches on his wrist. Could be a defense wound when Roger fought off Lyndon's attacks."

"We need to get a sample of Lyndon's DNA to see if we've a match."

The fax rang into the silence of our thoughts, and moments later Graham read aloud the SO's finding of the boot prints in the tower. "Matches size and type found outside in a thawed piece of ground. Most likely worn by a smaller person than the boot size would indicate. There was heavy pressure on the ball of the foot, where the toes would press down as the person walked."

"Another bit of stage dressing to cover up the real shoe size and make of the murderer?"

"Seems a bit elaborate, but again, if you watch that fictional stuff on the telly, you'll believe we can discern anything from an atom."

"So, the killer was over cautious and used someone else's boots to disguise his presence. Fine." He paused as Mark joined us again, a half-consumed mug of coffee in his hand. "Any guesses as to how the killer got Roger's boots?"

Mark said, "He could have pinched them, if they were left in the barn or somewhere."

"Or," I said, "Roger could have given them to Lyn. A gift from uncle to nephew."

Graham nodded. "The soles are quite worn. Maybe Lyn wanted them and good-hearted Roger gave them away instead of resoling them. Then, when planning the murder, Lyn remembers the boots and thought they'd blend right into Roger's other prints on the ringing chamber floor." He smiled at the thought, grabbed his phone, and gave the person on the other end of the line the particulars for a search warrant. When he'd rung off, he called to Scott. "I know you're about to pick up your own search warrant, but could you get ours while you're at it?"

Scott nodded, saying petrol and time were precious enough without wasting either. When Scott had left, Graham said, "I hope you two haven't tired of hide-and-seek."

Jo A. Hiestand

CHAPTER TWENTY-FIVE

"Do you remember Erik Davidson?" I asked Mark minutes later when we were outside. Graham had insisted we take a tea break while we waited for the search warrant, and I'd found myself following Mark outside to get some fresh air. The sun kissed the brow of the western chain of mountains, tinting the dried grasses along the foundation of the building an orangey-red and the remnants of snow a deeper hue. Twilight soon would claim the depressions of the landscape and creep slowly eastward along the alleys and through the churchyard. Shadows from the headstones had already lengthened and covered the graves not resting beneath the canopy of outstretched oaks and spruces.

Mark screwed up his mouth, as if trying to remember. "No. Doesn't even sound familiar. Should I?"

"No," I said as we walked over to the low brick wall that separated the adjoining car parks of the community center and Boot's. "I was just wondering."

"A person just doesn't bring up a name without a reason. You infer I should remember Erik Davidson. Who was he—a criminal I arrested who's now returning to punch my lights out?"

"Oh, no one in particular. I'm just curious if you remember him."

"I don't. Who is he?"

"One of the constables stationed at Silverlands when we first arrived." I paused, remembering the first time I'd seen him at divisional headquarters. He'd been chatting to a mate of his, turning the corner in the hallway, and bumped into me, sending me sprawling in one direction and my shoulder bag and sack of lunch in another. Luckily, things had improved on our longer acquaintance. I tried to sound indifferent. "It's no big deal."

"Must be a big deal for you to ask about him. What'd he do—ring you up for a date?"

"Hardly," I said, feeling it too close to the truth. I was already sorry I'd started the conversation and didn't know why I had. Perhaps I had just wanted to talk about something other than murder, something gentle, and Eric was the first subject that popped into my mind. "I just thought about him and wondered if you remembered him."

"Well, I don't. And I don't think I want to."

PEARLS BEFORE SWINE

I shrugged, trying to look nonchalant, and watched a mistle thrush hop along the ground, then grab a yew berry in its beak.

Mark stooped down next to the wall but turned slightly and looked up at me. "Isn't he the bloke who moved on to the firearms section and got all those accolades for shooting that kidnapper?"

I muttered that I hadn't heard of it but it sounded like the type of thing Erik would do.

Mark broke off a dry piece of grass and wrapped it around his finger. He was busy for several moments trying to tie a knot. Then, as if the reason behind my question became suddenly obvious, said, "You're not thinking of going out with him, are you? God knows I got off on the wrong foot with you at training school, but I'm trying my damnedest to repair the damage." He tugged the grass from his finger, tossed it onto the ground, and looked at me. His eyes stared into my soul. "Just a simple dinner. That's all I want, Brenna. Time to get to know each other away from the job. Just a nice meal and conversation. No pressure for another date, no good night kiss. We don't even have to shake hands at the end, if you don't feel like it. I just want to take you to dinner—a belated Valentine's Day celebration. No hidden meaning, no hidden agenda. Nothing romantic even suggested. A nice dinner on an evening when you should've gone out with your best bloke. Good enough? Or have you already by-passed me for Erik?" There was no suggestion of humor on his lips or in his eyes. He stared at me, waiting to be shot down or lifted up.

I said, "I'm not dropping you for Erik, Mark. I just thought of him because something came up that reminded me of him. I'm looking forward to our dinner—really. I thank you for asking me."

He seemed satisfied, for he started whistling "Pretty Woman" and sat on the edge of the brick wall.

I wasn't going to admit I had asked Erik to live with me, that even if we hadn't been working on Valentine's Day I would've had no romantic date. Mark was nice to want to take me out, and I sensed there was no implication in the asking. He wasn't expecting to end the evening with me in his bed.

A breath of wind stirred the branches of the trees behind the community center and tussled Mark's hair. He absentmindedly pushed it back into place, still concentrating on the cars passing us. The breeze died down, and the tune had changed to "I Wanna Hold Your Hand," but for that brief second he reminded me of Graham. Not that he and Graham looked similar, but it was the way he moved his hand, the brief frown as he watched a driver turn without using his turn indicator. Even his whistling. I averted my gaze to the woods behind the building, aching to wander in its dark depths and leave behind the dating game. Had Graham taken Miss Universe out on a Valentine's Day date? If so, he would have to be fairly serious about their relationship. Had he kissed her yet? Had he asked her for another date? I could feel my breathing grow more rapid as I fought back my jealousy. Granted, Mark was taking me on a belated Valentine's dinner, but we weren't going to any place nearly as elegant as Bovary's. I glanced at Mark, wondering if some Deep Dark Plan had been kicked into gear now that I had accepted the date. But he looked like a small boy, interested only in cars. Graham was hard to read. I told Mark I was going to the pub for a coffee, and walked quickly down the street. Maybe the voices of a dozen simultaneous conversations would drown out the whispers in my head.

AN HOUR LATER, Scott returned with the warrant giving us permission to search the Fitzpatrick house, plus an order compelling Lyndon to give us a DNA sample. I could see no other reason why he'd have those scratches on his wrists other than from struggling with Roger. If it were true, and Lyndon had killed his uncle, I didn't know how I was going to react. I liked the boy and I sympathized with him, even sided with him if he couldn't deal with Roger's monetary unfairness. But if Lyndon had killed Sibyl merely to keep her from talking...I sighed heavily, hating the extremes of the case.

Scott mentioned he would have his mobile on when I went out for my dinner with Mark, "in case you need me," then strode back to his patrol car. Now that Graham had secured the search warrant, Scott returned to his usual work.

We were a silent group as Mark drove us to the Fitzpatricks'. Graham seemed mesmerized by some notes he was reading; Mark whistled tunelessly, as though it was a release to keep him from boiling over; I stared out of the window, worrying about Lyndon and his mother, wondering if he would willingly give us a DNA sample. I did not want to see it come down to a fight. It would upset the family and us—especially Graham, who abhorred violence.

The car headlights washed over the front of the Fitzpatricks' home as Mark drove into the driveway. The same statue was in the front garden, but this time it did not leap out of the darkness. It remained demurely where it was, a pale, umbrellaed lady waiting for spring in the twilight of a winter's evening.

Noreen wasn't at home; Lyndon said she was in Chesterfield. But he let us in and stood in the doorway, watching Mark and Graham poke through his things. I could only imagine what he must be feeling at the intrusion.

Their search yielded nothing we sought, so Mark and Graham went through the rest of the house while I searched the garage. A row of shelves ran the length of the far wall, and a small workbench and rack of hand tools occupied the opposite side. Various sizes of boxes were stacked in one corner to accommodate a bicycle, treadmill and rolled up canvas tent. Several milk crates of old magazines and newspaper waited by the garage door.

In one of the cardboard shoeboxes, I found a pair of leather riding boots. When I called them to Lyndon's attention, he said they'd been given to him by his uncle. "It doesn't prove anything," he added, leaving the workbench and walking over to me. "So what if there are boot prints in the tower? Uncle Rog could've made them before he gave me the boots. Those prints could've been there for ages. And I don't believe it about the smaller foot inside the boots, either. How can anyone prove that? Sounds like a lot of rubbish. You lot must be desperate to get a solution to this thing."

I turned back to my search, wondering if we'd ever find any piece of concrete evidence to tie anyone to the deaths. Lyndon was wandering around the garage, muttering that we were manufacturing evidence to convict him. I opened another box and saw a Rolex watch, the second hand still moving. As I picked it up, I noticed a small fiber of yarn caught between two links of the watch band. It was the same color as the cardigan Roger had been wearing. Jens Nielsen had found watch band indentations on Roger's right wrist, and Geneva had said Roger's Rolex was missing. I stared at the watch, then at Lyndon, and asked whose watch this was.

"Mine. What of it?"

"You always keep your watches, especially expensive watches, in cardboard boxes in the garage?"

"No. Nobody does. It's just that, well, I realized I had it on when I was bundling up newspapers and sorting through this rubbish. I didn't want it to get scratched so I took it off and stuck it in the box because it was handy. Forgot all about it. Thanks for finding it." He made a step toward me, but I stopped him with another question.

"How can you afford to buy a Rolex? You know what they sell for?"

"I didn't buy it. Uncle Rog gave it to me." His voice was high as panic claimed him.

"Lord Swinbrook was a very generous man. Leather riding boots, this Rolex. Anything else?"

Lyndon shook his head. "Not lately. He always gives way too much at Christmas. And my birthday. I try not to accept it all, but he likes giving stuff away. He likes to make people happy. You don't know about the computers and stuff he gives to the schools?"

"Outfitting a school is one thing, Lyn. This is something different. Your aunt said she couldn't find your uncle's watch either at home or when she went to the mortuary."

Lyndon shrugged. "He must've taken it off when he was going to ring. You need to do that, you know—not wear jewelry and scarves and things. They could get tangled in the bell rope. Did you look around the tower? He must've put it somewhere."

"I think I've got it here," I said, holding the watch for him to see. "I think you took it from him when you killed him."

Lyndon's face flooded crimson and his neck muscles tightened as he yelled, "That's a bloody lie! I never did!"

"I think you did. I think you were protecting your mother from his on-going beatings. Maybe you hadn't planned it, Lynn; maybe you just wanted to talk to him, ask him to stop assaulting your mum, but in the heat of the argument, you struck him—"

"I'll have you up for slander if you go on. You watch your mouth!"

Jo A. Hiestand

"I'm taking this and the boots, Lyn. These items are on the search warrant." I started toward the door to the house, Lyndon's voice in my ears, his anger spilling over into fright. As I turned to open the door, I noticed a crate of Duvel beer on the floor. A wooden box of glass bottles, with one bottle missing, imported from Belgium, addressed to Kirk. As I turned to the boy, he was slowly walking over to me. I called loudly for Graham.

In the split second when I angled my body to pull an evidence bag from my shoulder bag, Lyndon grabbed my arm and pulled me against him. His right hand was on my bandaged wrist as he applied pressure to make me compliant. I screamed at the pain coursing through my burned hand and nearly crumpled to the floor. Lyndon pulled me to my feet and spun me around. He was a tall, muscular lad, and I could feel his strength as he held me to his chest. The other hand pointed a knife at my throat.

Whether hearing my yelp or his name called, Graham rushed into the garage with Mark fast on his heels. Graham's puzzlement melted to shock as he saw the situation. Mark's expression told me he was going to try something, which he did a moment later, moving away from Graham and approaching Lyndon.

"If you value your colleague's life," Lyndon said, gripping me tighter and pressing the knife point against my neck so that I could feel its sharpness, "you'll stay where you are and save the heroics for the telly characters."

Mark swore but took a step back toward Graham, who held out his arms to keep Mark behind him.

"Fine," Lyndon said, trying to make a brave front. His voice quivered. "Now me and your 'tec are gonna take a bit of a ride. And, I shouldn't try anything, if I were you two. Not, as I said, if you want your cohort to live through this day. Comprendo?"

Lyndon pulled me to the car, opened the door on the passenger side, and pushed me inside. He prodded me over to the driver's seat as he got in. Angling his body toward me, the knife still in his hand, he looked at Graham. I glanced up at the rearview mirror to the driveway and street behind us. Noreen hadn't returned from Chesterfield, so she hadn't parked in the drive, blocking our escape. I silently cursed my luck.

Lyndon said, "We're taking a little ride, and I don't want anybody following us—not you two, not panda cars, not helicopters. *Nothing* if you want her to live. Got it?" To make his point, he gave me the knifepoint again. He suddenly got halfway out of the car but kept the hand with the knife still pointing toward me in the car's interior. His right leg was bent, still inside, and his left hand patted his jeans pockets for the car key. He glanced behind us, looking terribly scared and probably having the same idea. Even though his stance was awkward, I didn't want to try anything. I was afraid if I tried to shove him, stretching across the car seat to get at him, he'd use the knife on me. Or on Mark, if he tried to lunge for the kid. So I remained where I was, hoping I could think of something during my kidnapping. In those brief moments while Lyndon was off balance and hunting for his key, I eased my mobile from my open shoulder bag to the palm of my right hand and held it up, angling it so Lyndon wouldn't see the small phone.

As I grabbed the mobile, I winced from the pain, but managed to turn it on, punch in Graham's phone code so his phone rang, and drop my mobile between me and my bag, wriggling just enough and covering the thud of the phone with a cough. I stared at Graham, made the sign language gesture for 'telephone,' then stroked my thumb leisurely across my jaw as Lyndon turned toward me.

Seeing I was sitting there quietly, Lyndon jumped into the car. He tossed me the key while still threatening me with the knife. "Okay. Your mates are gonna stand here and watch us leave. Now, back this out and drive. I'll tell you where. Just get outta here!"

I glanced at Graham as I backed the car out of the garage. He was nodding his head, indicating that he understood my pantomime. The last thing I saw on driving away from the house was Graham and Mark running to Mark's car and Graham grabbing his mobile.

Once away from his home, Lyndon settled into the seat, though he still kept the knife pointed at me. His hand was shaking, and he kept glancing out of the side and rear windows to see if we were being followed or if Graham had phoned for some cars to stop us. I was extremely nervous, for I didn't know what Lyndon would try if he got frightened enough. Or if he would wound me accidentally while he was waving the knife around in a show of bravado or power. It didn't take police training to know he'd never kidnapped anyone before; his voice quivered and he kept clearing his throat. He was probably sorry he'd abducted me, for now he had to figure an escape plan that wouldn't get him arrested and would leave me alive. Or so I hoped.

He indicated what roads I should take, and impressed upon me that any traffic violation that would get me noticed or stopped would jeopardize my life. I believed him, for his eyes held the fright of a cornered animal.

"So, Lyn," I said, speaking unnaturally loud. I wanted my voice to carry to my mobile so Graham could hear me and pinpoint our position. That was probably the only way I'd get out of this unscathed.

Lyndon stared at me, his eyes wide, his mouth slightly open, and grunted, "What?"

"Where are we going?"

"What's it to you?"

"Just wondering if you've enough petrol."

"You've only been driving for a few minutes. Don't get your knickers in a twist. Just drive."

"Just keep going on toward Hathersage?"

"Yeh. We haven't time to see Little John's grave, if that's your next question."

"No. I was just wondering."

"Yeh, well, don't. I'll tell ya when to turn off."

"Sure, Lyn." I concentrated on the traffic for a bit, for it was rather heavy on the A625. I prayed with everything I had that Graham was hearing me and was working out how to stop the car and take Lyndon into custody without bloodshed. I also prayed the phone's battery wouldn't quit at the crucial time. I kept glancing out the rearview mirror, not that I expected a panda car tagging behind us, but it would've helped subdue my heart rate if I'd seen Scott or Graham.

When we approached Hathersage, I said, "Ever stay at the George Hotel, there? We're just coming to it."

He shook his head, staring out the window.

"Charlotte Bronte stayed there, or so the hotel claims. They've a desk and room preserved. Interesting, if you're into literary figures."

"Who? Charlene Brotty?"

"Bronte. She wrote *Jane Eyre*. The family's associated with Hathersage and this area."

"Never heard of her. Or whatever she wrote. A film, is it?"

"It's of no importance, then. I just thought, you growing up here—"

"Yeh, well, I haven't. Keep driving."

"Just keep going west, like I'm doing?"

"You catch on quick. Yeh. Keep on the road."

I let a few minutes pass in silence, then asked Lyndon why he'd killed Roger and Sibyl. He didn't say anything, but kept looking at the countryside, and I thought I'd have to ask him again, when he said he had got fed up with Roger giving things to everyone else—the school, the village, but nothing for him. Ever. "I got so damned angry," he said, looking at me, his eyes dark with emotion. "I've got several part-time jobs so I can save up money for my career, and Uncle Rog can't even give me a hand-up with that. He dumps his money on football jerseys and such. He can't even help me, his own kin." He lowered his head and wiped away the tears that were spilling down his cheeks.

"And the pearl necklace—why that?"

Lyndon wiped the back of his hand across his cheeks and said, "I heard him at dinner at the pub that night. He was bragging about the Valentine bell ringing and the fur coat he'd just given Aunt Gen and such. I got bloody mad. All that money, and he gives me a worn out pair of boots! So I went home real quick, got the necklace out of mum's jewelry box, and brought it to the tower. Soon as he was dead, I threw it on his chest. See how *he* likes second-hand gifts, the pig."

"And Sibyl?"

He turned his head and spoke to the window. "I didn't want to. But it was something I had to do if I was gonna keep Roger's death a secret. She'd found out—I'd let something slip and she figured it out. I didn't want to hurt her, but I had to, so you wouldn't find out I'd killed Uncle Rog."

I nodded, trying to understand the pain he'd been through. Seeing his uncle lavish others with expensive gifts and yet not a penny for his own future must have hurt him deeply, made him question his own self worth. Perhaps the Rolex was the gift Roger had never given. Several moments passed in silence, then I asked Lyndon what his plans were.

"When?" he asked, turning back to me.

"Right now. I can't keep driving forever. Where's your ultimate destination? What're you going to do when we get to wherever we're going?"

He tapped the knife blade against his thigh and said, "I haven't thought that out. I wasn't exactly expecting you lot today."

"So you don't know where we're going, then?"

He rubbed his forehead as though his head hurt. The knife blade glinted in the light from a passing car's headlights, looking entirely too menacing. When he looked at me, his face was skewing up, as though he were about to cry. "If you'd just let me alone for another day," he said, his voice threatening to break. "That's all I needed. One more day to figure out what I was gonna do, where I would go. But you had to force your way into the house, poke around through my stuff. It's *your* fault you're in this fix. You cops always mess things up for *everyone*. Why can't you mind your own business? You—" He gulped for air, trying to calm his voice and perhaps his nerves. He lifted the knife and jabbed the air near my left shoulder. "You're always messin' about with people's lives. Why don't you just stay the bloody hell away from us?"

I tried to look at him while I talked, tried to calm him down, but I had to watch the road, too. I said as evenly as I could—for my voice, too, was on the verge of cracking from panic, "The cops aren't the bad guys, Lyn."

He frowned, perhaps not expecting my answer.

I could've reminded him that society now labeled *him* a bad guy, that he'd killed two people, which didn't exactly thrust him into the sainthood category, but I didn't want to antagonize him. He was already too jumpy. I continued, "We don't enjoy messing with people or giving people a hard time. The job's demanding enough and risky as hell, with too much to do, too few resources, and not enough time to get it all done. Why should we want to get involved when we don't have to? Why make things harder on ourselves? We're not the bad guys. Anyone who'd risk getting killed, who goes out in the middle of the night, in the cold and the rain, leaves his wife and kids to go to an unknown, possibly dangerous situation isn't the bad guy."

He stared at his lap, his head lowered, and nodded. The knife lay on his lap now, and he clasped his hands as though needing some sort of physical reassurance. On looking up again, he stared out the window, the knife momentarily forgotten while he sorted through my words and his situation.

"I've got to dump you, I know. I didn't want to do this, but I didn't know what else to do, how else to get out of this mess. I—I'm sorry, but there it is. Now, I don't know how else to end it. I've got to get away to figure this out."

"So you're making for Buxton or Manchester to get lost in the crowd?"

"As good a place as any. But let's make it Manchester. That's bigger. I won't get spotted there so quickly, and I can hole up somewhere and make plans."

My mind reeled at the suggestion. If I let him go in Manchester, we might never find him. He could hide up or travel to any large city from there. I said, "This road is closed the other side of Hope. There's been a lorry involved in an accident. I heard the report as we drove to your house."

"Where are we now?" He frowned and turned in his seat, trying to read the road sign we'd just passed.

"Just outside Hathersage. All I have to do is make a small detour before we get to Hope. Swing south on the B6049 to Bradwell, then west and catch the A625 again at Castleton. Just make a big loop. It's not that much longer."

"Yeh. Fine. Whatever. Just get me to Manchester by tonight."

"Ok, Lyn. Whatever you want. Ahh, we're just coming to Hope. It's best in the long run, taking this alternate route. We'll avoid sitting in traffic while the accident's cleared."

I turned south, hoping my lengthy 'detour' would give Graham enough time to barricade a road or establish some type of vehicle impasse. He'd get the personnel and equipment from Buxton, which was west of our position. If they responded quickly to his call, they'd be set up somewhere—hopefully in The Winnats, that steep-sided mountain gorge in the heart of the dales country. The road was single lane in both directions, with a sharp right-hand turn inside the pass. It would be a perfect spot for a police roadblock. And if Graham set it up properly he'd have Lyn, and my nightmare would soon be over.

I slowed the car considerably as I turned onto the small lane parenthesized by low, stonewalls and dense hedgerows. Patches of snow and ice clung to the base of the walls where the sun didn't penetrate at its lower winter angle. The setting sun flooded the land in a golden wash of color and tinted the lichen black. Inwardly, I was glad my ruse was working. Anything to gain time and slow our trip. When we turned onto another lane and headed north again, I glanced at my watch. Graham would've rung ahead to Buxton for officers and equipment, driving straight from Lyndon's house to the Winnats, canvassing the area and establishing a barricade before the equipment, Lyndon and I arrived. I concentrated on that image as I slowed our drive through the Hope Valley.

I don't know what I talked about during those last few minutes of the drive. Lyndon responded in grunts or single syllables when he did respond at all. I was feeling sorrier by the minute for him, for he had panicked when I had confronted him with the watch, and we wouldn't be here now if I had handled it differently. But all I had envisioned on discovering the Rolex was

PEARLS BEFORE SWINE

Sibyl's crumpled body. She'd had such a bright future, and I was angry that Lyndon had taken it from her.

We had just entered the Winnats when we saw the police roadblock. I slowed up, nearly stopping the car, and Lyndon asked what I was doing.

"There's a hefty line of police vehicles and a barricade, Lyn," I said, tapping the windscreen. "What's it look like to you?"

"Okay, okay." He angled around so he could see the road behind us. It lay like a white snake twisting through a dark gray landscape. The weekend traffic was starting to queue up, waiting to get through the barricade. He turned again, glanced out the front and side windows, then pointed the knife at me. "Move it."

"What?"

"Go on. Drive."

"I can't! There's a barricade, plus there are cars behind us. I can't back up."

"You can drive over there," he said, indicating the flat land on the other side of the opposite lane. "Turn around there and head back east. We can head to Sheffield. Turn around."

"I *can't* turn around there, Lyn. The police are letting cars through the other side of the road block. We'll get hit if I try—"

"You've got time if you move fast enough. The cars aren't coming *that* quick. Come on, get going—like *now*." He poked the knife blade into my left side so I could feel the point. "No one's coming. *Move it!*"

I took a deep breath, prayed to every saint I'd ever heard about, and stomped down on the accelerator. The car's tires grabbed bits of gravel on the road, skidded for a moment on an icy patch, then found traction. I headed the car toward the empty piece of earth at the base of one of the rock cliffs, then yanked the wheel sharply left as the rocky base loomed within feet of the car's bonnet. The brakes grabbed and spun the car nearly halfway around. I thought that would've been enough for me to escape, but Lyndon was quicker.

Jo A. Hiestand

CHAPTER TWENTY-SIX

LYNDON GRABBED MY arm and literally pulled me across the car's front seat and out the passenger-side door. He encircled my shoulders and upper arms with his right arm, pinning me tightly against his chest, while he held the knifepoint at my throat.

"Go on. Over there!" he yelled, yanking me toward a boulder that had fallen from the top of the rocky cliff. His legs hit the backs of my knees, forcing me to move forward. There were two barricades in the valley—the one at our end, and one farther down the road to stop the oncoming traffic. Between the two barriers was a no-man's land with police vehicles lined up and officers now crouching behind their cars.

Lyndon walked backwards to the rocky protection, placing me between him and the police contingent. Great. Every girl's dream job—a human shield. I knew there were expert marksmen in the group, but it did little to relieve my anxiety. I had no idea what Lyndon would do, and he obviously felt trapped and desperate.

I glanced at the top of the mountains, hoping, yet dreading, to see a police marksman silhouetted against the sky. It was a deep ravine, this section of the Winnats, and I wondered if even an expert marksman could get off a shot from a one thousand-plus foot elevation. Especially at dusk. No, I thought, the best bet for such an operation would be from the barricade or close to the side near the boulder where Lyndon was pushing me. As nervous as I was, I had to maneuver Lyndon so the police marksman could fire off a clean shot.

Of course, all this takes longer to explain than it happened. In the few strides from the car to the boulder, I had thought this out, and I acted in the last yard or so from the rock.

Wasn't it Robert Burns who wailed about best-laid plans going wrong? It certainly happened to me. I had planned to yell as though I were in severe pain and double up in what I hoped would look like a faint—the idea being my dead weight would be too much for Lyn to hold and, devoid of his human shield, he would be an easy mark for the tactical team. But as I started to go limp, Lyn's arm tightened around my shoulders. His muscles pressed against my body, holding me upright. He hissed into my ear that I would be sorry if I tried something like that, then he yelled at the contingent of police. His words echoed and rose, spilling over the mountaintops and into the reddening sky.

"If you want her to live, back off!"

I stared at the cluster of police cars, wondering if it would be the last thing I ever would see. If so, I wanted my life to end focused on someone I loved. I sought out Graham. He was crouched behind the bonnet of a police car, his head angled as if he were speaking to someone beside him. I closed my eyes, afraid I would die either from my exploding, pounding heart or from the knife thrust.

Lyn stood his ground, his arm imprisoning me against his body, not allowing me to breathe, let alone move. At nearly three-fourths of his height and half his weight, I didn't know how I could angle myself for a police marksman's benefit. I was afraid to think of the mere inches separating a clean shot at Lyn and a disastrous miss that would wound or possibly kill me. I tried to call out to Graham to let us pass, but Lyn had moved his hand that held the knife to rest on top of my chest, the knife blade pressing into my neck.

As though feeling my tightening neck muscles, Lyn yelled, "I mean it! I'm not fooling. You want me to slice her right here to prove I'm serious?"

Graham moved slowly, snail-like, standing up so he could talk to Lyn. He stepped away from the far side of the car but kept his hand on the car's bonnet. "What do you want, Lyndon? Don't hurt Sergeant Taylor. It'll go worse for you if anything happens to her."

Lyn's heartbeat banged against my ear, terrifying me all the more. I prayed he was not about to do something stupid. He pulled me up straighter so that I was standing up, and yelled, "Her well-being is in *your* hands. You let us through and she won't get hurt. Now, I want all your cars to pull out. *Now!*"

Graham turned, as though about to confer with someone. He evidently took too long, for Lyn screamed, "Move it! NOW! Or she dies inches by inches in front of you. *MOVE!*"

He jabbed the knifepoint into my neck, bringing a trickle of blood that ran into my collar. I jerked my head away from his shoulder, terrified and in pain, screaming to Graham.

In those few seconds of exposure, a police marksman got off a shot. The rifle retort echoed against the rock faces, splitting into a hundred sounds, boiling up and out of the gorge, dying what seemed hours later. It blotted out every other sound, so intense and frightening its consequences. As I felt Lyn's arms give way, I sank to the earth, not knowing if I were shot, stabbed or had escaped unscathed. In the awful dead silence after the rifle's crack, I lay still, unable to think, hardly daring to breathe in case Lyn would see I was still alive and grab me again.

But, in what must have been seconds later, I heard Graham's voice yelling at me. At that moment, I gave way to my emotions and sobbed. Unashamed, relieved. The tears soaked my jacket sleeve and the snow beneath my head. Footsteps ran up to me, and a voice urgently called my name.

When I gingerly lifted my head and looked to my left, I saw Lyn's body on the ground, the knife several feet from his hand, his head completely blown away and his blood painting the earth and snow.

I tried getting to my feet, but my knees betrayed me, and I fell again to the ground, still crying. Mark rushed up, his handcuffs shining in the last rays of the day's sun like the Keys to the Kingdom, but jammed them into his slacks pocket when it was evident they wouldn't be needed. Graham jogged up, his face white and grim, calling out in his urgency, "Brenna, are you okay? Are you hurt?"

His hands were under my arms before I could reply, pulling me firmly, yet gently, to my feet. I nodded, looked at the front of my trousers and jacket, which were now muddy from the wet ground and melting snow, and said in a quivering voice, "I—I'm in the wrong job. I'd be of more use if I—if I were a dry cleaner."

"You'd be bored within one week," Graham said. His eyes looked at me as though discerning my well being, then he took my good hand and led me to the cluster of police cars.

I leaned against him, gulping in air. As my crying ceased, I murmured my thanks to the group and wiped the tears from my cheeks.

Scott was walking over to me, a rifle in his hand. I glanced from him to Graham and said, "Did his new assignment come through?"

Graham shook his head. "It's not official. But he was handy. I didn't have time to get a marksman. You weren't driving all that long, you know."

"Isn't it next year?"

He ignored me. "And when you indicated you were headed toward the Winnats, a perfect spot for the road block...well, you'd be through them before I would be able to get a tactical team up from Ripley."

I blinked in disbelief. Now that Scott had seen that I would be all right, he had turned away, his face several shades of gray. I wanted to thank him, to ask if I could help, but he wandered back to the barricade and sank to the ground, his back against the cliff face, his knees bent, his head lowered. I hoped Lyn's death wouldn't affect Scott. Taking another human life, no matter if it was justified, was always serious and sometimes affected officers for many years.

"Plus," Graham's voice continued from somewhere behind me, "I knew Scott was a superb shot, and he was here. So I used him. I didn't think you'd mind."

Graham opened the back door of Mark's car for me and told me to sit down. But I leaned against the rear wing as he opened the boot and grabbed a first aid kit. Staring at Scott, I said, "Is he going to be all right?"

"I sincerely hope so. He's a splendid officer. I'd hate to lose him before he even starts."

PEARLS BEFORE SWINE

"Will he need to see someone? I couldn't stand it if he's hurt—emotionally or mentally—just because I let Lyn grab me."

Graham took a roll of gauze from the kit. "Hold still, Brenna. I need to bandage your neck."

In the excitement of the last few minutes I'd forgotten that I was bleeding. I moved my hand to my neck and gingerly touched my wound. When I removed my fingers, they were sticky from blood.

"Hold still," Graham said again, his voice firm. He grabbed my hand and wiped my fingers clean with an alcohol cleansing pad.

"I'm fine," I said as he finished with the washing, repacked the first aid kit and replaced it in the car. "I'm worried about Scott. Please have a look at him, sir."

Graham laid a hand on my shoulder and forced me inside the car. He glanced at Scott before saying, "I'll talk to him, certainly, but he'll have to talk with a counselor, too. Mandatory therapy, of course, in instances like this, but I've seen nothing but stupendous results. No matter how justified an action is, there can be years of emotional and psychological damage due to thoughts that plague the officer. He keeps replaying the scenario, wondering if he could have done something differently to achieve the same outcome but without taking a life. I don't want Scott, or any officer, to be haunted by that. So he gets his time on the couch before he's had his time with his phantoms."

I had never had to undergo the compulsory sessions, but as I watched Scott wipe his eyes I knew he would need them. For all of his bravado about catching bad guys, Scott was a sensitive, caring individual. Lyndon's death would indeed haunt him for years if he didn't talk to someone about it. And as much as I would have conversed with him over cups of tea or pints of bitter, I knew that 'someone' should be a trained counselor. Scott didn't need a well-meaning amateur, no matter how sympathetic. A professional would know how to talk him out of his depression. I asked Graham if he thought Scott would recover.

Glancing at Scott, Graham said, "He's incredibly strong. And sensible. I think he'll be fine. But you may not be. You're going to get checked over and that other ruddy bandage removed. It needs air."

"Who's going to contact Lyn's—" I stopped, my voice failing as I sought the words.

"His parents? I'll do that. God knows it's never easy—especially now, with this tragic ending. But I'll do it. I'll find the words somehow."

I knew he would. His ministerial garb might be shut away in a closet, but his training wasn't. He would more than find the right words to tell Noreen and Kirk; he would do it with grace and dignity, part of his Cleric Sparkle, as Margo and I had come to call it.

I glanced at the barricade, at the cars and police personnel. At Scott, bent over and crying into his hands. Scott, Noreen and Kirk weren't the only people who would be wounded by Lyn's death. It would affect us who had been here, Lyn's friends and extended family. It would also affect Scott's family if he didn't get counseling help.

Graham got into the car, started the engine, then turned to look back at me. "Congratulations on the mobile phone bit. I heard everything you said. Good bit of police work, that."

I stammered something and lowered my head, pretending to examine my bandaged hand. When I felt in control again, I looked at him. He was smiling.

"After seeing the doctor, how about seeing me?"

My mouth dropped open and I made some intelligent response such as "Sir?"

"Only, it won't be 'sir' then. It'll be 'Geoff,' if you can manage it. And you'll be Brenna, not Taylor."

"Pardon?"

"I've been wanting to get to know you better. Only if you'd like to, I mean." He glanced away for a moment, as though choosing his words carefully. Or shielding himself from seeing my reaction. "No pressure or anything, don't worry. Your job doesn't hang on your answer. I just—well, I thought we could chat over coffee, or have dinner or something. As formal as you'd like it to be. I don't want to pressure you." He raised his eyebrow, waiting for me to say something, then quickly said, "Life is precious. We never know what will happen. Friends are the most valuable things in my life, and I'd like to—" Again he paused, coloring slightly. "Well, this just emphasized it, didn't it? We could have lost you. Even before I'd got to know you—as a friend, I mean. I'd like to get to know you. But only if *you* want to. Oh, damn. What a hash I'm making of this..." He trailed off, looking uncomfortable; not at all like the man who commanded a murder team or examined hacked bodies without flinching.

I took pity on him, smiling encouragingly for him to continue.

He sighed, looked at me, and said rather haltingly, "Well, this is as good an excuse as any, I guess. To ask you out, I mean. I, uhh, I have to keep an eye on my Top Cop."

Though the surroundings weren't exactly romantic—a few lads from the uniformed unit, response drivers, detectives, police barricades, lines of impatient motorists, and a bloody corpse—at least it was a start.

Photo by: Chris Eisenmayer

Books, Girl Scouts and music filled Jo's childhood. She discovered the magic of words and the worlds they create — mysteries, English medieval history, the natural world, and biographies. She explored the joys of the outdoors through Girl Scout camping trips and summers as a canoeing instructor and camp counselor. Brought up on classical, big band and baroque music, she was groomed as a concert pianist until forsaking the piano for the harpsichord. She plays a Martin 12-string guitar and has sung in a semi-professional folk-group in the US and as a soloist in England.

Such a mixture of adventure, foreign delights and music laid the foundation for her writing. A true Anglophile, Jo wanted to create a mystery series that featured British traditions and customs as the backbone of the plot, while combining the traditional flavor of an English police procedural and the intimate atmosphere of a cozy. The result is the Taylor & Graham series, featuring Detective-Sergeant Brenna Taylor and Detective-Chief Inspector Geoffrey Graham, C.I.D., of the Derbyshire Constabulary. Brenna is a nature lover and amateur folk musician, while Graham loves early music and playing the harpsichord.

In addition to these hobbies, Jo enjoys photography, her backyard wildlife, reading and change ringing. She founded the Greater St. Louis Chapter of Sisters in Crime, serving as its first president, and is a board member of St. Louis Community Tower Bells, a non-profit organization obtaining change ringing bells for the St. Louis region.

She has combined her love of writing, board games and mysteries by co-inventing a mystery-solving game, P.I.R.A.T.E.S., which uses maps, graphics, song lyrics, and other clues to lead the players to the lost treasure.

In 1999 Jo returned to Webster University to major in English with an Emphasis in Writing as a Profession. She graduated in 2001 with a BA degree and departmental honors.

Years of British travel have provided the knowledge and detail that fill Jo's books. With one-month intervals separating each book, the reader can experience a year of customs and holidays flavored with Murder Most English.

Her three cats —Thackeray, Chaucer and Dickens — share her St. Louis home. (Learn more about Jo and her books by visiting her website: www.joahiestand.com.).

Printed in the United States
58963LVS00005B/97